THE BLOOD SERVICE

A SCI-FI ACTION ADVENTURE

THE CAPITAL ADVENTURES
BOOK 1

ALLEN A IVERS

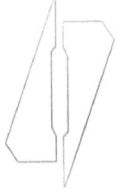

FOREWORD

This is the first book in *The Blood Service* trilogy.

This book contains the following content matter:

- *Graphic Violence & Traumatic Injuries*
- *Frequent Foul Language*
- *Sexual Activity*

We're here to have a good time with characters we love. If any of this material distresses you, it's okay to grab another book instead.

Hope you enjoy!

MAP & CHRONOLOGY

The Solar Imperium, also called the Gnostic Empire by the more faithful citizenry, stretches over a fifth of the Milky Way Galaxy. This map features the primary locations featured in the series thus far.

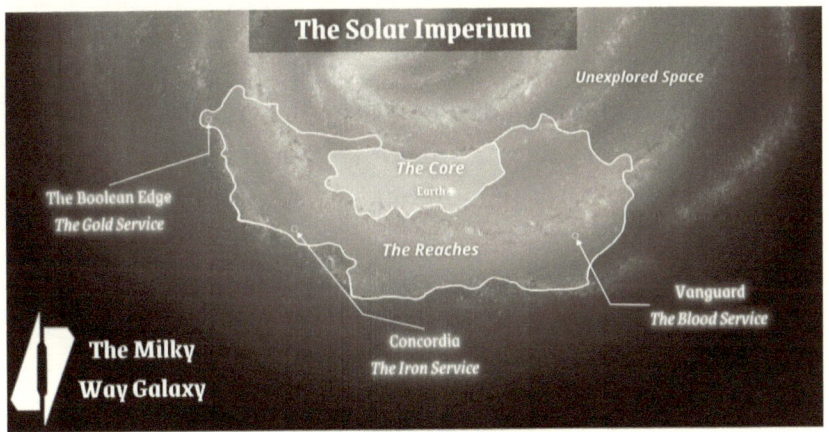

Map of Solar Imperium controlled space, 2241 CE

The events of the Capital Adventures occur entirely within these borders. Events from one book may be mentioned in another, or characters may cross over from one trilogy to another. Think of it as a shared universe, with the individual stories having unique tones and flair, while building an overarching plot.

You may enjoy each trilogy independent of the others—and I've meticulously built them so that your enjoyment is not contingent on having read the others! But if you want the full experience of the Capital Adventures, I do encourage you to pick up the other books to get a full sense of the Imperium's reach. The official reading order would be to read the trilogies starting with The Blood Service, then The Gold Service, and finishing out with the upcoming Iron Service.

If you're like me, however, and you were looking to read the novels in chronological order, the events of all nine books are as follows:

————

1) THE GOLD SERVICE
2) THE BLOOD SERVICE
3) THE IRON SERVICE

4) RANKS OF THE BLOOD SERVICE
5) COST OF THE GOLD SERVICE
6) SWORDS OF THE IRON SERVICE (COMING SOON)

7) COMMAND OF THE BLOOD SERVICE
8) SHARDS OF THE IRON SERVICE (COMING SOON)
9) POWERS OF THE GOLD SERVICE

WITH EVEN MORE TO COME...

The Blood Service Trilogy has a darker tone than the other two members of this series, with frequent and graphic military violence and confronting concepts like slavery, child soldiers, and war crimes. If you're looking for some weight in your space opera, this trilogy is going to scratch that itch.

"Do not be afraid; our fate
Cannot be taken from us; it is a gift."

DANTE ALIGHIERI, INFERNO

PROLOGUE

AARON

THE HOWLERS WERE like something out of surrealist art, and two of them together flying in formation had often been depicted in patriotic posters slapped around the city, usually against some backsplash of blue and white of the Imperial flag.

On Earth, those posters were mystically immaculate amongst the debris and grime surrounding them in the streets, as though frequently cleaned or replaced. Never a tear at the fringe or bleached by the sunlight. People kept a fair distance away from them, the healthy concern one gives around curses or predators.

Aaron had seen a few hanging around Vanguard. They were practically tatters.

The vehicles depicted were about as unholy as they come. The DH-55 DeHaans suborbital military transport, to be particularly accurate, was a nightmare-inducing silhouette. The primary engine socketed in the tail, with two maneuvering jets slid into the stubby wings, all wrapped around a bulbous fatted chassis, like the big metal bird bore a disquieting burden.

The smooth skin of the hull more resembled something organic than the alloy it was, and the engines—where the metal birds got their 'Howling' nickname—confused the ears. They sounded more like

1

someone had fired them up deep in the back of a cave, and all that could be heard was their echoes. It came from everywhere and nowhere all at once.

Twelve tons of military hardware could sail right over a residential district at Mach 2 and nobody on the ground would suspect a thing unless they looked up. What a frightening sight that would be. Who wants to see this metal beast lancing over their heads, heralding the arrival of the Empire's finest?

Aaron picked at the collar of his uniform. The one-size-fits-all jumpsuit was all they gave Capitals, and the tactical rig had been made for someone a few sizes smaller. The chest strap was riding up his front, with some devious plans to choke him out in a moment of pique.

The ground beneath them blurred together into one sandy color palette. The city's spires stretched up behind them, three towers reaching toward the sky like outstretched fingers. It was so far away behind them, it appeared to be stenciled onto the horizon. The bulky frame of the original Aurora colony ship could barely be made out against the apartments, warehouses and cranes surrounding it.

The sliding doors were sealed, so flush against the hull there wasn't even a seam. Soon those doors would rip open, the floor would drop away, sending two dozen men to face whatever awaited them on the ground. Who knows what would happen next?

"One minute out."

"I have visual on the AO."

The Oskie in charge—a robotic man named Lieutenant Holmst—consulted a monitor, barking into his radio intermittently. He was on a different channel and the acoustics of the Howler ate whatever other noise he was making. The pale ghost might very well have been placing bets for all they knew.

The harness yanked on Aaron's throat again, as the stress cables drew taut.

The Howler slowed and dipped into a deep circle of the landing zone, strafing the area. Out of the small double-paned window by his elbow, Aaron caught glimpses of the ground below.

A plume of smoke. Bodies. Blood. No movement.

Holmst glanced back at Aaron and the other Capitals. Scanning over them. Then he nodded.

He closed the monitor and pivoted to face the team. "AO is quiet. Capitals: hit the ground hard and secure the area, search for survivors. Oskies and the Howlers will provide air support. Gather anybody you find, bring 'em to the primary homestead for extract. Mission time no longer than fifteen minutes. Set your watches. Clock starts on the drop."

The team reached down to their wrists, setting the digital timers. No heads-up display, not for the Capitals. They had solar-powered panels that were often concealed from sun by gear and uniforms—real intelligent design.

Holmst worked his way aft, checking the cables on each Capital as he went. Awfully kind of him to give that much care for expendable munitions. Perhaps it was just habit.

"You miss the extract, you will get left." Holmst gripped the drop lever. "Earn your place, Caps."

He pulled and the floor dropped away.

The whir of the dozen or so pulleys vanished immediately, replaced by the air howling past his head—maybe that's the reason for the nickname—as he plummeted to the ground below, held only by the thin aircraft cable on the back of his harness. The tension on his thighs and crotch was tight enough to make his toes tingle. Although the sudden G-forces may have something to do with that, as well.

As it turns out, they weren't that high up to begin with. The pilot must've done a low pass over the landing site before Holmst unceremoniously kicked everyone out.

The cable yanked hard, pinching important things, but slowing his fall moments before impact. And just before the ground, the computers above knew to release the lock and drop Aaron safely to the ground. His feet hit dirt with all the laughable force of jumping down the last few steps of a stairwell.

For all of that drama and intensity, the team was placed on the field like pieces on a chessboard. The dozen folk landing kicked up dirt, creating a wide cloud, blinding Aaron to the world around him.

He scanned the area for any silhouette he didn't recognize. Anything big or menacing. But there were no monsters in this closet, not any that would show themselves. This was it.

He had to get focused now.

Aaron looked up at the Howlers overhead, as silent as a child's kite barely a hundred feet up. The doors slid open, revealing the demon's teeth—a mounted automatic plasma-launcher that threw off enough energy it could throw the ship off-course.

Nothing to fear. The hand of God was watching from above.

Aaron started the timer on his watch—fifteen minutes. "Two by twos," Aaron shouted, "Search the buildings. Eden, you're on medical. Nora, keep her safe. Check your fire, we have friendlies in the neighborhood." Aaron keyed his throat mic. "Team 2 is on the deck."

As crisp as if he was right next to him, Carmona chimed in, "Team 1 is on the ground. Start the clock."

Damn, it sounded like they practiced that more than once. Aaron could only hope that luck held. But in the hoping, he was certain he had jinxed it and doomed them all. That would be his luck, after all.

The homestead wasn't terribly large. A few converted storage sheds, some silos. A large pit had been carved into the ground, an excavation more akin to a mine than a farm.

Every few dozen yards, the dirt had been carved up by conflict. Blood caked the ground in thick streams, dried up.

Aaron could see a human hand in the dust nearby, severed above the wrist, but its owner was nowhere to be seen. In fact, there was a great deal of blood for there to be no bodies.

On the far side, Aaron could see Carmona's team milling about, trying to decide how to breach the central housing unit. It was subterranean, a large hole carved into the ground—not uncommon for these homesteads. The dirt was soft and malleable, making excavation easier than construction.

But something was wrong. They were hesitant, circling. They didn't want to go inside.

"What've you got, Carm?" Aaron asked.

There was a long pause.

"Watch your footing."

Aaron's team hovered about for a long moment, pairing off in their duos.

Quinn staggered up to Aaron's shoulder, limping on his sprained leg. Apparently, Aaron made a face. "Hey, you got me into all this," Quinn justified.

Fair enough. "We'll check the perimeter for stragglers, see if anybody hauled themselves out of the mess. Everybody else, hit the structures."

The terrain was almost dreamlike, flat and level, like someone had come along and beveled the surface to match. The ground was dry, but loose and dark, thick like clay. And it cracked along the surface, the pattern stretching forward for miles.

They walked for almost a minute in agonizing silence, staring at the open field. Anything that had been here was either still hiding somewhere or had fled long ago.

"What were they farming?" Quinn asked.

"No idea." Aaron was a city boy. He just ate the food. Didn't much know or care how it came to be.

"I mean, you can't grow much in this."

In what? Aaron looked back at him.

Quinn smiled. That sight was refreshing in itself. Quinn stooped down and palmed a bunch of the loose dirt in his hands. "This topsoil is garbage. Contaminated. You see any grass out here?"

Now that he mentioned it...there wasn't a damn thing growing, not even weeds. In any direction. They said this was a farm. And yet, there were silos for storage, packed with supplies. "In the pit, maybe?" Aaron asked.

"Possible," Quinn said, "I'd have to go look, but ya might find usable soil if you dig deep enough."

"You a farmer?"

Quinn's look soured. "My parents were." And that was all he wanted to say on that subject. His jaw tightened, and his eyes went back to the horizon, on patrol for motion.

"We've got a live one!" Eden chimed in over the radio.

"Christ, he's jacked up." That would be Nora.

"Cut the chatter!" Holmst ordered, "What's their status, Capital?"

Aaron looked back toward the Homestead, a good hundred meters behind them now. Nothing he could do but continue his own search, but he couldn't make himself move. He waited with bated breath for the report that might predict their own futures.

Maybe they had just hit their head, or beaten the demons back with their bare fists?

"What's their status?" Holmst enunciated, frustrated that he had to repeat himself.

"Hypovolemic shock," Eden responded, much more clinical than she had to be, "Traumatic amputation and...a likely spinal fracture." Aaron knew maybe half of those words but enough of them to draw his own portentous conclusion.

"Do what you can," Aaron ordered, "Nora, don't wander off. Whatever did that might still be nearby."

"Too right," Nora said, nausea tainting her tone. It must be quite the sight to get her riled up. She was acclimatized to violence. This was a woman not easily shaken. And yet...

Aaron turned back to his patrol to see Quinn frozen in place, chewing on his cheek.

"Are they gonna be okay?" Quinn asked, trying to hide the quiver in his voice.

"Who, Eden?" Based on Quinn's sudden shrug and pursed lips,

Aaron gathered an either-or quality to the question. "Nobody's gonna be okay after today."

All he could picture was that arm bone he found in the mine—the length of it, its weight, and the tapered edge to it—like a medieval scythe. He could see that being swung down to sever a man's limbs, with the appropriate force and willpower. It wouldn't slice, but it might crush or tear, like a powerful vice might.

He'd seen enough similar injuries with the mining rigs where careless folk would lose a hand to an apathetic and unforgiving pulley system. They were never cut or torn so much as removed.

The stories told of these critters, the local wildlife, eating their prey. Perhaps there was some truth in the tall tales.

Aaron pulled the charging handle back on his rifle, just enough to check if the chamber was hot. The last thing he'd want to do is look death in the face and impotently click at it like a cricket being introduced to a lawnmower.

"I don't know about you," Quinn stammered out, "but I'm all for ditching the perimeter and linking up with the others."

Aaron scanned the edges of sight one last time. Nothing but dirt and more dirt. Even the blood spatter didn't extend out this far. "Yeah...I think you're right," he said, grasping his throat mic, "Team two perimeter, falling back to extract. How copy?"

The Howlers swung overhead like silent phantoms, two dogs herding the Capitals back to their pens, "Negative team two," spake the crisp voice from on high, "Mission time is not expired. Maintain your search pattern."

Quinn shivered. "Oh, great. Wonderful."

Aaron tapped the boy's shoulder as he resumed their casual march. In retrospect, Aaron preferred the perimeter. The sights and smells inside the homestead proper were liable to haunt dreams.

Out here, he got a beautiful view of the rolling mountains on all sides and the comfort of seeing any attack coming long before it got to him.

What was there to hide behind out here?

The ground cracked, a thin gossamer line silently dancing its way backward between his legs.

His eyes followed back toward Quinn, but all Aaron saw was the two outstretched scythes wrapping around Quinn's midsection, and the boy's horrified eyes yanked abruptly into the ground.

When the dust settled, there wasn't even an imprint in the ground where the rupture had occurred, the dirt settling back undisturbed.

A monster from under the bed had reached up from the ground and pulled Quinn down into its lair. No sounds of struggle or screams of pain; it was as though Quinn had never been.

He scanned the ground and the cracked clay in every direction. Cracks everywhere.

Oh, no...

Aaron fumbled with his radio. "Perimeter contact. I repeat, perimeter contact!" He hissed into the mic, afraid to disturb the air more than necessary.

"No shit!"

The Howlers zipped by overhead, finally low enough for Aaron to hear their disquieting engines, the jet wash kicking Aaron's hair about his head. The dirt flung about stung his eyes, and he tried to blink away through the cloud, worried he might be taken in the distraction.

What he saw stole the breath from his chest and froze his fingers.

They moved as one, too many to pick out one particular shape. In the single moment of Quinn's abduction, the trap had sprung. Hundreds of twisted shapes emerged from all around the homestead, swarming the Capitals.

Gunfire and cries for help were drowned out by the baritone staccato of chattering jaws, gnashing teeth, and dry breathing emanating from the unified morass of leathery nightmares.

The ground cracked again under his feet. And Aaron could feel it rise up behind him.

A Jergad Drone.

It had to be eight feet tall, even in its hunched over state. A thick brown carapace over an inch thick covered its flesh like banded iron, camouflaging it with the ground as much as protecting it from assault. Its narrow thorax tapered down to a waspy center but was still thicker around than Aaron's shoulders, plated with a half dozen articulated scales.

Its two recurved legs bent backward like a bird's, with a wide-set foot made for stability and strength. More than enough to rend Aaron's stomach open in a single strike. As though it needed the help of its feet, with two searching arms ending in jagged blades, scythes articulated to slash. Its stance was wide and low, keeping its massive weight balanced.

Most of the body was occluded behind its fan-shaped skull crest —likely evolved that way to shield its core from frontal attack. Its lower jaw split open at the center, hinging open to reveal a wide row of large crushing teeth.

And its growling breath—a sound he'd remember through any dementia—came out in a surreal drum roll, a dissonant collection of angry notes assailing his ears.

Its pale blue eyes stared right through him, with no focused iris or pupil, as though nothing could escape its cold sight.

And its arms reached for him, twin bone scythes articulated at the wrist, ready to rend him apart. Eager, as if they had patiently waited for this satisfying moment and were now to be rewarded for their obedient restraint.

The Howler above opened fire, its door gun unleashing a dragon's breath of translucent green fire into the creature's broad head.

The crested skull snapped off at the half-mast, spraying the air with a thin mist of red blood. It cried out in agony and rage, flailing madly for Aaron, just out of reach. It leaned back, instinctively trying to catch its fall —

And exposing its plated chest.

Center of mass.

Aaron shouldered his rifle, snapping three clean rounds through, carving clean lanes through its vital organs and silencing its screams. It crumpled to the ground, slipping halfway back into the tunnel it leapt from.

"Quinn?!" He called out into the tunnel, trying to ignore the chaotic radio chatter screaming in his ear.

Maybe the boy was still in there, wounded and frightened. He needed help. Maybe he could pick out the whimpers of a farm boy.

No answer. Too much to hope for.

Aaron turned back to the homestead. The blood and the screams and the roiling bodies—it looked like the Mouth of Hell itself had disgorged a legion of its troops onto the field.

They were going to die here. They were all going to die here...

TWO MONTHS EARLIER...

ORDERS FROM THE MINISTRY
EARTH DIRECTIVE

ALL REGIMENTS
MESSAGE FOLLOWS

RE: BORDER WORLD SKIRMISHES
BY ORDER OF THE MINISTRY OF CIVIL DEFENSE, ALL
UNITS ARE TO MUSTER TO
OUTLANDER STATION

FOR DEPLOYMENT TO THE FRONT
ALL OTHER COMMAND DIRECTIVES ARE RESCINDED

ZU GLORIAM

SPECIFICS FOR HR-2056

MINISTRY IS AWARE OF HOSTILE NATIVE WILDLIFE
IN REGION

ARTICLE 6-58 s.2 INVOKED —
ALL UNITS ARE TO ABANDON POSTS AND
PROCEED TO RALLY WITHOUT DELAY

ALL COLONIAL ASSETS DEEMED EXPENDABLE

DAMAGE ESTIMATE FOLLOWS

PROPERTY ESTIMATE: TOTAL
MATERIAL ESTIMATE: TOTAL
HUMAN ESTIMATE: TOTAL

PART ONE
CHAINBREAKER

CHAPTER
ONE
RILEY

MARCUS RILEY BORE little respect for any man that cried, with distinct exceptions for patriotism and dogs. He rationalized that this instance was the former, as he fought the beads of salty water betraying him up behind his eyes.

For all the insanity of the last thirty-two hours, this moment of calm was the worst. The hustle of soldiers marching past, rucksacks on their shoulders, might have been soothing, but for the fatted transport that hummed on the launchpad, nose tilted gently skyward.

When each man filled his seat, workers crammed every other available space with crates from the supply warehouses. Somebody in there had the unlucky jump seat with a rocket launcher in his lap.

He dragged his feet as he trudged up the ramp, less a sailor on the gangway and more like a prisoner to the gallows. The crate in Riley's hands bore his personal effects. He rubbed his thumbs back over the studded tabs, as though he could put his commendations back on the wall, the picture of his sister back on his desk, and the server back in the rack.

Just two days ago, everyone had been surly and disgruntled, maybe even bored. Now, Imperial citizens were shooting at each other on the far side of the galaxy—and they had called Colonel Riley and his men to come join in their nightmare.

It's like they forgot why he was in this particular corner of the universe in the first place. The innocent citizenry packing the streets behind him—people he'd grown quite fond of—now hurled everything they had at his exposed back: epithets, threats, promises & tears, in that order. Just on the cusp of hating him.

He didn't blame them one bit. If he didn't go, they wouldn't have to suffer. His loyalty was going to kill them all.

Conditioning can only do so much for a conscience.

No amount of after-action reports could reflect what he'd seen firsthand on this forsaken dustball—those that died on the front-lines, civilian and soldier alike, did not meet their end with glory or meaning. They died brutal deaths, screaming for their mothers, and it would take entirely too long for those voices to quiet in Riley's memory.

Riley had been drilled and trained to march men in the streets and enforce laws and customs; theories had been discussed and debated on how one might cull the population to a manageable size; humanity had even enslaved entire planets before turning their greedy eyes to distant stars with an unquenchable thirst for something called 'dominion.'

On the far side of the galaxy, two opposing forces tried to enforce their own vision. But this enemy had no such relatable design, no human relative thought—they would butcher the colony down to the last child. They would do so because that's what they were for. Riley hadn't seen much of the universe in his six months out of the Academy, but this had to be one of its bleaker corners.

Riley stopped on the gangway, throwing one last glance up at the Aurora Building at the center of town. His office had been on the sixth floor of that towering complex, the structure retrofitted from the original colony ship's hull—set into the earth like a rusty knife. Riley often marveled at the engineering forethought that had to happen behind a functioning ship gliding through an unstable atmosphere just to plop down as a stable structure—and do so reliably.

What hadn't been stripped away from the vessel's superstructure to build the initial surface modules became the colony's administrative offices, manufactory, food & water habitat, and power grid. They were self-sustaining from the moment the rockets cut out.

Now some five years later, the colony was a thriving metropolis all to its own, with farmlands and mining and schools and hospitals, leaving the Aurora as the seat of the local government. Mankind had turned colonization into a tidy little business, efficient and profitable, with minimal risk.

Someone had lost money on this particular wager.

The dry savannah had been considered a prime location for mineral mining, designated HR-2056 by the bidding corporations. The official title was Vanguard, the most solid outer reach territory the Empire had stamped out.

The locals called it the 'Hellmouth.'

These colonists needn't concoct bogeymen for their children; they had but to simply watch the evening news. This bogeyman was quite real, quite vicious, and it snatched far more than ill-behaved children.

Riley sighed, putting his crate down in the middle of the gangway. Aides and other passengers simply parted around him, no one going to question the young man's intent—he might've been the youngest person there, but the white cords on his Orbital uniform gave him all their respect.

He clicked his crate open with his foot, relishing in that satisfying sound, before snapping it shut again. This place would have to find a way to manage without Riley and his soldiers.

It was a death sentence, but orders were orders—he followed just as many as he gave. And he would carry these out.

Leaving thousands to the whims of the local animals. Their feral executioners.

He had prayed on this, sought to conjure some wisdom his

instructors had forgotten, but none came. He read the words from the Gnostic Librum: "Aspire not for the self but for the Whole; the clean and the dirty; the sinner and the saint; the neighbor and the stranger..."

This order ran contrary to every bone in his body. This wasn't what he had been trained to do.

He let his eyes linger on the crowd below him, their watery eyes glittering in the mid-afternoon sun like a thousand diamonds in bright sands. A chorus of voices reaching up to his retreating form.

Save us.

This exodus would doom each and every one of them. For Consul and Empire. *Zu Gloriam.*

Those dispatch orders weren't meant for public consumption, but it didn't take too long for the locals to notice every soldier in every barracks packing their slate-gray duffel bags and crews scuttling about fueling the transports. Demonstrations packed the streets, having grown to the dull roar of chants that now echoed up through the city spires.

These weren't riots, not yet. They were pleading for their lives. The rioting would come next, as their last hope trailed up and away into the blue sky. Anyone who died in that early wave of violence should consider themselves blessed.

The Colonial Administration—the elected Governor and representative Statesmen—were likely to have strong opinions on the matter, but they wouldn't dare challenge the Consul's orders.

Or would they?

Governor Christopher Dedria all but jumped the police line. It was surprising agility for the older man, a portly gentleman in his fifties, with balding hair and a second chin asserting its dominance. But desperation makes athletes of everyone. Sweat already stained the hand-stitched linen shirt and its violet filigree. That ornate rag would likely be disposed of shortly to join a pile of soiled seasonal clothes that the dilettante worked through weekly.

Whatever voices of objection from the peace officers were

drowned out by the raucous cheers—Hell, Riley almost shouted just out of surprise. It's not often an aging dog delivers a trick like that.

"Ri-ley!" The Governor bellowed, popping the two distinct syllables. It sounded more scolding than he probably meant. "Colonel!"

No matter. This conversation had to happen eventually.

Riley stretched his eyes open wide, hoping to dry his eyes before this fight gathered steam. No one wanted to see their military weepy, circumstances be damned. They wanted the solace and calm of a hardened general, stoic and stone-faced no matter the odds—it was a psychopathy that was somehow comforting to the uninitiated.

The civilians were allowed to be emotional. His instructors had belabored that point: the people are under all kinds of stress, duress. You are their balm, their shield. They can explode; you must maintain.

The Governor opened the conversation by skipping some levels. "You're killing us!"

"Want to keep your voice down?" Riley asked.

"No, I don't think I will, Colonel!" Christopher snapped, "Your men leave on those transports, and we're all dead by the new year." For all his vitriol and spit, this was a man imploring mercy.

It was an accurate prediction, if even a tad hopeful. Riley's own analysts had it just under eight months. The structures would become a cosmic gravestone for the unburied, a sign for passersby to breathe soft as they sail on to safer shores.

Tread not on this cursed land.

Riley crossed his arms and squared up on the Governor, devoting his full attention. No more use for formalities. He was issuing this man's fatal prognosis—come down from the mountain for just a moment, speak man to man.

"I'm sorry, Christopher, but they need every gun hand they can get."

"Oh, I'm sure!" He spat, "One pretender hopping onto her pretend throne on some dark rock—and while you're out defending the honor of a sixteen-year-old *boy*, fifty-two thousand of *your* people..." The Governor lingered on that designation. "...will be cut to ribbons!"

That boy.

Riley bristled at the term, tilting his head. Maybe it was Riley's full and dark beard or the ramp making him appear that much taller, but the Governor seemed to forget that Riley himself was a mere nineteen.

"That *boy* is your Consul General," Riley hissed, trying to lower the Governor's boiling temper by denying that fire any room to breathe. He may have a colony of fearful screaming voices at his back, but Riley had an Empire to protect. "And I'll thank you to speak of him with respect."

The Governor paused, swallowing hard, nervous. Had he gone too far and damned his people?

Riley smiled then, amiable and warm. "And we train our sixteen-year-old boys very well."

The Governor squared his shoulders, rolling the kinks out of his creaking neck. "There has to be a compromise."

Steel toed boots approached from up the gangway, ringing off the titanium alloy floor. A commanding baritone shot through the noise of the crowd. "Any compromise would defy direct orders."

Lieutenant Ilern Holmst marched up to them, crisp and precise, folder tucked under one arm and rucksack over his shoulder. He might as well have stepped right off the Academy floor.

Two years of deployment and he hadn't lost a single step, nor grown cynical of his mission. His crew cut stained his pristine dome with a blanket of brown, so thin and fine it appeared painted on— revealing the surgical scars betraying his many implants etched onto his neck and hairline. His small frame and lean build packaged him as a coiled spring, a single muscle fiber from end to end, with visible veins popping from his biceps.

Riley could probably take his blood pressure from eyesight.

He was the cookie-cutter example of a soldier. A champion of deterrent by calculated escalation. Not the voice Riley needed right now.

"A compromise that would save lives, Lieutenant," the Governor countered back, not to be bullied. Not today. There was no more ground for him to give. They were quite literally standing at the harbor.

Holmst slid past the Governor like he was any other piece of landscape, presenting his folder to Riley. "Full roster, medical deferments tabbed."

"They'll have priority for Sol circulation."

The Governor exploded. "The orders are wrong, and you know it!"

Holmst turned around, setting his icy reptile eyes on to the Governor. Riley found his own glare tracking on to target as well. Even the crowd seemed to hush at that pronouncement.

No one knew what would happen next. By Colonial Code, they would be within their rights to place cold steel into the Governor's chest cavity—a kindness given other Judicial options.

But outburst or not, the Governor's life expectancy was short. Why wouldn't he throw out the rulebook if there were even the slightest of chances?

The man had tried deference; he had tried throwing fire; now to try hurling some blasphemy.

"Orders from the Dunsweir," Ilern snarled, "are not 'wrong', Governor."

"Blessed be his steps," the Governor intoned, call and response. "For his road is long." It almost sounded mocking, because it absolutely was.

Riley had been considering the math on this all morning. His detachment included over a thousand Imperial Regulars and a platoon of officers from Orbital Strike Command. They would likely make little impact on the course of the intergalactic conflict—the regiments in Sol were several million strong, and the locus of the fighting was nine jump points away.

Half of the war would be done before Riley arrived. He'd spend his entire deployment ferreting out enclaves of routed merchants who bowed toward the wrong person. The Governor's words were treasonous and heretical, but they weren't wrong.

Riley sat down on his crate. "Make your case, Governor."

Holmst stiffened, but the discipline etched into his bones locked him in place. His very marrow prevented him from objecting with the Governor's same brand of recklessness. He may as well have; that small motion bore out all the same intention.

The Governor tented his hands as he tried to phrase his pitch. It would've been more accurate to say he was on his knees. "You don't need to leave immediately. Let me draft up a militia, and you train them for a week, two at the most."

"They'd be an undisciplined mob with firearms," Riley dismissed it. "It'd be like setting fire to the town as we pull out of dock."

"A month then?" The Governor asked, shivers shooting up his spine like he could feel a blade's edge kissing the back of his neck, dragging along the stiffened hairs with a metallic hiss.

Riley shook his head. He wouldn't ask the real question, the impossible ask.

He needed Riley to become a co-conspirator.

"We're wasting time," Holmst chided.

"I think the ships will wait for us, Lieutenant. Do you have a proposal?" Riley quizzed his aide de camp, "Or do you fail to see the problem we're faced with?"

Holmst took a heavy, guilty breath. "I've read the BDA, Colonel. But we have our orders."

Those pesky orders. Wartime orders at that. Failure to adhere, and a court-martial would be the least of their worries. The battle damage assessment was galling: the word 'total' occurred about two dozen times. Hell, it occurred three times in Riley's deployment orders.

His instructors' voice rung through his head: the Orders are Gospel, and you will be asked to write your own verse.

Riley looked up at the Governor, studying the grey bloodshot eyes. He had cried when he heard the news, from fear or grief or rage. And he wouldn't ask for help.

The Governor hung his head, unable to bear the weight of Riley's gaze.

Riley sighed. He was going to catch a whole new Hell for this.

"What is the Oskie Creed?" Riley asked, invoking the words etched onto the marble floors of the OSC Academy at Holkstad, on the side of every Naval cruiser, and in a bold font on the walls of Riley's office high above them.

Gospel words, ones that every junior officer in Orbital knew by heart, and often were compelled to recite it under incredible duress: sleep deprivation, temperature extremes, even toxic shock. Riley himself chanted it as a young cadet, knee deep in freezing mud while carrying his bunkmate on his shoulders in a cold October wind.

Holmst would know the words better than his own name. "Service to the People, for they are the Kings. Service to the Crown, for he is the Sword. Service to each other..."

"For we are the Shield." Riley stood up, giving the Governor a good-natured clap to the shoulder. "We're not going anywhere."

The Governor perked up. Even he didn't predict this outcome. "Colonel?"

"A volunteer program," Riley declared, loud enough for the crowds, "The transports will leave as scheduled. Any Regulars that wish to remain—in violation of our orders—will suffer no consequence. I will bear all responsibility."

The crowds erupted in cheers. The Governor almost melted to the floor, a combination of gratitude and gravity. "Oh my God..."

Riley's fierce eyes scanned over him. "It's what you wanted, isn't it?"

"It's..." The bureaucrat couldn't find the words. The frightening implications of Riley's pronouncement weren't lost on him. He knew as well as Riley that the Ministry of Defense would not take kindly to their orders being so flagrantly defied. It addressed their current problem in exchange for an Imperial one later.

While Riley's absence on the field would bear no real impact, his dissent might inspire others to do the same. It was a single slip of snow that may cause an avalanche, and the Ministry needed to snuff that out before it escalated. Riley's deep connections in the Ministry would only protect him so much. This might be seen as its own act of rebellion, a brand new faction in the Civil War, if mishandled.

Riley would need to tread carefully.

It was a reality of command. Blending morality with circumstances often came with biting results.

Holmst squared up with Riley, a strange bounce to his step. No weight in his heels, all forward present. Was this cast-iron man actually pleased about something? "We won't have enough to staff a full watch, let alone engage in skirmishes."

"We?" Riley questioned, with a smirk.

"Goddamn right, sir," Holmst shot back with a crooked grin, "And patrols beyond the Wall will have to end immediately."

Riley nodded, having arrived at the same calculus. He turned to the Governor. "Tell your farmsteads they are to evacuate. Leave everything they can't carry and retreat to the safety of Vanguard."

"Some would rather die."

"And they will, Governor," Riley affirmed, "We can't cover them out there. Make sure they're aware of that. You'll net a few dozen families with that threat. Every single one that elects to retreat is a life saved."

The Governor sagged, all power in this world sapped from him. He faded down to sit on Riley's crate while the two officers paced away, deep in thought. "We'll need to fill out our ranks somehow. We won't have blood to spare," Holmst posed.

That was an intriguing problem requiring some moral flexibility of its own. Most of the Regulars were loyal patriots, and many would fear retribution from Sol. Riley would likely be left with a handful, maybe a few hundred volunteers to man the Colony wall. Hardly a reasonable force.

The local wildlife would take advantage of that weakness, and this sacrifice would be for nothing if they couldn't bolster their numbers.

The creatures had harried the palisades and nearby settlements since Landfall. Towering creatures, ferocious and organized, but primitive. An Oskie properly equipped was more than a match for four—maybe five—of the brutes in close quarters.

But should the creatures sniff out the diminished presence, they might press the advantage, overwhelm the fortifications. Riley needed to put bodies in the line of duty. Now.

"Do we follow the Governor's proposal?" Holmst offered, "Civilian enlistment?"

Riley shook his head. "Most of the colonists are scientists, doctors, farmers. They can't be made to fitness in time. And many won't pass medical. They'll fight, but they're not soldiers. They'll just get themselves—and God knows the people right next to them—killed. What about equipment retrofit? In the Academy, we defended an outpost by bringing farming and mining equipment up to military grade."

"Clever," And yet Holmst's lip curled at the thought, "But I don't think we have the expertise on hand, let alone the hardware."

"But we do have the Mining Pits..."

Riley and Holmst eyed the Governor. They had just dismissed the chance of robotic shock troops. So, where was he going with this?

The Governor nodded, talking himself through his own moral gymnastics. Suddenly he popped up to his feet, gliding over to the officers with a hushed tone to his voice. Even he wasn't comfortable with his suggestion, not enough for the consuming public a dozen yards away. "There's a few thousand Capitals in the Pits. They're fit, desperate. They might relish the fresh air."

Capital laborers brought to the colony to work off their crimes. He was suggesting they draft up a slave army.

It was an abhorrent concept; one the Empire had flirted with in the past. Service was, after all, a kind of labor. Riley had written one of his first officer candidacy papers dismissing the possibility—he had been eleven.

Severe enough crimes made citizenship null and void; sufficient service might win that citizenship back. And as they are not citizens of the Empire, they are not subject to its protections. They could be pushed harder and farther than a colonial militia. And they had spent their entire deployment under incredibly harsh physical conditions.

Those that survive the crash-style training might be workable soldiers. But they lacked dependability and loyalty, just as likely to turn and revolt. Textbook logic indicated that they would bite the hand with newly given teeth.

A child could see this was a bad idea. But this was not a textbook moment.

"Let's take stock of who we have."

CHAPTER
TWO

AARON

THE WIND WAS HARD ENOUGH it might blister the skin, but for the thick cake of dust protecting him, an incidental barrier between him and the harsh elements.

Aaron Havenes inspected the towering rig buried halfway into the rock—an HML Model 68 Autonomous Mining Drone. It had been squealing not half an hour before, when the Gearmaster threw the switch. It had earned him a mild beating at the hands of the Foreman before the emergency had been made apparent.

That used to frustrate Aaron, the abuses and knee jerk violence of prison guards. Now it glanced off him before sliding down his grimy jumpsuit to the dusty ground. The smaller injustices didn't even slow him down anymore. Not worth the trouble it brought.

The Gearmaster had done the right thing, cutting the power. Gearmaster—the term was frowned upon by the establishment. It granted the Capitals too much authority, but Aaron knew expertise when he saw it.

Gearmasters knew machines like Aaron knew his own hands. They could hear when the mining rigs were off, well before they broke. It was like they spoke a proprietary language that could not be taught.

It was a talent well respected in the Mining Pits, but the guards saw the title as a sign of authority. And nobody held authority in the Hellmouth but them.

Aaron was not a small man, but smaller than most in the Mining Pits. A stocky man well under six feet, he was strong enough to climb up into the rig with ease, and small enough to slide past most of its moving parts toward whatever offending piece of detritus had gummed up the works. Should someone turn the rig on, he'd be mashed into chili in short order.

It wasn't unlike spelunking into a cave, working his body through seams and crevices. All of the open space the moving parts needed were large enough to accommodate his small frame. He knew of a few pockets where one could hide from the cranking levers and pistons, but he was nowhere near them now.

And the sadistic Foreman might enjoy the sounds his mashed potato body would make.

This wasn't trust he placed in authority, but a lack of options. Even prudent hesitation to plan the next action might be interpreted as willful disobedience.

Aaron could see the problem now. A chunk of rock had been cut up, then tossed upward by the ten-foot wheels sliding against the silt. The drill bit at the head of the machine would have freed it up from the rock face, and over the three-hour process of grinding forward, the tires would've tripped up on it and hurled it up into the Rig's guts wherever the whims of fate dictate.

Normally, there is a faceplate to prevent such natural sabotage. It had been removed for repairs, after one too many high-velocity impacts, but the Foreman had directed they continue working. This was the natural by-product of missing safety measures.

If this hadn't been caught, the entire forty-ton rig would likely have seized, with pent up energy snapping a half dozen hydraulic lines, throwing the magnets out of alignment, and maybe even started a fire.

Nobody would've died; not from the accident anyway. There

would have been a public display, with every opportunity for fatal results. They wouldn't stay their hand for fear of damaging the property—Capitals had no value.

One outstretched hand, and Aaron managed to snag the fossil. It was caught up on the drive shaft, the one piece of the rig that didn't have excess torque. As it was, the rig couldn't move forward. Had it been tossed up into the drill bit's system, the rig would hardly have stuttered as the gears pounded the bit into dust.

No such luck. Aaron had to worm up inside an industrial goliath for the most invasive kind of exams.

Aaron plopped back onto the dirt, prize in hand, to the mild chatter and applause of the few prisoners who dared show emotion.

Just as Aaron had given up fighting the mild abuses, the guards had given up instilling maximum discipline. They had found the smallest of celebrations allotted to the workers increased their efficiency, not lessened it. It's the bigger shows that might inspire rebellion and discord.

Let them have their small joys.

The offending stone was a small piece, part of something larger shattered by the drill. It was fresh too, despite its depth in the ground.

Stone fossils chunked and split like sandstone, but this had splintered like wood—or bone—with one sharp spire stretching out to a point. The body of it curved back on a smooth line, as though made to cup against the human waist, and a natural edge that would cleave that waist in half with a single swipe. It felt porous and light, as though it might be hollow or some other material entirely.

This was a Jergad arm bone.

He had heard the descriptions but never seen it in person. Belonged to one of the natives. Big burrowing bastards, must've died before the colonization and been uprooted by the rig.

A guard's eyes narrowed, watching Aaron's study of the trophy. His hands fell to his sides, where he unlatched the taser on his hip.

Aaron tossed the bone to the side, lest it appear he was growing a spine.

The 'Gearmaster' stepped forward, inspecting the work. Jensen Davila was his name, and he was properly big, head and shoulders over Aaron. He was also the only one Aaron had met that made the labor teams' mandatory shaved head look good, with his chestnut skin glowing in the sunlight. He looked sculpted, all curves of broad muscles.

Despite the regular beatings, the drab uniforms, and the oppressive atmosphere, Jensen seemed to have his trademark grin tattooed on his face, ever a source of warmth for everyone around him. He even swapped jokes with his guards sometimes.

Making the best of a bad situation, Aaron supposed.

Jensen clapped his big hand across Aaron's back, his palm so broad that his fingers stretched across both of Aaron's shoulder blades. "Like tamin' a dragon!"

"Says you!" Aaron shouted over the rig's idling groans, "You don't have to climb up its *gulaw* ass!"

"I'm too pretty to do that, shortstack," he snarked back, resting his arm on Aaron's head like he was a chair back. "Ugly work for ugly folk."

"Yeah, yeah," Aaron shrugged, cupping his hands to his mouth to help project, "Gears! Loud!"

"A-yup," Jensen blurted, with an almost contrarian melody, "Fire 'er up!"

The metal titan soon roared to life again, absent the ailing groans that had once beleaguered it. It resumed its perpetual task of chewing through the ground, filtering out waste from useful ore, its gnashing teeth rejoining the orchestra of machinery in the mile-wide pit.

There were nearly a hundred of these rigs, each requiring a small maintenance team to keep running. The Foreman didn't tolerate even one hiccup in his great symphony, despite them being unavoidable and natural to an operation of this size.

The planet's odd thirty-hour day cycle made for long work days, and finding time for food or rest was hardly a priority. The benefit of using Capital laborers meant the Forman didn't have to reserve much time for worker safety. But even the guards knew to allow breaks for water and bread in between the incessant beatings, so that maintenance and repairs to damaged rigs could be completed without error.

The workers may be replaceable; the rigs were expensive.

Jensen mimed a few commands, indicating Aaron should take his water break now. To be heard in the Pits, Capitals had developed a form of sign language—quick and broad gestures of the arms—to communicate over the noise and great distances.

It became rather colloquial and most of the guards had picked up the critical phrases via repeated interrogations; they didn't enjoy the prisoners having a silent language all their own.

A water break—it was a wise choice. Aaron wouldn't likely have a better opportunity, and he needed to wash the soot and grime from his throat.

He waved to the nearest guard and mimed splashing water on his face. The guard consulted the holo-display that projected up off his wrist, checking to see if prisoner 626-B9 had already used his ration time.

Satisfied, he ticked a little glowing box, and the display flickered away down into the projector on his wrist. The guard jerked his head, ordering Aaron to move out, but he kept his hand on his taser.

He wasn't worried that the prisoner might try something. He wanted to remind everyone who had power in the relationship, and who could exercise it whenever their sick mind so desired.

This guard had a taste for it. Aaron could see it in his eyes. The perverted glee sparkled in the pale whites, as if the threat of violence sent an erotic shock through him.

Aaron had kept his head low. Despite being a smaller, leaner type, he had also managed to not be that remarkable. It was a conscious decision to avoid the more aggressive kinds of trouble. The guards picked on those with spirit, or without it, taking pleasure in breaking the prisoners like wild stallions to be tamed. It was an exercise in power, and the invocation of it for its own sake, as though the wielder had to be reminded of his own importance.

He walked the narrow ridgeline between the Pits back toward home. Previous Pits that had been mined out were now filled with the tailings from the current operations—pools of acidic sulfide slurry kept dammed up in man-made lakes. The fall would be a few bumpy stories down, and the pools below masked a hundred feet of hole.

Dozens of Capitals died every year from the fumes, and more than a few had 'fallen' into the mix and never been retrieved. Only one had fallen in out of stupid; the rest had been dropped into the mire, by guards and rivals alike.

It wasn't murder if there was no body.

Aaron imagined the day when they drain that swamp and find the mass grave in its depths, some Colonial bureaucrat would feign outrage with hands on hips at whatever bad man allowed this, before writing some long op-ed in a local rag and sipping their beverage of choice.

The apartments dedicated to the mining complex might be considered lavish by that same bureaucrat. The five-story structure had been early colonial housing, but since the expansions provided citizens with more comfortable beds and softer floors, the aging industrial walls had been relegated to housing for the Capitals.

What furniture and furnishings existed were bolted to the walls, installed by the engineers in the factories back at Sol. The cement foundation had only a few major cracks, like dried out skin cracking in the brutal sun. Prisoners used them as a semi-secret storage, hiding food reserves or personal belongings out of immediate sight. To have a room with a two-inch crack in the floor was a luxury, despite having to share the small space with half a dozen others.

The confined space gave swift rise to tribal mentality, with people from different floors and distant wings hoarding supplies from one another. What little manpower the guards had was kept to the Mining Pits, leaving the Capitals to police themselves inside the apartments.

This worked in surprisingly long spurts with inevitable small skirmishes. There was even a religious sect that had formed on the top floor, what started as a Gnostic prayer group selected their new idol in a charismatic guest speaker who rose up from the basement two years back.

The poetry of that was just too much for them to handle, Aaron supposed. People need their heroes wherever they find them, qualifications be damned.

The two guards at the checkpoint—Anatoly and Kipling—were wrapped up in some conversation, with a handcuffed inmate on all fours as their footstool. Based on the bruising around his head, there had been some minor brawl, and this was his punishment—for losing, of course.

The winner would've been long gone before the guards arrived, and they rarely gave enough of a damn to pursue; they surely weren't motivated by fairness, after all.

Aaron didn't recognize the punching bag, but he could make his guesses as to who painted on his bruises. "Where is she?"

Black & Blue spat a big wet one at Aaron's feet, "*Fra tow paz ki lomar!*" Aaron knew a bit of the Colonial creole, and curse words were some of the first he picked up.

"Such a creative individual, this one," Kipling slurred out past his cheek full of ration bar. The very notion of a condensed dehydrated protein mash, even deep in this rotund prick's cheek, was intoxicating to Aaron's malnourished mind.

A day of hard work notwithstanding, he hadn't eaten a proper meal in a month. Capitals often traded whatever materials they could find for a single bite of the soldier's daily allotment. And these lonely guards were often in a bartering mood.

A handful of well-known marketers had long since worked their abuse instinct dry and had instead turned almost chummy with their charges—provided they weren't using them as furniture.

Anatoly propped his heel upon the prostrate man's shoulder, like a human ottoman, steel toe leaning against temple. A reminder of the Capital's status. "His friends brought this little fella out, then went back inside."

Okay then, in this instance there had not been a discovery; there had been a delivery.

Aaron went for the door, but Kipling stopped him with a raised hand. "Pay the toll, 626."

Aaron rolled his eyes. "Take a swing."

The game had sprung fully formed from Anatoly's big brain and spread through the Pits like plague. The Capitals had little documentation about their past lives, and both prisoner and guard alike tried to deduce the prior lives of their fellows. Only the Foreman had access to confirmation, and he had agreed to stipend the winners.

A correct guess and the guards could 'own' a Capital for a day and a night. Helped with morale—the guards' anyways. Whoever guessed correctly dictated the results, and the range of punishments were...wide.

Kipling and Anatoly, however, mostly liked casual abuses. They were lazy bastards and enjoyed service of the more utilitarian type.

After all, they were using bag of bruises here as a footstool.

Anatoly rubbed his hands together. "I think you were some artsy guy, like a...guitar guy!"

Kipling and Aaron looked at him quizzically. The fat lunk shrugged. "Y'know like the..." He strummed his gut with his hand.

"No, I—I understood," Aaron said, stopping short of correcting him further, "But that's not it."

Anatoly snapped his fingers in cartoonish dismay, before nudging his 'stool' in the kidneys for slacking.

"My turn," Kipling said, stroking his nonexistent beard, fingers scraping across stubble, "I'm thinking you have the bearing of the educated, but too young to have gotten far. You were...a research assistant."

Aaron shook his head and Kipling fired off his last shot from the hip, "It's a trick question, innit? You didn't have a job, you *skel*!"

"Don't worry, Kipling, you're zeroing in," Aaron said, gliding past the guards toward the checkpoint doors. "I have a good feeling about you."

"We got everybody else, 626!" Anatoly called out, "We'll get you too!"

Kipling had a few good guesses under his belt, but Aaron would be surprised if Anatoly had correctly guessed his own lunch an hour after eating it. And with his restrained approach, Aaron had made himself neither easy nor a sought after trophy. It was a delicate balance he learned in his first cell block—this was the only place in the Universe identity was a weakness.

Numbers are lost; names are remembered.

The entrance of the apartments was large and vaulted, though it had become claustrophobic with the grime and mold. There had once been a lift system in place, now overtaken as the impromptu trash chute.

The central stairway wrapped around the caged elevator shaft, now half buried in refuse and excrement. The rotting morass would probably make a half-decent mortar if left out to bake. It had long since stopped turning Aaron's stomach, but he could still taste the burn at the back of his throat.

After all, if he was going to get ill, he'd have gone feverish, delusional and died months ago. He was probably inoculated at this point to whatever foul growth festered in that mess.

He jogged up the steps toward the fifth floor. There was no one to negotiate around at this hour—most of the residents were out in the mines. At night, he'd be stepping over people on these steps.

Late arrivals—or those excommunicated from their tribe—were Dwellers, living only on the steps, caught between worlds and without homes.

Not that having one was that much of an upgrade, really. It mostly offered allies to insulate from the more aggressive patrons. After all, this assortment of inspirational folk weren't sentenced to back-breaking labor for their work in children's charities.

Each floor bore the marks of the colonists that had once deemed this structure home—some abandoned furniture, worn decorations, and loose cloth littered every room. The mining dust and garbage tracked in by every Capital's boots didn't much help with the general scum that now clung to every edge and corner like artificial shadows. The well-walked path around the mess lined each long hallway as though it had been drawn with felt-tipped markers by drunks or children.

Aaron slid down the hallway, turning only to slip past other Capitals. The fifth floor was comparably clean when measured against the rest, with a garbage detail organized to remove the worst of the refuse. After a few outbreaks and even a fatality, the entire floor decided that sleeping in filth produced poor results for everyone.

He cracked the door on his room, waiting the requisite half second before entering. While he'd seen nearly everyone on his floor in some state of undress and even seen a few mid-intimacy, he always felt it polite to allow that single breath of time for someone to bellow out a warning.

Absent that, Aaron proceeded inside.

It was a small room, maybe only ten by six, and housing a good eight people at night. For the moment, there were only the two he expected.

Nora Silva held a wet rag to the side of her head. She gave as good as she got this time, it seemed, with stains of red tainting the edges of the damp cloth.

She had popped the faceplate off the gas heater, exposing its pilot light. Back and forth, like a bow across strings, she waved a threaded needle through the tiny flame.

She was a short woman, but solid, with a dancer's frame. This caused a number of people to underestimate her and each individually make the enchanting discovery that this little raggedy blonde could unscrew the human neck with a properly thrown elbow.

"What did he do?" Aaron asked, more curious than concerned. One too many broken bottles in a pub brawl is how Nora found herself Capitalized, anyway.

"He was an evangelical prick," Nora blurted, with a tilted grin. Maybe she was picturing the state in which she left him.

40

"Yeah, but what did he *do*?" Aaron reiterated.

She shrugged, "Should've listened to his own speeches, maybe he'd still have his two front teeth."

"He cornered her at the mess." The rich soprano tones and proper bedside manner cooed from the corner. Eden Neria squeezed out another dirty rag, the murky water darkened by the fresh blood.

The fae little woman was half of Nora's already small size, never clearing five feet tall, but that pitchy voice could command as much as calm. Her shoulder length hair—an allowance from working in medical and not around heavy machinery—had been tied back out of her face some time after she arrived five months ago and might not have been touched since.

It had gone oily and matted but her concern had always been for others before herself. Her soft brown eyes never seemed to darken, despite the ever-darkening circumstances she found herself swaddled in.

Aaron snorted at Eden's brief explanation. "Yeah, that's a mistake made one time only." He turned back to Nora, "What, did he try to share the Good Word?"

"Some choice words, really," Eden huffed, "about his exceptional genetics."

Nora smiled, some of her own blood still stained to her teeth, "I expressed my distaste."

Aaron glanced at the rancid water bowl Eden worked the cloth in and out of. "Did Nora leave us with any drinking water or..."

Nora clucked her tongue behind his back, as Eden dug for a bottle in the floor cracks. She removed a plastic bottle, half empty, the top crumpled down to save on space. She tossed it to him, checking that task off her list so she could focus on the real problem. "Progress?"

Nora pulled her soiled rag back, revealing the ugly abrasion to the side of her head. She had cracked her skull—a slam against a chair or table edge, maybe—but the bleeding had largely abated, revealing the soft tear in the tissue.

Eden settled next to her, taking the heated needle from Nora and gripping her hand with the other.

"Bite down on something," Eden instructed.

Shaking her head, Nora just smirked back at her, "Do your worst, seamstress."

Eden slid the needle under the skin. Nora didn't even need to squeeze the hand. She just stared at Aaron, more out of a game than a challenge.

Mental focus. She knew it unnerved people, and that amused her. Whatever pain she was experiencing paled in comparison to the pain she was inflicting with that downright Spartan display.

Give more than you take.

"You want to gawk, shortstack, you gotta pay," Nora taunted him, presenting the fresh zipper along her temple.

Aaron snorted at the quip: 'Shortstack.' Nonchalantly, Aaron leveled his hand at his height and swiped it clean over Eden's head—illustrating the stark difference.

Nora just smiled back. Whether it bothered him or not, she just liked taking up rental space in his head.

Not many stitches were required, and Eden was soon finished with her sanguine arts. It was not the first patchwork she had done in this space and, if Nora continued to pick fights, it would not be the last.

"If you're just marking time," Eden said, "Quinn's never without a deck of cards. Across the hall."

"I found a Jergad arm bone."

That stopped them both, backs stiffening and necks craning up as though a string lifted them to the roof.

The Pits were a good ten miles behind the colony Wall. Nobody they knew had ever seen one of the creatures in person. But they'd heard horror stories related by the guards: towering monsters, with scythes for hands, that could rend an entire platoon to pieces in seconds. They jumped from the ground and disappeared again like sharks in water.

No one believed the tall tales, but there had to be some brand of truth, some origin to the myth. And their curiosity never wavered.

"And?" Nora asked, masking the quake in her voice.

Aaron shook his head. "Got kicked up into Jensen's rig. We're lucky it didn't pull half the gears out of alignment. Would've torn the cliffside down." There was a hushed, almost reverential, tone to his voice. As though he feared invoking the image of the beasts might summon them to that very spot.

After a moment, Nora whispered, "What did it look like?"

"It looked like a bone," Aaron blurted, the words racing past his lips with the uncommon velocity of a jailbreak. "But it had this claw on the end, like one big finger."

"Metatarsal," Eden chimed in with the infuriating 'actually' tone that only came packaged with specific education or complete lack of one. People never talked like that when they had just half of a clue.

"Whatever," Aaron said, "But it was long, flat. And sharp."

A chill filled the air. They had all heard rumors. Aaron never trusted rumors. That bone was no rumor.

But the other two were still frozen, as if they were unplugged, slumped. Their minds elsewhere.

"Not as big as the fairytales but...big enough," Aaron murmured to the two statues.

He pushed the plastic bottle to his cracked lips, letting just a touch of the drink dribble down his lips. He could feel it seep into every crack of his throat and soak into the gristle of his thin beard, as if every part of him were eager for the drink. The moisture sank into his skin, doing little to sate the thirst banging on the alarms in his head. But the migraine will have to wait its turn.

Eden's big brown eyes locked on to his, as though hollowed out. "Carmona was looking for you this morning."

"He say why?" Aaron probed.

She nodded. "Army's pulling out. Got bigger fish than little ol' us. But they still have that Wall."

"Car knows more," Nora hinted with a natural lyricism, "He gave us the sales pitch a little bit ago."

Aaron did all the mental gymnastics himself. "A draft?"

"Volunteers," Eden corrected, "Serve a tour...go free."

"They goin' to give us sharp sticks or..." Aaron trailed off. When the two didn't answer, he wished he was back in the Pits. "You two idiots can't be thinking—"

"Not one to say 'no' when someone asks," Eden said.

Aaron rolled his eyes, "Just want to remind you, you *can* though."

Nora inspected the stitch work with her fingers, rough pads tapping along the beveling, "And do what else? Get shipped off to another border world sludge pen?"

"So you choose military service? They don't even see you as a living person!" Aaron was dumbfounded by the logic. This was lunacy to even entertain.

"It's just nice to *have* a choice, y'know?" Eden pointed out with a half-hearted smile.

"Choose what?" Aaron chuckled, miming out some floating text crawl from a propaganda video, "Death or dishonor?"

She didn't even blink. "Freedom."

Nora stopped just short of pointing and laughing, "Ah, they should slap your flat ass on a recruitment poster!"

Eden ignored the color commentary, stepping in closer to Aaron. "They're offering full clemency. I didn't choose this spinning rock any more than you did, but after this...maybe we could pick literally anywhere else?"

That notion gnawed at him. 'Freedom.' No more mining pits; no more sadistic guards; no more idle punishments. He could hold his head up for a change.

Go somewhere nice. Start over. With her.

Now there was something worth some pain.

CHAPTER
THREE
RILEY

THEY HAD WORKED ALL through the night to prepare the fields.

The parkland had once been a welcome respite for scientists and laborers to bring picnics or energetic children, a gathering point for the community. The grass was a local fauna and had been trimmed and maintained for both safety and aesthetic, with the dirt running track around the circumference kept packed and level.

Bleachers and other uncomfortable seating options were usually stacked around the various games, but workers had pulled them aside sometime in the night, the swift action carving six-inch troughs in the ground where they were dragged. They were now piled together at one side of the arena, forming a kind of control tower for the military, local government, and peacekeepers to have a full clear view of the basin.

What was once a two-square mile field for competition and recreation had been overtaken with nearly a thousand terrible examples of humanity. Murderers, thieves, and undesirables alike lined up for Riley's approval—as though their kind would ever deserve it.

But desperate times asked for moral compromises.

Cables dangled from the back of the bleachers where sleep-deprived technicians grunted out the last few adjustments. They were over an hour behind schedule, but they were badly understaffed.

Nothing to be done about it.

Several computers had been strung up to provide the most basic of database management for Riley and his crew. They would need to direct the field officers through the varied exercises to provide the most accurate information possible.

And in the event of an uprising, their vaulted position offered excellent lines for the twin mounted GA-57 repeaters on either corner. There wasn't enough ammunition to stop them all, but a given amount of falling brass would make any body politic reconsider their futures.

To put down a rebellion, a master need only bleed the crowd a sufficient amount. If fear can overcome hate, one man could control a thousand.

In Riley's experience, hate always trumped fear. And after all, wide-scale slaughter did not harness an animal; it left the master with a dead horse.

"Colonel!" A demanding alto voice dogged at his heels.

He knew the owner of that voice like he knew knee pains.

The Governor's daughter, Talania Dedria, held a minority post in the Governor's administration. He wanted to keep his activist daughter occupied with her passions. Unfortunately, they were many.

The human manifestation of spunk trotted up to Riley's side. Her strict ponytail like black silk pulled high on her head made her only seem taller. She looked down on him from her six-foot altitude. Her 'princess' voice and forced formality induced eye rolls from his staff every time she knocked on his door with the aggravating weight of a privileged woman in search of the shift manager.

Her clothes were minimalist, a simple white blouse with power trousers, but it was clearly off-world make. She had her expensive tastes, and her father did little to dissuade her.

As though he could; she was the power in their home, both a more genuine leader than her father and a greater pain in the ass. Her piercing green eyes felt more akin to a venomous snake, never blinking and just waiting for the moment you do.

"Colonel, you can't really intend to go through with this?" Talania demanded of a military officer who had trained from adolescence to serve with Imperial Infantry, Joint Command, and Orbital.

He wondered if the newly minted adult had completed something other than a five-page op-ed in her entire life.

Riley paused, sliding into what little decorum he had to spare. "Wasn't my idea, but a man works with what he has on offer."

"They signed up for hard labor, not *combat*," she spat at him, pointing toward the field now packed shoulder to shoulder with bone and sinew and meat.

Signed up. That's a laugh.

He had to admit, with the casual glance, they bore more than a passing resemblance to raw recruits. They may not all be as young, but they were fit and eager. This might not have been such a bad idea after all.

"Ms. Dedria," Riley chose his words, "It's an all hands on deck situation."

"Get it from the citizens," she was almost pleading, "There are more than enough people begging for the chance to defend their homes."

Riley glanced back at a nearby aide. "I feel like I've had this conversation before. Oh wait—I did!" He spun back around. "Your father beat you by fourteen hours. Step up your game."

"There is no need for—"

"They would die." Riley stated the fact as simple as breathing the air around him. "The mind may be willing, even brave, but the common folk are soft and comfortable. Criminals know hardship, pain, and determination. A starving thief will fight for long after the baker runs out of breath."

"So you'd rather send slaves to die in their stead?"

47

"My preferences don't factor into it," Riley began, "My job is to protect the citizenry, not throw them to the wolves. This is a voluntary program. Any one of those Capitals are free to take the jump seat back to Sol."

"Colonel, these people haven't been 'free' for a long time," Talania sniped back at him.

That was the key word, though not the one she thought it was. He could no longer stop his mouth from running off the reservation.

"People?" He blurted, "Ma'am, I guaran-*goddamn*-tee you, that those 'people' on that field don't think you are a person."

No answer? No pithy comeback, just a pouted lip and hand on hip? Fine.

Riley pointed at the assembly. "They see you, and they see an opportunity. They do not have compassion. They do not have empathy. They do not have their *humanity*. And those that once did, lost it in deep in the Pits. You and I and everyone else on this field are giving them a chance to prove otherwise. If they can sacrifice for us, as much as they have *taken* from us, then maybe they can go home. That's an offer the Empire would never make."

"But you would?" She caught him up.

There was the truth of it all. The world may not be, but he was gracious, kind, charitable. How dare he try to do two good things at once!

Frustrating, maybe, but she was right. He had overstepped his authority. This wasn't a promise he could keep, not really.

Riley ground his teeth, hearing the molars squeak against each other. "Please tell your father I'll need an accurate estimate from the silos before I can make rationing recommendations...Ms. Dedria."

Riley blew past her, taking the steps up the bleachers two at a time.

She didn't usually wind him up this much. Her previous complaints had been of the more adorable variety, seeking comments on whatever sob story of the week her Press office was towing at the time. Maybe it had something to do with how correct she actually was.

Slavery.

Even besides that, they were gambling the survival of the colony on the backs of criminals with guns.

This only ended one way. Eleven-year-old him would be ashamed.

Riley trudged up toward the post commander. He was a broad-shouldered man, built like a brick or a block of slate, with no edge or curve to his muscled body. His blonde hair was cut close, giving an unsettling brighter tint to his otherwise dark and leathery skin. His tan & brown BDU stuck out amongst the gray steel all around him.

The Gunnery Sergeant had a storied history written in his chest candy; there were ribbons from half a dozen armed conflicts, Purple Heart with Cluster, and a Bronzed Bar with filigree—singular heroism in defense of his post.

This man had likely seen more combat than Riley had read about.

He must've heard Riley's approach. "Ten-HUT!" The man barked with the gravel of a few bad habits and a lifetime of shouting. The technicians dropped their work and snapped to a crisp attention.

"Sergeant Bray," Riley affirmed, "Stand at ease. We've work to do."

"Yes, sir," Bray effused, a devilish smile locked away behind that drill instructor's iron mask, "We've put together a program that oughta thin out the field for us."

Riley's lips tightened, souring on that thought. "If we don't find enough talented folk on that field, Sergeant, our stay may be shorter than planned, so let's not take such glee in 'thinning the field.'"

Bray nodded, keeping whatever dissenting opinions he held back behind his teeth. That's not very useful. Expertise is only useful when shared widely and frequently.

"Speak freely, Gunny," Riley ordered, his eyes tilted to the floor.

He wasn't entirely sure he could keep a straight face if Bray had any truly colorful objections.

"Due respect, Colonel," Bray started, "If I speak free, you're going to frog march me out to the firing squad. So why don't we stay focused?"

Riley managed to choke back the laugh that leapt up in his chest. The man twice his age was trying everything he could to show due deference.

Bray was a career rifleman and Riley an officer crafted from birth. But while Bray knew more about the world, he also knew his place. A good commander would use Bray like the well-tuned instrument he was. "No, Sergeant. Let me have it. You also disapprove of our recruits?"

Everyone was watching now. They would sell tickets if they could.

Bray ground his teeth, his hand forced but deciding with how much passion he wanted to present. "Sir, Capitals aren't trusted when holding a toothbrush. You want me to gather together a regiment of them, train them, arm them, and trust them with border security?"

Riley's head bobbed from side to side, weighing his own screwball response. "I don't disagree on any particular point, but I trust you to... whip the prospects into shape, Sergeant."

"This is a *gulaw* farm animal prom, sir."

"Ain't it just?" Riley agreed, dropping into his seat, "Rest easy. Nobody's comfortable with it, Sergeant. But I think when you put them on that Wall, and they measure their adversary...they'll decide where their loyalties lie very quickly."

Bray chewed on his cheek, masking a twitch.

"At Holkstad, they used to say each Command has to reinvent the wheel for each theater. That's all we're doing."

"Can an old grunt share a bit of his wisdom?" Riley gestured for him to proceed. "The Academy trained you, but they ain't here. Use your head, not theirs."

"Do you why we're here, Gunny?" Riley asked the veteran, "I mean—why did you volunteer to stay?"

Bray shuffled a bit, uncomfortable with the line of questions.

"It's not a trick question. There's a lot of good answers. I'm just curious."

Bray swallowed hard before answering, "Just seemed like the right thing to do."

"Defying your orders in wartime?" Bray was silent, so Riley pressed on. "That's what makes the right thing hard. You don't do the right thing because someone's got a biscuit for you. You don't do it because it makes you warm and fuzzy. You do it, even when you know you're going to get hit for it. Because it *is* the right thing to do."

Bray opened his mouth to say one more word but resumed his parade rest.

But Riley wasn't going to let that slide. "You've manned the Wall?"

Bray looked up and away. The only answer that was needed.

Riley nodded. "They're not Regulars down there, Gunny. But tell me the few folks we got left wouldn't give their left nut to have a few more bodies between them and the wild? Let's give 'em everything we have in stock, huah?"

"Huah, sir." Bray nodded, softening his stance a bit. Sour disposition aside, he turned to his radio to begin the exercises.

There were a few simple and tactical truths about the Capitals that Riley knew, foremost among them that if these criminals remained they would be made assets or deleted liabilities. The mining platform and accompanying Pits were to be shuttered.

Those that could not be enlisted, would be shipped off-world in packing crates, bound back to their host prisons to serve the remainder of their sentences. They were too dangerous to leave unattended and every hand worthy of a gun had higher priorities than babysitting scum.

And they deserved all the creature comforts of a bag of cement.

Two separate incidences of unrest had already been put down at that news—one of which involved some deaths. A faction of Capitals felt they were entitled to their hard labor and modest accommodations.

In all fairness, a day working was better than a day stewing in the hot boxes on Charon. But they forgot the most critical of penalties they suffered upon their convictions: they weren't entitled to the air they breathe, let alone anything else.

This was a gift, a mercy, an olive branch from the civilized to the monster, to coax it back from the abyss. Reject that kindness, and there was no reason to tolerate the existential threat they represented. They were alive today because of the Empire's mercy, not because of their long-lost 'rights.'

Riley didn't need these Capitals to be much. Expectations weren't high. He needed them to be functional, cooperative.

And desperate.

If the Capitals could match the physical requirements of a soldier, Bray could fill in the rest.

The first challenge was a simple cardiovascular exercise that Regulars ran twice a week. With forty-pound packs, troopers would hard march in the morning cold three straight miles before stepping up the pace. Rough terrain and inclement weather would neither defer nor delay these exercises, sometimes forcing the march through hard rain or dust storms.

The Capitals were given stones, something more familiar to them. After being broken into loose groups, they were herded in a circle around the field, like a Sisyphean hell-march. The computers kept time and distance as the giant Ouroboros wound its way about the track, an undulating mass of the two conflicting feelings: hope for a future and a dire regret of the present.

The monitors in the bleachers quivered on their moorings. Nearly a thousand feet pounding dirt in a circular march was enough to shake the ground.

The acrid stench of sweat and fluids assaulted Riley's eyes. He blinked it away, refusing to let any water flush out the toxins. Too many years of training and too many badges to give a patriot's shower over a little rancid air; not with Bray so close by, anyway.

Not every person was capable of making such a forced march. Dozens were setting down their stones to catch their breath, only to be driven on by cattle prods.

The Capitals could resign this opportunity at any time, and march off the field to the bloated transports that waited outside the Stadium gates. They would be tagged, indexed, and chained for their shipment to a more fitting cell.

Some were smart enough to recognize their limitations and choose the prison.

Others simply protested the shocks. They spouted off about fairness or health or safety before being driven on by their taskmasters' prods. They spat back at their shepherds, shouting epithets that Riley lip-read through the video feed.

How charming.

But to most, the prospect of freedom was too enticing. They marched until their feet bled. The dirt warmed to a bronze with the reddish stains left by hundreds of blistering footfalls.

This was no senseless parade; it was a trial of mental fortitude. The average mind could not will itself past injury to continue: a feat required daily for soldiers. Outrunning, outlasting a threat was important, no matter how much the feet begged for pause.

Riley found himself surprised—though he shouldn't have upon reflection—that the Capitals bore this trait in great numbers. Their everyday involved working through injuries and past exhaustion. They lived without water and food. Warmth was the something mothers would beat them to sleep with. Hardship was their crucible and their nightly bed.

Though chaos was barely averted near the end of the march. The Capitals began dropping; the mind could push only so far. It cannot make a man walk when a tendon snaps or a knee buckles. The exhausted and spent were swiftly buried under the thousand footfalls of their comrades, reducing them to paste before anyone knew what had happened.

The sheer density of the crowd overwhelmed and subsumed them, painting streaks of red along the already sanguine sand.

The Capitals grew uneasy, restless and distressed, shocked at the discovery of their compatriots under their toenails. Their perseverance and the prodding of instructors had caused fatalities.

Murmurs were rippling through that crowd.

Bray's guards opened the ammo cans, ready for the worst.

A small Capital collapsed in the middle of his group, a wounded deer and a foregone conclusion. But for the quick action of two of his fellows, he would surely have also been trampled.

Instead, the flow broke around the fallen man like a river bend. The two heroes reached down amongst the pounding feet to snag the man and his stone.

But the sand of the track had gone thick with sweat and gore, clinging to clothes and flesh. Just a few inches deep, but it seemed to suck the little one back down to the ground. And with each failed attempt, the two Capitals redoubled their efforts.

Before their group had advanced, they had heaved the man back to his feet and returned his load, urging him onward.

It was almost inspiring.

Riley leaned over to Bray. "Make a note of those two," he said, indicating the two champions on the screen.

Bray tapped at his keys, triggering the facial recognition software and comparing to what he found. After three failed matches and some mild cursing, he found the two faces in question. "Franklin Carmona and Aaron Havenes," he muttered, scribbling notes. "Violence convictions both, but no marks on their prison records."

"Stamina, awareness, concern for fellows, executive action under duress..." Riley smiled wide with self-assurance. "What do you think, Sarge?"

Bray didn't answer, preferring instead to chew on the discovery.

Riley had spoken too soon. The forced march was only the first challenge.

The Capitals laid down their stones, thirsty and exhausted. Some even stooped to suck on the moist ground under their feet, unthinking or uncaring that it also contained the blood of their colleagues.

But there would be no rest. They weren't testing for physical fitness, alone.

Bray instructed over the loudspeaker, the Capitals were to pair off. With one friend across their shoulders, they would now run across the field. At the opposing side, they would switch places and run back. Failure to complete this action within forty minutes would result in immediate failure.

Exhausted, tired, and afraid—with all of these mental handicaps, could they still coordinate?

Some picked up the nearest person they could find without so much as a friendly greeting. One giant of a man picked the smallest feather of a human he could grasp. Riley could only laugh at the giant's simplistic perspective. Did he really think that his wee little load would be able to carry his girth all the way back? His impulsive behavior doomed the both of them.

Others burned precious time trying to select the most ideal person to carry. They debated body weights and lifting strengths, while others blazed reckless trails across the field. Some even began scuffling over the desirable partners. They were willing to fight for their tickets to freedom, even if it meant each other.

This was more of what Riley expected. Selfishness. Violence. Malice. Hardly a soldier's temperament.

The first duo came back across the field. A thin man, but lean and with a blank expression, moved with slow and deliberate strides. The weight on his shoulders was a woman twice his size, tall and solid, with a shaved head but for a single long braid of blonde hair thicker than a fuel line. That was a weapon in itself.

They had made their moves early and with calculated precision, deliberate caution, never rushing but never hesitating.

"Our first winners," Bray huffed, "Solomon Lipkin & Keira Ladd."

Riley snorted, "He looks like her child."

"Lipkin killed fifteen men with a spoon," Bray deadpanned. Riley tilted his head around, uncertain if Bray was pulling his chain. Bray's eyes were the only thing smiling. "Not all at once, sir."

"A serial killer? Or just resourceful?" Riley lamented, "That's an auspicious beginning."

"Yes, sir," Bray conceded, "And Keira Ladd was the lineman for a bank heist team. They hit seven locations in two systems before the team was captured." He paused, "They had to be separated after they were *re*-captured."

Riley snorted at that.

Bray didn't hide his own smirk, consulting a nearby display. "Says here these two were known associates inside the Pits. Rarely ever separate."

Riley had asked for coordinated people in peak physical shape. They fit the profile. Perhaps he needed to be more specific.

What was curious were the two heroes—Aaron and Carmona. They huddled around the little one they had saved from the stampede. There was discussion, some kind of heated haggling. There was no way the exhausted and beaten child they had ripped from the river of death could complete this next task. Carmona was urging him to quit the field.

Aaron was having none of it. He heaved the boy onto his shoulders and began the march. Cursing, Carmona wove his was back into the crowd in search of a partner, not to be left behind.

Was Aaron suicidal? Or had he some delusion that this would work?

Aaron made his leg of the journey without much trouble, trying to balance the time leftover for his diminutive partner and giving the boy plenty of time to catch his breath.

But at the far end, when they were to trade their duties, something happened. The boy refused.

As duo after duo passed them up and the clock wound down, the tearful little man tried to walk off the field toward the waiting transports. But Aaron wouldn't let him leave, physically keeping him on the field with hands pressed to chest. If his partner quit, Aaron would also be disqualified. He could not let that happen.

He would selfishly endanger the boy to save himself.

The guards noticed this as well, readying their weapons for any surprise. Riley sat forward in his seat, peering at the display. The image vibrated with the hundreds of footfalls on the field, but he could make out the general attitude of the exchange. The boy had no heart for this; Aaron had heart enough for them both.

The image stilled just enough for Riley to make out one phrase:

"Do you ever want to go home again?"

After a weighty pause, the boy dropped to one knee, as though to pledge service to a long-dead King. Aaron laid himself across the boy's shoulders. Groaning under the load, the boy stood back up and joined the dregs of the Capitals trudging their way back across the field.

Some collapsed halfway, feuding and crying. They blamed each other and their weaknesses. They turned their hot fires inward.

Through it all, through muck and torn earth, Aaron and his little squire hobbled forward. They were among the slowest, passed up by those racing time and fear. But they never stopped, their bickering at an end.

Carmona and his partner overtook them, shouting words of encouragement as they slipped by. Everyone they passed near called out to them, and feuding pairs were soon back on their feet.

The little underdogs might as well have been carrying a battle flag, bearing inspiration itself forward to the top of a distant hill, and leading forward the charge behind them.

Bray looked at his stopwatch, as though to confirm the giant digital clock ticking down on the glass wall was accurate. This was going to be heartbreaking.

If they took too long, they would be turned to those transports regardless. And all that faith and belief and fire would turn to ash. Bend the rules for them, and those that already fell would demand satisfaction. Shut them out, and those inspired by the exhibition would turn sour.

Either way, the crowd might boil.

"Weapons free, Gunny," Riley murmured, seeing the nightmare as it stumbled forward.

That's when the little boy fell to one knee. Aaron screamed in his ear. They were too close, had gone too far. Just a few dozen more steps. He had done more than this before. Pain is discomfort, discomfort can be ignored.

Stand up. Do it now.

The little squire screamed, knees shaking to and fro so hard they might click against each other. But up he went.

The crowd cheered. And as though he might draw strength from their enthusiasm, the boy's walk broke into a jog.

They crossed the line with 2.8 seconds to spare. They slid across it more than anything else, with the poor boy flopping onto his face in the blood and grime. The exultation was intoxicating, and even the observing commanders and citizenry found themselves applauding the Cinderella story.

Riley let out a sigh of relief. No uprising today.

A total of 758 Capitals qualified through the program. The remaining hundreds were escorted at gunpoint to the waiting transports. There were no goodbyes. There was resentment and vitriol, even a few scuffles to break up.

They all felt entitled to a uniform and a duty roster, to the freedom they had long ago sold at the altar of immorality. Just under half of the assembly had earned the right to earn it back.

Riley would be surprised if as many as ten survived to claim it.

CHAPTER
FOUR
AARON

QUINN HADN'T SPOKEN to Aaron since the Stadium. He was likely embarrassed. The kid never did like being so much as adjacent to the spotlight, let alone in the center of it.

He had suffered an ACL sprain from his final push and, while not quite bedridden, had been instructed by Eden to minimize his activity. Jensen and Carmona were kind enough to haul the few possessions Quinn owned to their new lodgings.

Everyone had been very supportive.

Precisely what Quinn didn't want: his name being mentioned with uncommon frequency.

Aaron pushed open the double doors like a cartoon sheriff entering his favorite saloon. The doors didn't swing with that classic fluidity; instead, they clacked hard against the back wall and hung there, like they'd lost their childish spring from ages of use.

The hundred or so Capitals inside were far too busy ensconcing themselves in their lush accommodations to notice his entrance. And Aaron, himself, found his jaw loose at the majestic barracks he now called home.

One of three longhouses on the premises, their facility more resembled an empty warehouse. In a past life, it had been; when materials and munitions had been cleaned out for the transports, furniture had been hauled in.

Cots had been bolted to the ground and walls with rusting three-inch iron spikes, as though the paranoid hasty designers were afraid the furniture might run off of its own accord.

Now there was a thought—that one of the Capitals might hoard the allotment of bedding, sitting atop a throne made of threadbare linens and treated rebar, issuing edicts to his followers and granting favors in exchange for but a few hours with a creaking foam mattress.

The authorities really didn't trust them at all, with the intentionally obvious security cameras tacked into the ceiling, ominous bulbs every dozen feet or so.

Tucked in the corners and along the dimly lit walls, Aaron could make out small colonies of rats trying their best to make no noise, but having left nowhere to hide between half-inch steel walls and a cold cement floor.

What once had been a haven full of crates and supplies was now a wild safari, with scant cover and too many dangers. The few entrances and exits available to them—cracks in the aging floor or creaking steel panels—were staked out by the more enterprising Capitals, doing everything possible to look nonchalant before pouncing on any measly critter that strayed too close.

Where humanity went, these little hitchhikers always seemed to follow. And the little critters rarely considered that they may be more prey than opportunistic parasite. Aaron made a note that the disease-ridden fleabags would have to be purged to prevent outbreaks. Fresh meat wasn't worth the bubonic consolation prize.

The Capitals congregated in their usual clans, with border disputes between neighbors and hierarchical spats over the top bunk. There was little more than shoving and yelling. No one wanted to jeopardize their meal ticket, but they wouldn't compromise their status either, hard-won in the Pits.

Even the eighth-floor cultists were holding a special prayer meeting on the Westside, using the hard-won good fortune from the Stadium Trials to recruit more believers. 'They had won nothing that had not been given by God,' the speaker intoned over and over again with different terminology each time. Pilgrim, Dunsweir—what's in a name, after all? Whatever Power In The Sky, they owed it their fealty.

And of course, by extension, to the speaker. They owed their speaker devotion should they wish more windfalls. That curveball was forthcoming, near the end of the service. But the hopeful and the hungry would swallow any pill if it meant more promises of less suffering.

It was far more difficult to convince them that they were being fooled than it was to fool them in the first place.

Aaron set about looking for young Quinn. He was likely somewhere near the rest of the Fifth Floor crowd.

He could spy Jensen and Carmona in a friendly contest of strength. The two had pulled aside a trunk to use for their arm wrestling challenge—the prize obviously was who got to sleep top bunk.

Their hands clasped and arms swollen as they fought each other. Their shoulders rolled and gazes locked in a sweaty display more suitable for the hedonists from the sub-basements.

It was a brand of masculine preening that Aaron never quite wrapped his head around, a strange cocktail of dominance and dignity stirred up with a dash of sexual insecurity.

Eden and Nora stood nearby, shouting encouragement to their competitor of choice; often both.

"Are you going to let that little piker show you up, Jensen?!"

"Stop helping him!" Carmona barked back through clenched teeth.

Jensen grinned to hide his grimace, "Gettin' a bit tired, are ya?"

"It's all about the leverage," Carmona smiled, resetting his grip and slamming Jensen's hand to the table.

Nora cheered, more excited by the tension than the result.

Jensen worked out his wrist and immediately reset. "Best of three?"

"Left hand?"

Jensen shrugged, trading his sides and the two were back at it again.

Even Solomon and Keira were watching from their nearby bunks, hungry eyes and icy stillness. The psychotic pair of attack dogs were rarely motivated to do more than was necessary, and found the flailings of their compatriots downright adorable. 'Efficient', was the word Keira had used.

Aaron had trouble telling her apart from the machines they used to work with.

Solomon caught Aaron staring, his dark eyes widening with recognition and pale lips curling back to reveal his stained teeth. Was he happy to see Aaron, or willing him into cardiac arrest?

Oh good. That was a ration bar in his hand. For a moment, Aaron could've sworn the man was eating one of the rats as casually as a child would candy.

Then again, it really wouldn't surprise Aaron if Solomon was just using the oatmeal as a palate cleanser. He could swear, half of Solomon's behavior was meticulously designed to be unsettling, like there was a puppet master somewhere behind a curtain pulling strings on his marionette. Every motion coming just a half second delayed so as to be as jarring as possible.

It didn't bother Aaron anymore, not after a year of exposure. But those first few months were chilling, catching the creeper refusing to blink for hours at a time.

Aaron sauntered up to the melodramatic monster with all of the formality of a backyard barbecue. "Quinn around?"

Solomon nodded at a bunk on the far side of the dick-measuring contest.

"Give him space, ya?" Keira advised, never taking her hungry eyes off the action. Her consumption of the gladiatorial foreplay could not be disturbed by anything short of an incoming attacker. It was then Aaron noticed he could only see one of her hands.

Aaron nodded and marched away in the indicated direction. Privacy may have long since been jettisoned as a concept, but that didn't mean courtesy had to go with it. Proximity had exposed him to all kinds of behaviors and none of it fazed him anymore.

At the edge of the clan's borders, far enough from the shouting gladiators and the jeering audience, sat Quinn. The young man could barely be called that, still with his soft boyish features and frame.

He was short and lean, like a loaf of bread that hadn't finished cooking. Give him a few more years and a healthy diet, he might grow up to be a person, but as of now, he might not even know how to shave.

He played with his deck of cards, bridging them and ruffling them from hand to hand in an idle dance to occupy his mind while his eyes traced over the opposite wall. He was propped up in his bed, leg immobilized to prevent further injury.

Aaron had to applaud Eden's ingenuity. There was no plant-life taller than waist height, and what metal was available had been reserved for other uses—most especially not for Capitals.

In lieu of this, Eden had bundled some grass together and tight woven it into a stiff rope. This makeshift bamboo did not want to bend in any way and when lashed to his knee, effectively locked Quinn's leg fully extended. There was no way he could further injure himself. It was a creative solution.

Quinn didn't even look up. Another person trapped in their thousand-mile stare. "Bunk's taken."

Aaron looked at the empty space above him. "You sleepin' in both?"

No response.

Aaron leaned against the bed frame. "You can do this, Quinn."

"Do what, exactly?" Quinn asked, grey eyes turning to fixate on Aaron like there was some accusation being withheld, "I—I've never even thrown a punch before!"

It was Aaron's turn to have no response. What's the appropriate response to that? 'First times' and 'rising to occasions' and 'meeting challenges head-on' did not fit the circumstance. Aaron all but crowbarred the young boy across a finish line where he would be trained to fight an alien menace for a whole year. Two hundred some odd days of combat was not this boy's skill set.

Quinn smelled the indecision. "I shouldn't be here, Aaron."

"But you are," Aaron quipped back, "Your sister doesn't want you in jail for the rest of your life."

Quinn clapped his hands, folding the cards together like all sixty were one object. "I won't be," Quinn snarled, "None of us will. You know why?"

"Well, not with that attitude," Aaron crowed, deflecting off of Quinn's apocalyptic prediction. This was a bomb that needed defusing.

Quinn settled back in his bed. Progress, maybe, but Aaron hadn't cut the power on this explosion. He'd just reset the timer.

Aaron dropped to the floor, sitting against the wall beside Quinn. "Nobody chose to be here, Quinn. But this morning, we chose to be anywhere else. We're willing to fight for it, and I don't know about you...but I've got enough fight in me for at least a few others that run dry."

"I'm used to talking, man...and when I'm not talking, I'm running," Quinn's voice quaked, "That's all I know how to do."

"Don't worry about that," Aaron reasoned, "They're gonna spend some time teaching us how to do the other thing."

"What was it like?"

"What was what like?" Aaron whispered, knowing full well what the kid was asking. What was it like to kill? But he wanted the kid to say it. Get comfortable with it. It was going to be his trade for the next year.

Quinn glanced down at Aaron's shoes, like he was afraid to meet the gaze. "Well, I'm not gonna ask Solomon!"

Aaron chuckled at the thought. He'd most assuredly get an

answer, but one that would haunt his waking moments and lurk in his dreams for at minimum a decade. Aaron, on the other hand, got up every morning and went to bed every night as a human being rather than an anthropomorphized act of bloodshed.

But of the Fifth Floor folk, who else could Quinn ask? Carmona was an innocent man; Nora punched one too many people; who knows what Jensen did.

Eden didn't much relish talking about her old patients. She had viewed her crime as a kindness. The families agreed. The Ministry didn't.

Aaron was the only approachable resource Quinn had.

So Aaron settled into that memory and the fleeting joy of his own internal wit abandoned him. He could feel the moisture in the air, heavy and gripping his throat, choking him. The sun blanketed behind a thick cloud bank, and the smog tinging the little available light a baneful orange.

The towering structures that vanished into the fog overhead reduced to a texture of urban architecture, a skybox full of dreams lifted out of reach by soft, moneyed hands. The grime and detritus under his feet slushed together, congealing into the mud of a city— the sludge that forever marked the cloth of the impoverished. It was the stain worn only by the meek.

His clothes clung to his skin, heavy and layered to shield against the bitter cold and the howling winds. A chain link fence rattled against its bindings. The market had been packed shoulder to shoulder as families strained to load down their bindles with necessities.

The gaggle of half a dozen languages called out in a kind of somber chorus of desperation but quiet contentment.

It had been such a good day.

The man had been fast, impossibly fast. Maybe if Aaron had only been watching closer, he'd have seen it all coming. But suddenly there had been a gun.

And Aaron had to make a choice. The drunken man may have

been fast, but speed was no substitute for good decisions.

The blood hung light on his fingers, as though he were too full for it to fully soak in, its warmth toxic and foul against his skin. The crowd parted around the deed, disassociating from the action but somehow unable to flee. There was a horror in their eyes, predictions of what would follow.

No one helped him then. No one tried to hide him or shelter him. He found nothing but their remorseful eyes beaming wishes for clemency.

They were not to be blamed. There was no one in that crowd that could help carry the Atlas weight that was about to fall on him.

"Aaron?" Quinn probed, cautious and wary. Had he just stirred up something he shouldn't have?

Aaron gave him a kind smile, easing the young boy's wary thoughts. "It's not very poetic, I'll give you that much. The closest thing I can tell ya, it's like...somebody cuts the strings. Turns out the lights. And suddenly they're just laying there. Nobody's home."

"I'm sorry," Quinn preempted, trying in vain to take responsibility for Aaron's discomfort.

"Nah," Aaron dismissed him, "Guy didn't exactly leave me much choice."

He could still see the striations along the gun barrel. Somewhere down that channel was a focusing lens and a capacitor and a trigger and a callous disregard for human life. They were all directed at Aaron, and a breath away from execution.

Stand and die. Or fight.

How was Aaron to know his prospective killer's bloodline, whose father sat in which Ministry? How justice would upend upon an act of self-defense in the face of the 'right' victim? How an off-duty cop loaded on vodka can have any violent circumstance excused by superiors? How paperwork gets lost in the databases and memories curiously purged? How every domino settles into place as dictated when the correct sequence of levers precedes it?

He'd seen it flow so smoothly before, with compassion and gravitas for the task at hand. He'd witnessed kindness.

But his own court had seemed to share the same contempt as Aaron's attacker. What other explanation could there be for the brutal speed of his trial, the urgency behind Blind Justice's dispensation?

It was one thing to kill, but to kill someone important—well, that just won't do. Aaron was doomed from the moment that little bastard thumbed the safety. And how fast he was in doing so, so casual and dismissive in his execution. Aaron could only act on reflex.

Quinn shivered, "I'm not cut out for this."

Aaron blinked away the memories, smiling past bitterness he had put behind him. "One thing you're forgetting, little man," he said, "You're not doing this alone. We're all gonna be here, every step."

"You don't really think that's true, do you?"

Yeah. They were all probably going to die in pursuit of this impossible promise. And Quinn was no fool.

"Wouldn't have it any other way," Aaron lied right to his face.

"You gonna stare down a Jergad with me?" Of course. The kid wanted to know about the enemy, what he'd be asked to kill.

"Damn right I will," Aaron responded, with more of a pause than he intended.

"I heard they're ten feet tall and eat the dead. You're gonna stand up to that?"

Aaron smiled, "You'll stand a lot taller when you're standing with us, Quinn."

"You're in my bed." A new voice, cold words loaded with a familiar malevolence.

Quinn's head snapped around. A half-circle had formed around Quinn's bunk of raggedy men, all torn cloth and unkempt beards. Their jumpers bore mostly tags of machinists but there was one Gearmaster at their center: Michonne.

His shaved head was knobbly and dented, an aesthetic result of genetics and old injuries alike. This was a pit fighter, an attack dog, who knew little else.

Aaron remembered him from the Pits, but he lived in an entirely different wing of the Capital apartments. Most of those assembled with him were Dwellers—curious. Michonne should be over with his own folk. Instead, he had put together a little clan all of his own and set out to stake territory with cracked knuckles and stern glares.

They must've excommunicated him and recently. And now he had brought his brand to the Fifth Floor crew, to carve out a space for his own.

Border disputes, even here. Fantastic.

"You light in the head, *Skel?*" Michonne spat at Quinn, referring to Quinn's light frame. "I said 'that's mine.'"

"Strictly speaking," Quinn's voice quivered, but it's not like he could flee, "That's not what you said. You said 'You're in my bed.'"

"You correcting me now too?" Michonne couldn't let that challenge, however minor, stand. Men like him never could. Could've just rolled his eyes and pressed on, but this tribal bestial bullshit would have its day.

"Move it along, Michonne," Aaron said, loud enough to draw attention from those nearby, "I'm not in the mood today."

Michonne ignored him, choosing to kick at Quinn's good leg, "Get up. Now."

Aaron cocked his head and blinked a few times, almost amused that Michonne had yet to acknowledge Aaron's presence, almost as though the kid was alone. Bullies have to single out their target for it to work, after all. If the target has a posse, it's just a brawl.

Cue the meat brigade, answering the summons.

"How's everybody doin'?" Jensen sidled up to the conversation, hanging off the top bunk's footrest. The five to one odds didn't seem to concern him at all.

"Go do some more push-ups, Jensen," Michonne retorted, "It's about all you're good for."

"Oh, ho ho ho—this is gonna be funny." Jensen popped off the bed, immediately stretching out his taut and veiny forearms, "Yo! Carmona! Eyes up!"

Carmona rolled over on his hard-won top bunk, grasping a lead pipe between his palms—where the Hell did he get a lead pipe?!

For all his machismo and muscles, Carmona bore a consistent cool head, with piercing brown eyes that made him the most suave and full lips that he had somehow protected from splitting in the dry air of the Pits. His shadow of a beard had already grown in on his face, spackling the debonair man with even more handsome. He rolled the pipe in his fingers, feeling its every detail as he eyed his targets.

It was pure peacocking, trying to illustrate to Michonne—and specifically his goon squad—why this was about to be a very bad idea.

Jensen smiled, warm and broad, as though he wasn't about to make a bodily threat, "Michonne, I need you to scurry along now before my friend over there has a chance to a rearrange your teeth."

Michonne bristled, muscles coiling up. He knew how to posture too. "Your friend moves, and I will put that pipe right down his throat."

What Aaron noted, was Michonne's hand sliding into his pocket. Quinn saw it too.

It was all talk, it had to be. Disorderly conduct amongst Capitals wasn't generally tolerated; it reduced work efficiency.

Aaron threw a glance at the cameras overhead, the tiny lens tracking on the standoff—a computer somewhere automatically picking up on body posture, lip reading threats, tracking increases in body temperature. It could even detect the battle lines being drawn, as two groups squared off. The guards would know exactly who, where, and how to respond within seconds.

So where the Hell were they?

Through all that bluster, he didn't notice that Solomon and Keira had swung around behind them, cutting off Michonne's escape. This had all the ingredients for a disaster.

Solomon threw a wink in Aaron's direction, as though the risks of the moment were completely lost on him. Was no one else seeing what Aaron was? Or did they not care?

"We've been more than polite, Michonne," Jensen affirmed, "Move along."

Michonne boiled over. "Maybe I make *you* move!" And he pulled a cement shard from his pocket: a shiv. He dove for Jensen.

Aaron gripped the bed frame, bracing himself against the ground as he swung his leg up, kicking at Michonne's hand as it lanced forward. The brutal sideways strike was rewarded with a meaty crack, the fragile stone dagger shattering. Michonne's cry was more of surprise than pain, but Aaron was certain pain would take over when he had time to take stock of his bent fingers.

Jensen shoved Michonne backward into Keira, who snagged the injured hand and cranked it around into a wrist lock. The curious blossom of dislocated fingers could almost touch his shoulder blades.

Keira leaned in, "Situational awareness...saves lives."

Aaron watched the barracks doors, waiting for them to swing open. Guards would pour in, armored and armed, ready to reinstate discipline and fear amongst the population.

But it never came.

Quinn let out the ragged breath, his nerves almost making him giggle.

The Dwellers looked about, waiting for instruction.

Carmona sidled up, pipe in hand, "It seems about time you all soldiered on elsewhere."

They agreed with his assessment and scattered into the shadows like a morning fog against the sunlight. Michonne watched them go, in too much pain to countermand that order.

Carmona stepped up to Michonne, crushing the shards of the shiv underfoot as he advanced. He leaned in close. "I believe you had some plans? They involved you, me, my discipline stick? And things you wanted to do...to me...with my discipline stick?"

Somehow that fire in Michonne's eyes had not abated, fed by an unseen and endless kindling. His eyes burned the only response Carmona would get.

Carmona nodded to Keira. She let go and Michonne whirled

70

away from the group, eager to get all of his attackers in front of him. It was only then he took stock of the swollen thumb and twisted index finger. And that fire consumed some kind of a fuel, glowing brighter and hotter. Simple distaste had grown to actual hatred.

"Go away now," Carmona instructed with a flick of his wrist.

Swearing some silent curse or blood oath, Michonne slunk away to lick his wounds and find easier prey.

Nora flopped onto her bed. "He's gonna be a problem."

"Nora the Oracle!" Carmona chuckled with a grin, "Are you looking forward to that problem?"

"He's got such a punchable face."

Jensen offered Aaron a hand up from the cold floor, and with one bicep curl heaved the smaller man to his feet. That wide, diplomatic smile swept from ear to ear. "Thanks, shortstack."

"Should I even have bothered?" Aaron asked, "Or were you just going to flex and bounce it off?"

Jensen snorted at that image, before softening again. "I owe you one, boss."

"Oh," Aaron cringed, "You start keeping score for the next year and everybody's going to be in trouble."

"Yeah," Eden beamed from her distant bed, perched on the edge like the cat that ate the canary, "Would you guys like to pay me up front or...?"

In fairness, the resident medic may not have the more glamorous saves, but her every day was going to be founded in rescuing idiots and heroes alike. Stitches and antiseptic may not be as sexy as sharp shooting or load-bearing, but they were quite a bit more clutch.

Jensen clapped a final thank you onto Aaron's shoulder, before giving a comfortable nod to the motionless Quinn. "You want to get a game going, or you just giving those cards a lover's touch?"

Quinn burped the stomach acids back down his throat, "We...we could play. Yeah."

CHAPTER
FIVE
RILEY

DEFENSE MINISTER CALDWELL took the news about as well as predicted: he cursed, he fumed, he threatened total annihilation. It was his theme song at this point.

He claimed Riley had deputized himself as Monarch of his own little world, something far and above his mandate. The promise made to Capital prisoners was wholly unacceptable and would never be honored by Sol. The Capital Militia was to be disbanded immediately, and Riley's troops were to obey their Consul and board a transport bound for the front.

And after all of that, he listened. Riley was not about to leave these people defenseless and he would use all tools at his disposal to protect them.

He would always bend the knee to the Consul and the Empire and would bend that same knee before a Military Tribunal. As for the Capitals, he promised to keep detailed logs of their performance —the Minister of Defense may do as he likes with it all. Riley's sole mission was to preserve and defend his Empire's borders and the lives of its citizenry.

Riley found value in the call, despite its sour tone. The temperature of one Minister was rarely reflected in his peers. They were all too commonly feuding with one another for dominance in the Cabinet and for the ear of the Consul.

Perhaps the Ministers of State—or even Energy—might be valued allies. Vanguard was a mining colony, after all. In any event, the primary military forces were occupied, and it would be some time before Riley was relieved.

Or arrested.

The Capitals were to made ready as soon as possible. As soon as they could be trusted to hold a rifle, they would be posted to the Wall.

Riley had toured the fortifications just the night before. The Wall itself stood thirty feet high, with alternating Repeater watchtowers and gun-nests every few dozen yards. The foundations ran deep, dropped down below the clay—halting any subterranean advance by the locals. The burrowing little bastards didn't like to work in the slate and sandstone below that.

A few previous surges had been caught at that depth by the tectonic sensors and snuffed out with 'thumpers.' The giant stationary hammers were designed to stun incoming burrowers, but field units discovered they also collapsed the deeper tunnels networks, blocking the secretive advances in their tracks.

The multiple crossing fields of fire prevented any one failure from opening a hole in their lines. Explosive charges planted in the ground thinned the oncoming horde. And on top of all of this, the Wall was hot with electric current.

It was an efficient defense that the aliens had learned to respect. There hadn't been a push that made it to the Wall in over a year.

Riley had come to observe the Capitals' morning calisthenics—he didn't need to, but Bray had reported that his very presence caused the Capitals to throw their engines into overdrive.

Riley didn't mind terribly much; it was good to get out of the confines of his office and this sight brought back many fond memories for him. Despite their status, they were pounding dirt like proper fighters. The air was thick with their salty sweat, and the chorus of atonal grunts was music to his ears.

For a blissful moment in that ear-piercing cacophony, Riley really felt at home. This was a base full of real soldiers in a real battlefield. It quickened his blood and lifted his heart. A commander needed soldiers, a battlefield, and a cause worthy of their efforts.

It was all very poetic.

Sergeant Bray had designed an impressive regimen. The Capitals began with a crash course in basic tactics and movement, as well as an attitude adjustment. They worked mostly at instilling teamwork under physical duress and lack of sleep. It was modeled it after Basic Combat Operations for the Imperial Jump Troopers, albeit watered down.

They awoke the Capitals at 0200 Hours Local Time. Many had only gone to sleep a few hours before, having been celebrating the first step on their journey out of perdition; the intelligent few among them had secured their spaces and grabbed the sleep that was available, something of a commodity even during their labor camp days.

Pre-dawn physical training taxed focus, but the aim was not to break them. The new troopers had to be acclimated to sudden demands on their system.

They had proven their physical aptitude. Now to mold their minds.

The first day had surprised no one with its terrible results. No amount of shouting or threats would break through the haze. Repeated instructions twisted about between ears and brains. Simple calisthenics taxed the Capitals to their limits.

Bray's growing anger was on full display, but mostly for the show of it. This was all expected. Motivating the Capitals would come with time and investment.

Even under ideal conditions, new soldiers took months to grow into the demands placed upon them. Citizens who selected this path out of desire and patriotism failed in the face of these challenges.

Being thrust into this environment, even by choice, could not hold a candle to those that trained for it from birth.

Morning PT was supplemented with marching, but unlike their

qualifier, they were drilled here for coordination. The distance in question was longer and further than anything they'd experienced. But now, every footfall must match its neighbor and beyond. If the snare drum of their march slipped even a little, their march was extended.

Whinging and bitching increased the march again. Bray denied the cattle prods any access to his recruits. These were not Capitals any longer; they were soldiers of the Empire and would be treated as such. Even if that rise in status meant more marching.

It was a good while before anyone in the regiment noticed that Bray was not setting the pace—they were. As the march dragged on further and further, Bray instructed them to observe their comrades. With practice, they would almost feel their friends fading, and could adjust to match.

Riley allowed himself a smile when he read the brief: he was teaching the little criminals how to be a team. Any skepticism soon vanished, as leaders soon cropped up amongst the crowd to help motivate.

Some of the Capitals led from fear, and they didn't last very long before they themselves were pleading mercy from Bray. The Gunnery Sergeant nourished himself from those moans, filling his cup and drinking readily.

The afternoons were given to the Capitals to recuperate, but at different times each day, they were assembled again for the evening's activities—they were never allowed to develop a habit and were often worked long into the night. Bray and his team assembled obstacle courses, with muddy waters and rusty razor wire coverage.

This particular evening had been promising.

The Capitals were given surrogate gear—backpacks loaded with stones and weapon analogs—to carry through their trials. At first, they were to simply complete the course. Crawling under barbed wire while beams of cauterizing light and deafening gunfire sawed the air above them. Climbing uncooperative nets and stomping through hostile terrain.

If their gear was perceived as too dirty, often from the Capitals' own sweat and blood, they were instructed to run the course again. Generally speaking, Bray made whoever he wanted to run as many times as he felt appropriate. An extra run could be assigned simply for having a foul look.

After the teams had grown comfortable with the course, Bray started timing them. If even one member of a fire team ran the course too slow, the whole group had to run again. It was a whole new metric to teach unity.

Some started to help each other along during difficult hurdles. Others grew to hate the weaklings dragging behind like an anchor.

The haters got more running. They would stamp that out like a stubborn ember.

Bray paced down the line, as the tired recruits climbed a rope wall. "Let's go, Jensen!" Bray shouted at a lumbering giant, who was struggling to even get started, "Tiny Tim over here is kicking your ass!"

The skinny little boy—no more than fifteen—had swung hand over hand up the rope, hopping up on his one good foot. He grinned from ear to ear like he was back on the jungle gym.

Despite a busted leg from the qualifier, the kid was downright rocketing through the course.

Jensen huffed and puffed with each movement, face red and neck strained. Bray was half the man of this big one but the Sergeant loomed over him just the same. "You know why he can do that, Hercules?"

"Because he's a little squirrel, sir?"

"And you are what, Capital? You ain't a little squirrel. What's your excuse?"

"I'm a workhorse, sir!"

"I don't believe you! Show me that you work! Huah?!"

"Huah!" Jensen let out a shout and grimaced as he tried to haul himself up.

The boy sat at the top, stretching out the heel on his bad foot, "Come on, ugly! Be a hero!"

"Quinn..." the man grunted, "I catch you, I'm gonna—"

"So catch me!" Quinn jumped down the other side of the structure, rolling down the rope net like his injury was naught but inconvenient. "Workhorse! Whoo!"

Lo and behold, the big guy was pulling himself up faster. Competition was a fantastic motivator; resentment was better. Jensen hauled himself up, and practically dove over the other side after the 'squirrel.'

Riley felt it in his feet. But that wasn't a human body impacting the ground. This was seismic, several miles away, rolling through. He felt it in his left before his right, as it passed by him, North to South.

It came from the Wall.

The whole training ground came to a hush. They all felt it too. Then together, they all felt it again. And again. The drumbeat of war.

The Thumpers had engaged, the titanic magnetic hammers slamming the ground. It meant only one thing.

The Jergad were attacking the Wall, just a dozen miles from where they stood.

The training grounds had frozen into a graveyard, scattered stony figures, all eyes turned to the North. Even Bray peered out at the horizon, and the dust cloud just beginning to rise up into view.

The murmur in his post fell to a hush as they all realized it at once. Riley spoke as clear and declarative as possible: "Get me a munitions and casualty report. Right now."

They needed to feel the calm of someone in control of the situation, who knew the gravity of what this meant, and wasn't frozen by it. His instructors had called it the Father Instinct—no matter how bad it was, a commander could be shaken but he never faltered.

The attack was repelled, but four Regulars had been killed and the Wall had been damaged—requiring additional security while it was repaired. They didn't have any more time for these team-building exercises and Bray's long-prepared tirades.

These reinforcements had to be deployed post-haste. Casualties wouldn't be avoided; they were a prescribed part of the process.

Bray objected, but mostly to formally lodge the complaint—everyone knew these troops weren't ready to see combat. But there was nothing to be done; they would see combat, or combat would soon see them.

Riley arrived at the training camp after the morning's PT. Riley's observation tower had a beautiful view of the base, with large pane glass windows to allow for maximum visibility. His view was obscured only by the mounted Repeater on the tower's corner.

Make no mistake, this may be a barracks, but it was still a prison yard.

That sweet smell of human sweat and effort had been replaced with a noxious stench more akin to that of a meat-packing plant, as though farm animals had voided their bowels and died amongst the assembly. The more time this many people spent in close proximity, the worse it would get.

Desires for indoor plumbing in the base were well-warranted but the limited technicians available were already working over-time shoring up defenses and repairing the wear and tear to the Wall itself.

The Capitals were plainly not a priority.

Gasping for breath—some even bent over retching—the Capitals waited for their absent Drill Instructor. They shared glances back and forth but no one said a word, their energy too precious to them right now.

The muted whine of Bray's vehicle rose up from the motor pool, as a trio of loaded Maglev Cruisers approached the formation.

Bray hopped out of the lead car before it came to a complete stop. He cradled something in his hands, a design Riley had known only from textbooks back at Academy.

It may as well have been a museum artifact, to be treated with care.

"This," Bray called out to the formation, "is the JP-36 ballistic assault rifle. It is a *gulaw* relic, an unholy fusion of replaceable parts, consigned to the scrap heap. Much like all of you! Huah?"

The crowd snapped back a crisp "Huah!" Heard, understood, acknowledged.

These rifles had been phased out of Core World use decades ago, but so many had been supplied to Ministry reserves that melting down just half of the stock took nearly four years. Those that hadn't been destroyed had been funneled to the border world colonies that couldn't afford more current technology.

They had been collecting dust in a dark corner of the Inventory and discovered only during the primary military exodus. Bray refused to give the Capitals anything better. A slave doesn't get his own whip.

"They are semi-automatic, firing thirty caliber steel jacketed rounds at over eight hundred meters per second," Bray bellowed, "The barrels overheat, making them inaccurate the longer you fire. They need constant care and love, or the bolt will refuse to cycle. The magwell is steep and deep, making it hard to feed fresh magazines in. They are weak. They will jam. They will break. And they are the only thing standing between you and the wild."

The crowd barked another "Huah" back like good little dogs.

With that, Bray shouldered the rifle as though he had been wielding the weapon since childhood. The shockwave from the gases escaping from the muzzle brake tossed the dirt around Bray like he was shaking off some invisible cloak.

Riley had forgotten the deafening sound a ballistic rifle could make, instinctively reaching to cover his ears. One Capital fell to their knees in shock and pain, their position markedly closer to the controlled explosion than Riley's observation post.

However obsolete the weapon system may have become, gunpowder-fueled ballistic munitions still commanded attention.

Bray thumbed a switch, dropping the detachable magazine from the underside of the weapon and slapping a fresh one into place before the old one had even found its final rest in the dirt.

"Yesterday," Bray shouted, "you learned to run. Today, you learn to fight."

Somehow, the rifles firing in unison felt quieter. Perhaps the shock of the initial gunshot had taken Riley by surprise, or perhaps one of his lieutenants had dropped a noise curtain around the post.

The thought behind the rifle was something out of the mind of an evil genius living inside an active volcano. Burning an explosive powder inside of a steel container—only one way out—using the compressed gases to expel a hunk of metal forward towards a meaty target. A civilized man would've used magnets, but this psychopath needed more explosions.

They had grown the design to be quite efficient, user-friendly, and safe over the centuries. Riley hoped the lunatic who first thought of this technique had been killed by his own creation before he willed any other technological monstrosities into the world. Humanity was not ready for the raw volume of brutality that twisted mind could have produced.

The Ministry had purchased these antiquated designs more for their price-tag than their effectiveness—what happens when a spreadsheet calculation dictates procurement.

It was obvious who among the crowd had operated a weapon system before. There was a modicum of operational discipline, although not refined.

The firing range had opted for steel silhouettes rather than typical holographic scorecards. The steel was to simulate the native beasts' leathery hides. Direct hits onto the targets dented and tore the metal, while anything askew glanced off. Capitals not on the line were put to use maintaining it. They hammered the damaged targets back into shape with large mallets and deployed them up from their berm for further abuse by their comrades.

It was a decent replication of real world results. The Jergad hides had a tendency to deflect most ballistic fire.

The Oskies preferred their weaponry battery-operated for that reason. Natural armor lost its advantages against something cooking flesh to carbon in under half a second. Short-range effectiveness, be damned.

When Orbital wants a job done, they want it done on the first attempt. Under their operational requirements, there was never room for second chances.

The voice of Riley's aide de camp broke Riley from his idyllic daydreams, "You have a visitor."

"Don't say it," Riley whispered without even turning to see. He didn't want to see. He prayed it wasn't true.

He could almost hear Ilern smile behind him. Because it was her voice again. "Marcus Riley." Talania sidled up next to him with two cups of black liquid. "Peace offering."

He didn't realize it until it hit him, but goddamn did that coffee smell good. He gingerly plucked the cup from her hands. "You don't mind if I have my aide test it for poison?"

"Chock full of it," Talania said, without a moment's pause, "But your liver will do just fine."

A quick second sniff confirmed the presence of a not-insubstantial amount of alcohol. A peace offering and a bribe all at once. "Isn't it a little early in the morning for a drink?"

"It's a little early for me to be seeing you, so I compromised."

Riley passed the cup off to someone—anyone—nearby. He didn't need to be dulling anything right now.

"How do they look?" She asked, slurping from her steaming cup of morning medicine.

"Is this your bleeding heart asking or is this a formal inquiry from the Governor?"

"Well, now it's both. Should I be taking notes?"

Riley sighed. "Their training has been advanced to meet operational needs."

"Do I need to be worried?"

Talania wasn't watching the training below. She was watching him. Riley ground his teeth, barking the order, "Audio from Lane 29, please?"

The technician didn't even acknowledge Riley's words as he processed the request. He filtered the cracks of gunfire out and brought up the dialog below. Their chatter was muffled by the gunshots drowning them out, but they could at least be understood.

Riley pinched the window in front of him between two fingers, telescoping their view down to the lane in question. Capital Carmona had left his lane and was instructing a fellow, under careful supervision from the rangemasters.

Carmona popped the action open so as to safely instruct the technique. "Don't tense up. Both eyes open."

"But I can't see down the sight right with both open." A display ran through vocal recognition software, before popping the name and ID photo of Aaron Havenes. It was a good picture. Usually, the mugshots were on the worst days of their lives. This one almost had composition to it. Even Talania perked up at the sight, studying the narrow jaw and bright eyes.

Carmona tapped Aaron on his left shoulder. "You're also blinding yourself over here, shortstack. Get practiced with 'em open. Breathe in, hold it, then exhale...and squeeze on the exhale. It'll loosen you up."

Aaron settled in behind the rifle, taking his time and exhaling as his finger tightened on the trigger. Crisp, single shots were singing off the metal in no time.

"See? Look at that. Make a badass outta you yet. Remember: aim small, miss small."

"What?" Talania blurted over the lip of her coffee cup.

Riley leaned over, a warm superiority filling his chest. He plucked at the lapel of her shirt, "If you aim for a man's button, and you miss...you still hit him. Aim for the man...you just miss."

Aaron rolled out his shoulder, stretching the bruises left by the unforgiving stock. "Newton's Third is a bitch."

"Ain't it just? Muzzle downrange and let's show off some, huh?"

Riley couldn't help but laugh. Talania shook her head, as she picked his full coffee cup off an attendant's desk, trading it with her empty one. "They need help operating their own gear."

Couldn't disagree with that. "Not all learning is theoretical, ma'am. I'm a firm believer in tactile education."

"When are they posted?"

"Tomorrow morning."

Talania almost spat out her coffee. "We're sending them up there with bang sticks and a week's worth of gym classes? Commander, due respect, are you *high?*"

"Oh, how I wish."

Both Talania and Riley turned to glance at the source of those words, as Ilern looked up quizzically. "Dammit. That one slipped out, didn't it?"

Riley pursed his lips, trying to not snort laugh at the blatant insubordination. Not of him; even he had lost his patience with Talania's patronizing attitude. She didn't have a proper solution to the dilemma; she was just there to shout at them from the moral high ground.

Riley drew attention back with a raise of his hand, dismissing Ilern's interruption. "Yes, Talania. I have several pages of literature about how silly this whole program is. I can forward you the packet."

Nobody saw the shot. Too lost in conversation or buried in their work. But the crack of glass and the snap of metal screaming past Riley's ear at supersonic speeds quickened the blood like little else in the world. The steel jacketed slug snapped past him and into the wall before anyone could even register its presence.

But Riley wasn't just anyone. The imminent threat kicked his senses wide awake. He could smell the sulfur that hung over the field. He could feel the tremors of a hundred gunshots tearing the air and rolling along the hairs of his forearm. But that was all background.

He could see the waves—the cavitation—as the air buffeted around the advancing bullet like ripples on a pond.

No naked human eye would never track something moving that

fast. The magic trick of a steel trigger creating a hole in a target at distance was an illusion beyond the average person's capability.

The various subdermal microchips embedded throughout Riley's body elevated him far beyond average. He watched the bullet approach with such clarity he could identify it individually in a courtroom.

Talania was not so fast. The bullet was going to split her ribcage.

Riley slammed two hands into her shoulders, fast enough he might have dislocated something. But he was certain she'd appreciate his work. In the time allotted, she moved a scant two inches—the bullet passed by, her clothing billowing in the shockwave, sliding under her crooked elbow and shattering the coffee cup in her hands.

The crowd of aides, technicians, and civilian bureaucrats ducked behind whatever they could find long after the threat had passed. To a casual observer, Riley had to be a soothsayer to avoid that shot. And the collection of eyes around him reflected some version of that title.

Talania looked up at him pained and offended before her own senses caught the pattern of sounds she'd heard and spied the ceramic shards still clattering to the ground.

Without a word or order, all fire on the range ceased, as though the entire regiment was holding their breath.

Down below, a Capital held his rifle aloft by the lower receiver— no hand on a trigger, but the barrel pointed at Riley's bleachers. It was not shouldered, nor braced in any way. Perhaps the rifle had a hangfire, or the boy had poor trigger discipline. This was just an accident, albeit a lethal one.

Riley snatched a radio from a paralyzed aide. "Single him out. I'm coming down."

He stuffed the handset back into his aide's hands and marched toward the ladder.

He had maybe thirty seconds to consider what he wanted to be done here. It was an act of violence toward a superior, worthy of a public flogging and a day out to be burnt under the sun.

But this was no Army Regular; it was a Capital, and one that hadn't even served a full week. If a laborer had struck back at a prison guard, the warden had full authority to terminate the problem and requisition a replacement.

Who was Riley going to requisition from, with Minister Caldwell already spouting for Riley's head and all the remaining Capitals shipped off-planet in the exodus? This was blood meant to be spilt, but blood, in general, was in short supply.

As Riley stomped over, he could see Bray drop the Capital to his knees and draw his sidearm from his chest rig. Of the hundred men on the range, nobody dared move, but Riley could make out a dull hum from the crowd, as though they vibrated on a hundred dissonant frequencies.

He could hear their indecision. Good. The last thing he wanted right now was an angry mob with high caliber weaponry.

As he drew closer, his decision almost made itself. The Capital in question was Quinn Josimovic—the squirrel—the boy that had been all but dragged through his qualifier. Over the body odor and gunpowder, there was a scent so thick Riley could almost taste it: fear.

Riley settled next to the boy, giving a show of examining the subject. Quinn wouldn't look at anything besides Riley's boots.

No spine. No courage. No discipline. This child was already dead, just looking for his place to rest. The only open question was how many would die beside him and because of him.

Riley reached for Bray's weapon and found it pressed to his palm. He thumbed the safety and it warmed in his hand as the capacitor charged.

Movement. Someone on the line. A flinch, nothing more. Riley looked over to identify the rebellious spirit that was so eager to die.

Aaron Havenes, brow furrowed and jaw tight. While neighboring Carmona was stiff as a board, Aaron would like nothing more than to rip that pistol from Riley's hands. But without any interference, he had stopped himself.

Curious.

Riley smiled at the man, at that lit candle that so eagerly extinguished itself. Would that fire spark anew if confronted or challenged? Would he deign to flinch twice when given an opportunity? Riley held his gaze on that young soldier, waiting for the subservience he was owed.

Aaron dropped his eyes back to Riley's boots, where he might study his proper place on this world.

A corporal somewhere was likely already pulling the prison files on today's players for Riley's perusal. Tonight's reading had been set, at least.

Riley held the pistol out to Quinn, shoving it into his field of view and displaying the side of it. "This is an AP-8 focused laser sidearm, but the principle is the same. Finger off the trigger until you're ready to fire." Riley tapped the handle, releasing the battery from its housing. "Unload before handling behind the line. And if you don't know what else to do..."

Riley leaned in close, but made sure to project for the entire assembly, "Put it down!"

"Yes, sir." If little Quinn had anything left in him, he let it out right there. Every muscle, every rigid structure holding him upright, let go and he relaxed backward sitting on his heels.

And with one violent heave, he vomited onto Riley's boots.

Riley elected to study the sky and reaffirm his mercy. Bray threw a side-eye glance at Riley before turning back to his troops. "You heard the man! You know what to do! Range is hot!"

Huah.

CHAPTER
SIX
AARON

AARON COULDN'T GET that sight out of his head. That shot should have killed that woman. And yet Colonel Riley—Master & Commander Local Allied Forces—slid her out of danger as though the high caliber supersonic death sentence were a may fly at a dinner party. The career soldier behaved more like he was offended at its presence than what it might've represented.

Nothing alive could be that fast.

Aaron couldn't shake the sight, that blur of motion, that ghost that he had assumed was flesh and blood. It was unreal, unbelievable...unsettling.

And familiar.

The Capitals had been informed they had passed basic proficiency and were to be deployed to the Wall the next morning. Given the display of 'competency' that Quinn illustrated, Aaron could only surmise there was some kind of grading curve at play. Gladly, their training would not cease, but units would rotate up to serve time on forward outposts while off-hours would be spent further honing their skills.

It would be a deadly first day. Undisciplined criminals with firearms asked to lay down their lives. Their freedom was bought in blood to be paid sometime soon. How much blood? And when? Who would pay the price that their neighbor might go free? And who decides who dies?

Aaron could still feel that blood on his fingertips, washing off in that faint rain four years ago. And yet, so palpably warm today, as if it might burn him.

The rest of the Capitals hadn't made that particular suffocating conclusion, or if they had, they didn't seem bothered by it. The entire Barracks had pulled together, a show of inspiring unity. They had dragged a half dozen trash barrels to the center space and improvised a bonfire. Boisterous chatter and even laughter echoed in the hall. Two different groups sang songs from memory, like competing choirs. The religious zealots led a small euphoric group in a prayer chant, which had a nonzero chance of ending in an orgy, as supplicants shouted gibberish in their ecstasy.

Even Michonne and his outcast Dwellers were welcomed, partaking in a downright reckless use of the rations available. This was a time for celebration, forgiveness, a holiday to be marked on a calendar kept only in memory: the first day of the rest of their lives.

Fitting.

Aaron laid on his bunk, studying the warp of the barracks' ceiling and trying to shake the image of Riley's supernatural speed. The gun in Riley's hands. The calculations behind his eyes. Riley could have killed Quinn before Aaron could even take a breath, and Aaron would barely have had time to process the murder before he shared that fate.

It was like being in the presence of something greater. Something terrible. Riley's cold eyes boring into him, amused by the mere mortal in his midst.

It was a look Aaron had seen before.

Jensen knocked on the wall next to Aaron's head, shaking him from his reverie. Despite a week of sleep deprivation and hard labor, he still had that warm smile. "Everybody else is having a good time."

Aaron's eyes slid over to the crowd. Everyone, even Quinn—especially Quinn—were deep in festivities. The squirrel had his deck of cards out, ruffling them back and forth in his hands in a distracting display. The crowd around him watched his mark more than his sleight of hand. An inebriated Nora hunched over a trunk, watching his hands move carefully.

"Where's your card?" Quinn asked, "Where do you think it is?"

Everyone laughed, as Quinn had slipped the card out of the deck and stuck it to his own forehead—but the vigilant Nora was far too focused on the elegant card play to notice anything had happened in her periphery. She stared down at the table-top, studying and oblivious.

"Nora..." Eden began.

"No!" She said, "I'mma—I'mma get it."

"No, Nora, it's—"

"Don't help me." There was a tinge of desperation to that. She knew that she'd missed whatever trick was at play but didn't want to admit it.

"Where's it at?" Quinn asked, expertly swallowing his own laugh behind that smug little mug. Everyone else in assembly was less kind, Carmona issuing loud and violent guffaws, sucking air between each huge laugh.

Solomon studied Quinn's hand movements the way someone might watch a medical textbook—he enjoyed the fluidity of the pattern, the practiced dance of fingers and crisp paper. He was practically salivating.

Keira enabled Nora's disability, as she refilled Nora's cup from a jug of—God he didn't even want to know what was in that. It was not...entirely fluid. She pressed the cup into Nora's hands with a word of support and Nora downed the cup in one swoop. Keira clapped her on the back, drawing forth some rancid coughing.

Quinn smirked, card perking over the crown of his head like a feather in a cap. "Any guesses? Window's closing."

Nora closed her eyes to swallow pride, before tilting her head up to see Quinn's stupid little face and his stupid little trick. There were almost tears in her drunken eyes, as her confusion overtook her. "How could you possibly...?"

Their joy was infectious. It rippled from group to group as if they were all one bacchanalia. It was a good night. For this one night, every clan and tribal barrier had fallen.

But something pushed down on Aaron's chest, like a weight he couldn't see holding him down by his shoulders.

The joy was premature, undue and malapropos.

"Come on," Jensen urged, "You'll feel better off the wall."

"I lost my invitation," Aaron said, dismissing the nonverbal welcome.

"That makes sense. That's what I get for leaving Solomon in charge of outreach," Jensen chirped, leaning against the wall, his bent arm flexing that disgustingly huge bicep. "Need to let something outta your skull?"

Aaron shook his head. "Just got a big day tomorrow."

"They're all big days now, boss."

"I'm not your boss," Aaron grunted.

"Always struck me as one. Maybe on a construction site?" Jensen leaned in, studying the reaction.

Aaron craned his neck to stare directly at Jensen's ugly mug. "How old do you think I am?"

"Plenty of people work as kids," Jensen said, "Age don't mean you're not somebody's boss."

"Are you doing the guessing thing now?"

"Was I right?"

"No. Who else is doing this?'

Jensen shrugged. "Quinn was a con-artist on the boardwalk, he was easy. Nora was a bartender who did more bouncing than her bouncers did. Carmona - news flash - was a police officer."

"Bullshit." Carmona? Riding blue?

Jensen smirked. "Hand to God. His whole soap opera involves a cartel, friends on the take, and ultimately a frame-up."

"He was awful eager to be back in Imperial service." Aaron

studied Carmona across the room, a jovial father, claps on backs and big laughs.

He looked back at Jensen. "And what do you win?"

"Bragging rights?"

Aaron snorted. The big guy had coopted an institutionalized abuse and made it into an ice breaker. "Eden was a medical resident. You...auto mechanic?" Aaron raised an eyebrow.

Jensen scoffed. "Yeah, for the low hanging fruit." Jensen pointed at Solomon and Keira, perched at the edge of the firelight. "Those are the tricky ones. Who were they before organized crime and the..." He paused on Solomon and his crazy eyes. "Less organized crime?"

Aaron tilted his head, studying the odd couple. Jensen side-eyed him, a proud smirk, like the proverbial cat a few canaries later. Finally, Aaron shrugged, eliciting a full toothy smile from Jensen. "Waste disposal. Both of 'em."

"Get out of here!"

"You wanted to know what they had in common. She was an electrician and he was in administration for the same company." Jensen leaned on the mattress. "You're the only one we haven't cracked."

"Sounds like *I* have the bragging rights," Aaron said.

"Maybe I wingman you a bit, and you just tell me. I mean, you are very ugly and need the help."

"I'm fine, thanks."

There was Jensen's toothy smirk again, self-satisfied. "You're in the dark over here, tucked against the wall, you like your words—you were a poet, but unpublished."

Aaron couldn't help but laugh, eying the party with an envious tilt of his jaw. It's true, there hadn't really been a routine or calm to his life since the exodus. If this was the new normal, perhaps he should rise to the occasion, live in each moment.

Jensen's smile slipped a bit, Aaron's contagious depression starting to bleed off. "There's always an open chair for you, and not for nothing, but I think Eden *was* kinda hoping you'd turn out."

His eyes picked her out of the crowd easy enough. She was floating near the edge, chatting with Nora but keeping a close eye on Quinn. The watcheye instinct of a doctor could never be shaken off. She caught him looking, and gave him a nod, calling him over.

The summons of a friend.

"Well," Aaron sighed, "We'll have plenty of time to talk at the Wall." That was harsher than he meant.

Jensen pursed his lips, taking a step back away from the surly man, "That's fair, but—and hear me out—you look like you need the company."

He didn't.

The clang of swinging doors broke the tension of their moment. Sergeant Bray hung in the opening, examining the space and the festivities before him. His nostrils flared, at the sight or the smell, and his lip curled back with the unmistakable disgust that comes packaged with a dose of pity.

The singing halted like the power had been cut. The chatter softened as everyone picked up on the presence, a slow wave of silence blanketing the space.

From the half-dressed debauchery to the casual reveler, they were all wondering the same thing: had they somehow overstepped? Was their freedom never properly real and the slack in the choke chain had been confused for autonomy? They were waiting for the whip. The anxiety of anyone who has served time in chains—were those bindings ever really gone?

But Bray did not speak. He did not bellow or scold or chastise. He did not sling insults or slam down instructions. He stalked into the room, one foot in front of the other, a methodical invasion. His eyes scanning the faces before him. With each subsequent step, he picked up speed and...confidence.

Something was different.

Target lock—Bray saw Aaron sitting off to the side of the bacchanal—and the Sergeant's path swerved to intercept.

Jensen nodded, and wanting no part of whatever was to come,

92

clapped Aaron on the shoulder as he peeled off back toward the silent tableau. "Have fun."

"Thanks," Aaron scoffed, as his friend abandoned him to whatever was in store.

Bray kicked up dust as he approached, dragging feet but firm strides. He stopped next to Aaron, eye level with the top bunk. It was a curious stance, somehow rigid and fluid at the same time. Was this how Bray looked when he was relaxed? It had the terrifying stillness of a sculpture.

"Why did you try to stop Colonel Riley?" He asked.

Uh oh.

Aaron dared not move, lest it be seen as hostile. Stay still. Stay docile.

He swallowed hard. "I didn't, sir."

"Yes, you did," Bray scolded, "Your first thought was to leap into the middle of an ongoing execution. Your second thought was smarter than that. What prompted the first thought?"

The tone of the question perplexed Aaron. This wasn't a reprimand preceding a punishment. Bray was genuinely curious and had sought out an answer.

Aaron took a liberty and propped himself up on the bed. "Quinn made a mistake."

"A deadly one," Bray shot back.

"That's because he's not ready," Aaron croaked out, "None of us are."

Bray took a deep breath and settled down onto the nearest bunk. "No. No, you're not."

Aaron blinked at that revelation. "Then why are we going?"

"You're a smart man, Capital. Take a guess."

He didn't have to think very long, but Aaron threw a glance at the party. Noise had started up again, but in that cautious good behavior manner. No one wanted to draw attention and everyone wanted to listen in. Aaron lowered his voice. "We're supposed to die, aren't we?"

Bray pursed his lips again, licking his teeth. "No. But we don't really care very much if you do."

"So why didn't...the Commander...kill Quinn? If we're so expendable?"

"Because you've figured out by now," Bray began, "That Colonel Riley—nor anyone in his sphere—were ever in any real danger."

That blur. It flashed across his vision like something out of a nightmare. He suddenly remembered why.

The officer Aaron killed four years ago had been that fast.

"How?" Aaron begged, "How was that possible?" He had to know. What kind of demigod was that fast? Why had Lady Justice blinked? Who was so important that they banished Aaron to the Hellmouth?

Bray locked eyes with him. "The best soldiers get the best gear. You Capitals are getting crap we tossed out a generation ago. The guys we spend real money on...the best guns, the best armor, implants, cybernetics. You sink enough money into somebody and we don't much like losing 'em when we can avoid it. Trainin' and gearin' 'em...gets expensive."

There was an acidic tone in his voice, an undercurrent of distaste. Riley was elite. Aaron's victim had been elite, in some form or another. Elites didn't think much of those beneath them. Bray happened to also be underfoot, just as much as Aaron. Everyone is beneath people like Riley.

"Our lives..." Aaron connected, "are going out there to protect people that we can't *afford* to lose?"

That was the reason for it all, wasn't it? Aaron's incarceration was out of property damage. It wasn't an important son of an important man, nor the gangland mentality flipping against a cop-killer.

Aaron broke it; he then had to buy it—with his life.

"Quite literally," Bray affirmed, "You're cheap, Aaron. They're not."

Aaron thought he was going to throw up. "Come here to break my spine specifically, sir?"

94

"No," Bray blurted, brow furrowed with surprise, "I...I came here to apologize."

What the what?

Bray continued, "I thought this was a waste of time. I thought this was dangerous. You don't take someone who's stabbed you, give them a knife, and trust 'em not to stab you again. I fully expected the entire Regiment to rebel. You're all dangerous criminals we were entrusting with *security*? Command was outside their *gulaw* minds. I'd have packed every colonist I could, slammed 'em into their jump seats like canned meat, and left you all behind to die at whatever cosmic horror God decides for ya. It's only what you deserved."

Aaron studied the Sergeant's face over this. He wasn't used to being wrong. Experience, careful study, and practice had kept him alive. Instinct told him one thing, and evidence told him something contrary. That was difficult to reconcile.

"Smart man once told me...that doing the right thing ain't often the popular thing. And you might even get punished for it. Still the right thing to do."

Aaron smiled. "So you're apologizing to a Capital."

"I still think it was a gamble," Bray hedged, covering his weakness, "But you were ready to eat a shot meant for somebody else." Bray shook his head at that profound discovery. And, in a truly unsettling development, Bray smiled. A full row of coffee stained teeth, more than a few chipped and cracked from a hard life.

"If we can get a just few dozen like you..." Bray declared, "If that ain't *exactly* what we were looking for."

CHAPTER
SEVEN
RILEY

MAYBE A TENTH READING would reveal the secrets to him. Riley flipped back to the front of the personnel file, scouring the pages for some footnote that he may have missed in his arduous research, some scribbled hieroglyph that might reveal the secret history of the Hero of the Hour.

They actually printed it onto physical paper—downright archaic. Suppose some clung to the old ways as though they deserved some kind of reverence. That musty smell was enough to drive him mad, and he'd even managed to cut his palm on the razor-thin edges.

To think, in eons past, this was what entire Empires had been made of—tree pulp. Supposed the proper term was papyrus, as this was made from the local grasses. It still stung like the worst bug bite.

It took three Lance Corporals two days to track down the file. Civilian government always found the most expensive and least useful way to conduct itself.

Bureaucrats were allergic to efficiency. Thankfully, whomsoever in the Colonial Administration that held pressed carbon sheets in such high regard had been issued their farewell stipends with the rest of the Governor's deep bench of sycophants and redundancies.

There had been plenty of parachutes available for the assemblage of empty suits.

Riley silently wished they could've just pushed a few of these bastards out of a window, as he sucked on the stinging wound again. Cathartic, but probably not helping it really.

Riley flipped to the cover page again.

'Aaron Havenes // Convicted of Capital Murder of a Peace Officer in the Year of the Pilgrim 2237 // Transferred from Fort Augustine Prison in 2239 // Began Indentured Service in the Vanguard Copper Mines 2240.'

His biographical information was limited even by Correctional standards—even previous profession and educational marks were absent or redacted. All that remained were the quotations from his Trial Defense.

The whole proceeding had lasted seventeen minutes before the tribunal rendered a verdict. A full transcript along with written affidavits and sworn statements collected by fellow Peace Officers waited in the tail end of the file.

It was a rock-solid case, almost unusually clean-cut. Aaron was a murderer caught with the blood still wet on his hands and a dozen witnesses lined up to testify.

The sensational Greenglad Bomber that had captivated criminal justice diehards for two whole years only had three witnesses, and one of them had been expunged due to the history of institutionalization. And that was a case that positively reeked of a Ministry scapegoat.

So what did Aaron do to deserve such a thorough burial?

And despite all of that, Aaron had proven himself a perfectly proficient soldier. Had the Ministry found him during his youth, they might've trained a useful officer.

Although, to be completely fair to his incompetent colleagues, they eventually found him; it just happened they found him standing over the corpse of a Peace Officer.

His door barked at him, as a clenched fist hammered on the steel frame. There it was, that urgent entitlement that sang with the infuriating music of a haircut in search of your superior.

A few voices chattered on the opposite side, but that banshee bellowed over the others: "Riley, open the damn door."

Riley slumped in his seat, regretting the coming expenditure of energy he just didn't have available today. He thumbed a switch on the tablet computer mounted on his wrist. "Lieutenant, can I see you for a minute?"

Talania slid through the creaking doors as soon as there was enough space for her tall frame. "How could you do this?!"

Two officers rushed in behind her, trying to pull her back out the door, but Talania backed them down with a bulldog's stare. This woman had all of the finesse of an orbital bombardment.

Riley waved the officers back out the door, before gesturing for Talania to take a seat in the only other chair. "I see the honeymoon period is over," he said, flipping back to the front of the file for the eleventh time. "You're welcome, by the way."

"Very cute, Riley," she snapped back, "You can't fire me. The Ministry is going to have your head for this!"

"The Ministry is occupied with the other side of the galaxy," Riley intoned, "And they've wanted my head pretty much since I graduated with suboptimal marks. Trust me when I say, in our line of work, you only survive this long if you know how to duck."

Talania leafed through the papers on her clipboard—was she the one carrying the torch for these heinous artifacts? She began reading from a branch of statistics longer than her arm. "Six accountants, three policymakers, twenty-three--"

"I know all of this, Ms. Dedria."

"Twenty-three community outreach officers, and my *entire* communications office!"

"You know how I know all of this?" Riley groaned, hoping beyond hope he could make her stop, "Because I wrote the memo."

"You're diverting one hundred and sixty pounds of rations specifically to the Orbital detail?!" Talania barked, "That's like fourteen people, but you're starving entire families in this breakdown!"

"For Orbital, that is starvation rations," he said, "With all our upgrades, we cook a little hotter than you do. It's a military situation, Talania. I'm sorry, but these are difficult decisions with harsh realities."

She reached forward, ripping Aaron's file from his hands, "You can't just melt the Colonial Administration because it's annoying."

"So you admit it's annoying?"

"Oh, granted freely!" Talania nodded, but she wasn't going to be turned aside, "But these are critical—and might I add Constitutional—offices. The Governor, the Statesmen: they won't stand for it!"

He pushed out a breath, trying to push the growing anger out of his chest with the same action. "And Daddy's got your back, does he?"

Her nose twitched but she stood her ground. Political power, much like physical power, came from the foundation. Any equivocation weakened the stance. Talania learned that lesson early and applied it well, often finding strength when there was nothing to back her by just standing hard.

It was an illusion that made her an effective politician. But the quiver of her lip betrayed the truth her otherwise immaculate poker face tried to hide: that imitation of power had been silenced.

A shape at the door, answering Riley's summons. "Lieutenant Holmst," Riley asked, "Would you find Governor Dedria and bring him to my office? His daughter has some questions for him and I would like to minimize the injuries from the judicial duel to follow."

Holmst nodded and marched off down the hall. Riley gestured to the open chair, as he plucked the file back from Talania's grasp. Such shows of civility had never calmed her before but giving ground might reduce the amount of violent attitudes in his vicinity.

There wasn't a whole lot of ground for him to give her. Riley's office was marginally larger than a tin can, and Talania's high pony-tail was already brushing the roof. A small porthole behind Riley offered a little natural light, but it only served to highlight the lack of decoration adorning the bulkheads. His desk was bolted to the floor, no pictures on the blue-gray walls, and a small cot that folded up into the bulkhead

The only real art to speak of he had hand-painted over the door jam: "Service to the People"—a reminder.

Talania took what little was on offer, easing herself into the open aluminum seat. She looked like a child, her knees crooked up higher than the armrests. Space travel was not made for the statuesque.

"What's to become of us?"

"A skeleton crew will maintain the necessary administrative functions," Riley droned, "They will need proper management, and I know you're looking for work."

"So you shove me into a corner where I can do the least harm?"

"Where you can be the most helpful, actually," Riley said as he reopened the pages to resume his study. "Talania, you've a brilliant organizational mind and it would be a shame to sideline that."

The compliments felt strange in his mouth, almost chewy. False. And he couldn't shake the feeling of her stare, that she was well aware of his discomfort. Talania's fleeting patience had been exhausted and she had resolved to stare at his head until his thinning hairline retreated back over the horizon.

"Has anyone ever told you, you look like you tortured animals as a child?" Riley mused.

"Better to look like it than have two Naval Medals in the field," Talania shot back.

"I've only got the one," Riley said, "And it's an Academy Merit, not a Medal."

Talania leaned forward, propping her elbows on her knees. "What do you gain by establishing martial law in Vanguard?"

"I don't have to do two and half hours of stand-up material in front of career morons in order to justify saving your life," Riley said, "These aren't normal circumstances, Ms. Dedria."

"And what about tax collection?" She asked, "Road maintenance? Will your office be handling law enforcement too?"

"There's a reason you still have a job. If you even want it."

"So building you a throne is left to Stage Two?" She taunted, with a raised eyebrow.

"No thrones, Ms. Dedria," Riley assured her, "One day, I'm going to lead from the bridge of an Eisenclad Dreadnought. But today, I chose to stay here, ever the servant."

She scoffed, retreating back in her chair to study and hate him from the safety of a few extra feet. Her ivory tower had crumbled under the weight of her own righteousness and she blamed a so-called despot on the neighboring unrelated high ground.

This was too perfect. If the Princess pouted any harder, she might regress back into Grade School. Fitting, for a woman who never left that esoteric cradle where all conflicts are conceptual.

He had no doubt she felt for those that were hungry but had never been truly hungry herself. She had never missed a meal, and not once had she eaten some stale shards from a can.

It was all well-intentioned, to be sure, but it rang hollow.

He leaned back in his chair. "Ms. Dedria, if you expect humility from your authorities, you're in for a very depressing adulthood."

She didn't miss a beat. "Maybe my leaders should start measuring up."

For all the annoyance she provided, her pure gumption went unrivaled. He wanted to put it behind glass to preserve it for future generations to dissect. It would be such a shame to watch it extinguish in a gasp of smoke.

"Tal?" The Governor peered inside, the fat man leaning against the doorframe, a hollowed-out remainder of a once powerful man now sapped of stature and vitality.

She didn't even move, her eyes still locked onto Riley. "You agreed to this, didn't you?"

Riley almost laughed out loud, incredulous and amused all at once. She had gone sniffing for a fight before she had even shored up her support. No wonder this political bulldog had never gone beyond the charity arena—she couldn't keep her own house in order, let alone convince a dissenter to fall in.

The ashen man took the few steps over to his daughter like he might collapse along the way. Riley could swear his hair had gone grayer since this morning, the experience of the last few days showing their toll.

The Governor scooped up his daughter's hands in his own. "If we all die down here, does it really matter if we died standing up? We'll still be dead."

Her eyes flashed, back and forth from Riley to her father. She had drawn the conclusion, that her formerly impressive father was now repeating someone else's words, a hollow echo of his previous power. Didn't much matter that this was Christopher's genuine opinion on the matter.

Her opinion of her father was higher than that; the notion had to come from some outside corruption.

And with that breath of air, the fire in her kindled anew. "Do you really think you can crown yourself a monarch so easily?"

Riley fought the urge to speak, pinching the bridge of his nose as though he might stem the flow of acid pumping up his throat. The burn in his chest and neck forced a cough out of him.

"Tal, please—" The Governor tried to refocus her but she swatted his hands away.

"No, I think I deserve an answer. You abolish everything that makes us a Republic, you defy the Ministry and the Consul-General, and you assure us that it's for our own good. You draft the miners with promises while offering their deaths; you invoke curfews and starvation rations. But we should be grateful because the very nice man who just wants the best for us might leave us all to die if, say, one little girl raises her voice at him? Oh, please!"

"Well, not when you put it like that," Riley blurted back.

Riley's desk chirped, indicating an incoming message from a secure channel. For the briefest moment, he didn't know what to do with all of this asinine paper, before sweeping it gingerly to the side and out of the way.

He flicked the newly exposed toggle, allowing several console monitors to rise up from the desktop surface on a single crane arm. The fact the whole apparatus could vanish into his desk had never stopped surprising him. It was as though the whole thing existed in an alternate dimension but phased in just to give him his mail.

"Do you really think you can invoke monsters under our beds, and we will just happily surrender our freedoms to a man like you?"

"Talania! He's the only reason you're still alive!" The Governor's objection was both empty and too late. He had long since lost any muzzle on his daughter, likely around her thirteenth birthday. This late and futile effort was so weak it didn't even deserve appreciation for the attempt.

"So what, do I kiss the ring now, or did that window close?"

"I have a security briefing being relayed through two satellites," Riley said without looking up, his eyes scouring the monitors, snap reading the by-line of the message and studying the video. He pointed toward the door. "If you don't mind?"

The Governor tried to pull his daughter out, but Talania refused to stand from her chair. "What is it, Colonel?"

Pursing his lips, he pinched the video message wider on his screen and spun the console arm around for them to see.

A smoking homestead. A silo burning. Bodies littering the ground. Some still twitching.

Blood staining a camera lens.

"I told them..." The Governor murmured, "I told them to evacuate the outer homesteads. I did!" His head whipped from Talania to Riley and back, waiting for someone to absolve him of responsibility.

Riley tapped the edge of the monitor, scrolling the image to a man splayed out in the dirt, his body torn in half through the midsection. He was still breathing.

"This is what happens when you don't listen to me."

CHAPTER
EIGHT
AARON

IT HAD BEEN A TRAP.

The Howlers had brought them to a homestead on the edge of the colony, far beyond the Wall. They had set the Capitals down to search the site for survivors.

And the Jergad sprang from the ground—not camouflaged or hiding, but from tunnels beneath the rock. They had burrowed up into position and waited for the humans to take the bait.

And now hundreds of the damn things swarmed the Rimpau homestead, gutting and cleaving and hissing and snapping.

Aaron kicked the dead beast at his feet, its flesh still sizzling and snapping from the plasma blasts, like bacon in cast iron. Its two blue eyes stared vacantly at the ground. It looked possessed or hollow, like some evil force had been driving it forward.

Don't fixate, Aaron. His friends were trapped, a hundred more of these to go. This was the first of many.

The Howlers' overhead unleashed their fury, door guns beating upon the back of the swarm. Dozens of individuals fell, but the horde ignored the sky-nuisance. They couldn't reach it, and besides—they had other toys to play with.

The mob pressed in towards the homestead itself, surging over the sides of the pit.

He could hear the distinct voices over the radio. Holmst calling out for ground reports. Carmona calling out targets. Eden instructing someone through triage. Nora tossing insults at the ugly beasts. Jensen bellowing encouragement like a Viking general on his way to Valhalla.

Then suddenly nothing. And he was just watching it happen.

Aaron broke into a jog, rushing toward a roiling mass of blood-thirsty critters that had evolved from the dirt up to butcher and cleave. They hid in the grass and snatched the unwary.

They were every bit as horrible as the stories.

Some of the Drones saw him—heard him—felt him—approaching. They turned to face him, their jaws unhinging, as though to swallow him whole.

Aaron slowed to a stop, shouldering his rifle and taking careful aim.

Click.

Nothing. A stove-pipe jam—a shell casing was stuck, not having cleared the chamber & crunched by the collapsing piston.

The Drones hissed and charged, their feet slapping the ground, beating on the skin of a war drum. They stooped low, hiding their bodies behind the crests of their skulls. It was like some kind of demonic bulldozer had been bred with a wheat thresher.

Aaron pulled the action back, letting the jammed casing fall free, and slapping a new one home. He shouldered the rifle again.

The beasts loomed over him, even with their hunched postures.

The rifle spat fire and kicked into his stomach, somehow harder than it ever had before. He had dropped his stance in his panic.

But the thirty caliber round slammed into the lead Drone's face. It slumped, dragging against its neighbors.

Aaron dropped to one knee, shouldering the rifle properly, before cracking off a fusillade of follow-ups. Some shots skipped off the leather carapace, chunking bits of the natural armor, but refusing to bury any deeper.

Others hit square, the lead round tumbling deep into the crimson juices underneath. They collapsed in a pile a few feet in front of him.

Either by cruel fate or sheer determination, one still reached for him, waving its clawed arms at him from underneath its limp brethren.

Aaron dropped the empty magazine to the ground, fishing a fresh one from his harness as the beast hissed at him, helpless on the ground. He chambered the fresh magazine before snapping the first round into the helpless Drone's head, ending its futile thrashing.

As Aaron pressed forward, he passed many fallen Capitals' bodies—if what remained could be called as such. For every dead Capital, there were four or five open tunnels large enough for a pit miner's drill bit. These industrious little buggers had quite a network under the homestead and had laid in wait for fresh prey.

He made his way towards the homestead's central pit unmolested, the body of the horde having already spilled inside.

The Howlers swung overhead, their own gunfire having ceased for some chilling reason. He jogged up to the lip of the maw, breath hitched in his chest for what he might see. What presented itself was both inspiring and terrifying.

Two stories straight down into the Earth, the farmers had carved their home and their crops. Various holes in the walls, either excavated or natural, had to be the living spaces, with the pit floor acting as the farmland, with solar reflectors lining the walls every few feet.

Whatever crops had been their craft were trampled into dust under what had to be over a hundred alien feet...and just under a dozen remaining humans. What remained of the Capitals had formed up at the center of the farmland, standing at the center of the crop circle.

Nora and Jensen were back to back, screaming taunts and threats at the nightmare swirling around them. Keira and Solomon picked their targets with care, both soaked from head to toe in the blood of their kills. Eden tended to a wound in Carmona's arm as he directed fire at the alien surges, pushing back on the rising tide every time it swelled.

The aliens seemed happy to let them exhaust their munitions, testing and probing responses.

An alien lunged forward and snagged a Capital with a claw through the leg like a hook through a fish. They dragged him back before anyone could react, sucking the poor soul into the body of the horde. His screams were garbled and silenced by splashing liquid and crunching bones.

In a matter of seconds, the leading edge of the monstrosities had turned back toward the survivors, spitting a chittering roar that was somehow synchronized like a chorus of moist thrumming.

The horde was playing with its food.

Aaron keyed his throat mic. "Holmst, drop the cables now!"

"I drop the cables, they'll yank the birds right out of the sky," Holmst snapped back.

"Give 'em air support!"

"We melted the barrels, Capital. The mission is scrubbed. If you want out of there, fall back now!"

Carmona dropped his rifle, drawing his sidearm to shoot down an advancing Drone. It crumpled at his feet.

Jensen dead checked the beast with the last few shots in his rifle. Empty, he grabbed the barrel and beat on the monster's face with the rifle butt in a vain attempt to stop its death throes.

Aaron checked his magazine: nineteen shots. Make them count.

A Drone rushed a distracted Jensen, too occupied with hammering on his current target.

Aaron shouldered his rifle.

Center of mass. Breathe out. Trigger. Aim small, miss small.

The shot clipped beneath the back of the skull, snapping whatever cords held the creature up. It crumpled like soiled laundry at Jensen's feet, next to its cousin.

A few of the monsters turned and hissed at the threat from

above, trying to reform their battle lines and present a shield for the back ranks. But the sheer size was too much, and Aaron had a view of too many vulnerable points, peppering his shots across the mob.

"Now!" Carmona called out, seizing the opportunity.

The survivors directed their fire at the far side of the ring, spraying whatever remaining munitions available into the distracted horde.

It was too much, too fast for the body to respond. The Capitals cleaved a break in the circle and staggered with their wounded toward the homestead's interior caves. Whatever awaited couldn't be worse than their current state.

Keira and Nora held the doorway, while Eden and the others lurched over the threshold, a trail of blood and shell casing behind them.

Before the Drones could push past their mounting dead, the Capitals slammed the blast door down.

Heroism accomplished. Time to run.

Aaron chucked his rifle aside and fumbled with his sidearm, firing random blasts into the assembly below him. Their attentions were split, but the horde was now advancing on Aaron, and he had the distinct disadvantage of being alone.

He stepped back away from the lip of the pit as the monsters clawed their way up the sides as though gravity were a just a stern suggestion.

Oh, he'd done it now.

"Holmst?" Aaron stuttered, "Cables? Maybe drop me a cable?"

Their claws dug long troughs in the lip of the pit, as the Jergad host heaved their skeletal frames over the edge. Somehow, some Drones were climbing on the backs of the others, their scythe arms sliding past each other and climbing up without injuring their comrades, a devil's ladder of hissing blades.

Drones came up over the cliffside two or three at a time. His shots glanced off their skull-crests like arrows against a shield wall, sparking and chunking bits. He may as well be throwing firecrackers at a bulkhead.

The pistol slide slammed back one final time, resting open and leaking smoke, like an exhausted runner exhaling steam on a cold morning.

Aaron thumbed the magazine loose and fished in the pocket he knew was empty.

The ground cracked. Because of course it did.

Aaron felt his footing give way. He tucked into a ball and leaned to the side, rolling away from the grasping claws of the Drone that slashed the air behind him.

He didn't look for the strikes, just scrambled madly away. He felt the blows hitting the earth behind him, jackhammering through the soft earth and tossing arcs of dirt into the sky.

In a bizarre moment of clarity, he felt the pressure first, before the surface tension of his uniform and flesh gave way and that scythe drove down into his thigh like an ice pick.

His scream was cut short as it hauled him backward, further tearing down his leg as it dragged him through the dirt toward a collection of thirsting maws. Aaron grabbed at his harness for something, anything.

His combat knife was a serrated utility tool most commonly used to start campfires and cut rope. But it was steel and pointy.

The creature rolled him over. A single angry face stared into and through him, its eyes a cool and pale blue, no iris to betray depth or focus. It breathed in his face—stale and heavy—with its guttural vibrato pushing the foul air over his face. The split jaw quivered, as if eager to feast but savoring the moment.

Aaron simply sat up and pushed the knife directly into the creature's eye socket clean to the hilt. He felt it skip off of two separate somethings inside before finally stopping.

The creature huffed, as if considering how to respond.

And then, every muscle in his body seized, a shock grabbing hold of him and throwing him backward to the ground, like he'd just gripped hard with both hands on to the leads of an alternator.

His vision went black, then white, then black again in an epileptic surge of overwhelming intensity. The first thing he noticed was the tears falling down his face, a grief-stricken fall drenching his cheeks.

He gasped for air, sobbing without cause or reason. It was like he had been given everything he'd ever dreamed of, and shown it again destroyed and ruined by unseen hands. It was the kind of heartbreak that came coupled with heinous cruelty pitched downward on an innocent child or the grief of a widow standing over their beloved's crumpled body.

It was more than simple sadness, but the absence of joy on the edge of memory, how recalling a time before the pain only magnified the suffering.

What was this feeling? Where did it come from?

And with that, the slain creature fell to the ground on top of him. He could hear something valuable crack, his muscles tightening in a futile attempt to protect his failing body, but he didn't feel the pain that should accompany his undoubtedly fractured legs.

It was as though he had been blinded by a white-hot iron, silencing his nerves and stealing his voice. It drove blunted speartips behind his eyes, and with his last coherent thought, he presumed his skull had spilt its mealy load onto the dirt.

As he bled from his leg and cried into the clay, he waited for the cacophony of angry blows to follow, a syncopated succession of talons rending him to paste. He wrapped himself in his misery and sought solace only in that his end might be quick.

But it never came. They denied him that comfort.

The silence of the battleground and that haunting echo of the Howlers overhead was the only thing he could hear, as though the natives had given him his sentence, and had carried it out. And with their work done, they quit the field.

Aaron shivered under the body of the beast, as darkness finally claimed his sight. The last thing he saw was the Howler hanging in the sky above, unfurling a rescue he did not deserve before all vanished behind a blurry shroud.

He could feel the creature exhale one ragged sigh against the ground and deflating atop him. He closed his eyes, hoping to awake far from here where comfort was simply known by the absence of suffering.

Behind his anguished tears and clenched eyelids, in that empty void carved in the stone of his memory, were two blue eyes, lidless and alien, staring back at him. He saw them, as much as they saw him, taking in his face with careful study.

Those eyes flitted back and forth, absorbing every detail, every blemish, every stain, every scar.

They could see him.

They knew him now. And they would make him know their pain.

PART TWO
PARAGON

CHAPTER
NINE
RILEY

HE WAS DAMAGED GOODS.

The money would have been better spent on fresh munitions, requisitioning equipment from the black market, or feeding the living. Aaron Havenes should have been consigned to a scrap heap, tossed unceremoniously into a grimy ditch, where he would mercifully perish before his festering wounds could take hold.

The man had served his purpose.

Unfortunately, a certain charity case in Administration had other intentions for the Hero of the Hour.

"We had to induce a coma," the doctor said, with the infuriating calm of someone who dispensed with their human empathy decades ago.

Riley stared past the doctor in towards the surgical ward, where the third batch of surgeries was commencing. The surgical team would be wrist deep in their patient for the next six hours.

These doctors could be treating sick colonists or saving injured soldiers. Instead, they would spend their combined time and their extensive expertise patching up a man recruited solely for his ability to bleed.

Princess Talania had taken a special interest in Aaron. His story had spread through the colony like a particularly virulent plague.

The Capitals had rescued a single civilian farmer and his mouth had been left annoyingly unscathed. The man spoke endlessly of heroism—quite innocently and completely lacking in activist coaching, of course. He spun tales of a man standing against a force of nature, holding the proverbial flag high over rising flood waters.

Talania caught wind of that tall tale and spun up her considerable energies, hoisting Aaron up as a symbol to the people. She excelled at this: find emotional lightning rods, raise them up into the storm until they cease to draw the ire of Zeus, discard, repeat.

It was a talent, he had to admit, and one that could be bent to the needs of the people and the state; she regularly bent it for her own ends.

Riley supposed the Imperial Flag had long since lost its flavor for her. Not a patriot to anything other than herself. He should've let her take that bullet last week.

Now, now—that wouldn't be very nice, now would it?

As Riley watched valuable man-hours fritter away, Talania took in the doctor's reports like a brown-nosing teacher's pet. She scribbled notes on her ridiculous paper. Riley was certain she was busily composing some heinous public release that he would have to quash before it managed to leave the building.

The doctor was deep in the weeds, detailing the previous work that Riley couldn't dream of understanding and certainly didn't waste the energy to try on.

"Nanofiber cords were successfully attached to the left intracapsular ligament, and arterial grafts made to the femoral artery, where the damage was most extensive." The doctor explained in a patronizing tone that came packaged with advanced degrees and white coats. "Combined with the multiple tibial shaft fractures in both legs, and the sheer blood lost, he is lucky to be alive at all."

Riley couldn't control the scoff that huffed out of his nose. Lucky? He shouldn't be alive. It's improper. It's wasteful. How many citizens are these doctors *not* treating while they repair the leg of a Capital?

Talania resisted the urge to glare at him, blinking through her irritation. "What are we doing about the neurological damage?"

The doctor paused. "...We're not quite certain what's happening."

A learned man of science—while dodging the actual phrasing—actually admitting to their own ignorance? What was this now? Riley's eyes narrowed, and he declared a single curious sound, "What?"

More techno babble was his reward. "He is verifiably unresponsive," the doctor assured, "but we have recorded increases in rapid eye movement, heart palpitations. And CT scans indicate spikes of activity in his amygdala."

Talania could decipher it all. "He's...dreaming?"

"Vividly." The break in the doctor's tone intimated how impossible that result was. "But what images we've collected are...gibberish."

"Show me." For some reason, Riley felt an itch behind his ears. He had to know what the Capital was seeing.

"Sir, most dreamers have unusual imagery. It takes months to parse out--"

"Just show me," he snapped, fed up with the excuses.

The Doctor recoiled, and even Talania gave the Colonel a concerned eye. Every danger sense Riley had was firing, and he had to quiet them.

Pulling up his Entiglas, the Doctor was a few quick taps away from Aaron's file. He projected the images up on to the wall.

Most dream studies had been relegated to the farcical fringe, a technological wonder used in the same field as astrology, palm readings and astral projection. It was a simple matter to duplicate electrical impulses through an analog brain and any neural network of sufficient complexity could reproduce visual images from the patterns. They proved fascinating for experimental psychologists and generated genuinely stirring artistic pieces.

This was not one of those.

The pictures glittering off the wall more resembled a technical error, blending chaotic flashes of pastel colors at a confusing rhythm, as though keeping a musical time that fluctuated at the whims of a senseless composer fueled only by a glass of water and a cocktail of off-brand stimulants.

"Safe to say this isn't a glitch?" said Talania, asking the obvious question.

The Doctor shook his head. "We've run diagnostics backward and forward, and the data we collect is consistent. This is, as best we can tell, exactly what he's seeing."

It made Riley want to throw up. He turned his back on the wall, but to his dismay, the light was causing the whole room to flicker like a nightclub past midnight. "What can we gather from this?"

"Nothing conclusive."

That wasn't good enough. "What about the inconclusive things?" Riley said a bit more forcefully than he intended. "Any theories, wild guesses?"

Silence. Terrific.

"Fine," Riley sighed, throwing a halfhearted glance at Talania, "Let me know if your expense account wakes up."

He spun on the balls of his feet and marched out of the room. He couldn't stand to be near the projector color-test display a moment longer. It was unsettling to be in the presence of, let alone study. Something about it gave him the chills, like a cross to a vampire. To the doctor's credit, he did say it was gibberish. Aaron's brain was likely to be slurry if subjected to that display for any extended period.

Riley had grown comfortable visiting the wounded in military care, but this was a civilian hospital. It was downright busy by comparison, but not because of their business.

There were likely three times as many tools and staff. Everyone walked the corridors like their occupation was the least pressing thing on their mind, or simply pushing past mental and physical exhaustion. The regularly sanitized floor squeaked against every fall of his boots.

Couple that grating metronome with the dull apocalyptic hum of suffering that seemed to be generated by the walls, and all Riley wanted was to see the sky again.

Holmst waited for Riley outside the observation room, maintaining a parade rest. He dropped into formation, following a step behind Riley as they passed the somber civilian staff.

They all gave Riley a wide berth, keeping a respectful distance, groups even parting with his approach. They knew his importance without having to be reminded.

Or maybe it was that look of murder and urgency that they simply wanted no part of.

Good.

"My report is ready for you at your discretion," Holmst said, like he was submitting himself for penance.

"You made the right call, Lieutenant," Riley huffed, "Their role in all this is to bleed so your men don't have to." Riley flicked open his wrist computer, the projector beaming the holographic display to hover in front of his face. Despite the incorporeal nature of it all, subdermal implants in his fingertips allowed Riley to touch the image with his free hand and the implants would push back on him as though he were touching an actual screen.

He flicked through two news reports—the Civil War was going predictably poorly for the scrappy pirate Outlanders on the Boolean Edge. He called up Holmst's report to peruse as they walked.

Holmst proffered the top of his head, as though expecting a blow from a drunken father. Riley would not give him the satisfaction or resolution of his shame.

"Capitals barricaded themselves in a meat locker," Riley read aloud. "Oddly appropriate."

Holmst nodded. "We didn't even think to look for them on the first pass."

"Bray is on-site?"

"And teams at the Wall are triaging the wounded before transferring them back home. I took the liberty of signing them off for two days R&R."

Riley tightened up his jaw. "One day. After that, they're to be returned to the duty roster. Be sure we pay Sergeant Bray a visit. They're alive right now because of the work he put in."

"They're alive right now because of *Aaron*, sir."

Riley shook his head. Even his aide had swallowed Talania's efficient propaganda. That woman's reach was far. But this wasn't worth the blood pressure. "The Capital did good work," Riley conceded.

The two walked in silence for a long time, until they finally emerged from the hospital. The doors swung open and the fresh wind brushed his face like a kiss from the heavens, cool and calming. The claustrophobic halls full of sick and injured, the lack of urgency, and abundance of chattel combined to make for a singularly unpleasant experience.

Perhaps some of that equipment could be better used in Forward Wall Medical Stations?

As he stepped out from the hospital ward, the colony's structures stretched out before them. The Aurora tower stood just across the boulevard, its knobbly frame reaching high into the sky, with its heavy engines seated down underground to serve as a foundation.

What was once the tallest structure in the area had since been dwarfed by the three taller skyscrapers and a fourth going up. The gleaming daggers of glass and steel reached high into the sky, as if to taunt the conquered world beneath them. There was no seam or steel frame, just their glassy sleeves catching the midday light and lighting the entire city with an autumn warmth not previously seen outside of memory.

Beneath their familial embrace, shopkeepers hawked their wares, cafes served their fare, and maglev trains hummed their loads in a suburban ballet of peace and prosperity. They had taken a wildland and crafted civilization out of nothing but dust.

Even Earth wasn't this welcoming anymore, with permanent

storms rocking the coastlines and intense heat baking the Midlands. Colonies like Vanguard were comparably temperate, especially for those without the means to buy it on Earth.

People poured into these fringe worlds like they might forge their fortune from the very soil. There was a time when living on the Reaches was considered a rich man's retreat, a healthy and quiet retirement; until a few short months ago, it was almost the desirable choice.

They had names for colonials now: Dusters, people scratching a living from the dust. Minister Caldwell had a few more choice titles for them.

"May I speak freely, sir?" Holmst broke the silence.

"He's alive," Riley jumped on the moment, "For the low, low price of whatever Princess decides to spend on him. But so long as she doesn't divert any Military supply..."

"They left him alive, sir."

Who did? Riley pivoted on his heels, turning back to Holmst.

His aide had stopped in the middle of the boulevard. He was halfway between declaring his discovery and caught up in the act of it. His eyes were darting around, replaying the mission in his head, before bouncing back up to his commander's icy face.

"I had a pretty good view of it. And I've been going over it again and again. They had every opportunity to finish the job. They didn't."

He was caught up in the momentum now, closing the distance between the two. Thankfully, there was a break in the trains overhead, allowing Holmst to have his little moment.

"They don't have much care for their own losses. They come after us until we are dead and gone."

Riley sighed. "They're persistent. You're not telling me something I don't already know, Lieutenant."

"They had him, sir. I mean it, they *had* him. So he stabs one with his quick knife? What of it? They're made of the damn things. He should be hamburger. But he takes one last Drone down and they just...bugger off? It doesn't make sense."

Holmst took the last few steps toward Riley, the mental ball officially rolling downhill, avalanche warning in effect. "The civilian we rescued? He wasn't an accident. He was left alive to bait the trap. Pretty basic mechanic. Get us deep enough inside the jaws before they snap it closed on us: maximizes casualties. It's Guerrilla Warfare 101."

And now the thesis statement. "Sir, they're smart enough to make plans."

"Are you suggesting that Aaron is...boobytrapped?" Riley couldn't imagine how that would be possible.

Holmst pursed his lips, going over the instant replay in his head one more time. "We're missing something, sir. I know it."

CHAPTER
TEN

AARON

THEY LATER TOLD him it wasn't the first time he'd woken up, but it was the first time he could remember doing so.

The bedding was stiff, with pressed sheets and a heated blanket draped over him like a crusty & scratchy tortoise shell. He could feel the seams in the bed through the thin mattress, where sections could be pulled away to grant doctors access without moving him.

Diodes kissed his skin and the tell-tale beeps of a dozen life signs being monitored cut the air just a few feet away from him. A large diode clung to the back of his neck, right at the base of his skull, one long line of tape and cord that went from ear to ear. Tubes pressed against his skin, and a plastic reservoir strapped to his thigh, weighty and full.

He tried to flex his leg, but a tingling numb was his only response. He could only hope that was a painkiller and not a far worse discovery.

Aside from the chirping of medical equipment, the only sound was a dull hum that came from his right, modulating every so often, with the tell-tale rise and fall of city life. Wait a minute...where was he?

Then he opened his eyes, cracking the sand at the edges of his lids like he was breaking free of an eggshell.

Off the opposite wall, hung a calendar with a dozen scribbled notes on it. His eyes couldn't focus on any one word long enough before they would slide off.

The lights were dim, but a warm and welcome light beamed in through the window. The blinds had been drawn to allow that inviting glow to stretch out in the room.

The pale blue sky overhead, just like —

Those eyes

Aaron shook his head, adrenaline pumping. That dull hum had risen in pitch, a soft whine to match his tension.

He could remember the Farm, the shouting, and that horrible pain. He looked down at his bedsheets, where two distinct lumps sat. His legs. They had been so—

Don't pull the bandage, rip it.

He hesitated for a moment before flipping the bed sheet aside. Mercifully, his leg was there to greet him, albeit with a nasty jagged scar down from thigh to knee.

He had been hit from behind, so this was an exit wound—the back side of his leg was liable to be a real horror show. The damage had mostly healed, aside from the drainage tube still gurgling on his hip.

"We have to prevent infections," a voice called out, silky and low.

Aaron glanced at the door. A tall and slender silhouette hung in the entry, with clean clothes and a tightly kept ponytail. Her posture seemed closed, with one hand on hip and legs close together, allowing only tiny darts of light to slip through her frame.

The light from the hallway beyond blinded Aaron to more specifics but wrapped them in a kind of otherworldly glow, as though she might have come from some benevolent higher place to bestow kindness and forgiveness.

"Remember me?" The voice asked, with a chirp of playful to it.

"Where am I?" Aaron stopped short of demanding an answer. He had no reason to think he was in any danger, but he didn't much care for this person's flirty opener.

The figure stepped forward, letting the light from the window dance upward to reveal their face. A hard jaw with a perfectly curved brow and pale lips: it was as though they had been carved from marble in honor of something greater.

It was ethereal. Or maybe that was just the drugs.

"At Hospital, in Vanguard. You were injured out at the Rimpau Homestead," the alto voice intoned, "We've spent the better part of the last week rebuilding you."

Aaron looked back down at his leg. One week? That scar looked several months of healing old.

The figure smiled, predicting his line of thought. "Modern medical marvels, Mr. Havenes."

They took another step into the light, further from their divine backlighting. She was still beautiful, even in the fluorescents of the office, with bright eyes and high cheekbones.

Her look softened as he continued to marvel at her. Good, she thinks it's the medication. "Talania Dedria, with the Governor's office?" She said, offering up the freebie.

She spent the next hour answering his questions: The aftermath of the battle, the curiosity of his survival, and the fate of his friends. None of the Capitals had suffered such egregious wounds as he had; or at the very least, none had survived that experience.

But those that had survived the battle—including the patriarch of the Rimpau Homestead—had not ceased their talk of Aaron's heroics. They returned with stories of a man who belonged in ancient folklore, who would feast in the Halls of Valhalla and lay at rest behind the Pearly Gates before beginning life anew with the Pilgrim, to walk with the Dunsweir on the Great Sojourn across the stars.

It was like they had witnessed an entirely different battle than he had and constructed a magnificent fresco to commemorate the day.

Maybe it was the staging or the lighting, but Aaron didn't remember any specific act that required so much as a footnote in a history book, let alone a full chapter title.

Aaron felt a wave of nausea broadside him, and he buckled over, the acidic bile a rising tide in his throat. Talania looked out the door, "Um...can we get a—"

But Aaron quashed the impulse, waving her off. He hung his head over the tile floor for a long moment before sitting back on the cold refreshment of his pillows.

They patched his leg up good as new in less than a week; they had him hooked up to more computers than a ship's navigator; and yet, they didn't have a proper fix for nausea. It was always the most common problems that were treated as ordinary, unfixable, traditional.

"It's the painkillers," Talania offered, "Gives ya one hell of a case of vertigo. Up till now, you haven't been sitting up."

"Coulda warned me," he snarked, forcing a crooked grin.

Her only response was a shrug, awfully dismissive for the otherwise angelic entry she had made. Suppose she wouldn't live up to the mild case of deification any more than he would.

"It'll pass, especially if we get you movin' around," Talania suggested, "What do ya say? Want to take that new leg out for a spin? The sun's out."

"I can walk?" He asked, incredulous. He felt the phantom of that Jergad arm plunging through his leg.

She tapped her hands on the footrest of his bed. "Buddy, the talent in this building, you can probably tap dance. Not sure if you could before, but you probably can now. Just don't pull out the bag."

To go out into the city, amongst everyday people again: to argue with store clerks, banter with passengers on an El-Train, or just stand and listen to the passing of the world.

"Where are the guards?" Aaron blurted, nodding towards the empty doorway.

Talania smiled wider, just a hint of devilry on the curve of her lip.

Like a child breaking the rules while the family is away. And she was inviting him to join her. "You're not just a Capital anymore, Mr. Havenes. At some point, we have to start treating you like a person again."

Aaron swept his feet off the bed, dangling his toes over the harsh tile floor. His legs felt bruised and sore, creaking and popping with even small movements. A week of sedentary life had robbed him of even the most basic flexibility.

Extending his legs, injured or not, brought painful warmth to the muscles in his thighs. He took a moment here, rolling through the motion time and again until the pain subsided.

Talania waited with the patience of a garden statue, observing his routine and silently judging. Or was it appraising? He was more than just a curiosity to her. He could see it in how her eyes lingered for that half-second before politely breaking contact.

She had to have seen him dozens of times during his stay, but he couldn't shake the blush filling his cheeks as he felt her eyes studying the curve of his shoulders and the corded muscles of his back. Before it was clinical; this was something else.

He inched off the bed, letting his toes graze the icy floor. He did not expect to get a response from only one of his feet. His left leg felt the pressure and the texture, but the dissonant lack of the crisp burn nearly threw off his balance. He tilted on the bed, as his brain immediately assumed he wasn't level.

Talania squashed the urge to chuckle. "We repaired the neuropathy as best we could, but..." Made sense.

The drastic scar in his leg probably took out more than just bone and muscle tissue, and all of that would have to be replaced by farmed tissue or artificial material.

He was going to have to see what Eden thought of the work.

After the initial stomach turn, he was able to throw his weight onto his feet. A few testing steps later found remarkable stability. Not only could he walk, he could probably run if properly motivated. The fact that Eden made do with the supplies available to her after having this miracle factory at her disposal was a testament to her patience and commitment.

Talania held on to his wrist with a considerate touch, more guide than support. She walked him through the bustling halls of the hospital.

Staff cycled through holographic displays and stenciled information in the air with their fingertips, while Nurses followed autonomous beds toward the appropriate medical bays.

It was like wandering through the home factory where dreams were packaged for delivery to the masses: granting verticality to the paralyzed, clarity to dementia, and life to the dying.

These were angels and miracles trundling about like any other day, like the raw sorcery they wielded had bored them into an empty sleep.

"They process about two hundred patients a day," Talania volunteered, seeing his eyes wander off. "It's a rather quaint operation."

"So this is what qualifies as quaint?" He asked.

"Compared to a proper hospital. Ever seen one?"

He shook his head. "Too rich for my blood."

Every so often Aaron caught one of them staring as they passed. But they weren't gawking at his wound, neatly concealed by his neutral gown. They were watching him, like there was a spotlight tracking as they walked. One nurse's station traded whispers and sideways stares.

"We should sell tickets." He thought out loud.

"I'm sorry?"

Aaron nodded towards the gaggle of nurses, widening his eyes and leaning back in shallow mockery of their amazement. He'd be worried about offending, but it was rude to point, so turnabout's fair play.

Talania smiled, expertly swallowing the laugh. "You're a bit of a local celebrity, Mr. Havenes."

"For what?"

She stopped at the double-doors, tapping the giant toggle on the wall. "A mild case of valor above and beyond. Everybody wants to know more about the mystery Cinderella story. Some tabloids are suggesting you used to be military or a firefighter, first responder—the story changes page to page. You didn't save orphans or anything, did you?"

It seemed like everyone had concocted a more interesting life for him than he actually led. They thought awfully highly of him, or the barrier for entry on heroism was a lot lower than he first presumed.

Talania shrugged at his non-response. "Well, handsome, if you lie and say you were a paramedic, I could stand to win some money."

He didn't have time to absorb those words as the doors swung open, burying him in focused light. When his eyes adjusted he could finally make out the sources.

The sun was particularly bright that morning as if burning that much stronger to impress its guests, but that light was picked up by the three glittering towers overhead, that shone with equal luster. It appeared like mankind had intended to socket gems in the sky, but Aaron knew them for the reflector dishes they were—collecting sunlight to bounce down onto the solar farm below.

As utilitarian as they were, they were an intoxicating sight, like a trifecta of jewels in mankind's crown. Beneath their splendor lay a proper world, a band of steel and silver to carry those gems.

Shiny elevated trains whisked along their magnetic tracks, their sweet hum a calming serenade of industry and progress. They zipped in and out of buildings, ferrying who-knows-what to God-knows-where like a frantic hive, both neurotically furious and calming in their efficiency, like they could not be overwhelmed no matter the load.

The dozens of buildings in sight were a sampling of architectural brilliance, more art than function, with sweeping curves and shapes that defied any average understanding of physics. These were not structures made for explicit intent like the Mining Rigs or the Capital Apartments; these were elegant designs sculpted for their own sake, a pleasure drawn straight from the mind into the world, a testament to Humanity's command of the elements.

For sure, the gravity on Vanguard was less than Solar Standard, and the tectonic functions had long since quieted, but those buildings held a part of Aaron's mind hostage, a disquieting beauty as if to challenge the hand of fate: Witness Me and my Will.

Aaron's wonderment faded the lower his eyes went. On the street level, people walked with a purpose of mind, with not a single soul loitering. Perhaps they were numbed to this majesty? If a person was to see this kind of landscape on the daily, did they really cease to appreciate the madness of it all, the impossible wonder of the achievements on display?

No. He saw that familiar look now. He saw it in that Market four short years ago, and he saw it in their eyes today.

Every passing businessman or lab coat down to the youngest child bore the same purposeful stare, eager to be anywhere but here, so focused on the future as to ignore the present. It was troubled, quiet and reserved - not by the present, but by the possible.

It was the anxiety of a life lived in silence for fear of standing out. What did they have to fear, so far behind the Wall and amongst such grandeur?

Of course—count the seemingly ubiquitous cameras, the far-too-chatty security guards given a wide berth by passersby.

And the immaculately kept streets. Cities have poverty; poverty means grime. These streets were spotless.

Where was all the dirt?

Talania took up that furious pace again, leading Aaron down the road. The bouncy pavement gave back for every step he gave it, as if he wore springs in his feet.

It made walking downright pleasant, even engaging. Steps that might pound on the knees and toes instead propelled one onward to further steps. He thought he would have to try to stop, rather than push forward.

"We've been a bit frantic since the exodus," Talania sighed, "And many families weren't sure how to think about their futures. They came here seeking a life and then...many believed the Empire had turned their backs on us."

That was a naive assertion, Aaron thought, to think the Empire had ever been there for them in the first place. It was there for the whole, perhaps that could be argued, but for them personally?

Individuals were disposable, statistics on balance sheets.

"Colonel Riley..." Talania intoned with every diplomatic bone in her body, failing to hide the venom tainting every word, "Stayed to provide security, but that didn't do much for people's spirits."

She stopped, pivoting on one heel like the ring leader she was. Aaron preempted her, "Cue the heroism."

The finger guns from a grown woman betrayed her young age. "Bullseye."

"You're from a Press Office, aren't you?" He asked, eyes narrowing.

She lost some of the air buoying her actions, but she didn't lose her stance. "When there used to be one."

Aaron sighed. Of course, all of the repairs had a cost attached. He wasn't a person; he was a Capital. He was munitions. He was not expensive, and they had spent quite a bit.

In fairness, they had saved him. A little payback wasn't out of line. "What do you need me to do?"

She dropped her act, hands flopping to her sides. "I was going to do a whole routine."

"I'm direct."

"This doesn't have to be a transaction." The creeping smile told him that she was enjoying the patter though, a curve at the corner of her lips. She sparred with everyone she met and enjoyed every worthy opponent.

"What were you going to call it?" Aaron fished.

"Quid pro quo?" She offered with a shrug, "We donate medical, you donate a few words. It would do wonders for the people, let them know they're going to live out the year."

Yeah, but they might not.

"I've got a few events we can set up, nothing in stone though," Talania hedged, inching toward him, as though she was afraid to over-pressure him. She reached out, her slender fingers working against his shoulder, coaxing the yes out. "I could work with you and we'll build something with minimal stress. You *are* recovering still, after all."

"What about my team?"

Talania nodded. "We could use them."

That's not what he meant.

A crisp thud, metal on flesh. He knew that sound all too well, the cushioned blow of a baton striking a forearm, or that of ribs curling around a steel truncheon.

Aaron turned, searching for the source. It was out of sight, some-where hidden in the gestalt of the city's preoccupied masses. His were the only eyes that pricked up, as the civilians elected to instead quicken their steps and lower their heads.

Slaves avoiding the master's whip. The shadow in their eyes and the hollow in their chests looked all too familiar to him. No one wanted to have the Sight fall on their shoulders.

Talania's grip on his shoulder tightened, her own unconscious danger sense. "What do you say?"

No. Aaron wasn't going to be distracted.

The beating was coming somewhere to his left, down a bouncy plastic boulevard a few dozen feet off, shrouded from the lights and the traffic. Aaron let his feet lead him towards the noise.

Talania half-mumbled his name as she tried to guide him away, but he would not be deterred, pushing through her grasp and towards the threat.

With each successive step, the happy din of the city's life seemed to fall away. The light dimmed and cooled, as the mirrored daylight could find no way into this tight corridor. Aaron had to rely entirely on the neon store lights of nearby establishments.

He passed two separate store clerks on the street side who not only paid no heed to the repeated wet thuds cracking the air, but they also couldn't meet Aaron's gaze as he advanced toward the sounds.

They were ashamed, afraid, a cocktail of both.

He stepped over the threshold into the alley, and to her credit, Talania was only a few strides behind him, like she was following him into the mouth of a cave—but she was following.

He saw them then, not even trying to hide. Two Army Regulars—they wore pristine dress greens, with high collars and a meager spackling of medals and ribbons on their shoulders—stood over a middle-aged man. The gaunt drifter lay crumpled on the ground, a dribble of blood rolling off his lip and down his linen shirt.

Aaron knew immediately why this particular man had received such singular focus. The beaten man's blonde hair was cut shallow to one side, left to grow long to his shoulder on the opposite. His scratchy beard was cut evenly across but lacking in precision or choice.

The designs on his clothes blocky and geometric, but intricate and hand-stitched with a thick thread. Everything he owned was made by himself or friends, and every style done by the same unskilled hands.

He was poor, possibly homeless, a vagrant.

A deck of playing cards scattered on the ground.

The Regulars loomed over him, their stun batons out but not primed—preferring the kinetic satisfaction of the polymer. Wide stances, pushing their faces forward.

They weren't detaining this man or apprehending him. They were hitting him because they liked hitting him.

It was in that instant, Aaron recognized them—Anatoly and Kipling, two guards from the Capital Apartments. They had been so approachable, portly and lanky duo, with goods to trade and warm smiles.

They were the good ones; they sang a different song these days.

"You goin' to answer my question, *skel*? Eh?" Anatoly jeered at his prey. "How much you made? You out here, conning the good people?"

Talania pulled on Aaron's shoulder, but he refused to move. He wanted to see this, and he doubted the Regulars would like a witness.

Anatoly brought his club down onto the Vagrant's leg, hard enough to leave a bright red welt. "There's a safety reg, *skel*. No loitering. Do you know what that means?"

"No," Kipling chimed in, "You know the facts about these colonials. Their ears are stopped up, all dirt and dust."

A chuckle, as Anatoly tapped the Vagrant about the ears with his baton, pushing his head from side to side. "You got dust in the ears. Is that it? Dust in your ears?"

No more.

"What the Hell do you think you're doing?" It really was more question than objection, but Aaron's voice echoed in the space.

The two Regulars looked up, stiffening at the two silhouettes at the end of the alley. "We're enforcing the law, citizen. Go back to your business."

"I'm no citizen," Aaron sneered. "This what you volunteered for?"

Talania sighed, all escape lost now. She muttered curses, as she reached for the taser on her waistband.

The Regulars abandoned their quarry and marched on Aaron. They split wide, one to each side. Kipling sneered at him. "You volunteering for a lesson?"

"I think he's goin' to die." Anatoly snarled.

Aaron wasn't fazed. "We're all going to die. Just looking for a good enough reason to."

They didn't recognize him. The surroundings, the costuming, and the bearings were all absent. There was no clue to indicate all the past history they had.

No memories kicked up about cartons of cigarettes, or a bottle of Kevalkian Whiskey, or half a dozen pin-ups, or medical tape. These grey market dealers had forgotten one of their biggest customers because of time and place.

"I'm Government and this is my charge. Trust me, you don't want to do this, boys." Talania put some convincing steel behind that threat.

But the Regulars had the taste for it now. They were ready to take some chances. They were untouchables, heroes by ego alone.

Just as they were ready to pounce, Kipling's brains finally connected some dots. "Did you come by way of Hospital?"

"Yeah. You want to see the inside of it?" Aaron hissed at the genius.

"He really eager for some pain." Anatoly shot back.

"I'm sorry," Talania interjected, "If you're going to threaten us, maybe do it without whistling through your teeth. It kinda undercuts your whole strongman routine."

Oh my god. He did whistle through his teeth. He'd done it since the day they met and Aaron had never noticed. Aaron almost broke up laughing on the spot.

They didn't like that mockery one bit. "Give me your name, brat," Kipling spat, "So I know what to put on your tombstone."

The charismatic Talania knew when to make her introductions, firing for maximum effect. "Name's Talania Dedria, jackass." Their smirks dropped in an instant—yeah, they knew who she was and what that could mean for them. "And this is Aaron Havenes, hero of the Rimpau Homestead. Killed a dozen Jergad drones and butchered the last one with his bare hands."

"Well, that last part's not strictly true," Aaron chimed in, "I had a knife. Got a knife for me?"

Talania shook her head, crackling her taser in the air. "I got fifty thousand volts looking for a home."

"We'll make due," Aaron said, as he turned back to the grunts.

But they had dropped their hostile stance, Anatoly even holstering his baton. They stared at him, slack-jawed and brows furrowed. "...626?"

Aaron nodded, his fists tightening. He prayed this new leg would hold out.

"You..." Anatoly said, "You've seen those things?"

Aaron paused, studying the man's face. The grunt couldn't be older than twenty-five, but his bright eyes and clean face more resembled a child. There wasn't fear in his face, but awe.

Aaron nodded. Anatoly blinked a few times, processing that before speaking. "What was it like? Killing 'em?"

There it was, that moment's fear retreating in the face of a thirst, a hunger for glory and bloodshed. He wanted fearsome tales of valor and daring more common in propaganda than reality. In Aaron, he didn't see property or a prisoner or a soldier: he saw a paragon. Something to emulate, to admire and aspire to.

To revere.

The Vagrant struggled to his feet, stumbling away further down the alley. Aaron watched him go, as the two officers were too occupied with Aaron's battle-lore to care about their victim anymore.

This is who he was told to die for? Anatoly? Kipling? These were the examples of someone too valuable to lose, more expensive than Jensen or Nora? Or Quinn?

Huah.

CHAPTER
ELEVEN
RILEY

"IS SHE TRYING TO START RIOTS?" Riley pushed the monitor down into his desktop, closing off the view of the last few seconds of annoying footage. "Because this is how you get riots."

Talania had worked quickly and brought her bright-eyed war hero under as many spotlights as she could lash together.

To his credit, Aaron took to public speaking like he had been born in front of TV cameras. He may as well have been wrought from factory steel to be a sympathetic hero, and the crowds of Vanguard ate him up. He spoke of the Capitals and their struggles, their flaws and their desires, their dream of citizenship and what they were willing to sacrifice for it.

This was someone the Empire had deemed not worthy, not safe, not even human. This evidence ran counter to everything the people had ever known.

Contrarian evidence was dangerous.

"She's doing her job," Holmst muttered from his chair, eyes buried in the map that he has projected on the wall.

"Her job," Riley began, "as I recall, is to administer the civilian Government. Not stage campaign events that undercut support for Security."

Holmst bit his tongue, choosing to look over parts of his map he'd already looked at. It had the unmistakable look of a child who knew a secret.

Riley's eyes narrowed. "Say it."

Holmst closed the map, tucking the hologram into his wrist, and whirling about like a rubber band had snapped. "She's a small-town debutante who writes op-eds about people being mean to her. The more credit you give her, the more powerful she becomes."

The message was loud & clear: stop being so emotional, so child-ish. Think like a soldier.

Riley worked out his jaw. "I'm supposed to do...what about it?"

"Not a goddamn thing. She wants to keep tilting at windmills, let her. She's an empty shirt using the ammo you give her. Don't blitz every down. Let her have the underneath game."

"I give her the nickel and dimes, eventually she owns the store."

"Yeah," Holmst accepted, "but she's gotta save up for it. Meanwhile..."

Riley nodded. It was a solid approach: letting Talania have small victories kept her from making attempts at larger strides to under-mine the colonial stability. It would keep her busy in smaller affairs, but it was the persistence that got under his skin the most. "What's your recommendation for Specialists No Neck and Numbskull?"

"Anatoly is taking full responsibility. He'll receive a demerit, and both men will be rotated out to a Wall prefecture."

Riley raised an eyebrow. "They aren't going to be so bored anymore. I like it. I'd have gone with a good thrashing in the public square, taste of their own medicine."

"This is more poetic."

"Yeah, it is." Riley nodded. "We're going to want to loosen the curfew, let everyone cool off a skosh."

"I'll amend the Press Release and inform the Top Shirts. We need a repeat of yesterday like we need a hole in the head."

Riley leaned back in his chair, staring at the ceiling like he might bore through it to freedom. He never noticed that the dots in the ceiling tiles were actually symmetrical. "If Princess calls about it, I'm up at the Fort. If she calls more than three times, I'm pulling her transponder."

"Sir, I mean this with all due respect: you have an unhealthy fixation on that woman."

Riley nodded, rubbing his face like it was bread dough, hoping to push all of his stress out and push on to the next of the ten thousand problems on his desk. "I usually focus on anybody doing the shooting at me. But, like you said—next thing. Brief me."

Holmst slid his fingers along his wristwatch, 'throwing' his map back up on the wall and blowing the image up wide enough for Riley to see: a topographical display of the colony and surrounding lands, all tinted a pleasant golden yellow.

"Echomapping by thumpers along the Pierson Corridor confirms the prevailing theory. There is a deep network of tunnels in the mountains outside the Basin."

As he spoke, Holmst clicked a key, allowing the image to slide forward: a cross-section of the mountains with jagged lines criss-crossing toward a central point like the veins on a maple leaf.

Riley leaned forward, still rubbing the tension out of his jaw. "Thermal or LADAR pick up anything of note?"

Holmst tabbed his little slideshow forward again, adding a rather aggressive color layer to the map which burned the eyes. No wonder the amber glow was the default. This hurt to look at.

"There's a sixty-kilometer block of the mountain range that runs four degrees hotter than the rest, but nothing focused. And LADAR can't grab any useful readings."

Riley stuck his hand into the projection beam, cutting the presentation short. The map retreated into Holmst's wrist like it was afraid to be touched. "That's a lot of maybe, Lieutenant."

"Yeah," Holmst conceded, "which is why I ran down the after-action reports for the last six months. They've been hitting us from all sides, probing the Wall for weaknesses, but wouldn't you know it, they seem to hit the Northeast corner with a bit more regularity. Four times more regular."

"Shorter hike?" Riley mused, with a soft smirk.

"Smoking gun, sir. They're coming from the hot spot."

"Okay...give me your gut instinct: have we found the nest?"

"Or a forward outpost," Holmst confirmed, "Sir, these things aren't rocket scientists. They want to get somewhere, they have to walk. They have to be coming from somewhere."

Riley stared at the wall, where the map had once been, but his memory could recall it all like he was looking in the mirror. "What's your play?"

Holmst tabbed his wrist, bringing the image forward again, zooming in on a cross-section of mountain, a series of red dots popping up. "Thor's Hammer can't bombard from orbit with any kind of kill confirmation. We could drop CN-20 nerve canisters, but without knowing the volume of the space, we can't get an acceptable air density."

It was deep past the Wall, far beyond any support or rescue. The solid rock of the mountains might inhibit the Drones' freedom of movement, but they certainly had defenses in place. Holmst knew exactly what we he was asking, and with compartmentalization, he was the only other soldier on the planet who understood how completely short-handed they really were.

"I don't like where this is going," Riley murmured.

"Sir, we can't play defense all the way till the Empire comes home. At some point, we gotta go make them host the party."

Riley shook his head, more like a quiver than a clean rejection. "Their house, home field advantage. You go into their ground, and you surrender the one strength we have."

"Sir, we're going to keep bleeding until we step up in the pocket. Small casualties here and there, disputes between factions. How long will the Capitals stay loyal? The critters will wear us down, shave off folk wherever they can, until we're down to the bone. Let's go deep, make these little bastards back up out of our face."

Riley took a deep breath. It wouldn't be the first risk he'd taken since manning this post, but the dice have a way of turning on their shooter. "A recon mission."

"Yes, sir." Holmst pointed at a mountainside. "I'll take a small team, fleshed out with Capitals. We wait for a Jergad attack on the Wall, they make 'em three times a week. With the body of the horde on walkabout, we make our move. We insert here, laying thumpers as we go and extract before they come home for dinner. Ideally, we don't even make contact. The thumpers will relay data back to Thor and give us a better idea of what we're looking at. Total mission time no longer than four hours."

It was sound strategy, clear some of the fog of war and minimized the risk. It was still damn dangerous. Extremely so. People get killed on these missions. Commanders rarely had a moment with such certainty for blood.

He could be sure someone would die on this mission. Riley had just given himself chills. "Two Oskies, volunteers. Briefing is at your discretion. Get in, get out."

"Thank you, sir." Holmst pulled the map back down into his wristwatch and went for the door.

Not so fast.

"Two things," Riley said, stopping his aide at the door. "You're in their back ranks. Lots of HVT. Keep the risk to your team minimal, but if you get the opportunity at some infrastructure, cut their ankles out."

"Can do, sir," Holmst cheered right up at that.

"Number two: you're staffing up with Capitals. Take Aaron Havenes."

And that sucked the air right out of his sails. "Sir, that I'm not so sure is a good idea. Aaron's exposure to—"

Riley silenced him with a raise of his hand, as if he could cut the air flow to Holmst's throat. Aaron, Aaron, Aaron—Riley was sick of hearing that name. "Talania is using military hardware to undermine military authority. You're going to put her Hero on a Hero's mission. We need the best."

"Willco, sir. My only concern is--"

"Your concern is well founded, Lieutenant," Riley cut him off again, locking eyes with his subordinate. "No matter how minuscule, he is a potential threat. And you always have the authority to secure the safety of your men. Do we have an understanding?"

Holmst didn't move, his eyes flitting across Riley's face, as if trying to defuse a bomb with uncommon delicacy, before ultimately giving in. "I think I understand, yes, sir."

"Gamble with their lives, never your own. We don't have the blood to spare," Riley intoned like it was a chant, "Your op. Get this done."

CHAPTER
TWELVE
AARON

THERE WAS a sort of shelf at about shoulder height in the Howler, perfect for resting a tired head against. Aaron could lean backward and take all of the stress out of his neck and shoulders. He couldn't fall asleep standing up like that, but it was a relaxing position for a good daydream.

The others weren't so lucky—that shelf jammed 'em right in the back. Perks of being 'shortstack.'

On the opposite end of the sanity spectrum, Keira had properly nodded off, with her mouth hanging open like she was trying to catch rain on her tongue. Solomon cuddled against her shoulder, taking his own flight through Neverland.

Aaron never thought he'd be jealous of that pair, of all people, but they could sleep in an active warzone, so long as they were together. There was something oddly romantic about it, if Aaron wasn't quietly convinced they both ate human flesh.

Command had dangled sweet, sweet inactive hours in front of the regiment as bait and almost Aaron's entire team had jumped at the chance. No one knew the stakes until they'd been briefed, and then they regretted opening their mouths.

Nora had chosen wisely to stick with Wall duty; gambling on

dangerous missions for R&R was foolish. Can't take rack time if you're dead.

Aaron didn't want the R&R. He just wanted out of that damn city. Better to focus on his trade than consider the measures and costs of it.

To his credit, Holmst had picked this team well. He had gotten rather familiar with the individuals in the Capitals that stood out for competence and obedience both.

For all their bloodlust, Solomon and Keira were efficient machines. Carmona was in the jump seat next to the Oskies, the de facto commander of the Capital detachment. He waited with a stiff back, less like a lap dog and more of the patient attack breed, a stern-looking rottweiler awaiting instructions on who to unleash his particular brand of Hell on.

Jensen and Eden sat opposite Aaron, signing a basic conversation to each other to kill the time. It was a confusing long stare before he picked up they were playing a game—Eden kept grunting when she lost, drawing the attention of the Oskies who were more accustomed to the silence of a disciplined op.

The last Capital hadn't met anyone else's gaze since he boarded— Michonne. For all his usual bluster and venom, he held uncommonly still at Aaron's shoulder.

That animated aggressor from the barracks had somehow been stripped away. His eyes squeezed shut, as if chanting some comforting mantra inside his own skull. When Aaron had been bedridden, Michonne had racked up an impressive kill count on the Wall, five scratches in the stock of his rifle.

But that posturing and reputation were stripped away in the belly of the Howler. His hands trembled by his sides. The rest of the team were as relaxed as circumstances allotted, and they all had stunt and combat drops under their belts. Michonne was a Wall jockey who had never served forward of the line, and he looked ready to vomit.

Something was wrong.

Aaron nudged him, trying to draw his eye, give the man some

resolve. But Michonne shifted away, not out of annoyance or consideration. He snapped away, like he'd been burnt, shifting weight onto the opposite leg.

His skin pale, and his jaw tight. He didn't want to be here. Muscles tense, too tense, his knuckles wrapped tight on his rifle's grip.

Aaron nudged him again. He had to calm down or Michonne risked injury on the drop. Michonne sneered, but still refused to glance over.

Holmst whispered something to Carmona. He gave a crisp nod and turned back to the Capitals, grabbing his throat mic. "Two minutes out. We are silent running, no talking, no nothin'. We get found this deep in, and we are all dead in record time. Oskies are setting the pace, so if you fall behind, we will not hold up for you. Huah?"

The team nodded, tapping chests and gripping weapons, rather than bark their response. He did say silent running after all.

Carmona made the briefing concise and declarative, like a proper platoon leader. Aaron could swear Car had pitched his voice down to have more authority. Was he trying to impress the dignified First Lieutenant seated next to him?

Holmst held up one finger—one more minute. His eyes tracked over to the sleeping Solomon and Keira and he smirked.

Aaron gave Keira a good-natured shrug, jostling her and Solomon both. They sniffed, straightened and shouldered their gear like they had been awake the whole time. They didn't need specifics anyway. These two followed the leader, followed orders with silent efficiency, and killed whatever blocked their path; speechcraft was not their field of expertise.

Carmona moved around the cabin, swooping from person to person, checking their cables and rigging, like Holmst had done every other time. The Lieutenant had delegated some of his duties out. Whatever. It still had to be done. No room for mistakes. Not this far out.

But Carmona was awfully proud of himself, all chipper and bouncy. There was even some color in his face again, like someone had breathed life back into him. He was well rested. Alive. He looked like a different man.

Satisfied, Carmona took his station and Holmst rigged him up, giving a paternal slap on the shoulder to confirm before turning back to the cabin. He carefully drew everyone's eyes in, raw magnetism and pure adrenaline pulling the focus. He raised his hand, five fingers, counting down.

Four, three...Aaron closed his eyes. Relax or break your neck.

And the floor fell away. That grinding whine pierced his ears as he zipped down. Trust the cable. It'll say when to open your eyes.

When the cable jerked, he heard the snap next to him like a chicken bone next to his ear, wet and crisp.

His boots scuffed against granite, and the cable whirled away up. He opened his eyes—in time to see Michonne's limp body slip to the ground. If he felt his neck break, it was brief.

Aaron moved to check him, but Holmst waved him off and back to his position: every avenue had to be held and checked, lest the locals get the drop on them. Aaron shouldered his rifle and looked out over the mountain, feeling the Oskie Lieutenant slide up behind him to attend to Michonne's surely fatal injuries.

Aaron occupied himself with the vista. Bare unfeeling stone on a steep grade, with smooth beveled edges from the harsh wind. The consistent mottled gray was marred at irregular intervals by patches of black scorch marks and ragged barren branches, leftover from whatever plant had been cooked into glass. What remained looked like tiny black fingers reaching up from shallow graves.

The air was thin, promising refreshment for strained muscles and failing to deliver—Aaron was already gasping for a proper chest full.

Wisps of cloud grazed the boulders and outcroppings, like a bed sheet of cool air or a lover's hand caressing its curves. The Howler could still be made out between the rolling curtains, circling back away toward the refueling station.

They were all alone now.

The apprehensive platoon looked to Holmst for instructions, soon following his stare to the crumpled remains of Michonne.

When Aaron looked back, he found Holmst staring at him. For how long, Aaron couldn't be certain. There was a dilemma in his eyes. Maybe he was considering evacuating the dead, or calling off the mission to try again another time? This was an inauspicious beginning to hinge upon. They were down a man before they'd even touched the ground.

Did he blame Aaron for the drop-rook's injury? No, there was something softer in his eyes, something deep back there, and it was far more chilling than blame.

Regret.

Ultimately, Holmst sneered and got to his feet, leaving Michonne where he fell. With a nod, he took point and began his march up the mountain face. The two other Oskies gave hand signals to Carmona, directing the marching order and urging silence. Their quick-knives were at easy reach on their chest rigs and Aaron didn't doubt that they would deploy those knives to preserve the secrecy of the mission.

Jensen and Keira had the roughest time of it, as they were tasked with hauling the thumpers up the steep incline. They had all carried more under worse conditions—Hell, Solomon had carried Keira on more than one occasion—but they had to carry this load under cover of silence. They could not grunt, whine, or moan, nor could they scrape or scrabble their way up.

Each step had to be laid with precision. Worst case scenario, the beasts below could hear the breathing above them—no need to give them any help detecting the intrusion. A slight mistake might cause a tiny rockslide, just a tinkle of rocks dancing down the slopes that should not be that would give away the entire team, and with no support or escape route, they would be butchered like lost children in a dark German forest by the waiting bogeyman.

Aaron had enough trouble making the quiet climb without

hauling fifty additional pounds of reconnaissance gear. Silence isn't golden. Silence offers a blade and waits with bated breath for the owner to do the harm themselves.

Aaron resorted to counting his steps, curious to see how many it would be before they reached the caves, or his feet snapped off at the ankles.

His toes ached inside his ill-fitting boots, as his legs burned from the stress of each successive footfall. His shins bemoaned every motion, as though they might convince him to take a seat and drink in that vista until the sun set against the glassy fields below.

Don't think, count. One, two, three...

Why was Holmst so concerned with Michonne? A Capital died, he did so quietly and without disruption. This should be a moment of somber celebration for any full-fledged Citizen of the Empire. At best, it was a moment that should pass like hot fumes from a rusty tailpipe, lingering only to remind of the toxic effect its presence had brought.

Instead, Holmst had acted as though Michonne was important somehow, held value as a real human life. That was out of character. Michonne, the Banished and the Dweller—he barely held value to other Capitals. What currency he held had long been spent, frittered away in useless conflicts and fleeting pleasures.

He was physically capable but hardly exceptional; he was far from stupid but no intellectual; he had no real allies to speak of and more than a few enemies, and Aaron had numbered among them. He was an awfully big risk to put alongside a collection of safer bets.

Thirty, thirty-one, thirty-two...

———

It was no cave.

The stone surface was porous and pocketed, and it was certainly a natural occurrence, with jagged outcroppings and dips in the passage, but the eight-foot-wide hole in the rock face could hardly be described as a cave. This was not hewn by claw or machine, but something had spat forth from this point some time ago. This was a lava vent, from long ago when these mountains had been active.

That might explain why the Jergad rested here. The roads were already in place.

There might be hundreds of the big bastards huddling in the many corners of this labyrinth, waiting for the slightest disturbance to unleash hell. Or there might be none at all. Possibility was the enemy of calm.

Holmst picked at the wall with the snub-barrel of his rifle, as if to check if the pumice could take the pressure of his weight. It refused to give against his repeated probing, so he confidently took a stride into the mountain's belly.

Jensen threw a glance at Aaron. The big guy had misplaced his trademark smile. Through thick and thin, drenched in sweat and shivering in the cold, that man could bring out his infectious grin. He stood slack-jawed now, trying to gasp as quietly as his chest would allow, with eyes narrow and spider-webbed with pink capillaries.

The altitude was doing its damage, but the nightmare now presented to him was what finally robbed him of his joy. At least Aaron wasn't alone in that.

Holmst looked back out of the tunnel, his eyes seeming to glow in the dark as his cybernetic retinas caught the light and reflected a sickly yellow, like a pale gold. They seemed to pulse softly, a rise and fall of tide waters, a soft hand growing in insistence.

Aaron was reminded in that moment how far from human the Oskies had become. If the Capitals had lost their humanity for their crimes, the Oskies had given it up for other gifts.

They did not climb all this way for a nature hike, but nobody wanted to follow into that maw. Even stalwart Carmona found his newfound patriotism sapped away at the sight of it. Holmst could smell their fear and those demon eyes narrowed to slits.

The assembled crowd of Capitals in their loose linens and oversized boots were not as capable, not as dependable. They were just Capitals; no stomach for this. They needed motivation.

An Oskie's rifle probed into Jensen's back, urging him onward. He was the pack mule with the mission sensitive gear, after all. But every instinct in his reptilian nethers refused that order. But with a gun at his back, there was only one way to go: into Hell. No one voluntarily visits that establishment without four or five escape plans.

The Oskies looked at each other. No one wanted to carry Jensen's pack, but they were preparing to, as one reached for his quick-knife.

Aaron had to draw attention.

He took one big step out of the formation and over the threshold into the dark. Everyone watched as he sidled up to Holmst, vanishing into the lightless cave like a cloak had been draped about his shoulders to shield him from view.

Aaron looked back to his friends, first catching a mean glare from Carmona. He was Capital Lead after all; he should have been the one to take this plunge, but this was a little deep in the shit for posturing and protocol. Carmona did not relish this leap of faith any more than the rest, but Aaron had just shown him up and they were in no position to discuss the matter.

Satisfied—or perhaps he didn't want to stray too far from Aaron—Jensen adjusted his gear and followed Aaron into the black. Momentum gained, the rest soon followed, inching themselves deeper and deeper into the void.

They couldn't turn on torches, not without alerting the homeowners, but there was no way to passively see in that kind of darkness. Not even the Oskies' implants could pick up enough light.

Instead, Holmst dropped small infrared torches, sticking them in air pockets in the walls. They were just small sticks, really, barely the size of a pencil, but the fat tip threw off a faint glow, more than enough light this far removed from the sun.

The Oskies had their implants, but the Capitals resorted to using handheld monoculars to see in the dark, squinting through a bulky steel tube in one hand while feeling their way forward with the other.

Holmst would place the flares at regular intervals as they descended, lighting their way forward—and hopefully, their way back out. Aaron had no idea what the half-life on the things were and quickly conjured the obvious scenario where the flares go out, and the blind little Capitals were left to die in the hollows of a dead volcano.

They stopped only briefly for Jensen and Keira to set up their thumpers. The work allowed the others to catch their breath and draw from their rations. Carmona made sure that the two mules got fed and watered during the cumbersome task, because as soon as they finished, Holmst would press the group on, deeper and deeper into the mountain's heart.

There was a logic to it, not cruelty; the longer they were here, the more danger they were all in. Better to move fast and patch injuries after.

The silence was maddening, but what was worse was how that silence magnified even the smallest sound: the scuffing of a shoe heel or a heavy breath, the clank of polymer parts as someone adjusts their grip on a rifle, or even a squeak as someone wiped the sweat from their forehead.

Aaron swore he could hear his own eyelids as he blinked.

And whenever Aaron turned, he would catch Holmst turning away. In one sense, that would be normal, but with paranoia edging, it stuck in his mind. Every single time, Aaron would turn and Holmst would look away, like he was being caught staring.

Something was wrong. He could smell it.

Until finally sight deafened the senses, as a muted orange glow came from around the bend. They had only gone down, and still one thumper left to place. In the heart of a mountain, what could possibly be putting out visible light?

Aaron lowered his monocular, going so far as to pocket it. That small hesitant glow gave off enough to his starved eyes to light the entire passage. The team inched forward, wary but excited, with Holmst throttling the advance to avoid a misstep. Perhaps it was a trap, but what need would the Drones have for traps this far into their turf? They could simply overwhelm.

Eden was the only one who didn't rush onward, her head hung low, chin to chest. She was staring at the ground—the smooth, packed stone. The air pockets in the walls and ceiling had been pressed into an almost polished marble. When she finally noticed her solitude, she looked up to Aaron, swallowing her fear to follow.

She and Aaron stepped into the light, seeing their colleagues huddling at a breach in the wall. It was barely more than a splinter, split in the stone like rotting wood peeling back. The russet light positively streamed from that gap, and they all yearned for its secret.

Curiosity and that damn cat.

Even from his distant point, Aaron could make out something moving. He wished he hadn't looked.

Inside the dormant magma chamber of a long-dead volcano, they found the nest. It looked more like a city.

The golden light beamed up to them from enormous patches of moss, rows upon rows—some kind of bioluminescent process between rock and plant that made the most welcoming of lights, like a soft lamp in a library. There were whole fields of it stretching far down the length of the cavern. The stuff looked thicker than grass, hefty and peaty, like a sponge or baked bread.

A scant few Drones could be made out meandering through the paddies, probing the crop and harvesting up particularly lush bundles with their bladed arms.

They would then ferry their loads throughout the cavern, before returning to further tend the crop. One beast could be seen hoisting a patch to its demonic maw, where the levers of its split jaw gingerly picked the moss from its clumsy claws before passing it to the chomping teeth behind.

Beyond the farmlands, three artificial stalagmites rose from the floor, reaching their asymmetric spires toward the cavernous ceiling thousands of feet up. Aaron might've assumed them to be natural formations from the passing of an epoch of natural events.

Rather, a team of Drones pulled stone blocks from some unseen quarry to reinforce their newest project, and spit some mucus or resin that seemed to fuse the stone chunks into one cohesive piece. Simplistic pick points had been carved in the sides like a rudimentary ladder, allowing for the Drones to wedge their claws in for leverage and lift themselves up to the many small awnings and overhangs that dotted the vertical surface.

As one Drone clambered up with a patch of Moss, it passed a pair in their tiny hovel. They exchanged hisses before the climber had to recoil and climb on upward.

Aaron lifted his monocular, daring to zoom in on the towers. The moss gave off so much light that it nearly blinded him, beaming a clean white circle onto his face, but he could just barely make out the outlines of eggs amongst the dotted homes in the towers. They were cushioned with the moss, like a baby bird.

Perhaps it served as both protection and immediate food for the fresh infant? Dozens of Jergad ferried material up to the various aeries, the entire clan tending to everyone else.

This was no outpost; this was their home.

"Pilgrim, save us," Jensen murmured. He may as well have yelled, but no one reacted to it.

Aaron lowered his glass and craned his neck back, hoping to see far above where the towers might end.

High above toward the very top, suspended bridges connected the three towers to a massive platform at the center. It looked like a ball caught in a spider's web, an anvil suspended by mere threads. For all its weight, Aaron thought it surely must collapse. Any moment now he would hear the rocks creaking under that impossible load.

These industrious beasts seemed to defy conventional physics. What had once been an enormous magma chamber had seen the touch of construction and architecture, agriculture, even social castes.

This was no dark den of giant brutal monsters; this was genuine evidence of real civilization.

"Back the way we came. Now. Double-time."

No one wanted to dispute Holmst's order. They had stuck their heads far deeper in the lion's mouth than they ever intended to. The longer the stayed, the more they tempted fate.

Jensen and Keira dropped their remaining thumpers, more abandoning them than anything else. Ounces made pounds; pounds made pain; pain made delays.

Now was no time for delays.

Aaron helped Jensen shed his gear, pulling the straps loose as fast as his hands could work.

And that's when Aaron heard the spoon of a grenade spring free with a metallic happy ring, happy to announce its release to the entire cavern.

Aaron looked back to see Holmst dawdling at the window, cupping the smooth steel incendiary tin in his left hand—and staring at the moss farm below. Holmst considered the grenade for a moment, as if debating one final time, before turning his eyes to the window.

He was going to burn it. And every ear between him and the surface had heard that pin come loose. The noise of city life in that cavern came to a crashing silence, that ring still working its way down the cavern.

The thin red line had already been crossed.

"Run!" Aaron bellowed.

As if to countermand that order, Holmst hucked the grenade toward the moss paddies. The aluminum casing skipped off the stones with a hollow melancholy tune.

Fast, too fast, Holmst was right next to him—a blur of motion in between the melodic falls of the grenade. That look in his eye, regret and...shame?

Something hit him. Holmst? Why?

Aaron fell to the ground. His ribs screamed.

That is, until the flashfire caught and spat a dragon's breath through the stone window. Flames licked the air around him, and just as soon extinguished by the exhale of wind that felt like someone had compressed a storm gale into the room with him. Stone cracked and fell all around him, a bedding of shards.

Aaron shivered, shaking the chunks off of him and pressing himself up off the floor, his bad leg moaning as if it could remember the punishment from last time.

The once calm lantern light of the moss was now a flickering beam of orange. Had he been down longer than he thought? Even with just the dim firelight glinting off the stone, he could tell he was now alone.

And what was worse, the stone chips at his feet were starting to skitter along the floor, as if trying to crawl out of the way of the approaching horde. Their chittering screeches seemed to echo from inside his own head, as the shadows danced across walls around him.

They were coming.

Aaron fumbled with his rig, scrambling for his monocular. He had to find the flares, find his way back out of the tunnel. He ripped the eyepiece from his pocket, bracing it up to his eye.

Drone, front and center, framed in the window and searching the debris. It spotted his movement, and reared back, talons high.

Aaron snapped his rifle up, barely taking time to sight down on his target. The gunshot itself nearly threw Aaron back to the ground, with a piercing whine driving itself into his ears. The thirty-caliber weapon was a loud crack outside; inside the mountain, he might as well have shot himself for all the pain he caused.

He had no idea if the drone went down. He collapsed, trying to push his sanity back inside his head. The rifle was going to do him no good down here, and he may very well have summoned whatever remained of the sleeping horde.

Don't think. Run.

Aaron sprung to his feet, running toward what he hoped was an open passage. Up to safety or down into the belly—he wanted to be anywhere but here.

Sure enough, the silhouetted Drone stood up in his way—at least as best as it was able: his shot had severed its leg at the knee. Propping itself up on the stump, it took a wide swipe at him. The blade hooked his rig, slamming him to an abrupt halt.

He could feel the bone spear pressed against his spine.

It dragged him backwards, carving a trough through the stone scraps. He was dead without that night vision optic, but it was currently tied to a thing about to kill him.

Choices.

He clicked the straps off and slid out of the webbing just as the Drone's second claw came down, cracking the stone under it like a steel pick. For all of the Jergad's strength and tenacity, the smaller Aaron was a great deal more slippery.

He ran, boots pounding the ground, swinging his arms as though he might drag his body forward with each motion. He did not dare look back. The hellish sounds that issued forth from behind him didn't need a linguistics expert to translate. If they were violent and cruel on the plains, what would they do to him down in this spider hole?

His ankles creaked and shins burned, lifting the heavy load of his ratty boots with each step forward. That implied he was going uphill at least. That was positive news.

A Drone came into view, seeming to step out of the very wall. Its jaw swung open and hissed, drooling its thick mucus onto the floor. No time. Don't slow down. Aaron ran right at it.

The Drone waited for him, arms open to greet him in for the deadliest embrace. Perhaps it would cleave him down the middle, slicing his skull in two to minimize his ability to feel pain? Or it would take him at the midsection, to better guarantee a kill? What if it missed and took him at a shoulder, holding him just long enough for the brethren to arrive and feast?

What is it not expecting from prey?

Aaron charged the Drone, a creature three times his size forged from a child's nightmare. It lowered its head, displaying the wide skull crest like a leathery pauldron to shield its body.

Right. That.

Only one way to go now. Aaron jumped.

The Drone had filled the entire hallway; that is, until it had stooped. The space between the large beast and the roof was a mere three feet.

Aaron squeaked between monster and stone like a pub dart. The creature reacted but too late, slamming its head crest into the roof, sealing the opening and also wedging itself.

Aaron thanked the countless nights on the obstacle course before tucking his head to his chest and running. His chest ached from the lack of oxygen, his vision dimming, the cold mountain air piercing him to the bone. Each laborious breath felt like swallowing whole ice cubes.

But he couldn't stop. Do not stop. Sergeant Bray's voice barked some epithet in his ear.

Aaron wiped at the side of his face and up his jaw, smearing the sweat with a warm liquid that could only be his blood. The gunshot must've ruptured something. Or maybe when he hit his head?

Light. Sunlight.

Aaron shot out of the cave like he was rocket powered. He wished he'd died in the blast.

The Howler lifted away, the last of its cables pulling into the belly. Despite being a mere twenty meters up, the ghostly machine hovered in absolute silence.

He could make out a single voice screaming: Jensen, frantic and raspy, "I see him! He's right there! AARON!"

And just like that, he was silenced by the closing hatch and the aircraft's curious engineering, before it peeled away into the sky, like it had never been there at all.

That silence ripped out his guts.

They left without him. The mountain winds cried out in a louder voice than those engines did. The gnashing horror behind him was louder, bellowing up from the belly of the mountain like out of a trumpet announcing the approach of the executioner.

Aaron fell to his knees, his exhausted legs unable to hold him a moment longer. What would be the use of standing, anyway? The load would be relieved in short order.

They emerged all around him, from behind boulders and over cliff edges, slithering towards him with unexpected fluidity, like they might be wary of some trick. Or maybe they were just playing with their food.

Aaron glanced back at the tunnel, toward the fires they had lit far below and out of sight. Behind that curtain of impossibly black shadow he had trespassed through, a dozen shapes roiled and twisted, as though the darkness itself hungered for sacrifice.

He closed his eyes, listening to the approaching drums of a thousand heavy feet. Maybe it would be over before he opened them.

CHAPTER
THIRTEEN
RILEY

"YOU LEFT HIM!" The voice cried out, "You crazy son of a bitch, you *left* him!"

Riley had been at the Wall's Northern Hangar Bay by pure chance, performing a surprise inspection with a few officers. The recon team had not been expected back for another few hours.

Based on the growing crowd and the epithets issued from around the returned Howler's dusty frame, something had gone sideways.

Riley strode on over to the theatrics, as much curious about the outburst as he was annoyed. The crowd parted for him, allowing him to take his box seat for the unfolding drama.

A large Capital—memory said Jensen Davila—had been tackled to the ground, an Oskie dropping a knee onto his throat. Lieutenant Holmst eyed him with a kind of humor. But the shade over his eyes betrayed a rising remorse, that the thrashing fish on the deck was throwing barbs that struck true.

Riley couldn't hold back his smile. Clearly, the mission had been an unqualified success.

Jensen spat his words, trying to force his head up from the deck. "He was alive and you *left* him!"

"I stay ten seconds more, and we might all be dead with him,"

Holmst stated, with the boilerplate assurances of someone convincing himself first and foremost.

Jensen grunted some epithet past the knee on his throat. The big man had enough meat on him he could probably heave the Oskie off him, upgrades and all. He was choosing not to, or perhaps hadn't the presence of mind to try it.

It was the Capitals who straightened up first, a filthy-haired short woman spying Riley's gossiping smirk. The silence rippled across the assembly until all eyes were on him.

Riley studied the prostrate man, the grief that wracked him. Even with a boot on his throat, he was still twisting and pushing. He had to be losing consciousness soon, the blood flow cut off to his head.

And the soldier sitting on him wasn't doing much better. A long and arduous op, and now this—the young man was actually steaming. His cybernetics were overloaded.

Riley stepped into the circle, pushing the crowd back with his stare. "Corporal, what's your heat sig?" He barked.

The man swallowed hard, as he consulted the heads up display flashing across his left eye for a quarter of a second, "Hundred eight point four."

"Keep at it and your implants will cook you in your skin," Riley scolded him, "Lieutenant, have your men stand down for ice showers and refractory. Be in the ready room for debrief in five."

"Yes sir," Holmst nodded to the Oskie controlling Jensen's air flow. Without any further instruction, the Oskie released Jensen—and struck him aside the head with a rifle stock.

The Capitals jumped in surprise—some to defend their comrade, others to his aid. But all of them froze in place, stopping themselves from committing an even more egregious error. Every airman, every soldier, every technician in the building had their hands on their weapons.

He owned their fates, every step of the way.

Holmst and his team retreated through the crowd but Holmst's eyes still lingered on the situation he had created, unable to unhook himself.

Riley hovered, something magnetic in this moment keeping him from receding back into his scheduled events. Perhaps it was their eyes, the way the Capitals hung heads and furrowed brows betrayed their frustrations, their resentment—their anger.

"I have been...understanding of your situation," Riley lectured the Capitals. "I would even go so far as to say I have been compassionate. You are a volunteer force. This was a volunteer mission, and a dangerous one. Casualties are not always avoidable. It's not anybody's fault. Huah?"

Movement.

Carmona took two disciplined steps forward, falling into parade rest. He had carefully positioned himself in front of his vulnerable compatriot, possessive, defensive.

How very noble.

He had a very winsome look, shaved head and rigid bone structure—like a recruitment poster came to life. "Sir, permission to speak freely?"

Look at him. He thinks he's a real boy.

"Permission denied. Fall in, Capital."

"It's just that, the Lieutenant--"

Riley drew his sidearm. The only warning Carmona had was the dull whine of the capacitor charging before a concentrated beam reduced two-thirds of his head to a pile of ash, leaving his neck a carbon stump.

A Capital cried out in surprise before clamping her own hands across her mouth. There—now they were beginning to understand their place.

Riley holstered his weapon before his body had crumpled to the ground. He cocked his head at the Capitals that remained, curious if anyone else had brought something for show & tell.

Some dared not move a muscle, while others couldn't stop themselves from shaking, holding back tears. This shouldn't shock them;

death should be the blanket upon which they make their beds. They should be ready to face its embrace the way they would a lover, surrender themselves to its whimsical delights. Instead, they somehow had believed their futures bright.

Bray had been too soft on them.

"Report for R&R, and eyes up for future assignments, Capitals. Dismissed."

He would have to amend their training regimen, introduce some drills to increase their comfort with their mortality. Perhaps some good old fashioned capital punishment might better acclimate the crowd.

The Deck Crews saw to the body's disposal. The Capitals would be escorted by armed guards to their barracks for the promised rack time. But then, some new edicts would have to be issued.

Riley tucked his hands in his pockets as he marched up the corridor toward the Ready Room. He stared at the beams overhead as he passed through each hatch, the metronomic pattern soothing his nerves and buffing that metallic edge off of his breathing.

When was the last time he had killed someone? Had it really been Ostia? Fourteen months of a Colonial post and heavy desk work was making him just as soft as the Capitals under his command. He needed to be made of sterner stuff if they were going to make it through this ordeal.

Battlefield terminations were the unfortunate reality of battle-field command; those that serve under often lose their nerve or their courage, and it often required the heavy hand just as much as the softer touch. His instructors had often belabored this point, the mutual tragedy that came from a proper commander 'filtering' his flock.

He had failed that test as a boy. Repeatedly. He hadn't responded to their lessons. It was a cruelty he had been made to embrace against his better judgement. He had many an unfortunate memory tied to those lessons.

If it was so unfortunate, then why was his heart pounding and his breath so light? Why was he excited?

Riley heel-turned to a stop at a bulkhead door. The door guard snapped off a perfectly fine salute, but all Riley could muster for him was a simple nod. The silent guard didn't express any distaste, preferring to reach for the door handle. But the man didn't meet his eye.

He cracked the seal on the door with a hush, prying it open for Riley to slip through. The Ready Room was a small conference space, with a holotable presented to the eight seats terraced out against the opposite wall. Each seat had a micro-scale version of the table, personalizing mission details for each recipient.

Holmst leaned against the table, somehow already out of his gear and the tiny hairs on the sides of his head glistening from a fresh shower. But his eyes were hollowed out, his shoulders hunched.

"Was that really necessary, sir?"Holmst asked with a bowed head. It's like he thought the sword might fall down onto his neck next.

"Word travels fast, I see, " Riley muttered.

"Mostly the sound did, sir."

"Are you going to get in my face too?"

Holmst chewed on his cheek, carefully considering if it was worth poking the dragon today. Riley's heart leapt at the very thought, beating so hard it might bruise his chest. There was a small part of him that thirsted for another round.

"No, sir."

Pity.

"You followed your orders, Lieutenant. Struck a major blow to Jergad supply lines, reconned their fortifications..." Riley paused, considering how to address the elephant in the room. "...and you followed your orders. You'll be receiving commendations for your work today."

"Just used to my casualties being from hostile action," Holmst said. "That's all, sir."

"Realities of command, Lieutenant," Riley intoned his instructors' words.

Holmst blinked at that, as the gears in his brain slipped. "It was supposed to be the Capital, sir. It was supposed to be friendly fire."

"You adapted." Riley dropped into the closest chair, propping his feet up on the edge of the map table. "Now, give me the rundown, Lieutenant. What exactly are we dealing with?"

Holmst held his breath and his tongue.

FOURTEEN
AARON

Those blue eyes. Staring at him from the black.

THE CORNERS of Aaron's eyes itched, little bricks of sand scratching at the skin. Otherwise, he'd have assumed he was already dead. He felt the stone under his fingertips but it was uncharacteristically warm and pliable, like a firm cushion overstuffed.

The minor sounds of industry echoed in some distant place, as workers went about their schedules. There was even a soft scent on a mild breeze, something vanilla—perhaps someone was baking nearby?

Did they come back for him? Was he back in that quaint hospital being treated for more injuries? Or had he never left its walls, and this had all been some lingering nightmare?

He blinked his eyes open, the sand crumbling away. He was on some kind of stone plateau, a golden glow rising up from somewhere below on all sides.

Oh no.

He reached to push himself up—and the stone surface gave way ever so slightly, a sealing resin softening at his touch, like an organic latex. Aside from the instantaneous confusion turning his brain inside out, it was actually quite comfortable.

Unable to work his brain around this discovery, he elected to crawl. The edge of the plateau was a dozen feet or so from him. He wormed his way along the strange ground, hesitant to confirm the only conceivable possibility. With a bracing breath, he tugged himself towards the edge.

Hundreds of feet below was the magma chamber, the three towers, the devastated moss farms—he was deep in the Jergad nest.

"Oh...fuck me..." He couldn't stop the words from leaving his mouth.

Aaron flopped over, looking for a swift exit he could squirrel out of—coming face to face with a Drone, one eye darkened by a hideously familiar scar.

Aaron couldn't muster a sound, as it snuffled around him, chitters deep in its hungry throat. He watched its mandibles lick the air in a rhythmic flow.

Scarface just stared at him with its one good eye, a dozen ways to kill him. But there wasn't a mark on him, just the scuffs & bruises he'd received in his retreat.

Aaron pushed off the ground, inching himself away—and Scar barked, a harsh & sudden sound that froze him to the spot. It was a violent objection, and whatever the beast's reasoning, Aaron didn't want to test its patience.

Why would they take him alive? These roaches weren't exactly known for their planning or strategy. They ran themselves with more brutish tactics, numbers overwhelming. Taking prisoners had only one real purpose during an armed conflict.

They wanted what he knew.

"Nothing quite as sinister as that, *ak'thun*."

The voice came from everywhere and nowhere. It echoed off the walls of the chamber and inside his own head. It was kind yet firm, formal yet awkward.

His skin trembled and his eyeballs shivered. He could swear he could...smell the words—like freshly baked bread, lightly spiced and left to warm in the sun. It was comfort incarnate, yet unsettling, like his head was pressed into a vice.

It was behind him. He was sure of it.

He could hear a regular sound, the intermittent flow of breath grating past a surface.

His mind conjured a thousand monsters from a thousand childish nightmares, of beasts with no face or asymmetric horrors with a hunger unknowable. Whatever monstrosity spoke those words had to be ten times what Scar was, a Lord of the manor, a God amongst insects.

Aaron's hands shook against that impossible stone, as if they might tear off of his wrists and flee—every man for himself. They just have to run faster than the slowest team member.

That's how he got caught in the first place, after all.

He lifted himself up onto his knees. Don't look. Just run.

Aaron spun to his feet but found his great escape abruptly halted by a familiar face. Scar stood in his path, no anger or hatred in its stance, but its wide frame blocked any escape from the plateau. No need for bars in this place.

Scar barked again. It struck Aaron how bizarre that sound was coming from the Jergad's frame. He had heard their talk, their screams & chittering, but that sharp exhale and baritone thud...that wasn't a threat; it was an order.

There was only one thing to do now. He turned to face his jailor.

The light beaming up from the cavern below was dim and his eyes would likely never adjust to the subterranean space, but he could make out a form. Something bulbous, large, almost as big as the Mining Rigs.

How it even fit on the platform with him he couldn't tell. Perhaps it was dangling off the far side. How the platform held the weight was another question entirely.

There were four limbs tucked back over the top of its frame, perhaps gripping the ceiling of the cavern, but he couldn't be sure.

And the hallmark swept-skull fan reached high in the air, before bowing backward and out of sight.

Two pure pupiless eyes—solid blue like a kind of acrylic paint that shone brightly—reflected the little available light. Two vertical slits peaking out at him from the mountain of shifting shapes.

What's worse, was the entire titan hadn't been there a mere ten seconds before.

"We are not here now. We are far away. But we can be where we need to be."

Aaron bit his lip. Maybe those arms would sweep down to pierce his flesh, drain him of blood and knowledge. Perhaps it didn't need to touch him at all, it would simply shout him to pieces and collect what it desired from the remains.

The unknowable monster seemed to shudder, recoiling for a moment.

It was then he heard footsteps, clopping heels on stone. Those stunning blue eyes bobbed up and down, advancing away from the shrouded creature. In a nausea-inducing moment, the eyes tilted individually to rest more horizontally, to fit the face that stepped into the light.

"Whoa..." Aaron blurted, slack-jawed.

The shape was human in the most uncanny way. He could see Jensen's top-heavy frame, Eden's hair & Talania's hard cheeks, the swagger of Carmona in the gait. And unsettling of all, those solid blue eyes...

The beast at his back nudged him forward toward the doppelganger. Aaron stumbled, almost dropped to his knees before it.

The blue-eyed impossibility gave no reaction, a stoic and regal mask. "A projection drawn from your memories, *ak'thun*. You understood this person. We would have it that you understand us."

No words. This was absurd. Horrifying even. There was nothing comforting about what he saw.

It paused for a moment, considering him. Then the image shimmered, revealing a perfect replica of Talania, Princess of Vanguard.

At least the doppelganger had made up its mind.

Aaron felt the pressure from Scar at his back, but he was too off-kilter to consider escape anymore. "How is this possible?"

"We have spent time trying to understand that ourselves," Talania's ghost said. "You touched our mind. How did you do this?"

Aaron glanced at the wounded beastie that blocked his escape—and the white tissue that now sealed its wounded eye. Could it be that...? No. How would that even work? "I don't know what you're talking about."

"No *ak'thun* has ever known us." She took another few steps forward, the image shimmering again to reveal the softer Eden. Her soothing bedside manner was slipping out of the mouth of a monster. "You saw us. And we saw you."

That voice was so unsettling, churning his insides. He only just noticed the tears spilling down both of his cheeks.

She took another cautious step forward, and in an instant, stood a foot taller as Gearmaster Jensen. It was changing tactics, looking for a way in.

"They call you criminal. They call you ravager. They call you murderer. What do you call yourself?"

"What do you want?"

Eden again, soft and kind. "We want to live, just as you do."

Aaron snorted. "I don't know how I can help you."

The doppelganger huffed, the exhale drawing it back into the regal demeanor & form of Talania. She reached out to him, not quite lunging for his face. He jerked his head back, but too late. She gripped his skull between thumb and forefinger, squeezing gently.

No. Not there. He didn't want to go back there.

Amongst the flashes of color and maddening patterns repeated ad infinitum, Aaron could feel the rain on his head and the blood on his fingers. The city towering high over his head. The crowd parting around him like they were drawing back a curtain. The body crumpled at his feet.

And yet, there she stood—Talania was at his side, gaping at the dead.

"You killed your own?" She asked, almost confused by the equation.

All of the adrenaline of the day flooded through his veins. The taste of metallic in his mouth. The smell of ozone burning his nostrils as the laser pistol cooled in his hand. All the fear, all the rage, all the instinct that had boiled up in a single moment. Old scars ripped open with a rusty blade.

"...Yes." He barely pushed the word out.

"They wished you harm?"

Aaron shook his head. "I don't know what he wanted. Don't even know his name."

His lips quivered as he studied the dead man and the carbon scorch on his chest. The burn had etched a crater into the flesh and the snap-boiling of fluids had tossed viscera on to everyone nearby. The man's chest had popped like a water balloon. His eyes fixed open, staring into the sky to catch the abuse of a thousand raindrops.

They'd been the same age. One with rank and power and money.

Aaron doubted the boy had real hatred in his heart, just the desire for more things and the will to take them. And take and take and take some more, without worry of who he hurt. It wasn't malice that brought their conflict; it was a far more common crime: a callous disregard for others.

This boy would've killed Aaron and would likely have never thought of it again. Aaron never stopped thinking about it.

Talania's fingers released him and the memory melted away in less than a second. He collapsed right where his victim had been, only to find the stone floor of the plateau.

"We did not wish you pain," she said, her empty blue eyes softening at the sight. That was likely the closest to an apology he would get.

Was this going to be the duration of his captivity? Emotional torture,

forced vacations into his most painful memories? Was he to be a labora-
tory animal for an alien species, only for them to study his corpse when
they were done? If they were going to kill him, why not get it over with?

"What do you want from me?!" He bellowed at the dark shape.

Talania stepped into his sightline, kneeled down to his level, but
keeping a respectful distance, "Peace."

Ho-with the what now?

That thought had obviously twisted his face. It was all the
response she needed. She stood up and walked to the edge of the
platform, "Your people destroy our home, our food, and ourselves.
We are few now and persistence will render us to shadows. You fear
death, *ak'thun?*"

He wiped his face, scrubbing away the dried tears and snot, but
he refused to answer.

"Yes...It is difficult to fear your reflection."

Aaron took a step forward—into grasslands.

The doppelganger stood waist deep in the reeds, wearing Eden's
form as her hands caressed the amber waves of grain.

The grass seemed painted by a soft blue of the midnight air and
rolling along like a soothing ocean. Aaron could feel the tickle of the
individual blades brushing against his forearms, the cool air filling his
lungs. It was rejuvenating, like he was awaking from a refreshing
sleep.

The savannah splayed out before him stretched from mountain to
mountain, a picturesque landscape lifted clean out of a fantasy, like
some somber depiction of Heaven. The clear night sky wore ten thousand nameless stars, a coronet of white gems staggered across the
azure expanse all the way to the horizon.

"This was our place..." She whispered, reverential, like her breath
might disturb a sleeping child. "It had seen nothing but the simplest
life had to offer."

Aaron stole a refreshing lungful of that air, tasting the moist earth
on the wind and the smell of cut grass. He had never felt something

so lush before, like a cool rag draped across feverish skin. With every passing moment, unseen weights were lifted away.

A grunt, earnest and hungry, came from the grass at his shin. He looked down to see a Drone at his knee. It was pubescent—laughable, it was as big as he was. It sniffed at the ground, its claws picking chunks of the hearty grass and sliding the tiny bales to its waiting mouth. As the jaw bones sifted out debris and junk, the teeth worked to mash the barley with a quiet contentment.

The beast more resembled livestock than monster.

"We were one. Quiet. Still. At peace." She turned to look at him, slipping into Talania and her cold fire. "You were many."

He heard the unmistakable supersonic boom pierce the upper atmosphere. Aaron craned his neck back. Three stars were on the move, glowing brighter and brighter. The orange flash of reentry burn lit up the alloy hulls. They dipped low on the horizon, skimming the ground as they approached.

The sound caught the attention of the herd. Dozens of heads poked up out of the grass, curiously studying, all tracking the movement as one.

"How are you doing this?" Aaron asked with a hushed whisper.

"I showed you your own memory with clarity and honesty," it responded, "That you might believe this story to be as true as your own." Her calm veneer crackling with energy, as if her fury grew with the oncoming storm. Aaron could guess what came next. After all, this lush plain was not one he had ever seen.

The stars zipped overhead, silent as the night, with only a stiff breeze to ever signify their passing. He couldn't make out the ship or model, but Aaron could see the lights from the bellies exposing the interior. And small objects were falling.

Bombs.

He whirled about back toward the head of the basin where the ships had come from. Sure enough, a maelstrom of plasma and fire erupted, blinding the field with light. All went white—and the pain struck him.

This was it. The torture he knew was coming. It lit every nerve on fire from head to toe, white hot and electric. He couldn't see anything, couldn't hear anything over that writhing agony.

And just as suddenly, it stopped. Perhaps now the questions would come, the accusations and the guilt and the manipulations and then more pain. They would visit a personal brand of justice upon his head, laying countless deaths on the feet of the one. He was all they had to exorcise their pain upon and they would have him bear it all.

But nothing. He lay curled up on the bare earth, black and scorched to a cracking glass. He checked himself over, but for all of that suffering, there was no visible injury to him. His clothes were unmarred, his flesh untouched.

That endless rolling field had been scraped off the ground, plowed under by hellfire, leaving smoldering ashes every few dozen feet. The young Drone lay toppled over next to him, what few bones left recognizable were charred and fused with the earth.

The bombers had laid it all to waste, paving it over to make way for the Aurora Colony ship most assuredly waiting in orbit. It was the first strike in a war they had no idea they had started. Simple, efficient, and brutal.

Memory. This was her memory, and their memories were hers—the summation of an entire species' physical pain wracking her in a single moment.

Eden looked down at him, her glowing eyes boring through him. "We would share of our story, *ak'thun*, that you know what we know. And we know too much of pain."

The wasteland faded away, returning them once again to the gloomy shadows of the magma chamber. It felt claustrophobic by comparison, the air stale and heavy. Yet, it was rank with the same burning smell from the field that had once been so sustaining. The moss fields below must still be smoldering.

Eden lowered her head, and the shrouded alien behind her mimed the same. "Make it stop. Please."

CHAPTER
FIFTEEN
RILEY

THEY LOOKED DRAINED, like acrid water at the bottom of a tapped out well. The Capitals were dragging their feet, shoulders slumped, and gasping for a moment's breath. Whole platoons stopped their marches to redistribute loads. They even traded words with their instructors.

They'd gone soft at the edge of a softer hand.

Riley hadn't held out any hope to see grand success stories, but in his wildest dreams, he had not predicted such extensive deterioration. Their fortitude paled against the most basic expectations. And with the casualties mounting, the failing Capitals were tasked with tighter and tighter rotations. By the grace of God, the alien attacks had lessened in the last week, but field accidents—and even some friendly fire —continued to sap their numbers.

The day seemed particularly gray, even before this depressing discovery. The Thumpers laid by the deep recon returned a nightmare scenario. The compacted slate of the mountains might have spelled doom for the locals, but after an epoch of dead tectonics, the stone had fused into one solid block.

That mountain was a literal fortress and any sufficient orbital bombardment from the Thor's Hammer satellites risked fallout on the civilian population. Enough kinetic breakers might do the damage, but there wasn't a proper battlefleet orbiting the planet. And there wasn't enough nerve gas in three systems to dose a chamber the size described. Those creatures were dug in like ticks, and nothing short of a manned assault was going to remove them.

Conservative casualty estimates ran in the thousands—Riley had less than two hundred good men.

These Capitals weren't going to break the margin, even if they stood up to muster. The only hope was to last long enough for the cavalry to show up.

And arrest him.

No. Worry about that time when it comes.

Sergeant Bray trudged from his barracks, a reluctant answer to a rather stern summons. The grizzled veteran looked more salty than usual, with heavy bags under his eyes and puffy cheeks, like he was hiding the rest of his mounting failures from view. His sickly look didn't stop him from snapping a crisp salute to his commander.

"What do you have to say for yourself, Sergeant?" Riley asked, in no mood for delays as his eyes scanned over the pathetic excuse of a regiment.

The Sergeant's eyes narrowed, as if to close the gates on any treasonous thoughts that might deign to show themselves. "They're Capitals, sir."

"So this culture of hugs comes from the Mining Pits, does it?"

Bray glanced over at the heavy-feet of a passing platoon. Despite keeping time, their feet scuffed the pavement with each step, grating on the ears. "Soldiers have to fight for something, sir."

"Soldiers, sure," Riley pointed at a stumbling Capital at the rear of a formation. "They're not soldiers, Gunny. Not yet, they're not."

"They bleed like soldiers, Colonel."

Riley raised an eyebrow. "You gone native on us, Bray?"

"I bleed Blue and White, sir," the Gunnery Sergeant retorted with a bit heavier grain than he should have, and he began to follow with an even sterner salvo, "And it was my understanding that disciplinary action was--"

Riley pivoted hard to come face to face with Bray. The veteran shut right the Hell up, stiffening like someone had jammed a rod down his back. "Mind your tone, Sergeant."

It was the age gap again. This career man thought he knew better than his betters. Don't tolerate that, his instructors had warned. He is older, not smarter.

Bray had been well trained. He stood at attention, awaiting permission to pull oxygen again.

Riley didn't owe him anything, but a stern hand worked best when coupled with paternal love. "Your Capital spoke when his voice had nothing to add. He needed to listen, and his fellows needed an example."

"My days are devoted to the glory and the service of the Empire, sir." Hardly a pledge of fealty.

"I have to ask: what do you do with the nights?" Bray remained stoic, eyes up and away, focused on nothing. Riley wasn't going to let him off that easily. "Perhaps you need time to adjust your thinking?"

Bray blinked but remained still. "Shall I take up my rifle, sir?"

Riley leaned back, picturing the old man operating a Repeater on a Wall prefecture, his weathered hands shaking with age and arthritis. "For death and glory?"

"For the Empire."

"A minor refresher for you, Sergeant: out here..." Riley sneered, "I am the Empire."

Bray twitched.

Finally. Of course, the Gunnery Sergeant didn't respect Riley's authority.

Age and experience had a way of cementing opinions and locking up the mind. Tradition and procedure and repetition was their morning gruel and their evening bed. The youth pushed out of the

Naval Command Academy had been a hundred-year practice, but human bias could not be so easily reprogrammed.

It wasn't his fault; it was evolutionary.

It was Riley's responsibility to confound that instinct. Talent, knowledge, and strategic thinking were not granted by virtue of surviving longer than the rest; they could be instilled, like writing to a drive. Riley was ten times the tactician Bray was on his best day.

This relic needed an object lesson of his own.

Riley turned towards his waiting car, waving Bray to follow. "Your orders stand. Give me a fighting force that can save lives and kill bugs. Do you think you can do that?"

"*Zu Gloriam*," Bray blurted from reflex.

For glory. They were all so fixated on glory and honor and legend and high-minded principles. They lacked pragmatism.

Maybe that was the problem.

"Effective immediately, the regiment is to resume Hell Week schedules."

Bray stopped. "Due respect, sir--"

"I feel whenever someone says 'due respect,' they never actually mean it."

Bray took that hit to the chin before continuing right on down this stupid path. "Due respect, sir...You don't get better soldiers by breaking their legs."

Riley sighed, leaning against the side of the car. "Gunny, for the last time...If they make it out of this alive, that is nothing short of a miracle. It is not your Command Directive to keep them alive. They're not soldiers. You are not a drill master. That is not a barracks." He pointed at the structure to their right, the boxy warehouse disgorging bands of malcontents playing at discipline. "Do you know what that is?"

Bray shook his head.

Riley sneered, "It's a tomb."

Bray said no more, only saluting as Riley climbed in his cruiser and zipped away. He could only hope the words stuck with the

Sergeant. It was far past time to cut the brakes off and get to real work.

The military base was a few miles short of the Wall, so it would be a brief ride back to the City's warehouse district, with nothing but the back of a Corporal's head and blurry sprigs of depressed grass to stare at.

The hovering cruiser's vinyl seating did little to cushion the metal structure underneath and the vibrating rig was numbing his hips. These junkers were fuel efficient and light, but hardly built for the comforts he ached for. Perhaps he could have one of the Corporals rustle up some padding, or even just a thick blanket.

Maybe then he could get a solid night's sleep.

But Riley would have no rest. His wrist tablet chirped with an incoming call.

Riley keyed his pin code into the surface, calling up a familiar scrunched forehead. Riley could feel the bile pushing up his chest, burning and warm. "Lieutenant Holmst, you bring me the very best of the nightly news."

It must've been a sour connection, as Holmst's lips were out of sync with the audio, and the amber projection flickered with every skipped data packet. "Talania Dedria issued a public declaration, calling for the reinstallation of the Statesmen."

"What is this, the third time?"

"Kids these days, I tell ya."

Riley rolled his eyes. "And she's calling me a sadist and a fascist, I suppose?"

"She stays away from the pronouns, sir," Holmst said, pulling his lips tight.

"I'm running out of reasons not to arrest her, Ilern."

"It's what she wants you to do."

"We can carve out a special block for her, even make room for her precious cameras." Riley could see it now—the Dark Room Morning Report, about that time when we remembered what sunlight was and how it felt and how sorry we are.

"We need her quiet, not martyred," Holmst said, expectant.

Riley nodded his head. "Agreed: Pull her transponder, requisition it for a forward outpost. Make sure that makes it into the daily: 'Colony Security.' Make sure we snag at least two others, so it's not so targeted. And extend the curfew to include radio broadcasts outside of emergency channels. She wants to slander me, she can do it in the privacy of her own home. Her father might even listen to her wail and moan. But public challenges in the body politic? Just sows discord."

"Yes sir," Holmst swallowed the rest of what he wanted to say.

Riley glowered at the floating amber head on his wrist. "Spit it out."

"Due respect, sir..." There's that phrase again. "If we act like despots, we only prove her point."

The cruiser dropped to a low hum, slowing as it entered the city limits.

A crowd had blocked the path, pushing on a nearby warehouse like an unseemly growth, ebbing and rippling as their tiny fingers ought entry.

The driver clapped the horn, but all this did was get their attention.

"Lieutenant, if I were to be a despot, I'd be a damn good one." Riley's focus had shifted from the call to some of the crowd now advancing on the cruiser. A few more determined than others. "Apologies, Ilern, but I'll have to call you back." Riley pushed the display closed, directing his full attention to the oncoming storm.

The corporal thumbed the strap off his hip holster. He was young, only a few years older than Riley, with a jittery look about him.

"Stand easy, Corporal. No need for blood today."

The words did little to calm his nerves, as the advancing few were gathering followers—a new object for their ire. One colonist pointed a meaty finger. "You're feeding those criminals?! While my wife goes hungry?!"

"Hungry men don't keep your wife alive, and if you think I'm feeding them well..."

Wrong answer. It rippled through the crowd, as they all shouted objections on moral grounds. They lived better lives, more just lives, honest lives. Why are the criminals rewarded while they sit at home hungry?

It's like these people forgot what the other half of the equation was.

"Let me fight!" "They're criminals!" "You're a monster!"

The first man shivered, his thin jowls quivering while the others spouted. Riley's driver stopped himself from turning fully back to face his commander. Does he drive on, back away?

Push through?

"My boy's sick," the man's quiet voice somehow picked over all the other shouts. "If he don't eat regular...he gets bad."

Face one mob, or twenty people. A mob is just rage. People are many things, least of all strong.

"What's your boy's name, sir?" Riley said with all of the smooth demeanor of a viper.

"Wynd."

"Wynd...a good name." Riley studied the man's...well-built frame. "And how many meals are you missing, sir, while your son goes hungry?"

That quiver was an earthquake now, fists clenched and jaw tight. He was going to jump into the cruiser and beat Riley with his own two hands.

The heads-up display flashed across his eyes, diagnostics and interface options in the blink of an eye.

And Riley was out of the car, fast, suddenly behind him before the man could speak up. The crowd jumped back, away from the unnatural display, afraid maybe that they might be churned to mash if caught in the path.

The man froze, his senses telling him the impossible, that the officer from the car was now behind him. Riley pressed his palm into the man's lower back. "It's either a cruel father, or a terrible liar. Your boy starves...and look at you."

Eyes darted from the cruiser to Riley to the accused. Their focus broken and with it, their will to resist. Without a drop of blood.

Pathetic.

CHAPTER
SIXTEEN
AARON

IT WASN'T A FOUL TASTE, but it clung to the sides of his mouth, cementing with the moisture and refusing to vacate. He could no longer taste anything else: a grainy paste, bitter, with tiny flecks that lodged between his teeth, scraping against the gums.

It was surprisingly hardy stuff. He never thought he'd be able to go full vegan, but the stuff did, in fact, satiate the grumbling in his gut.

It was, however, full of fiber. And he had little privacy. It was a tight race, but after his first escapade with no bathroom, he decided he preferred what remained of his rations to this cleanse.

At least the smell from the fires had abated, replaced by the rank leathery sweat of the beasts. None had approached him, or even stopped by with even modest interest. They lumbered about with maddening focus, completing a single task before moving to the next.

Whether they were tending to the moss paddies, ferrying supplies, or fortifying the cavern—they had sealed the window Holmst had attacked through with that strange cement—they handled their challenges with precision and efficiency.

If they gossiped to each other, drew satisfaction or enjoyment from their work, they weren't showing much of it to him.

He had been in prison before. This was all too familiar.

The only reaction he was able to draw from them came on the third day when he dared to leave the platform. Scar emerged from nowhere, stepping out from a pocket dimension to herd him back. Without his weapons, he was no real threat to the big guy, his protestations drawing no distinguished response. It walked forward, and he had to retreat or be trampled.

Once, he planted his feet, halfway wanting them to trample him underfoot. Instead, Scar barked and gingerly picked him up with its claws—careful not to squeeze hard enough to harm him—and set him down back at the center of the platform, before retreating to his unseen post.

Well, at least this iso cell had a view.

There were a half dozen tunnels in the cavern, spiraling off to God knows where. Perhaps there were other nests around the mountains, or those were the highways toward Vanguard—there was no way to know for sure. With time, Aaron might be bored enough to tally the incoming and outgoing traffic to draw some conclusions.

He could feel her arrival, as his ears popped and his jaw clicked, like a hand squeezed on his skull. He glanced over his shoulder at the bulbous shadow and the blue-eyed form of Talania.

She studied him in silence for a time, head tilted to one side. Aaron stood up and advanced on her, confident strides, a touch too fast to be considered peaceful.

She simply watched him walk up and past her toward the shadowy form, his outstretched hand finding nothing at all, his fingers grasping at an image that always seemed far away. No matter how close he got, it was always a city block from him.

He chuckled. "So what? You're just a figment of my imagination?"

"We are a projection to your senses, to aid in communication."

Aaron pursed his lips, looking back at his captor. "I don't get how that works. If you wanted to negotiate, why not just 'project' yourself to all one million of my friends back in Vanguard?"

"You are sixty thousand," she corrected, "With a mere handful of fighters in your ranks."

Interesting. She may not be arrogant, but she is eager to share what she knows.

Aaron made a show of a big sigh. "You didn't answer my question. Why not talk to someone in charge?"

"They are not you, *ak'thun*."

"And I'm special, am I?" He said wryly, "Is '*ak'thun*' some kind of momentous title? Am I some prophesied hero that's been spoken of in a thousand years of oral history?" He was just about done with this pomp and circumstance. He'd been eating moss alone in the dark for nearly a week.

She turned to face him, those soft blue eyes looking right through him. If they focused on anything in particular, he would never know it, and to be studied by that empty space unsettled him. "It means 'without height'."

Alright then, she's calling him short. Everybody's in on it now.

"We do not entirely understand what binds us to you, *ak'thun*, but one can only seize on opportunities when they present themselves."

"'We' meaning..." Aaron paused, trying to parse out her strange syntax. "You and me, or just you-you seize on the...?"

She stared back at him, blank and expectant.

"Yeah, it's the whole third person thing, it's..." Aaron said, waving his hand nebulously in her direction. "It's confusing. What can I call you? You have a name? A title? A collection of noises the rest of the clan associates with you?"

She looked out toward the cavern in a rather noble profile, with the light glancing off her cheek at just the right angle as to make her glow. "When you speak to one, you speak to all."

He blinked, waiting for her to break the pose. She did not. "Alright, your Highness, exit stage left."

She looked at him, brow twisted up. She knew how to look confused, at least. "We do not..."

184

"Overdramatic. You coulda just said 'Hive Mind', that's all."

"Highness. Yes, one assumes everything is high from your...perspective."

Aaron nodded. "Okay, I deserved that one." He shook his head, and tried to brush away the entire exchange.

She took a couple meaningful steps toward him. They were ginger steps, fluid and soft, almost sensual. It was like she was trying to linger in each step before pushing closer.

He scoffed at the display; she was able to project more than just words, but posture and picture: every action was a calculated decision, nothing accidental. This was all in his head, his brain painting something for his eyes so that he did not go mad, and the brain was doing so under explicit instruction.

Almost by definition, she could not be genuine.

She froze at that. "You do not trust us?"

If what her story was at all true, about a desire for real peace...there hadn't even been a discussion amongst the colonists. First contact with the Jergad had been down a gun barrel.

But of course, the person telling it shades the story to their light.

Aaron tongued his cheek. "Okay, whether...you're in my head or I just have a shit poker face...no, I don't trust you."

"May we ask why?"

Not a topic she should have opened. "You've killed friends of mine."

"As you have killed ours." She responded with no hesitation.

"Then why haven't *you* killed *me*?!"

Scar cooed from his dark post nearby, almost a purr deep in his throat. The Queen sat in that accusation, bathing in its implications. He had been a singular threat and a potent weapon against her. By all reason, she should have torn him to gooey bits and painted the walls with viscera.

What was staying her hand?

Aaron turned away—no. Make her do it.

He whirled back around. "I am no one! You've been in my head, you know better than most. I'm a criminal, a murderer. I have no value. I have no rights. I am not special or interesting or important. I am only alive because they *allow* it!"

He softened at that pronouncement, taking a moment to absorb it himself. The truth hurts.

She actually smiled at him. "Those are their words. Not yours."

The Queen of the Jergad strode over to him. He recoiled as she reached for his face, but she did not hesitate, cupping his cheeks between her palms.

They were soft, warm. Real. No images came flooding in, but rather the soft comfort of a warm blanket toasty from the dryer. It almost drew tears from him.

Was he just that thirsty for human touch, or was this some power of hers to sap his will to resist?

She pulled on his cheek, lifting his eyes up to meet hers. "You are alive. That simple fact makes you valuable. Life itself *is* the treasure."

"Wouldn't say that if you knew my life," he blurted. How absurd. She knew his life, every waking scrap of its pitiable path.

Her smile drooped, heavy with intent. "Ancient heroes are nothing more than myth...but they are about people. And when those people lived, they were not 'heroes.' It is in the crafting, in the telling of their deeds, that they are lionized and deified: their actions in which they are now remembered. But in their day, they were nothing more than 'alive'. Nothing more than you are now."

Aaron snorted. "So, you guys do have stories, huh?"

"We have our history as we remember it."

He swallowed all of his fear before he could speak again. "I can't just get up and end a war," he whispered to her.

Her hands dropped to her sides, a small smile edging on her face. "Who can know...until we try?"

"But I don't have any power!" Aaron broke in, pulling away from those intoxicating hands, "Nobody will listen to somebody like me!"

The Queen straightened up, the motion pulling him up straight with her. "You know much of rank, of position, of the lower place they put you in? Who would listen to us?"

Aaron blinked.

Of course. She'd kept him alive all this time for information. She was buttering him up. He could provide intelligence on the humans' fortifications, equipment depots, capabilities.

She wanted targets. He was a resource to be used and exhausted.

"A-ha," he said dryly, "So you don't care about me at all. You want the big fish."

The Queen's stoic facade twitched, almost like a video feed had skipped some frames. "What more could we show you to convince you of our cause?"

Aaron decided to test her. "Let me go, right now. No muss, no fuss."

"And you will bring our case to the humans, *ak'thun*?"

"I can't promise anything," he jabbered, "I'm-I'm a Capital. But it would go a long way to show you mean business. I go back, I'm gonna tell 'em how I survived..."

He sighed, computing the inevitable result of that conversation. "And they're just gonna love that story. You know, the one where I held court with an alien shadow blob—" Aaron stabbed a finger at the shifting morass behind the regal Talania. "—and how the vicious natives showed me nothing but hospitality: smelly, *rancid* hospitality! I'll be lucky if my CO doesn't lash me to a big stick for target practice!"

"Why would they do that?" She asked, quizzical.

"Why..." Aaron gasped, barely able to understand the question. "I've been trying to tell you, I am a Capital! I surrendered my basic right to be 'alive.' Those people down there don't owe me shit! I have no value to them! My word is nothing!" His voice echoed off the walls of the cavern, punctuating his point.

Futile, as the nest continued its work unabated. It was like shouting at the rain.

The Queen was similarly unenthused, barely reacting to the

outburst. She took a bracing breath, an unabashed bit of theater for his benefit. "We shall stay our hands."

He blinked. "Stay your hands?" It finally clicked, lightbulb moment. "No more attacks on the Wall, on the farmlands...you'll stop attacking Vanguard?"

"Our assault will cease. You can bring them this news. Surely, then they might be willing to listen." She made this declaration with a soft voice but a firm stare. "That is our trust in you."

"That..." Aaron fumbled for words, "I'm touched by the confidence you have in me but...you should just know, it's a tall order."

"Yes. *Ak'thun* may even have to jump."

Oh my God, stop.

PART THREE
LODESTONE

CHAPTER
SEVENTEEN
RILEY

HE HAD ARRIVED one dry morning, stumbling out of the horizon a ghostly mirage.

Despite the roiling heat of the day and the peeling sunburns that lined his hands and lips, reports read that he was shivering. The sun damage had sent him to heatstroke, rendering him completely unable to regulate his body temperature.

His clothes hung off him, made looser by a few key rips, either from battle damage or abuse. He had pulled up his tunic to shield his face from the blistering wind, but it did little for his nose, the skin already peeling back.

Dehydration and exposure had nearly finished him.

The guards took him into custody without a thought. Their basic thinking had been limited to purifying silhouettes on a horizon.

They couldn't be expected to know what Riley knew. If he had seen that ghost walk out of the desert, he'd have ordered a marksman burn two symmetrical holes in center-mass before they could make out his face. Human or not, all friendly forces were accounted for and rules of engagement were quite clear.

At the very least, Aaron should have been held in quarantine to await a battery of tests—where he would most assuredly have been found contaminated by some hostile pathogen, forcing Riley to purge said threat. It would have been a tragic but altogether necessary end for the Capital and safety precautions exist for a reason.

Instead of reducing Aaron to a slag heap from two hundred yards, the Regulars lent him a blanket, their food, and their ears. The detachment of Capitals and the Regular fools listened as the walking dead man droned on about his experiences, about how genuine hell demons nestled in the foothills actually bore us no ill will, that these bladed monstrosities that could not be manufactured in a mad scientist's lab to be more horrifying, creatures that had slain hundreds of their kin, sought only an end to the bloodshed.

Aaron made outlandish promises, how the creatures were going to cease their offensives and retreat back into their holes to await our response.

How did he know all of this?

They talked to him, he said. The critters barely capable of strategy were sapient enough, civilized enough, to trade words with an entirely different species? It was far more likely the governor's daughter would personally anoint Riley with oil and crown him Regent than there was any truth to Aaron's outlandish aspersions.

He was a POW held by an enemy force during a time of war, released without negotiation or trade, and Riley was supposed to accept this gift without inspection?

The room was barren, just an empty storage closet the technicians had hastily converted to an interrogation space. The Wall's fortifications were capable of hosting triple the standing troops and munitions, so a half hour of heavy lifting freed up a small space at the Prefecture.

Two technicians plugged up the single air vent with sealing foam, allowing only minimal refreshment, and barred up the one open window, reducing the light to a single slit that draped across Aaron's bare back.

They bolted two empty shelves to the floor and walls, securing them as racks for Aaron's restraints. The ropes lashed to them were drawn taut and bit into Aaron's wrists, pulling his arms wide to match the ankle-bar that locked his legs open. This spread eagle position kept him open to the litany of abuses at Riley's disposal.

All in good time.

Riley observed Aaron through a camera from the room next door, along with a half dozen doctors and officers—it looked like a collection of professors had brought their children out of Academy and directly to a slave box.

Holmst leaned against the back wall, unblinking, as he studied Aaron's stripped form. His pale eyes traced the lines of the man on camera like he was looking at a ghost.

Or was he looking at a stinging rebuke of his talents? The lieutenant's deep-socketed eyes betrayed more guilt than frustration.

The Capital hung against his restraints, letting his flesh bear his weight; the cords on his wrists were already cutting into his flesh, letting little rivulets of blood drop down his arms. Riley had seen this before: the prisoner was using the pain to keep himself awake and cognizant. Aaron was more than a simple slave with a gun.

Caution was never too high a price.

Aaron glanced up at the camera lens, letting out a sigh and a raised brow. Oh, was Riley's deliberations an inconvenience to the prisoner?

"Any theories?" Riley asked the room.

A murmur rolled through the group as they all debated who should speak first. Riley rolled his eyes. No executive function to be found, high nor low.

One doctor finally chirped up, a wiry little woman. "He claims the Jergad Queen spoke to him through a projection...this would indicate some kind of non-linear connection between the Queen and the rest of the hive mind, their gestalt consciousness."

Her eyes danced up and left, as she started to fabricate the rest of the reason for opening her mouth. "Perhaps she uses some inaudible low-frequency sound or an electrical current—something that could influence brain activity with enough sophistication to create and manipulate such an illusion."

"Impossible," another egghead spat at his colleague. "Basic commands to simple creatures is one thing, but complex audio-visual hallucinations in a hostile cerebellum?"

"That's assuming he actually saw what he claims he did."

"Precisely! It's far more likely he's lying."

They were about to break down into a full committee on biological markers and entomological implications if Riley didn't recapture their focus.

He pressed his knuckles against the wall, giving them a ripping crack like he was rolling them over nutshells. This redirected everyone's attention.

An ambitious little dissenter stepped forward. "Sir, our physiology is just not evolved for such things. It's much more likely he's fabricating this story."

"So," Riley cut off the debate, "There's absolutely no reason at all behind the lack of Jergad attacks on forward positions? Zero contact for seventy-two hours? That's just a happy coincidence?"

"...Yes?"

Riley peered at the original scientist, a mousy little woman twice his age positively withering under his gaze. He took a moment to soak in her embarrassment, what self-abuse must be running through her head.

He threw her a rope. "Talk it out, Doctor. There's a ration card in it for you if you make my day."

She swallowed hard, feeling the pressure for a heavy moment, as all eyes came to rest on her. The older the eyes, the more dismissive they were.

But Riley's eyes were the only ones that mattered.

"It is generally accepted that, uh...the Jergad drones receive instructions through a combination of pheromones, sound, and chemical markers left by their comrades. But they achieve actions far too complex for what these elements can likely achieve. A more...fringe theory...involves their cerebrospinal fluid."

The whole room shifted at the mere mention, with her dissenting partner loudly scoffing at the words. "I'll be the judge of its merit," Riley scolded the man into silence. "What's your name, Doctor?"

She coughed the nerves out of her throat. "Lisa- Womack. Dr. Womack."

"Dr. Womack," Riley smiled, nodding to her, "Room is yours. Give us a show."

It took her a solid few seconds but she was able to get in gear. "In Jergad skull cavities, we have found an abnormal amount of nickel and iron—magnetic metals—suspended in the fluid. It's possible... microfluctuations in a magnetic field could transmit communications by vibrating those compounds."

"We did it for nearly a century," Holmst chimed in, the idea piquing his interest. "Morse code. Tapped out electrical signals across wires in a universal cypher, you could send...petabytes of data that way."

"More or less," Womack agreed, "But this would be over the air, using the planet's own magnetic field. All she has to do is influence that in minor ways."

The doctors collectively sneered and scoffed, until Riley leered back at them. "That's *more* outlandish than the drivel you spin every other day?"

"Sir," the leader of the dissent brigade stepped forward as if to present himself for further punishment. Perhaps he had a fetish for it. "Our instruments would certainly have detected any such shifts in the magnetic field near or around Jergad hordes."

Holmst perked up in the back, stiffening at some notion in his head. Riley glanced over. "Lieutenant. You're doing that thing with your face."

Holmst lifted himself off the wall and into a parade rest. "Colonel, Aaron's first symptoms of alien intrusion began after he stabbed one in the head with his quick knife...his steel quick knife."

195

The Doctors immediately huddled up, running equations and wild hypothesis as easily as Riley could put on his shoes. Murmurs of electromagnetic influences, the metallic composite of the knives, amplitudes of current across the human body and a dozen other terms were tossed into the open air, but Riley gathered what he needed.

Aaron had rather crudely—and literally—hacked into the aliens' comm-net. And now, they could talk to him.

So was it possible? Could the aliens really be suing for peace for the first time because they were finally *able* to? The last two years of tactics had hardly betrayed a defensive stance, let alone one seeking to minimize conflict.

But new opportunities present new choices.

"Thank you, Doctors, that's all fascinating. Womack?" Riley tapped a command into his wrist. "Lunch is on me. You?" Riley pointed at the lead dissenter. "Don't get to have lunch. Let that be a lesson."

"But—" It was Womack speaking up for her rival. How quaint.

"That'll be all, Doctors. You have patients to tend to," Riley declared, choosing instead to stare into the camera feed of their guest.

The Doctors funneled out of the small room muttering and grumbling at their female peer, like she had somehow unduly undercut their prestige simply by being correct.

Or maybe they just wanted her meal.

"Due respect, sir," Holmst cajoled his commander, "this could be a Godsend. We could turn our attention back to the Empire and—"

"You really think it possible these things won't come for us in our sleep?"

Holmst's face twisted and froze, caught between two equal impossibilities. His eyes darted to the screen and their irenic prisoner.

Aaron's return upset a very basic principle of the aliens' behavior: they hadn't butchered him with a hateful fixation. Either of the conspiracy theories—of a peaceful resolution to the conflict, or a human operative for a hive mind—would have born the same rolled eyes from him not a week before.

Now, olive branch or dagger, everything they'd taken for certain had been shot to shit by one solitary wanderer in the savannah.

"Why don't we ask him?" The lieutenant finally said, turning his eyes back to Riley.

He could swear, the aide de camp might actually have had a glimmer of hope somewhere behind those ice blue eyes, a lightness under his brow.

How disappointing. Riley could have sworn that was a seasoned soldier at his arm, not some naive member of the diplomatic corps. Soldiers lived in permanent residence amongst the worst realities of the modern world. Lifting your head up from your foxhole to gaze at the shapes in the clouds got it removed from your shoulders.

Riley gave his lieutenant a soft, patronizing smile, trying to remember how his own teachers used to belittle his youthful missteps. "Lead the way, Lieutenant."

The two marched the short distance in toward Aaron's makeshift cell. The open door flooded the room with light from two floods triggered by the hinges—intentionally blinding the occupant to hinder resistance.

Aaron didn't even look up, his eyes cast to the chipped stone floor.

Riley squared up in front of the Capital, arms folded. "I trust we've made you comfortable?"

No response. But Aaron's eyes flitted across Riley's pristine boots, studying and absorbing.

He was listening. Good. Time for the two-punch.

Riley pursed his lips as he fished in his pocket. "They strung you up? That's just bad staff work. Lieutenant, would you mind?"

He pointed at the restraints, and Holmst delayed the requisite half second before swooping forward to undo the restrictive knots.

The sudden slack sent Aaron to his knees, as the awkward wide leg restraints kept him from holding himself up. The prisoner rubbed at the sores and blisters on his wrists. Standard pain response, unconscious behaviors.

The crinkle of a wrapper pricked up his ears, his neck craning up to see Riley chewing on a ration bar: steel oats with a bitter chocolate and stimulant injection.

He wasn't even hungry. He just wanted to show the Capital food.

Riley gnawed on the end of the bar, breaking off a malleable chunk. "I apologize for the accommodations, but we have some protocols that...quite frankly, we've never had the opportunity to observe in this particular theater. The bugs don't typically leave survivors."

He pointed at Aaron with the bar, letting it linger with grabbing distance. "And they let you go twice."

Before Aaron could reach for the food, Riley pulled it back, breaking off another bite.

It was the unspoken offer for comforts, the waste of a badly needed necessity. It was better than any torture, any pain.

In his final exam, Riley had brought a mangy dog. The instructors were disappointed, assuming physical violence. But Riley went through his motions, before inevitably giving the ration to the dog. The starved animal swallowed the thing whole right in front of the prisoner.

The implicit threat coupled with the abject waste was devastating to their psyche. No amount of shouting or sensory deprivation would best a wasted cigarette or spilled water.

Torture steeled the will; waste crushed hope. The real game was not in invoking so much pain that one begged for release, no—a man will tell you the sky is made of ice cream to quash a fire.

But a seduction, if he believes you his only friend in a God-forsaken world? You silence all hope, and then position yourself as the sole source of store-fresh, brand-name, farm-to-table relief.

People will confide their darkest secrets in their friends.

"You know who I am?" Riley asked between bites.

Aaron nodded, shaky from exhaustion and nerves, but his eyes never left the ration bar. "I'd like to hear you say it, if you can."

Aaron's dried and cracked lips seemed to pop apart, the dirt and saliva having dried into a sealant. Finally free, he sucked in the stale air like it was a cool drink of water. "...You know who I am?"

There it was. The aggression, the pride, the belligerence of a prisoner. He was not yet broken, but would need the softer hand and patience. 'Do not cede the higher ground; instead, give enough to build a bridge that you own.'

"He speaks!" Riley said, glancing at Holmst with a happy smirk. "Little victories."

"If you're going to torture me," Aaron croaked, "I'd rather we get to it already."

"Torture?" Riley played up his appalled expression, "Aaron, we're just happy to see you."

"So the ankle irons and the tanning rack were just...?"

Riley nodded, with rolled eyes, as though he too found it ridiculous. "Part of the protocol."

Aaron sneered, a thin smile wrapping up around his jaw, "I'd love to meet the guy who drew up that bit of the rules."

"Work long enough in the Armed Forces, and that sentence becomes a bit of a refrain." Riley quipped, drawing up a chair from the shadows. He eased into it, settling in like he was building a nest. Aaron was not going to be easily persuaded by that, but a proper foundation had to be laid. Interrogation was a patient man's art.

Aaron leaned back, like his body was slack in a rope line. "They don't want to fight anymore."

"I believe you."

Aaron blinked, clearly not expecting that response. "Really?"

"I'm skeptical of them, but I believe you," Riley said, gesturing for Holmst back in the shadows. The lieutenant produced his canteen, careful to remain out of sight. The senior officer who had abandoned Aaron in the mountains certainly wouldn't create a further bond.

Riley took a theatrical swig of the contents, relishing the refreshment as it cooled his throat. He offered it to Aaron—the first official gesture of connection. Aaron took it—hook, line & sinker. He plucked it from Riley's hands and took a strong belt.

Riley began, "Some of us have been fighting these things for years. It's not so easy to rationalize that they suddenly want peace."

Cracking voice, relishing the refreshing water. "It didn't make much sense to me either."

"Why's that?" That's it. Unravel his own logic, so even he doesn't believe himself anymore.

Aaron froze up, clutching the canteen like it was a teddy bear and he was a small child laid up at sundown. "They'd killed friends of mine."

Riley gave the smallest of nods. "Mine too. It's been a long war."

Aaron glowered up at Riley, under his ragged brows. "You have the power to stop it."

Give ground. Be humble. Let them be the ones to overreach.

"You think very highly of little ol' me," Riley smirked, all contrite as he leaned back in his chair. "But we're the ones defending a Wall. They're the ones hitting us."

"Not by what I saw." Aaron didn't have to look at Holmst for everyone to know where that jab was sent.

Damn it. Riley had been arrogant bringing the lieutenant in here.

Damage control. 'They will flail. You must direct.'

"Lieutenant Holmst was acting under my direct orders," Riley jumped in, "Turning the blade to them saves lives on the Wall, and by all accounts, it has completely blunted their assaults."

"They stopped," Aaron flared, "because they want peace--"

"They wanted peace at Rimpau?" Riley asked, "When they cut your friends to ribbons?"

Riley let that image hang in his head. Riley had seen the body-cam footage from the Oskies. The Jergad had been ten-to-one, and they had torn through the opposition like a hungry Hydra, more a single legendary monster than individuals, as they pulled the hapless into a waiting maw to experience the kind of suffering reserved for mankind's worst offenders before silencing their screams with blood.

"Aaron," Riley soothed, "It's not an action I take lightly, but we had to start punching back."

"They're defending themselves..." Aaron whispered. "This was their home."

"Is there any action we could commit that justifies what they've done?"

That was apparently a land mine. "We glassed their whole planet!" Aaron shouted, "We killed billions!"

Ay, there's the rub. That's the root of the tall tale.

Riley got up out of his chair, kneeling down in front of Aaron. Vulnerability—putting himself within range of Aaron's grasp was a show of trust, kinship.

He was not a prisoner and Riley not his captor. This was more intervention than interrogation, and a delirious Aaron would lose sense of his allegiance.

"Says who?" Riley met him at the same level. "The telepathic monster that personally executed your friends, my friends? It's claiming victimhood? Really? Oh, please, Aaron! You're smarter than that! It's in your head! It's been there for months! They didn't let you go out of the goodness of their heart. They're lying to you!"

Riley sat back on his heels, letting Aaron stew in that. The Capital squared up, but his lip was quivering, his hands shaking.

Aaron was moments from breaking.

"Aaron, protocol insists I terminate you as a threat," Riley stated, with gloom. "I'm trying to save your life right now."

"You don't care about Capitals..." Aaron stammered out. "No one does."

"Do this right, and you won't be a Capital, Aaron. You get through this...and you're a citizen again. More than earned it. You could go back to your life or build a whole new one, if you want. But not if you die out here."

Aaron lowered his head, eyes darting across the floor, like he was speed-reading something scrawled into the foundations.

"You've come a long way," Riley said, "That's got to mean something."

"...They lied to me?"

"The best lies are sprinkled with some truth," Riley equivocated, quoting from some high school philosophy textbook. "We may not be angels. But they're not victims. And given a chance, just the smallest chance...I understand why you trust them. They spared you. But *why?*"

"Because..." Aaron croaked out, "I can speak for them."

"To what end, Aaron?"

Aaron shivered, sinking backward into his restraints.

Turn out the lights and last one out, get the door. Show's over.

Riley made some effete promises for creature comforts, physical therapy and observation, of how the Doctors were going to help rehabilitate him, even that he could see his friends just as soon as they could make assurances he was safe for general exposure. Riley spoke of fresh clothing and a hot meal—nothing luxurious but sorely needed. It was a kindness bestowed.

None of it would come true, of course. He was a Capital. Riley would likely never step foot in that room again.

After a few performative farewells, Holmst slid the door closed behind them. He fell in stride beside his commander, but he moved like someone had strapped him with cement boots.

Better get this over with.

"You've got comments?"

"We went in there looking to get answers," Holmst fretted, "Not supply them. What if he's telling the truth?"

"You want to know what the oddsmakers say about that?" Riley asked, a growl behind his cynical question.

Holmst bowed his head for a moment, before bucking up the courage to support his objection, "Sir, it's a possibility we shouldn't dismiss, is all."

Riley stopped in his tracks, blocking the hallway, "There are only two possibilities, Lieutenant. Either they are actually suing for peace, or they are trying to trick us. Either way, the prescribed response is 'let your guard down.' There are thousands of innocent lives in Vanguard and I will not *gamble* with their safety."

"Then why not execute him and move on?"

"Because he's a gold mine of intelligence, and I wouldn't give that up for my own mother. We're not peacemakers, Lieutenant. We are Peacekeepers."

"I'm from Venus, sir," Holmst blurted, stopping in the hallway like an anchor.

Somehow, the gravity of it kept Riley from walking on. He turned back to his aide. "I'm sorry?"

"We get acid rainstorms. The ground has to be carefully cultivated, or it doesn't grow anything. We had...six famines growing up. But no matter how bad it got, we all knew we could trust a man with a flag on his shoulder."

"You looking for a demerit or just a smack in the face?" Riley asked, lip curled.

"Peacekeepers do a lot of torture where you come from?"

Adorable.

"That wasn't torture, Lieutenant. Believe me, when I start the torture, you'll know. There'll be a ledger. It'll be your job to take the minutes."

CHAPTER
EIGHTEEN
AARON

IT STARTED with simple blood tests. They unlocked his restraints, brought him water and a hearty bread, before setting him down in a steel chair. There was polite conversation, even asking about Aaron's future plans, what he'd do with his freedom.

He'd have to think about it. They found that charming. Or maybe, they were just wincing at the parched creak in his voice.

With a hypo, they drew blood from his arm—it felt like a lot, but what did Aaron know? There wasn't even a puncture site where the work had been done, but the primary vein collapsed after, a blue streak up his dark bicep. He asked about it, but the Doctors were more eager to talk about him.

They were never happier than when Aaron was talking about himself. He doubted they were actually listening to a word he said, but they almost never stopped with their questions.

He learned the name of his primary physician: Dr. Lisa Womack. She was a slender woman, short, almost childlike. She had solid shoulders and immaculate flowing black hair that hung along her angular jaw like curtains cut for the occasion. There was a strand of her bangs that kept slipping forward in front of her eyes, and she had to keep swiping it back to hook behind her ear.

She was a lively conversationalist, with a music to her soprano voice. It sounded so...familiar.

Aaron could not remember what they spoke about, but he grew to relish her visits. Womack meant food, water, comfort, warmth, and...

Touch. It was like a shot of electricity, a bolt that darted from end to end affirming he was awake, alive. It warmed his gut and cooled his sweat. It relieved the weight on his shoulders and anchored his feet to the ground.

It was so isolating without a human voice, but a human touch might as well have been a drug cascading through his veins.

It was nearly a week before she touched him the first time. She had stepped up to apply a topical antibiotic to the abrasions on his wrists. He had developed a fever and they were concerned for his health. He felt her soft hands graze his wrist and for that moment's embrace, he was in heaven.

"Thank you," he rasped, with more intensity than she likely expected.

She started at the words, blinking through the computational error. She had done nothing worthy of gratitude, so she thought, until the obvious result came to her.

She resumed her task without another look. It was bliss for a brief time, before they left him again.

Two days of solitary and smothering heat later, Womack returned with her team. She never directed their work; rather, she nodded to them at intervals, indicating they could proceed to their next task. She busied herself talking with him.

Distracting him.

"What were you thinking?" Womack asked him. "At Rimpau?"

Aaron's eyes fluttered as he struggled with parsing the question.

She had never asked about his time as a Capital before. It was always about before, his life as a citizen and his occupation and family, the Empire and Sol.

He swallowed on the dried mucus, trying to force a pathway for his voice. "I...I thought...was going to die."

She glanced at someone just out of sight, hovering somewhere to his left. They nodded to her, and she looked back at him. "What did you see?"

"I saw..." Those eyes. The Queen's penetrating stare. "I saw the Howler overhead."

She raised her eyebrows, like a teacher pulling an answer from a child. "Did you dream?"

Aaron shook off the mounting headache. "I saw her eyes..."

The shadow leaned forward, grunting with a familiar gravel that teased the edge of memory. "Whose eyes?"

Aaron lifted his head, searching the darkness for that voice. Womack couldn't let him. "Aaron, focus. Please."

Something in her voice, a bedside manner, a friendly tone, his own delirium. He didn't know why he associated the name, but all he wanted in that moment was to see her face, hear her voice. Was she there?

"...Eden?"

"Not her," Womack scolded, in that soft maternal tone, "The eyes. Tell me about the eyes."

He didn't answer, at least not fast enough for her liking. He blinked, trying to break the growing crust on his lips, and in that moment's hesitation, her team may as well have vanished.

He was alone for three more days after that. His abdomen had gone from hunger pangs to pouting silence, only to circle back with more pain. And every time that pain came, bread and water would appear with the warm face of Dr. Womack. Then he would be alone until that pain twisted up his insides.

He tried to fake it, aping the movements and groans, but they always knew when it was real.

Then they turned on the lights. Hot, white, blinding him.

Before he knew it, his restraints had been cut and hands pressed him into a board. Thick bindings lashed about his midsection and chest, pinning his arms to his sides, before tilting him down to a horizontal position.

He could hear the wheels on his gurney rattle as they wheeled him out.

He was leaving.

"Where are we going?" He croaked.

Dr. Womack's dulcet tones crooned into his ear. "We're moving you to a Forward Operating Room."

"Can I...talk to the cleaning crew?" He jested, his throat raspy from lack of use, hitching in a painful way every so often, "I want to... apologize for the state of my bunk."

She snorted. "Two whole months of isolation, he's still got a sense of humor."

"You should see me af—after a forced march. Jokes get filthy."

He felt a prick at his elbow and a chill shot up his arm and through his chest that made his stomach churn like cold laundry. This was not made for his comfort.

Womack leaned in again. "We need to insert two probes, one into your lumbar and another into your cerebral cavity. This should help us study the movements of your CS fluids. We got authorization this morning!"

She sounded oddly chipper for the assortment of words in that sentence.

"Maybe I just tell you about my dog?" Aaron gurgled out.

She hummed, choking back a laugh. "You don't have a dog. You've never had a dog. Maybe you can get a dog? It's not a complex procedure, but it is delicate. So we're going to be putting you under for it. Do you have any allergies or medical conditions?"

It was harder to concentrate, the passing lights glowing brighter and brighter with each successive pass, like they were swinging overhead on a string and getting closer and closer to his face.

"I'm squishy and full of blood. Try not to spill me on the floor."

He had a very limited view of the world from his bed, but he could make out the moment the cement pavers overhead dressed themselves in white and black paint. The lighting softened, diffused, like it was leaking through a thin cloud layer. And there was that acrid smell that reminded him of a cold shower, of the disinfectant the prison wardens used when clearing a new inmate through quarantine.

Machinery hung from the walls, with express purposes lying somewhere between medical miracles and medieval inquisition.

He pressed against his restraints as they swung the gurney into position. It shuddered as they clipped into place, metal clamps onto the legs raising it the half-inch needed to keep it from rolling off.

"I have to confess," Womack murmured, before leaning up into view, her medical mask failing to conceal the morbid flicker in her eyes, "We usually only perform this on cadavers."

"Well..." Aaron's eyes fluttered, fighting the blanket that cajoled his mind into silence, "I like doing...new stuff."

That flicker slipped away, a wisp of sadness peaking at the corner of her eyes. Or was it pity? "You're used to your cage now, aren't you?"

Perhaps she was quick off the draw, or he was now slower than he believed, but a new wave of cold crept up his arm before he could answer her pointed question. It inched up the length of his bicep and across his shoulder before worming into his chest, where it exploded in him. He was warm and cold all at once, relaxed but something troubled him.

It felt like a brick sat on his chest, compressing his ribs and squeezing his back against the bed. His own weight felt like it might crush him, unless he were to sink into the mattress and slither away.

He blinked. And he could no longer open his eyes.

They had been frozen shut, captive to whatever drugs Womack had forced him with. Despite the bewildering sensation, he could still hear them chatter amongst each other, muffled laughter and casual requests. It was as though he could hear them through a thick wall or with a pillow pressed around his face.

The dull whine of machinery filled his ears, dwarfing all other sound. At first, it sounded like it came from within his own head, but he realized it was in two places: one above and one below. It reminded him of the drill bits on the Mining Rigs, a kind of industrial grind coupled with the cry of a dying animal.

It pulled closer and closer in a delicate approach that might deafen him for life. He tried to pull away, to no avail. That weight on his chest kept him locked in place.

They hadn't put him under. They'd paralyzed him.

No restraint could keep him from twisting at the wrong time, but they still needed him...alert.

That's when he felt the first pressure on his lower back. And when he heard the first gunshot. The drills retreated like frightened rats and the doctors cried out.

Perhaps the Wall was being hit? No. That was close by. He'd have heard the Thumpers and the Repeaters sing their brutal arias before any rifle fire on the barricades.

Each successive drumbeat of high caliber gunfire was accompanied by the ring of an escaping brass cartridge, a harmony he was very familiar with.

Voices shouted and soon he felt hands upon him. A new voice—a woman's, muffled but shrill—shouted: "What did you give him?!"

That voice. Could it...?

A lyrical interlude that could only be Dr. Womack's deceptions responded with some incomprehensible chemical compound.

The demanding voice was not amused by the answer. "How much?" No response. The shrill voice demanded again, "How much, Dr. Haircut?!"

Womack tried to declare her superiority with an unusually haughty tone. "I have a Doctorate from Osiris Medical College—"

"I was a resident in Detroit's Lower Wards and you have the medical malpractice of a first-year *bartender*! Look at it—His BPI is 80 over 50, his kidneys are giving out, and he's suffering acute nervous shutdown! That's alarming enough, but hypotension? He *should* be clockin' on all cylinders ready to blow a gasket! And that's because you OD'd on your paralytic, you colossal moron!"

Womack tried to interject some excuse, of this being expected, and the new voice was having none of it. There was a tinkling of glass as someone lifted a needle. "If you don't give me what I want to know, he'll go tachycardic in less than a minute. After which—I guarantee—"

Another interruption from Womack and the voice was out of patience, turning almost to a growl. "*How much did you give him?!*"

Eden. He'd heard that voice in labor, in war, in play and in her sleep. It really was her.

Through Aaron's weakening hearing, he could barely make out Womack's defensive muttering, something and the number: "Ten."

Eden cursed, before cupping Aaron's head in her rough hands. "Aaron, I don't know if you can hear me, but there is an immense amount of pressure on your brain, and if I don't relieve it, you will wish you were dead."

Several voices grunted out indistinct commands.

Eden was having none of it. "Nora, with me! Solomon, Keira on the door!"

A familiar gravely voice bellowed over the din. "Alright! You heard the lady and you know your places! Jensen, barricade that window! I don't want to see any more pretty pretty sunlight! Huah?"

"Huah, Gunny!"

It was the team. They had come for him?

He could hear their voices, even smell their sweat. He wished he could see their faces.

But there was a blinding pain, white hot, right behind his eyes. It was so deep he could swear it was coming from somewhere outside of his body, from the gurney he was laid upon. It wasn't a spike of pain like a sprain or even a broken bone.

It was more akin to being boiled alive.

He could see those two blue eyes staring at him through the cloudy darkness. They stared a single commandment into his very bones.

Stay alive.

Nora huddled somewhere overhead. "What do you need me to do?"

"I need your hands," Eden barked, "Give me what I say, when I say it." Womack started to speak, but Eden promptly drowned her out. "And if this one says another *gulaw* word, put two in her *fra ti* forehead!"

"Eden, you've got three minutes tops!"

"I've got one minute, old man. Knife, now!"

He felt the slightest tug on his forehead, just under his hairline. Perhaps it was the chemical nightmare he was experiencing, but he could swear she was getting ready to scalp him. He could feel the edge of the blade slice through skin and meat, before it slicked against his skull, like a bowstring across a violin, playing a sour note in his ears.

"Give me that drill!"

That dull whine sang out again, this time in front of his face. She must've pivoted the rig and now lowered it down against his skull.

Aaron felt himself try to tense up, somewhere inside that chemical prison, while his body lay limp on the table. It was the most surreal feeling, like a lucid dream where he knew he could move but couldn't make it happen.

And all the while, that burning pain, scorching behind his eyes straight through him.

The Queen's stare grew brighter with each second, as if urging him to run faster and faster when he couldn't even lift his fingers.

What good was he?

The drill scraped against his skull before finding purchase and biting into the bone. That pain lit up like someone had doused his entire body in gasoline. It should've blown him away, reduced his sanity to shattered glass.

But he had felt pain like this before, he had weathered it. Those blue eyes told him so. The fires that fell from the sky and sanitized a planet was a pain far more impressive than this. He carried a thousand more scars than this horror could possibly inflict. He was made of steel now, wrought in an inferno and forged in a crucible that rendered mortal pain a shadow of real agony.

He survived the wounds of an entire species; he could survive this.

"Got it!"

The drill pulled back and Aaron could feel his forehead dampen, as though a cool cloth had been draped across his brow, dousing the painful fires and wicking away the heat. He tried not to linger on the notion of his brain's fluids were now exposed to the world and slicking his face, albeit through a very tiny hole in his head.

"Eden, we have to go! Now!"

Two quick straps of a tape locked some gauze over Aaron's head wound. "I'm done! Jensen! Ruck up!"

Jensen. Eden. Nora. Solomon. Keira. Even Bray.

Where was Carmona? Why wasn't Car with them? He should be barking orders. He should be leading.

His restraints flipped away, and his body slipped to the side, like a bag of sand.

The fall felt without end, an hour or a lifetime of free fall. It was a solid minute before he realized that someone was carrying him on their shoulders. They did their best not to jostle him, but no matter how small, the rhythmic roll of steps banged on the inside of his skull.

"We are mobile! I've got anchor. Solomon, Keira—let's get deadly!"

They related their heroics to him later with a unique touch of horror. Three army Regulars were killed in the exchange of gunfire, and Keira sustained a burn to her left leg.

Their initial plan had been to break in, secure him at his cell, and exfil by land cruiser to an arms depot to resupply. With Aaron mid-surgery, they had to delay their escape and were ultimately cut off. They reversed directions, with Gunnery Sergeant Thomas Bray now leading the insurrection—technical term. Gunny insisted they call it that.

Apparently, the Gunny was marching to a different beat these days. It must have been his gravelly-voiced shadow that visited a few days before. Perhaps he read the Doctors' reports or looked at an advance schedule.

Whatever he had turned up in the weeks of Aaron's captivity had urged a career veteran and loyal Imperial to turn terrorist hand-in-hand with Capital criminals.

Bray and Nora had disabled the nearby Repeater towers while Jensen and crew secured a land cruiser. Unfortunately, it was on the wrong side of the Wall. The team had to beat feet into the open Savannah.

Eventually, the small arms fire stopped and the Wall receded over the horizon. They had no supplies, no food, one working vehicle, deep in Jergad territory. And they had just launched the first attack in Vanguard's rebellion—sorry, insurrection.

The cruiser was still rolling when Aaron was finally able to open his eyes, staring up at Eden's soft face.

She inspected his head wound with a confident smirk. "I do good work."

———

"Scale of one to ten, Gunny—how jacked are we?" Nora was never one to mince words.

The crew huddled near the land cruiser, afraid of every little crack in the ground. Instinct and memory told them what to fear, how to protect themselves. They had no concept for how far their fall was bound to be.

Aaron stood out in the open desert a good dozen meters from the illusory safety of the cruiser, half hoping that a pair of bifurcated jaws might surge up from the ground to pull him to his due.

Everyone urged him to come back to their little campfire summit, but no one had the bravery to step out onto the hostile clay to retrieve him. They had sieged the single most impressive fortification on the planet, but they still feared the very ground they stood upon. The contradiction almost made him laugh.

Gunny threw a glance out at Aaron. "It won't be long till the LADAR satellites pick up our silhouettes out here, at which point a brisk orbital strike from Thor's Hammer will...obliterate us. It'll hit ya so hard, it'll be like you never existed."

"Can we camouflage ourselves, top cover or—?" Eden asked, to an audible scoff from Keira. Eden glowered at the woman twice her size. "Unless you got a better idea?"

Bray shook his head. "It'll buy time, but the satellites are thorough. Unless we can get back inside the Wall—where they're too nervous to drop kinetics—we're just targets downrange."

"What does the Hero think?" Solomon hissed, throwing a wry smirk out at Aaron.

"I think you all screwed up," Aaron said without missing a beat.

Jensen shifted in his seat, rocking the whole cruiser. "Aaron, we saved your ass."

"Did you now?" Aaron sneered, "I look real safe to you?"

"Bray said—"

"I heard what Bray said." Somehow the weakness in Aaron's voice, just the smallest squeak betraying his pain, was enough to quiet all objection. "And I know you believed him. But...Riley was right. The safety of the people has to come first."

Bray stiffened like Aaron had just burned an Imperial flag in front of the Ministry of Cultural Observance. He may as well have spat on a grave. "You really think that kid gives two shits about 'the people.'"

"He cares about keeping 'em alive."

Bray's eyes went dark, his voice like a knife's edge. "No, he doesn't. He never did. He just wants medals, merits, heroics. And you don't get those by following rules."

"Gunny, if we followed the rules," Aaron began, "you would have personally executed every one of us and thought nothing more of it."

The half a beat told him he'd struck true, but Bray was used to taking hits. "Riley is a country mile over the line. I'm a soldier. He's a monster."

"Doesn't make him wrong," Aaron spat back. "He's thinking about the big picture."

"That why they were gearing to crack you open? Jus' big picture?" Nora scoffed.

Aaron tongued his cheek. "Carmona would agree with me. Maybe that's why he's not here right now."

"Carm is dead," Jensen's face had paled, a burden remembered. He paused without breath, pushing the words out of his mouth like he might gag on them. "Riley killed him. Because of me."

"How does that even—"

"They left you on that mountain, we had something to say about it!" Nora snapped.

Somehow, Aaron's frustration only grew. The bodies just kept piling. Because of him. "Maybe next time, keep your heads down and your mouths shut."

"Aaron—" Eden started.

"Shut up. Okay, just shut up!" Aaron's voice echoed over the plains, like the very planet joined him in his objection. "I'm not worth all this! I'm dead, then I'm dead. *Leave* me there! You guys rocked up —I'm not that important, to risk yourselves like that. I am not worth your lives! None of this matters unless you get—out—*alive*! If Carm's dead, that's on him being stupid!"

Nora met his challenge with one of her own. "You haven't seen what we've seen, Aaron! You had your own little spirit walk, and that's fantastic! But we've been knee deep in this for a lot longer than you!"

Her voice scratched as she blinked away the angry tears. "Riley has been draining us dry. Not because he needs us, not because he has to. Because he likes it. He's starving us, hell marching us. He's one minute away from just setting up a battle arena to entertain the mob. He likes playing warlord, he gets off on it."

She paused to pull down air, sniffing away her outburst. "Bray told us there was a chance for peace. And Riley would rather throw us into the grinder for one last gasp of glory than even look a bit closer at it! Carm is dead, Quinn is dead—how many more?! We're supposed to die? To save them?! Those sadistic bastards?!"

Nora clambered to the other side of the cruiser, getting whatever distance from Aaron she could, setting herself down on the far edge to glower from the shadows, let her fire burn out.

Eden spoke up, ever the kind. "We came for you because we were willing to die to know one thing: are you for real?"

Aaron chewed on her words, his head hanging low. It was a long moment before he could bring himself to respond. "You don't even know who I am. I'm nobody."

"You're our friend," Jensen grunted.

"But why?" Aaron asked.

Eden considered him a moment, she hopped off the cruiser, her boots dusting up a small cloud from the cracked ground. Jensen almost dove to catch her, as if she might sink right through and down out of sight. But once Eden was out of reach, no one dared follow.

Eden marched over to Aaron, her heart clearly racing from the many horrible possibilities beneath her. But she marched on anyway, right to Aaron's side.

After a sharp breath, she whispered, "I wasn't going to leave you behind. That's my choice."

Aaron studied her almond eyes for any sign of weakness, any breach in that facade. She did not blink, scanning his face for the rest of the story he had dared not share. The midnight sky painted her eyes a soothing blue, almost pulling a river of tears right out of him, as every last string was cut.

He lowered his head. "I'm not worth..." His voice cracked again, hard, halting his objection.

"Nobody is," she said, "But we *want* to be worth it. Huah?"

Huah.

Aaron swallowed hard, looking up toward the cruiser full of eager soldiers. They waited with bated breath like they were about to hear a prophecy bestowed from a blind desert wanderer. "I don't know if she was telling the truth," he murmured, "I just...know what she said."

Keira shifted her weight on the cruiser, making the whole thing bounce like a rickety old spring. "And we ain't had any attacks on the Wall since your little excursion. So two plus two..."

She was right. The Queen held up her word.

Aaron straightened up. "What's the play?"

Eden hooked his arm and brought him back closer to the cruiser. "Riley's not going to stand down. No way, no how. So we gotta make him."

Aaron nodded along with the thought. "Sure, anybody got one of them wrist phones? We'll give just give him a call."

Bray smiled. "We have a fortress between us and Vanguard. No way through. Entire regiment of soldiers. Howlers, Repeaters, Thumpers...not to mention Riley and his Oskies. And we got the seven of us. Thoughts?"

"Seven people can't take and hold a city," Aaron said, stating the obvious.

"We won't have to," Eden said, gaining confidence. Maybe the fact that no horror had sucked her into the ground yet had tempered her faith. She straightened her shoulders. "Riley has more enemies than just us. The city's been boiling for months. We just gotta turn up the heat."

"Incite open revolt," Aaron murmured, piecing together the implication. "Overthrow the militia and turn the city back over to the people?"

"Is there anybody even left in there?" Jensen asked, hopeful and bright for the first time before human eyes. It was almost unsettling. "Riley has been thorough with his little coup. There may not be any resistance left."

Talania—the governor's daughter, no friend to Riley, and insti-gator extraordinaire. This might just work. After all, she pulled on two bloodthirsty Army Regulars; a little revolution won't douse her fire.

"That still leaves the Wall between us and Vanguard," Solomon cautioned. "S'all bullshit unless we can get through that."

"Maybe your new friends could lend a hand?" Nora grumped from her corner, pointedly. Every right to be.

Whether it was snark or good point, the group murmured their agreement, turning to see what Aaron thought of that theatrical proposal. Perhaps they just wanted to see what minor miracles Aaron had tucked away.

The ability to summon swarms of angry blade-monsters would be a hell of a parlor trick. And it would prove his story twice over.

They were in this mess because of him; it was on him to get them out of it.

Aaron shook his head. "They're kinda banged up and the Wall's been repelling them for years. We need to change up the game. What are they not ready for?"

Jensen started to smile: that big, toothy, stupid smirk. "They built that thing for war." He raised one big eyebrow. "They didn't build it... for industry."

Aaron had a feeling he was going to hate whatever very good idea he had.

CHAPTER
NINETEEN
RILEY

HE NEVER THOUGHT that such an open plaza could give off an echo, but some combination of the steel buildings overhead and the vast open air created a kind of drum for their voices, chants and stomps vibrating the air and feeding upon itself. It made for an eerie atmosphere, like there were thousands more than there actually were.

Riley stood his post, rifle slung and arms at parade. The presence of Oskies amongst the Regular MPs was a show of force, to be sure, but an arm need not be flexed to show its strength. By their mere presence, they could keep the peace in Dodge.

They stood at the edge of a stage, erected by the lovely Talania Dedria so the voiceless could have their precious moment to speak. Little did she know that there was a lot of stupid and entitled in the assemblage of man.

They had their turn as they demanded unicorns from thin air. The crowd that assembled to cheer on the demands grew unruly.

Riley shook his head at them: eating more now meant eating none later, but there was no explaining that to them. They coordinated their noise, chanting as one massive horde at Riley and his peace officers. The handful of Riley's men stood quietly, absorbing the abuse like a harsh rain.

Conservative counts had the protest at over a hundred, at least in the Pro-Starvation side of the aisle. Riley had eight men. If they decided to storm the stage...Riley's implants would cook before he could exhaust their numbers.

Talania stood to one side of the stage, 'in charge' of the event. What lunacy—no one was in charge here. This was a loosely choreographed shitstorm looking for a fan to glide into.

She consulted her papers, eying Riley ever so often—unable to ignore his presence, unable to act like it was normal. She didn't trust him to be harmless.

He should never have come. The people were incensed at the sight of him. It was her dream come true, and his presence had only made it better for her. The author of all their pain had stepped into the streets, just a common man—come tell him how you feel.

Riley quashed his knowing smile. He had made arrangements to counter her, and his team brought the big guns. A projector and a speaker system miraculously appeared when the Pro-Living side of the protest—or as Riley termed them, 'the Pragmatists'—arrived.

They were wrapping up what he could only describe as the most boring and visceral slideshow he'd ever seen.

Some elder Statesman who probably had nascent dreams of being Governor was at the podium, pounding his fist on the veneer. He was a wiry man, hunched. He'd have seemed weird with his no chin, but his jowls—nay, giblets—gave him three chins, like he had a food pouch he stored his day's collection in.

It quivered as he spoke. It was made extra awkward by the giant golden projection of him that lorded over him and aped his movements in unison.

Giant, golden giblets quivering over the crowd.

The unfortunate man pointed at still images of Jergad slaughters, fields of blood from Rimpau and Cassock. These were not creatures that could be trusted and their archon, Aaron, argued for insanity. The Capital's criminal record streamed past the display of gore, and all the while those giant golden giblets shook.

It was not the prescription for calm, but for ridicule.

He was getting to his greatest hits, too. He raised one frail fist. "We will weather this difficult time because we are strong; we are peaceful, and; we are...a family!"

"God," Riley muttered, "are we really?" He glanced over at Holmst, too exhausted to mock further.

Holmst smirked. "I've got a few uncles I wouldn't mind punching."

"I've got Ministry contacts."

"You'd do that for me?"

Riley chuckled. "Do it? Ilern, I can get you art commissioned of the before and after."

Some nearby Regulars had a good laugh, their amusement rippling just under the surface. But Ilern's smile faded a bit.

"I'm kidding," Riley huffed, raising an eyebrow at his aide, "You don't take pictures of the crime."

Giblets stepped down, prompting a minor mixture of applause and less-than-fond farewells. Another Statesman took his spot at the podium, a youthful face chiseled from stone, with perfect hair and perfect teeth.

He was a politician someone grew in a vat, but there was something uncanny about him, in the glassy look to his eyes—like the home-pond was probably in someone's bathroom and had previously housed an illegal vodka still. That plastic veneer looked even worse on the projection, like a featureless golem.

"I call on you, my friends and my countrymen..." he began, his voice exactly what some algorithm said would stir hearts and minds, but ultimately just made everyone cringe. "That's all I can call you, because I can no longer call you patriots."

Ah. Now we were on to the fate-taunting portion of tonight's show.

The crowd's reaction was immediate. Epithets were thrown, cursing, shouts, threats. What was worse...the crowd was at a roiling boil. Any one dramatic pull and the whole horde would follow toward disaster. Any single rogue actor could set it all off.

Yes. Anyone could. This wasn't dangerous; it was an opportunity. "Ilern..."

"Sir, this is a bad idea." His mind had gotten there just as fast. So how bad of an idea was it really?

"It's not an idea; it's an order."

Holmst sighed—awfully theatrical of him—before abandoning his post on the stage. Ilern was a ghost, slipping off his jacket and snagging a cap to cover his head.

Talania saw him go. "Lieutenant!" She called out, but he didn't even break stride. "Lieu-tenant!"

Her calling out to him drew attention, but it was fruitless. The crowd initially parted to avoid the advancing officer, but he seemed to vanish into them, and they just as quickly forgot about him.

Talania scanned the crowd, searching for where he must've gone. Shoving her paperwork off to a random set of hands, she dove in after him. Riley watched as she waded in, half-starting in one direction before darting off in another, trawling an open sea for a single man.

It stirred the blood to watch an Oskie work.

The political Golem was growing more agitated and animated, clearly enjoying whipping the hostile crowd with his controversial statements. He pounded on the podium hard enough to stutter the projection. "Where is your faith, your solidarity!? This Empire that has given you so much—it angers you?"

Riley recognized the tone of this man's diatribe. He wasn't proud of his Empire; he was afraid of it, and what it might do to him if his patriotism wasn't clocked at an 11.

The Golem slicked his hair back in a choreographed display of dismay. "This man—"

Uh oh.

"This man—" Golem pointed right at Riley, standing post a dozen feet from the podium. "This man put himself at incredible risk, and he is the only reason you draw breath today. You'd have your peace, all right—you'd all be dead."

Great, now the epithets were being thrown at *him* now. But Riley could use this...

He caught Ilern's eye in the crowd—and Ilern stared him down. His icy eyes narrowed in a single plea: don't make me do this.

Behind him, Talania picked her way through the crowd. Maybe it was his implant scars, or the pleat of his pants, but she finally identified the back of Ilern's head and lunged for him.

Riley blinked.

And Talania's futile swipe appeared downright lazy in comparison.

Ilern hefted a brick, picking his way around Talania's reaching fingers, and hurled it toward the stage.

Ilern's throw was perfect, the brick coming right for Riley's head. Riley let it sail on in, studied the beveling on it—a concrete chunk, loosened and leavened from the aging streets. It would weigh about four pounds, enough to crush Riley's skull upon direct hit.

He let it graze him. He slid just enough out of the way that it might scrape his forehead.

Had to make it look real. Show them blood and they will boil.

And did they ever. The crowd was immediately in a frenzy and projectiles came hurtling in from everywhere. There was nothing the bureaucrats at the podium could do, no urgings they could give. They had awoken the beast.

Riley slipped back behind the stage, ushered by the waiting staff. He could hear the batons snap out and the crackle of electricity. But the crowd wasn't attacking the stage; they were attacking each other; loyalists versus rebels, locked in a scuffle for 'who' started it.

Dabbing his fingers to his head, he felt the warmth of the blood and the rough bits of stone that had seated in the skin.

Perfect.

———

Riley would've wanted to be present when they pressed those irons onto Talania's wrists and ankles. He would've relished the chance to lord over the hundred meter march to her cell. And the clang of closing steel doors would have been the lullaby that sung him to sleep.

The Regulars responded to the attack by detaining threats—largely at random—and her crowd rallied to respond. The riot was put down and dispersed in under an hour. Seventeen people were injured, including two officers.

Dozens were arrested, Talania included. She was being charged with fomenting rebellion under the 'Fighting Words' statute, assault with a deadly weapon, and—Riley's favorite—treason.

He wanted to see her face when they read her the charges, but he had to have his 'wound' dressed. He had a part to play in this opera. And because of that, he missed a truly glorious moment.

They sent him a video package to commemorate the arrest and her arraignment, but it wasn't the same.

He'd have to pay her a visit. She wouldn't take to the canteen, but maybe a fresh meal and a sip of fine whiskey? Better yet, he could wallpaper her cell with all the fabricated evidence, until even she believed it. She'd testify in open court, swearing to tell the truth about things that couldn't have happened.

He could warm her right up—and tear her down.

One of his assistants announced an unscheduled arrival, a very predictable one. It appears the former Governor had swung by to make a direct appeal. How adorable.

Riley beckoned the broken man across the threshold. If he owned one, the fatuous Christopher Dedria would've been clutching a crumpled cloth cap between his hands, his head bowed as if to offer itself for abuse. He shuffled forward, some combination of deference and age taxing him of his strength. He looked pale, pallid, like a soft sweat brought on by fever.

"She assaulted a peace officer," Riley said without looking up, feigning absorption in more material matters. He had to hide his self-satisfied smirk as he read the witness statements that had been properly massaged for public dispensation.

"So you claim," the Governor snarled.

Riley pointed at his bandage. "I didn't trip getting out of the shower, Chris."

"Were you asleep at the time?"

"Excuse me?"

Christopher ground his jaw. "I seem to remember you types dodging bullets. You missed a rock coming at you?"

Riley lifted his head, trying to avoid gloating. "Implication being...?"

The Governor cleared his throat of phlegm and fear, hoping to cough cowardice back. "I am not here to defend or deny anything, Colonel. I just want you to let her out."

"Finally ready to break a rule?"

"I don't give a hot damn what the official line is, or what really happened. I just want you to let her out."

Riley glanced at the broken man from under raised eyebrows. "That woman has jeopardized the security of this colony and its people. They're hungry, they're tired—and she just riles them up, again and again. And that's ignoring criminal assault! When the crisis is over, I will review her case."

"When could that be?"

Riley shrugged. "Imperial forces have quashed the Outlander resistance, and brought the rebels to heel. After retrofit and dry dock for the transports...we could see reinforcement as early as a year. Possibly longer."

"What happens to us then?" The Governor was panting now, as though he had just sprinted some great distance. Panic had taken hold of him, and he was prying its fingers off of his throat.

Riley pursed his lips. "We may all be dead by then. If I'm being completely honest."

It wasn't a lie. The Jergad forces had never been numbered. And the one location they found may be the first of many such nests throughout the planet's crust. Any bleeding might very well be refreshed in a matter of hours.

Of course, no intelligence supported that theory, but what they had was markedly scarce. Riley found himself engaged in long-term conflict with a question mark, and he refused to underestimate those variables.

In a year's time, he may also face a tribunal over his actions, his defiance. But the people would live to see it.

Christopher finally raised his head, meeting Riley's eyes. His pale gray eyes were striated with red, dried tears staining his cheeks, and his button nose had been rubbed raw. "So...no peace? We're just... going to be under wartime rule...even without wartime conditions?"

There was the rub. The Governor had come under no official capacity, arriving with the proverbial hat in hand to argue in favor of insanity. He wore the banner of Talania's fanatics, towing a line suspended on nothing at all.

Riley didn't miss a beat, his lips tightening down to a line. "Lack of shooting doesn't mean peace. You've lived here even longer than I have. Do you believe for a *second* that it's possible?"

It was rhetorical, and he didn't much like the answer. "I know that she believed it."

"And she'll patiently wait for it. Along with any co-conspirators," Riley countered with a growl.

The Governor's brow furrowed as he considered that. "I was told they were all arrested at the rally."

"Many were," Riley conceded, "but I have repeated reports that the dissent has broad support. And with the day's violence, I have to prepare for similar attacks. Those that may have been...encouraged by her sedition."

"Sedition?" Christopher almost spat the word, "My daughter--"

Riley cut him off. "The Empire just got through with a Civil War. Do you think their response will be lenient, just because our lives here are hard?"

"The people are frightened, that's all," Christopher said, offering up his own hollow theory. "They will grasp at anything they think might stop their pains."

Riley couldn't contain his scoff, but Christopher continued, "It's been hard on them, Colonel. They're tired and afraid. They need a warm hand, not more judgment."

"Christopher..." Riley cautioned, "Your daughter is a malcontent and a traitor. These are facts, not open to interpretation. She *assaulted* me." He let that sink in before softening. "She will await judgment, and due process demands a nonpartisan arbiter. Since I cannot provide one—given that I'm literally a victim—she will await a proper hearing. That is what's fair."

Take it and leave, Riley begged from behind a clamped jaw.

Riley had broad and sweeping authority in a war-time battlefield. Her agitation had clearly defined punishments under Imperial code. A lengthy stay at their local Bastille was generous, even magnanimous. Minister Caldwell would've devised a painful and theatrical rebuke to be performed in the town square for a maximum audience.

Riley had simply defanged the viper. Riley didn't want to do anything more. Unless he had to.

A small part of him wanted the Governor to tease that line.

The Governor worked his jaw, considering the consequences of the words tossing in his head. He debated the consequences, making a measured risk assessment. Each further challenge brought with it requisite uncertainty. His life might be easier and more comfortable if he simply bowed his head without further protestation.

Riley might respect the casual question from a civilian, clarification absent imposition or insinuation. Talania had been an egregious offender in this manner. She didn't conjure that behavior from thin air.

Christopher opened his mouth. "She is a patriot. And begging your pardon, Colonel..." And what if Riley didn't give it? "What if you're wrong?"

The people need certainty. The people need certainty. The words positively bellowed in Riley's ears.

Riley closed his eyes, letting out an exasperated sigh. "I take it you intend to order her release?" Riley asked, refusing to bring his stare on to the human mistake standing in his office.

Christopher mustered his courage before whispering the words. "You *are* wrong, Marcus. You just...are."

Oh, Christopher.

Riley pushed himself away from his desk, rolling his shoulders as he stood up. Even at his stature, he still towered over the curled frame of the Governor. "Should've just made a public statement, Governor," Riley seethed, "I wouldn't have been able to stop the flood of public demand. But now..."

The Governor presented his wrists, ready for shackles, with a flicker to his eye as fear and courage fought it out. Perhaps he thought he'd get to be in his daughter's cell, wait out the disaster while maintaining their high-minded consciences. They'd get a room with a meager view, access to the digital libraries, and receive fan mail about their resistance to the big bad security man.

Riley looked down at the fat hands hanging in the air before him, skin spotted and hanging off of sausage links that had no obvious joints. "Dammit, Chris. I'm not the office you surrender yourself to. People didn't come into your office to turn themselves in."

The Governor wavered for a moment, his hands shaking before he lowered them back to his sides.

Riley shook his head. "You've done nothing wrong. What in God's name would I throw you in prison for? Speaking your mind? No, Christopher. No, you're going to walk these city streets a free man. Hold your head high. Because the Wall is high, our people are strong, and there is no storm we shall not weather together—despite our differences."

"Because 'we're family?'" The Governor scoffed.

"Not the way I'd have said it, but sure."

Riley clapped the man on the shoulder like they were old friends. He felt the bovine man's skin crinkle under his fingers, like a younger man who had suffered a particularly crispy sunburn. The last few months had taken a toll on him beyond his years, sapping him of a vitality he had little of.

He guided Christopher towards the door the way he might carry a trash bin to the street. "Take a few days, Governor, and think about all the lives we've saved. Then give my office a call, we can set about putting together a public statement."

"Alright..." Christopher exhaled the words like he was shuffling off to walk his last mile.

His days of relevance had long since passed; how much further could that useless morass stumble till there was no reason to keep going. He was waking and eating and speaking more out of habit these days than anything else.

Once the Governor was good and gone, Riley summoned Holmst into the office. He closed the door behind his aide, something that sent Holmst's eyebrows up. "What's the thinking, Colonel?"

"Is there a use to Christopher Dedria?"

The Lieutenant tried to hide his eyes widening and his jaw tightening by shifting his stance.

"You disapprove?"

Holmst stiffened back up. "Yes, sir. He's a bureaucrat, but he knows the Tower. Yeah, he was never one for leadership. More of a functionary."

"But when does his pain outweigh his function?" Riley asked.

"I don't see a day that happens, sir." Holmst hedged his bets.

"Hypothetically," Riley pursued this, "Let's say he starts to make a measurable amount of noise. What's our play?"

Holmst shifted again, uncomfortable with the entire line of questioning. "Sir, you'd be putting two hundred soldiers in the position of martial law, escalating the security responsibilities of an already understaffed garrison."

"The practicalities aren't at issue, Lieutenant. Pure hypothetical. Academic exercise."

Holmst's eyes darkened, knowing then that this was no exercise. "In any case, you would need to show probable cause he was an immediate and present threat to the colony. There'd be unrest, so we'd need to make our case three times over. We'd have to be able to convict him of crimes unbecoming—absolutely kill him in the court of public opinion—before we even approached a judge. And do so with such certainty that no one could do anything but agree. In short? He'd have to have a bomb strapped to his chest railing about the End Times."

Riley pursed his lips, like he was savoring the taste of that notion. "We could arrange that."

IT STARED BACK at them from horizon to horizon, a flickering fortress peeking out over the glassy mirage of the savannah.

Gun towers stood a good twenty feet taller than the palisade, marking the kilometers up and down its length with enormous automated repeaters at their masts. Driven by a targeting algorithm and two technicians, the ninety-two millimeter gaussian rifles threw canisters packed with superheated copper.

The molten slugs hit with enough kinetic energy to flip a tank. If the impact didn't kill the target, the heated copper would melt through any armor.

Aaron had only heard their chugging sounds once before, pattering away at a Jergad horde with the metronomic rhythm of a hammer to a nail, pounding with all the persistence of a forced morning march. And it had been just as effective, tearing apart the impressive alien beasties like they were but children's toys.

For their plan to work, they had to breach all three levels of defenses. And they needed an answer to those towers. Aaron had a theory, but it would require some help.

He felt her presence that night, as though he had never left that mesa in the mountains. Those blue eyes looked upon him from some distant peak, making the back of his neck itch.

The Queen had no understanding of technology and had never considered the possibility of sabotage, let alone that she was the sole being alive that might succeed at such an attempt. She withered a bit at the senseless loss of her people's lives, that this tactic had ever been an option and she had been helplessly blind.

But that soon faded at the prospect of defeating the purveyor of that violence. It was chilling to see.

She would await his call.

How would he signal her, he asked? She made some vague assurances. She would do her part when it was time.

Jensen and Nora that morning returned with the requisite vehicles they would need. And Aaron was almost happy to see the HML 68 Mining Drone. The titan had been scrapped and left to rot in the years before the Wall's construction.

Now, it was going to ring the doorbell.

Flanked by two land cruisers, they advanced toward the barricades with cautious haste, at a positively hair-raising speed of twenty kilometers an hour. At this rate, they'd be at the Wall next week and the garrison would have time to host a cookout or two.

There certainly was activity at the Wall, as the three-story vehicle lumbered towards their fortifications, a steampunk skeletal land-whale made of rebar and nightmares, with its drill tip hanging low like an elephant's trunk.

There had to be a mixture of feelings up there, confusion as well as genuine concern. The Miner could absolutely breach the Wall—but why was it out there and who brought it to heel? What were standing orders around autonomous civilian vehicles assaulting military installations?

Of course, the rig would never get there. The first line of defense blocked the way.

And here is where stage one of the plan went into effect.

Bray had asked for some rather suicidal volunteers—his own

words—to run a 'wild weasel.' Aaron had no idea what that meant, and Bray was too nervous about his own idea to explain in any depth. Suffice it to say, Bray wanted to stick his head in the lion's mouth and make it bite on a less interesting target.

Solomon and Keira salivated at the chance to taunt fate. They were always exponentially more frightening when paired together.

Jensen sat atop the rig, a Gearmaster astride his mechanical mammoth. The loose control system he had rigged up gave him the most basic control of the Miner's functions, but Aaron would have to operate the drill from below. And this left Jensen exposed, with a single steel plate as his only cover.

Aaron wasn't much better off, with no hull or bulkheads shielding the beast's interior. Any shrapnel or ricochets were going to be just as deadly as a direct hit. He was in a lethal pinball machine.

Aaron checked the chamber on his rifle, the action slick with freshly brushed lubricant.

What if they shot at him, the people on the Wall? Of course they would, with that cattle prod at their backs. He probably would in their shoes. But could he, without Imperial threats and hate biting at his neck?

Could he kill someone who just wants to go home?

He'll do what he had to and do the calculus later. Killing wasn't his job today, nestled in a spot where gnashing gears and levers would aggressively press him into a mealy dough.

Killing was just a hazard of his career.

Now the Wall was in a flurry. The distant klaxon could be heard sounding the call to arms. Aaron was a gear rat in the Pits and he was a rat now—he had to worm his way into a damaged beast and repair battle damage.

The trick would be doing it all without stopping the rig. No matter what happened, the rig could not stop.

Momentum was their ally.

Aaron leaned out of his seat, his shaved head poking out of the side of the rig's right flank. From his position on the mining rig, Aaron could see Bray's cruiser peel out of formation and streak ahead, loaded down with the psychopathic couplet.

They were going to die in a gloriously stupid fireball, or this was going to be a helluva light show to kick off the party.

Any attack on the Wall had to first confront several arrays of landmines. After the Thumpers forced the Jergad to the surface, there were shaped charges triggered by the watch commander. They thinned out the horde, often separating them into small platoons that the Repeater towers could decimate.

Those same mines would cripple the exposed treads of the mining rig, and might just send shrapnel up through to the very help- less Aaron and Jensen. They had to be dealt with first.

Keira and Solomon hucked a steel rake off the back of the cruiser. The sudden drag nearly tossed their vehicle end over end, like they were trying to do a backflip and the dust cloud it kicked up was easily four times the height of the cruiser.

And the rake was indeed sweeping up the mines—two meter wide bricks of steel and industrial hate press-formed into murder boxes. They tossed those charges into the air like the most terrifying confetti. There must've been hundreds of the things, ready to shred an encroaching horde.

The commanders must've sorted out their priorities. If the sweeper paved a road, the rig would advance unmolested right up to the Wall. Someone somewhere hit the button.

It was like a patriotic display from the West side of Hell.

Explosions lit up the air, masking the cruiser from view, but the continued explosions implied their work continued. Some from the ground, tossing dirt and metal in theatrical outbursts, while others still detonated in futile displays in the air, throwing their payload in random directions.

The explosions finally stopped. The cloud of dirt and smoke hung in the air like a veil.

And that cruiser shot back out of the smoke, a bit more ragged for its journey, humming along with the occasional cough and sputter.

Coated in soot and a bit of blood, Bray stood high like he was a force of nature. Keira cackled from her perch on the rear, an immortal Greco-Roman legend waiting for her place in the stars. And Solomon looked positively nonplussed; Aaron was convinced that Solomon had been dead at least once before as a purely recreational activity. There was nothing for him to fear but familiar roads.

Those three could probably drive a hammer straight through the Gates of St. Peter, and escape naked, coated from head to toe in the blood of their enemies.

Jensen hooted and hollered from above. "You like that?! Well, let's kick it up a notch!"

And with that, Jensen threw the rig into a lower gear. The giant mammoth cut loose a bestial roar, some blend of anger and anticipation. It pressed Aaron into his seat and sped forward toward the Wall. The tread tossed the hardened dirt like it was simply packed snow, leaving a trail that even a dead man could follow.

They were in range now. Those Repeater towers turned to bear down on the rig. All Aaron could remember was the slurry of meat and blood those guns had left their subjects in.

These Repeaters were pre-packaged flak cannons hot from a shipyard and refit for ground-based anti-material work. A single canister would impact the outer hull, and superheated copper would spray through the interior—killing drivers, maiming machinery, and igniting munitions in a hostile carrier.

The miner was not nearly so sturdy. In terms of effectiveness, they were duck-hunting with a bazooka.

Now or never, bug lady.

Aaron closed his eyes, and behind his lids, he found that piercing blue gaze. It called to mind the idea of changing the channel, away from the battlefield and to this strange communication. He didn't say anything, and neither did she. But he felt her influence. It hurt, at first. Like a headache that thrummed behind the eyes and at the bridge of the nose. If all the theories were correct, the Queen could bend the magnetic field of a planet enough to communicate.

And enough to flummox a targeting computer.

The first shot came.

Aaron saw the muzzle flash from the distant barrel a millisecond after he heard the 92mm canister howl past him. It whistled close enough for him to see the burning sulfur endcap tracing its white line across the sky onward to land harmlessly in the dirt almost half a mile behind them. It felt like an eternity before the second one came, zipping past the enormous rig, missing by a good dozen feet.

The rig was no small target. These turrets were, quite literally, missing the broad side of a barn.

It almost felt like the shots were bending courteously out of the way. Shot after shot sailed in, four or five per second, and all of them wildly off center.

"Alright, everybody, welcome to the Devil's Circus!" Jensen crowed over the radio. "Bray's car to the left, Eden on the right. Watch the rampart for snipers. Aaron, prime that drill. We're going in dry!"

Gross, man.

Aaron slung his rifle and began to worm his way forward. The engineers that built the rig did not plan for a human to be wriggling through the innards while it was active, but there was a designed pathway for technicians to go station to station, and Aaron was a small man.

Pistons mashed and gears ground all around him as he picked his moments to squeeze through gaps and passed swinging pendulums like the most spiteful obstacle course.

He couldn't see outside anymore, but he could hear the gunshots over the groaning joints, and the obstinate echoes of the Repeaters heralded doom with every drumbeat, coupled with the yawning whistle of the incoming and outgoing. Louder cracks of gunfire circled the rig, as Jensen and the others traded volleys with the garrison.

His radio chattered with ambient chaos: "High left, tap tap!" "I see him!" "Eden, don't get so close!" "Loading!" "Rampart, right. They're bringing up rockets!"

He found daylight again at the maw of the beast, the tilted bit exposed to the world. Aaron perched across the drill's shank, careful not to rest any of his weight on the three-foot-wide neck.

The bit itself was nearly ten feet across, all metal teeth and circular jaw, like an enormous steel wyrm that fed on anything in its path. He could stand upright in the space, with every moving part twice his size and ten times his weight.

Taming a dragon.

Sparks shot off the bit, coupled with the rings and gongs of ricocheting metal. Had something broken? No, someone was shooting at him.

Aaron tucked himself back for a moment, out of sight, before leaning forward with rifle shouldered. He craned his neck looking for the source.

The face said young, angry, even thrilled. The uniform said Capital. The gun said hostile.

Shoot him, Aaron. Do it.

He thinks killing means his freedom. He has no idea they're lying to him, and that freedom can't be bought, no matter how much blood he brings them.

His life is not up for sale.

Aaron pulled the trigger, the shot skipping off to the side and lodging in the concrete. The offending Capital ducked for cover, out and away.

The frenzy and excitement of battle blinded the Capital. He had no idea that Aaron had simply missed. Aaron breathed a sigh of relief, shaking out the tension in his everything.

"Heavy ordinance!" Bray shouted over the comms. "Drop that son of a bitch! Now!"

Jensen could only get a few words out. "Fire in the hole!"

They were mere feet from the Wall when the explosion hit, flames licking the rig's innards for half a second before the shockwave snuffed them out. Skipping metal and screaming gears burned Aaron's ears.

He felt the shard of metal knick his arm. The mild and brief gong of warping metal was his only confirmation he hadn't imagined it, although the trickling of warm moisture down his cheek was a more morbid corroboration. He rubbed his cheek: just oil spatter.

"Aaron!" Jensen called out, "You alright down there?"

"Yeah!" Aaron called out, "Rang my bell though!"

"My girl's whining. Sounds like the drive shaft!"

Aaron couldn't leave his post on the drill bit. He spun about, looking back at the mewling beast behind him.

A great deal of cosmetic damage—along with two gear systems completely shattered, but the worst of it was the motivator: the rotating piston arms were on an irregular rhythm, biting on the downstroke and loose on the upstroke. The bearings were loose on the floor, having been blown free of their casing.

The engine would eventually work itself to death, and then the rig would be a very impressive paperweight.

But the drill would still work.

"She's DOA, Jensen! Who knows how much time she's got in her."

"Like we weren't fully committed already!" Jensen shot back. "Dropping the hammer!"

With the minefield behind them and the Repeaters off-target, there was the third and final obstacle, the most literal of them.

The Wall itself was six feet of solid concrete, reinforced with rebar, and encased in half-inch steel plating. The Jergad had only made it this far a handful of times, and powerful conductors cooked any beasties that had managed to try and climb that steel barricade.

The drill would run electricity just as well, so that steel casing had to be cut free.

Aaron slipped a pair of goggles over his eyes, lest he blind himself with this task.

"Let's go, Aaron! Now or never!" Jensen was right. If the rig froze up on them, they'd never get going. The rig wasn't driving out of this firestorm; may as well get digging.

No mining rig in the universe cut its own hole. Three industrial-strength lasers were mounted on a reciprocating ring around the drill bit. Their range was minimal, but they could prime a cut through any surface known to humanity—they had been used on everything from diamond mines to the sides of comets.

Commanded from Aaron's seat, the ring lit up and started quivering. Aaron was a scant dozen feet from the Wall's exterior shell, watching as the three beams danced around a perfect circle, each laser cutting a third. They danced back and forth several times a second, boring through the third line of defense.

It was only time now. Could they hold the rig?

It was then Aaron realized, he couldn't hear the Repeater fire anymore.

"We're rounding third base!" Jensen called out. "Tell me you got that rocket-boy!"

"He's down," Nora crackled through the radio, "but I've got activity at the Eastern Repeater."

"They're taking it manual," Bray guessed. "You gotta start drilling now."

"We're working just as fast as we can! Ya can't rush these things!" Jensen objected, almost like an egotistical artist, but Aaron knew he was right. If they tried to drill before the shell was broken, the current would cook the computers and most likely kill all passengers.

They had to have a clear channel to dig into first.

Bray was less convinced. "You are out of time! They will sight you in! Let 'er rip!"

"Two more minutes! That's all I need! Give me two more minutes!"

Aaron watched as the metal glowed red, then to a blazing yellow. Sparks of molten slag spat off of the Wall as moisture boiled and burst, chunking chips of fire off of the block. Larger bits simply sloughed off, dripping to the ground far below.

The distant cacophony of gunfire and shouting and other bloody operas all paled against this simple quiet tableau, hissing metal and primary colors.

The howl of a Repeater round broke Aaron's reverie. That was close. Far too close.

By going manual, they had cut the computers—and the Queen's interference—out of the equation. It was a cumbersome method requiring the Repeater to halt all fire while they cranked the individual gears and locked it into its new place.

He would hear the ones that missed, followed by protracted silences as the turrets realigned. The shot that killed him would not so courteously announce its coming.

Finally, the half inch steel disc fell free, revealing the mottled concrete surface behind.

"Down and clear!" Aaron shouted.

"Follow the yellow brick road!" Jensen cheered.

The drill roared to life, the ancient dragon shaking off a years-long slumber. It whirled at first, stuttering, before spinning into a feeding frenzy, its teeth hungry for fresh stone.

It lurched forward, an impatience to its lunge, teased and withheld for too long.

Aaron waited with bated breath as the head lowered into the porous stone surface. This was either going to work, or their plan died right here.

It was harder to tell which protested louder: the Wall or the drill. It pulled the cement into its teeth like the Wall was made of plaster.

However, the drill was used to soft clay and sandstone, not reinforced cement. If they plied too much torque rushing it, they were liable to bind the bit on the rebar and debris. They had to push with just the right touch.

Aaron tried to shovel the crumbling bits out of the hole and away from the drill—his hands a scant few feet away from the gnashing monster. Aaron could only pray that the rig didn't snap a rod. They wouldn't be able to back the drill out, let alone have the time for it.

"Jensen, Aaron! Time for school!" Nora gave the order.

They were out of time. "Ten more seconds!"

Aaron watched the drill bit sink into the Wall, finally burying its pipe out of sight. They were nowhere near through.

"No more time! Get out of there!"

The drill whined, like a kicked dog. A bit of chunked rebar had caught in a flute, halting the spin. Ignorant of the blockage, the rig's computer pushed and pushed. If that shard wasn't removed, it would snap the drill rod in two and their plan would die with it.

Aaron glanced up at the shooters on the Wall. Everyone was looking out and away. It was a four-foot jump across the expanse into the breach.

He dropped his rifle and jumped into the hole.

"Aaron?!" Eden screamed, more surprise than concern.

He grabbed the offending rebar, trying to tug it out of the flute. It was hot, scorched by the midday sun and the friction of the cutting. And it was stubborn, locked into place by the pressure of the pushing drill.

Gunfire whistled past, shots dancing off the drill pipe. The garrison was trying to snap the pipe. Aaron could see Eden's car drift close, with Nora leaning off the tail.

At the peak of the arc, Nora was stationary—a perfect firing platform. She snapped two shots just before the cruiser zipped away again. The gunshots ceased, paired with a pained cry as someone fell from the Wall's deadly heights.

Aaron wrapped his hand around the pipe, his knuckles bare against the drill bit. This had all the ingredients for him to lose a hand.

And the rebar came free.

Like a monster uncaged, the drill roared to life again, hurling debris with renewed vigor. Ungrateful at his help or his presence, it tossed a chunk of concrete directly into his head.

Aaron keeled over to the ground. The reverberating pain filled his head with fog, his eyes unwilling to focus on any one thing for longer than a second.

He was sure he'd cracked his skull right open, and if he didn't push hard with both hands, it would uncork its load onto the ground like the most demented champagne.

Nope, just felt like it.

With a steel buzzsaw at his back, Aaron had no room to get a run-up. He was going to have to free jump back to the rig. Every moment he lingered risked something juicy and ugly.

He squatted low and frog-jumped the gap.

Not even close.

He landed chest first into the lip of the rig's drill bay, knocking the wind out of him like he'd been hit by a car. Shocked, stunned, out of breath, and bleeding, he promptly slipped to his fingertips.

"Aaron—goddammit!" Bray cut his own objection short. "Suppression fire, now!"

A shot snapped into ledge right between his hands, chunks of metal skipping against his hands and face. A few inches had been the difference between a shrapnel exfoliation and having no head.

His sweaty fingers slid along the edge, the metal lip biting into his hand. Nothing to kick against. There was no way he was going to pull himself up.

Far to his left, the Repeater tower had just finished anchoring itself to a new position. It would fire on him any second and take the rig out in a cataclysm of fire and molten metal.

It was an ugly twenty-foot drop to the ground, where he would most certainly be crushed by the collapsing rig.

But five feet down was a tear in the hull—where the first rocket had struck. It would lead to the rig's transmission assembly.

He would never dare crawl through it while the rig was active—but this lawn ornament was never moving again. And he was out of options.

Aaron let go, tucking his legs forward to snag the jagged lip, catching it like a kid on a slide. He slipped down into the inner entrails of the rig, banging off of gears and pipes as he went.

There was precious little room, not even enough for him to crouch, as he wormed through legs first. He scooted along, bracing himself on support beams and dormant gear systems, wriggling through whatever cavities were open to him.

That's when the first round hit, a deafening gong that robbed him of his hearing, but he could see the darts of fire and light slash through the rig above him like the spears of an angry God. Tiny beams of hot metal sprayed through, pinned open by rays of sunlight that now had entry into the bowels.

His hearing properly blown, he didn't hear the next shot, but the rig shook and whole bulkheads buckled with each successive hit. Sparks and hot metal rained around him, singing his clothes and scalding his skin.

He laid back against a steel pipe, his arms slick with oil and sweat. He would be crushed by the collapsing rig, shot through with molten copper, or cooked alive by the fire.

Beneath him was a curious sight—dirt. The rig was missing its underbelly plating.

Aaron rolled off the pipe and dropped to the ground. It was only a five-foot fall, but it was still like a swift kick to the gut, someone planting a foot into his abdomen and snapping all of the air out of his lungs.

The rhythmic chugging of the Repeaters continued, pounding liquid drives into the side of the rig. And Aaron could feel the metal beast start to groan, no longer able to support its own weight.

It swelled for the briefest of moments, like a collapsing star, all the repeated explosions pushing outward on the hull. Then it collapsed on itself, giving out one last gasp and crumpling to the ground.

No time to breathe or wipe the sweat from his forehead. Aaron rolled out from under the collapsing whale, scrambling to his feet.

Metal shards rained down around him, threatening to crush and spear in equal measure.

Perhaps it was luck, or maybe the Queen's strange power had some hand in it, but nothing struck home. What rained around outside of the rig was minimal, the steel beast preferring instead to sink down onto itself. This titan of industry simply deflated to sag in the dirt.

Cheering erupted from the fortifications above, the attackers plan thwarted. Celebrating too soon.

Because as Aaron peered through the dusty fog, the first thing he saw was the gaping hole in the fortifications, six feet across in a perfect circle—the drill had done its work.

The second thing he saw was a cruiser zipping in close, low and slow. Aaron could swear he heard the individual pulses of the laboring Maglev engine.

A single arm stretched out from the side, reaching for him. He grabbed it. The vehicle slowed just long enough for them to swing him aboard before tearing off through the cloud.

Eden sat behind the controls, her hands dancing across the dueling consoles, leaning over to tab a co-pilot's controls, before snapping back to adjust on her own. She was hard at work but hardly strained.

Nora gripped her throat mic. "We got him!"

"You're a psychopath, Aaron! A beautiful, beautiful psychopath!" Jensen shouted.

Aaron melted backwards into Nora, finally allowing himself to breathe easy but unable to tear his eyes off of Eden's impressive display at the controls of two different seats. "You used to play piano, didn't you?"

Eden smirked, almost charmed by the cognitive dissonance it took to make that connection. "Nora, concussion protocol."

That wasn't a no. Nora flashed her tac light across Aaron's eyes, before giving a casual thumbs up. It wasn't until she poked at his new head wounds, dipping her fingers in the drying patches of blood, that the examination hurt.

"You're leaking, bud."

"Yeah, I'm used to it at this point," he huffed back at her.

She pursed her lips with a tilt of her head, agreeing with the diagnosis and absent a pithy comeback of her own. "He's not dying."

"Keep him that way!" Eden snapped, as she spun her hand across the display.

The cruiser spun to, bringing its nose to bear on the collapsed rig —and the exposed hole in the Wall. "Triggers light!" Bray crackled through the radio, "Conserve your ammo!"

Nora handed Aaron a rifle—Eden's. It had been caked with dirt from a dozen other missions, spackled with old alien blood, and the polymer stock bore a carving of a square cross, itself collecting dirt in its grooves.

She tapped him on the shoulder, bringing herself close to his ear. "Full mag, no regrets."

Huah.

She slipped out from under him, head low to avoid the wind shear, as she settled up in the co-pilot seat. She shouldered her rifle, tracking for targets to pop into view, like the most demented carnival shooting gallery. Aaron's head lolled over, as he let himself catch his breath.

The second cruiser came up into formation beside them. Keira was bent over Solomon, tending to some unseen injury, while Bray and Jensen sat in the front. Jensen gave a short wave, greeting his friend in a lunatic contrast of battle damage and neighborly intentions.

Aaron waved back, urging his friends to take the lead position. Bray nodded and throttled up. The cruiser was perforated from its previous minesweeping run, but it still had enough heart for one more push.

The Wall was in full panic mode. A team desperately tried to rotate the Repeater towers to bear on the much smaller targets, perhaps hoping to cut them off with a fusillade of artillery they wouldn't dare cross.

The rest of the garrison took up their arms and drew down on the encroaching vehicles. They were the last line of defense. There had to be less than a dozen of them.

A Regular ran up and down the line, screaming epithets at his Capital regiment, waving a sidearm in their faces. He had all the inspirational vigor of an angry banshee. He seemed to give orders via gun barrel, waving it around like it was a magic wand or an extension of his anatomy. He either didn't know or didn't care about its deadly capability, as he pressed it to a Capital's head, shouting the call to arms.

One poor Capital froze, panicked and afraid of his entire environment. The Regular pushed the gun barrel into the boy's temple, screaming and spitting.

Nora shot first, splitting that officer's cap at a hundred yards with a thirty caliber round off of a moving vehicle going nearly a hundred kilometers an hour.

Aaron would've showered her with praise if the look of shock on her face hadn't betrayed how much that was not on purpose.

It was like she had uncorked a vintage bottle of compressed violence. Gunfire came raining in, skipping off the cruiser's hull and dancing along the dirt.

Aaron might've sworn they were trying to miss, shooting just close enough to say that they tried. Yes, these were small and fast targets, but they were on a clear predictable path with minimal ability to evade.

They were better shots than this.

Bray's cruiser hit the rig's body, using it was an impromptu ramp. The maglev transmission easily picked up the hard surface and climbed up toward the gap in the Wall.

And sailed through.

Eden pressed her left hand forward, throttling up for their own approach.

And that's when the Repeaters kicked in, spitting lances of fire across their path. They had effectively dropped a high explosive lattice over their gateway. The rate of fire made for an imperfect blockade but it was better than nothing at all.

Any attempt to cross would contend with the split second gamble of catching a 92mm canister to the chest.

But their aim was off, manually dialed in. It was a little high.

"Go low!" Aaron shouted.

"What?!" Eden had clear objections to this plan, but Nora simply smiled, her mind having followed the design just fine.

Aaron shouldered the rifle, popping off a few rounds at the Wall's palisade. "Can't stay here!"

After a moment's consideration, Eden re-centered the cruiser on the drill site and its new fiery gates. The plan wasn't wholly insane, as the Repeaters had set this up with some—albeit inspired—improvisation. There was a distinct pattern, that if timed just right, an interloper might dance between the shots.

Aaron scrunched low in his seat, as if ducking might protect him from the ordinance being lobbed into his path.

The side panels on the cruiser were half inch alloy, designed to be lightweight. He could peer out two sizable pinholes cut by the small arms fire levied from the Wall.

If a Repeater connected, the cruiser would become something only suggested by the most outlandish historians to have once been a vehicle. Most people will assume it was some kind of food storage container split open by its rotting contents in a hot summer sun.

Eden ramped up the miner's corpse, destined to either crash into the Wall or leap through the piercing gaze of Ares himself. Even the shooters on the Wall paused in disbelief, as they elected to rush the furnace of exploding fire.

Maybe they were holding out hope for a climax to the fireworks and held any shots that might rob them of the catharsis.

They were denied, for the Gods were pleased.

Eden took a low road, bouncing off of some crumpling rig debris.

The cruiser slid through the lower edge of the drill site, passing below the shots like they were riding under two crossed sabers. And if Aaron had been sitting up, he'd have caught a canister to the side of his head. It would've been a rather climactic way to complete the set of injuries for the day.

There was the smallest moment of hanging in the open air, where the car hung in the open that he could see the severed drill bit lying on the ground a dozen feet below. He wanted to prop the damn thing up like a flag.

And then the floor of the cruiser slammed up. His backache notwithstanding, they were through the Wall—and no defenses between them and Vanguard proper.

The cruisers formed up, kicking up dueling dust trails on their way to the glinting city towers on the horizon.

"Do you have any idea..." Jensen began, pausing for dramatic emphasis, "How absolutely *badass* that looked?"

"Oh yeah? Really?" Eden asked, her adrenaline building to pique and then her cup spilled over. "*Then you do it!* Do you have any idea how dead we should be?!"

Aaron didn't hear it coming, but he could see it hovering on the horizon. He pointed toward the silent phantom that made Eden's statement ironic. "'Bout that much dead?"

Everyone craned their necks to see the Howler on rapid approach.

Of course, they would scramble air support, wouldn't they?

"Somebody got a grenade launcher I don't know about?" Keira asked, more eager expectation than an actual question. She just wanted to notch her bedpost with a beast like that. It was like a big game hunter seeing a predator with blood in its eyes, and despite the tilted odds, they were still excited at the confrontation.

Trust Bray to keep them grounded. "We can't, we gotta lose it. We split up. There's only one o' him."

Eden scanned the pancake flat terrain of the Colonial Ranges. Plainlands far as the eye could see. "Lose it where?!"

"Bray, we split up and we're just rolling dice on which car it chooses to kill!" Jensen's objections weren't unfounded.

Without a way to cook the Howler, it would drop both cruisers with ease.

If the cruisers limped under ballistic fire, they would fold like paper against the Howler's arsenal. They were suborbital vehicles with proper EM shielding. Nobody had any heavy ordinance. And there wasn't enough ammo to waste peppering at the damn thing.

"We stay together, it kills us both and the mission dies with us. If you got a better plan, I'm all ears!"

Aaron sat up. "He's right. Heads down and pedal to the floor. Huah?"

He said more in that articulate grunt than he had meant to. It was all at once, a fond goodbye and a gracious thank you and a solemn apology and a gritty war cry.

People were going to die in the next few minutes.

Jensen pointed at him from the other cruiser. "I'll see you in Vanguard."

And with that, Eden and Bray banked the Cruisers apart. Both were battle damaged, with cosmetic holes and scrapes, but Bray's limped along with a chugging Maglev that had been excoriated by the claymore field. It trailed wisps of smoke from a leaking battery cell.

Nora pulled her last magazine from her vest, swiping bullets out of a half-spent magazine with her other hand. She was taking the moment to consolidate her last few rounds. "I don't know about you, Aaron, but I think we can take it down."

"Really?"

"Yeah," she said with almost confidence. "We both aim for the left engine, we might not kill it, but we can ground it."

That wasn't a half bad plan, but it was half baked. The idea that their rifles could damage the Howlers was more than far fetched. If they had something with a bit more punch, they might be able to wrench it out of the sky, but that was a tactical dropship meant for a theater of war—it was built to take fire. Attacking that ship would be an honorable and hilarious way to provoke a door-mounted plasma launcher to cook them alive.

Still better than being chased down like a rabbit in a field trying to outmaneuver the bird of prey lowering its talons into the grass.

As silent as an owl swooping past, the Howler turned to hunt its prey—it chose Bray and his crippled cruiser.

"We're just going to watch?" Eden demanded, furious and frightened all at once.

Nora gripped her friend's shoulder. "I wasn't planning on it, really."

Eden nodded with that, accepting the cruel reality of it. It was always a long shot, the seven of them against an army. They knew people were going to die, but it must be hard for the doctor to stand idle while it happened. It went against her blood. So she looked at the path ahead, the great circle they cut across the grass toward Vanguard.

They'd be long gone when the Howler turned back.

Eden and Nora might have been able to, but Aaron couldn't tear his eyes away. The Howler descended on Bray's cruiser and with a short burst of light, a fiery plume went up. The Howler paused over the cloud, a lion looming over its kill.

All Aaron could see was Quinn's face, a scared little boy being pulled into the abyss. It had been his purpose.

They were all picked for their ability to die in place of others, variables in a cruel calculus that accommodated for losses, and commanders that exchanged one kind of person for another. Numbers on a board.

Capitals could die—they were Capital criminals, after all. They could die without anyone's guilt.

The Howler dropped its ropes, lowering men to the ground.

And Aaron's eyes lit up. "Turn around."

"Say what now?" Nora blurted, more surprise than anything else. She had just finished pulling Eden out of this depressing boat, now she had to collect him too?

"I know how to do it. Turn us around."

Eden didn't need to hear another word. She spun the cruiser around, drifting along the dirt before flooring it directly at the silent dragon.

If he was wrong, they were all about to die. Trying to save his friends seemed like a good way to do it.

They bore down on the unsuspecting Imperial Howler—why would it prepare for an attack? The last known target was actively fleeing, and hardly a threat anyway. They would hunt it in due time. They had no reason to fear the vermin.

But they had made a crucial mistake.

"Talk to me," Nora demanded, with just a touch of eagerness.

She thought this possible, just because he did. And why not? They had thumbed their noses at fate all morning. What's one more time?

Aaron smirked, matching her spirit. "You said it yourself. We don't need to kill it. We just need to ground it."

Nora's eyes lit up. She immediately dug for their cruiser's minesweeping rake and set about turning it face up.

"This is gonna wreck the cruiser, y'know!" Eden cautioned, but she didn't ease off.

"I'm not worried about resale. Are you?" She shook her head, adrenaline trumping the abject terror in her eyes.

All the Howler had to do was notice their approach, spin about and glass their little petulant charge into glowing slag. This entire affair depended on their arrogance.

Nora locked the rake into place, tapping Aaron's shoulder. "Are we holding on or jumping off?"

Aaron looked at the blurry ground whipping past. "I really don't know which would be better, honestly."

"Ride it out? Let's ride it out." There was no convincing her otherwise. Aaron and Eden exchanged looks, a silent suicide pact. This was going to suck.

It was a haunting few seconds of roaring maglev before the

Howler team noticed them, far too late. They tried to pivot the door gunner to face the new threat. They tried to retract their cables.

They didn't have the time.

The cruiser zipped under the Howler at a hundred kilometers an hour and the minesweeper snagged two of the cables. The sudden force nearly wrenched the back half of the cruiser clean off, shredding the metal like it was a cotton ball.

It felt for the briefest of moments as though they were stretching the world's largest rubber band.

The two cables they snagged were on the same side of the craft, and the Howler tilted with the added force. Onboard computers tried to balance the craft, firing one engine in overload to compensate, but it was too late and too low.

The engine clipped the ground, and the silent beast suddenly shrieked. Chunks of monster were tossed across the plain and the beast itself sat hard into the dirt.

Their own cruiser collapsed into the dirt, sliding into home as the maglev engine was rent asunder by the effort.

Aaron inspected the critical damage and the belly-flopped Howler behind them. Intermittent coughs and groans implied that the crew at least survived the crash, but they weren't going to be putting up a fight anytime soon.

Familiar and bloody faces emerged from the pile of rubble that had once been Bray's cruiser—Jensen, Keira, Solomon and the eponymous sergeant himself.

Jensen stared at the crashed Howler with a mixture of disbelief and awe. Keira eyed the same wreck, but more amorous than shocked, as though the raw destruction and twisted metal were the eyes of an erstwhile lover. Solomon inspected the damage around him, as though this had all been a misunderstanding.

Bray just stared at Aaron, a wry smile cracking across his leathery face.

Aaron jumped as Nora let out a gravelly cheer.

Suppose they were going to walk the rest of the way.

TWENTY-ONE

RILEY

IT HAD BEEN a small thing to edit the paper records. No matter how complex the watermarks, or fine the threading of the page, modern technology made a mockery of those defenses.

They simply altered the colonial finance records from the past two years, fattening the government's balance sheet—and then skimming that same fresh dairy off into Governor Dedria's personal accounts. These files were then replaced, and then 'discovered' by a very moral bureaucrat.

What choice did Riley have? Not only had the Governor been implicated in a massive conspiracy to defraud both public and Empire, he had been doing so during a deadly crisis.

Details of extravagant meals and luxury items he lavished on his daughter spread through the colony's whisper network like electricity through water. Talania's revolutionary hobby was true progressive tourism, that of a dilettante descending into the mud to claim a kind of lease on systemic pain, before retreating to the comforts of three-course meals and off-world liquors.

While the people nibbled their monthly rations, the Governor's manor ate fresh meats from private stores purchased with taxes pilfered from their pockets.

Public opinion warped almost overnight.

The people were primed and ready to hate; all they needed to know was who deserved their ire. Talania had been pointing at Riley. Riley just pointed back.

They led the Governor from the Aurora Tower in shackles. A bit theatrical, even for Riley, but the mob needed a good display of leadership and moral authority. They needed to feel it was their hands dispensing the justice, that they were the ones in control.

Two Regulars marched on either side of the deposed Governor, one hand each latched onto their charge's spongy arms. He was lax, putty in their fingers, all fight beaten out of him by circumstance and sleepless nights. He dragged his feet down the few steps onto the paved streets, scuffing the expensive leather loafers all the way—not the best choice, given the charges.

The crowd had been slowly gathering all evening. What started as a few dozen curious onlookers had soon grown to almost a hundred angry faces.

The textbooks said that the volatility of a man was in direct proportion to the number of his compatriots; they took on the worst characteristics of their worst member, allowing a normally civic-minded professor of ethics to shamelessly commit a hate crime in record time. Shamelessly.

Riley waited with Holmst and a cadre of troops, probably a few more than was realistically required. The cruiser would carry the Governor to detention, where they would schedule him a hearing.

Riley would ensure such a hearing would never come.

The soldiers marched the Governor up to Riley, presenting him like a package awaiting signature. Riley looked the man up and down.

The stubble on his cheeks followed suit with the rest of his failed hygiene. He hung his head low, as if to present Riley with the top of his balding skull for abuse. His knees quaked, more from exhaustion than fear, ready to give in but for the Regulars holding him upright.

All animus had exited this man.

The Regulars called up the file on their tablets, sliding the image from their machines to Riley's wrist display. Riley made a show of reading the file he himself wrote, the glowing amber color playing across his face.

"Christopher Alexan dei Dedria," Riley began, "You are charged with conspiracy, embezzlement, and sedition, which carries with it a combined twenty-year sentence. Do you understand this charge?"

The Governor lifted his head, swinging slightly as if blowing in a nonexistent breeze or being hoisted up by an invisible thread. He pushed the single word out of his mouth: "Yes."

"Evidence of your guilt or innocence will be presented at your hearing," Riley continued the Rites, enjoying that blend of confusion and frustration on Dedria's face. Too exhausted to express himself and too weak to resist.

The Governor had started to murmur along with the Rites, words every citizen had beaten into them from all the way back in grade school. Fear was a powerful motivational tool, and a strict enough punishment kept the world an ethical place.

"The Detention Clerk will present you with a Duty so that you may continue service to the Empire. Performance of this Duty is a condition of your Citizenship. If you are found virtuous, you will be compensated for your time. If you are--"

"Why did you do it?" Christopher interrupted, quiet and soft.

Riley didn't even slow down, tapping a few confirmations into his display, savoring each haptic response the hologram pushed back into his fingertips. He was driving nails into a coffin with each keystroke.

"If you are found guilty, you will serve out your Duty to the extent the Court dictates. They may levy additional punishments as befits the crime."

"How do you think this ends for you, Marcus?"

Oh?

Riley's eyes slid off his display. The Governor's hunched form had curled into a ball. What had once been slackened was tightening up, such as it could. His arms bowed out, as if giving ground to the

Regulars. Even they could feel the temperature rising, sliding closer to their charge.

The Governor presented his chins, thrusting out the soft mass in a prideful display. It was as if he couldn't decide which to declare as the real one.

"They'll give you medals? Will they? Clap on the back? For *this?!*" He gestured with his shackles.

"This is justice," Riley quipped back, with just a twist of irony. "You're a criminal."

The Governor shook his head. "Justice is for the people, not for you. Service to the *people*, Marcus. For They are the Kings."

Riley stiffened. "You're going to quote scripture now?"

"I am the Governor of Vanguard," He spat back, "and you need those words. You've forgotten—"

Riley returned to his display. "Your hearing will be scheduled for the earliest convenience."

"So never?" Dedria fumed at the obvious result.

"No. At the earliest convenience." Riley pushed the display back into his wrist and forced a warm smile.

"Service to the People...Governor." Riley slid his eyes to the military cruiser behind him, reaching for the door handle to courteously allow the Governor to take a seat on the ride to in-house exile.

The Governor was never going to take that offer, and with Riley's back exposed, he lept like the obese tiger he dreamed that he was. Even with his arms bound behind him and his legs restricted, the man launched his whole body forward.

Poor fool.

Riley spun back around, catching the Governor in the throat with his elbow. The soft croak of the blubber soaking the broken trachea was all anyone heard.

It would have been a crippling injury if Riley had struck a bit softer. Instead, Riley drove the blow home, hard and through.

The Governor was still alive when he collapsed into his guards' arms, gasping and writhing. Without his windpipe, the man would find the singular horrors of strangulation without the comfort of a human face looming over him. No, this man was now gasping for breath staring up at the night sky, alone and afraid.

He thrashed for a painful few seconds before he lost consciousness. Prompt medical attention might've saved him.

Nobody called for it.

The crowd fell quiet, watching with horror as their Governor fell still.

Holmst glared at Riley, who offered a shrug in defense. "He lunged at me. What can you do?"

He felt it coming in—a ballistic object, slow and with decent mass, a brick or stone of some kind. His cybernetics kicked in, picking up the threat from the cries of the crowd, the flicker of an object passing a light source, and the sound of stone slipping off the pads of a glove. He could almost hear the irregular mass spin in the air, tumbling end over end. It was a solid throw, perhaps a bit lucky, as it sailed in towards the back of Riley's head.

It was the calling card of any anarchist in any century. And the second time in as many days.

Imitators.

Riley looked up at Holmst, confident smile.

The lieutenant whirled around Riley, snatching the incoming brick from the air. Riley didn't even need to blink.

It was a bit like someone had dropped a match into a pool of rocket fuel. The crowd swelled up in a tide of pent up frustrations and lashed out on the barricade. They cursed and foamed.

Perhaps without justice to be spent on the Governor, they now needed a new blood bag; or they objected to the manner in which justice was dealt out. But the audience at this execution had turned as easily as turning out a light.

The Regulars ushered Riley into the cruiser, eager to get him away from the threat. Riley found that rioting mob to be almost adorable. They were so wrapped up in their hatred, they didn't care who would absorb it, just so long as they could express it.

These were not people with ideas and conflicting dreams; they were simply cups overflowing.

Riley chuckled as the cruiser pulled away.

Holmst sat beside him, his brow twisted in confusion. "Sir, I don't think I can conjure a way that could have blown up worse."

"You," Riley began, "are just not having enough fun in your life, Lieutenant." Holmst settled into his seat, quashing his frustrations. Riley smirked. "Out with it."

"That was *murder*, sir."

"Is that the title of your autobiography?" Riley inquired.

Holmst ground his teeth, the only indicator of the boiling waters that roiled underneath, "You are an augmented Field Colonel with Orbital Strike Command. He was an overweight bureaucrat with his hands bound. There are a dozen different non-lethal takedowns you could have used from that position."

"And yet," Riley said simply, halting that line of inquiry in its tracks.

Holmst sounded like someone had let his soul leak out of the window like a wisp of smoke. "What are we going to do about the civilians?"

"Formally declare martial law. Riot control protocols, extend the curfew to business hours. Detain any dissenters. We'll need to requisition some space for all the time outs we'll be giving. There's a marketplace just off the Hospital." Riley perked up, a hollow imitation of inspiration. "In fact, requisition the Hospital space. They have bedding aplenty that could be put to better use."

"You've put some thought into this, sir." Holmst wasn't asking. That was an accusation.

Riley licked his teeth, tried to control his smile. "And tell Thor's Hammer they have clearance to fire just as soon as they acquire our AWOL Capitals."

"I'll let them know, but they won't," Holmst responded a bit too fast.

Riley cocked his head at that, picking up on all of the compact information those words conveyed. There was only one good reason to have Thor's Hammer hold their fire, and that scenario was statistically impossible.

Riley straightened his back, taking a steeling breath. He could feel his own frustration cup starting to runneth over. "They broke *through* into...How many Regulars are stationed on any one Wall prefecture?"

"Twenty, with a Capital support squad of fifty each." Holmst ran down the rest of the details, like he was running through a casualty report. "Two Repeater towers, a Claymore field, and the 'Iron Curtain' electric fence. Even scrambled a Howler for intercept." Holmst raised an eyebrow. "Thor's Hammer has a pretty good view of the wreckage. If they fire now, they'll risk civilian casualties in the hundreds, at minimum. Military assets would be among them. And that's if we could acquire them in the crowds."

"Screw the curfew," Riley said, "Full lockdown. Find them."

"Yes, sir." Holmst avoided Riley's gaze, sapping all of the joy from Riley's body.

The dead man was right. The Ministry would hang him; the locals would burn him. There would be no justice; there would be no awards.

He had done the right thing at every step—and they would now punish him for it.

Service to the people? Screw the people.

TWENTY-TWO

AARON

THEY COULD SEE the fires brewing in the city just after sunset, the lights dancing off the glass spires like ethereal candlelight.

"What have we done?" Eden asked, her voice so small, so distant.

Keira nudged the little woman with her elbow. "What makes you think it was you?"

Bray wiped the sweat from his furrowed brow, as he squinted at the glittering lights ahead of them. "Jergad swept around us, got to the city first."

Fatalist.

"No," Solomon whispered, his gravelly tone catching everyone's attention, "Would be nothing to see and a lot to hear."

"Jergad don't light fires," Aaron concluded.

This was something else.

The fires only grew in intensity as they marched in. Perhaps it was just the deepening night that made their glow more terrifying, as they cast dancing shadows up into the night sky. But that sinking feeling in his gut told him that whatever violence was going on was only getting worse.

They made the suburban edges of the city just as Nora blew out the heel on her boot. Rows of identical steel condos stood like prostrate worshipers before the obelisk of the city's towers, now positively glittering orange and red. All the lights were off in each home. Just silent gravestones.

The team traipsed from house to house, following the natural yard lines in toward the city center.

Bray raised a fist, and everyone paused. "Hide."

Everyone darted out of view, jumping in different directions. Aaron slid to a stop by the corner of a house, Eden flopping down next to him and clutching at his side.

She balled up his tunic in her fist, pulling it tight across his chest. Everyone found their comforts in every moment they could. Her cool fingers worked over the cloth, almost icy when they brushed his skin.

A long moment passed.

"What is it?" Jensen asked, calling across the street.

Bray snapped back hard. "Shut up!"

They waited some more. Sure enough, a cruiser rolled up the street—full of Regulars, hollering to each other. "Hey, *skels*! Not so smart mouth now, are ya?!"

They pushed something out of the cruiser as they sped along. It bounced and skidded along the ground, skipping whenever it found enough friction to hitch. The cruiser was out of sight when the package finally stopped—it was a man.

Eden rushed out. "Don't!" Aaron hissed, but it was far too late.

She dropped to her knees next to the man, staying low but checking his vitals. Combat medic. She had her training, her instincts.

The slump of her shoulders told everyone what they needed to know.

"What the hell are they doing?" Jensen asked.

Nora scoffed at him. "What? You never seen a gang before?"

"What did he do?" Keira almost laughed.

Eden shouldered her rifle and marched past the giant back en route to the city. "Nothing excuses that."

Everyone watched her for a second, before falling in line behind her. Whatever had happened here, law & order had long since been surrendered. Safety only came from joining in the chorus; dissent was abused from the whole; distortions were excised. Learn to sing or be made to bleed.

Yeah. That sounds about right. That's the home he remembered.

They finally hit the city proper. The orange glow had overtaken, like flickering spotlights that aimed to turn the sky back to blue. They shot out of alleys like beams of red, lighting the districts one shouldn't tread into. Aaron could see one of the fires, peering past the breaks in buildings.

Soldiers were fueling giant pyres, throwing whatever they could get their hands on into the flames. And they were forcing tearful citizens to watch.

Punishment.

"I don't think there's a whole lot of government going on," Jensen whispered to Aaron over his shoulder, "Do you?"

"*Fra ti mizu*," Nora cursed just loud enough to echo. Everyone winced but her.

"Your little government stooge is going to be a little hard to find in all of this," Solomon muttered.

"She wouldn't sit quiet while all this was going down," Aaron said. "Bray? What would you do with a mouthy young rebel?"

"If I can't silence them?"

"Yeah," Aaron nodded. "You can cow the people into submission, you can kill those who resist. But what about the people too important to kill?"

"You throw in prison," Eden finished his thought.

"We're not important enough to care about, so we go to jail," Nora heckled, "She's *too* important, so she goes to jail."

"Cut the chatter," Bray snapped. "Where would Riley put political dissidents?"

For some reason, Keira started to strip out of her uniform.

"Really, Keira?" Bray began his tirade, but she cut him off.

"We stick out," Keira said as she reached into a nearby dumpster,

"If you're not part of the racket, you're gonna be part of the take." She fished out a pile of clothes, dumping them to the floor. "Get dressed."

Aaron looked down at the uniform he wore: spackled with the dirt of the Pits, alien blood, his blood. He hadn't spent a day out of that jumpsuit in years. Attempts to wash it only set the bodily fluids into the cloth. His medals were scars kept and made.

This tattered cloth was the only thing that 'belonged' to him anymore. He left it in the bin with all the rest.

———

Riley's improvised prison was the city Hospital. While Bray knew how to get them there, Aaron knew his way around that building from the hours of physical therapy he had done during his recovery and press tour.

The broad corridors had been gated off at regular intervals, requiring key card access to pass through—they'd been reinforced with guard posts at choke points and steel bars over windows, but the reindeer games outside had lured most away from their posts.

The sterile floors had been scuffed and sullied with the inherent depravity of a prison environment. It was moments like these that Aaron regretted his sense of smell.

Former bank robber Keira had some experience breaking out of prisons. Breaking into one was largely the same principle. Unless there were specific protocols, barriers kept things out just as well as in. And Keira knew how to breach barriers.

She grabbed a guard and threatened to remove his particulars unless he relinquished his keycard. Bray and Aaron stopped her from taking his hand for any biometrics; just take him with us.

Annoyed, she schlepped the guard from checkpoint to checkpoint, walking them through each barrier. They passed violent criminals and the cravenly desperate alike.

Aaron paused in front of one room, peering through the small double-paned glass of the door. Talania had to be in one of these rooms.

Huddled in one corner, perhaps chasing warmth. Hair frazzled, clothes damp. They had hosed him off before dumping into the room.

He couldn't be older than ten.

"Let him out."

The guard grunted a response, only finding his words when Keira cranked his wrist further up his back, "Can't!" the guard warned. "They're killers and psychopaths."

Jensen looked over Aaron to see what he'd found. "It's just a kid..."

"He attacked a peace officer!" The guard slurred. "Used a knife! He's dangerous."

Solomon seemed to teleport from some dark corner right up to the man's ear, deep inside the man's personal space, whispering a simple assurance: "Me too."

Aaron shook his head. "How many more like this?"

The guard didn't answer. Keira applied leverage. He cried out and Aaron leaned in. "How many?"

"We don't exactly keep count. I just feed 'em. Okay?"

Talk about throwing away the key. They don't even know who they have, or what they've done. They did something, someone threw them here. And that was the end of the conversation.

"You're going to think real hard," Aaron said, "And we'll give you all the time you need: Tall, brunette, young, been on TV a whole lot. Where is Talania Dedria?"

"*Fra tow,* Capital." Now that wasn't polite.

Something in his arm popped and he bit his cheek to keep from screaming.

Keira whispered in his ear: "Wrong answer. Now, for the House in Andalusia and the hundred-foot Parlor Boat, answer the man's question."

"Do what you gotta do, *skel,*" the guard spat, "Colonel will eat you for breakfast! He's—already on his way with a detachment of Oskies."

"If you're gonna lie," Solomon sneered, "give it some conviction."

"Freeze!"

Aaron rolled his eyes—Of course this would happen. He turned to see—

Anatoly and Kipling, sidearms drawn and staring down their holographic sights at the crowd. Their hands shook, fingers wrapping triggers.

Nobody moved for a moment. Then Kipling lowered his gun. "626?"

"Kipling." Aaron nodded, "Anatoly."

"You look...different."

Of course. He wasn't wearing his Capital gear anymore. He looked like a person.

"We're looking for someone." He said, "Talania, Governor's Daughter."

Anatoly's muzzle lowered, but he kept his stance. "I heard what happened."

"What happened?" Eden demanded.

There was a moment in Kipling's eyes, something akin to pity. This was a Doctor too sad to deliver news to a critical patient.

He holstered his weapon, prompting Anatoly to do the same. "Let him go. He just handles the First Strikes."

"This..." Aaron pointed at the door, "is a First Strike?"

Kipling tongued his cheek, the shame positively leaking out of him. "She's in the ID Ward," Kipling said, "with the rest of the Seditionists."

Aaron grabbed their captive soldier's hand by the wrist and slammed it on the biometric scanner, the door locks on the boy's cell opening with a baritone clack.

It seemed like Jensen was inside the cell before the door even opened. He knelt at the boy's side, careful not to get too close. "It's okay. It's okay, we're here to help. It's over."

Eden caught Aaron's eye, watching as his vengeful eye drifted back to their captive. "You go right now. You tell Riley we're here. He finds me, or I find him. Huah?"

The man nodded so fast it looked like a shiver. He knew what his other options were. Keira let him go, and he staggered away from them, his injured arm hanging like drapes pulled half of their rod.

Anatoly looked like he might melt, a great weight removed from his shoulders. "I'm sorry," Anatoly stammered out, his whole body rocked by the release.

Bray clapped a hand against the soldier's head, perhaps hoping to tap the insecurity out of his ears. "You're slow, boy. But you did the right thing. That ain't so easy, is it?"

And with that, Bray and the others sidled on past, opening cell doors as they went.

A veritable mob started to assemble behind them. Sure enough, Anatoly & Kipling fell in with the crowd of prisoners and malcontents like they had always been there, consumed and subsumed by the river of people. It wasn't a move out of survival or confusion, but of exhaustion—two people lost in their world and seeking some reason or direction. They followed because they were done wandering.

Aaron found the whole thing disconcerting.

Deep in the Hospital's Infectious Diseases ward—where the quarantine procedures made for excellent cells—they found the object of their search.

The room had been much like his old hospital space, but most of the furniture had been removed. Two fixed track lights in the ceiling were all that lit the space, likely because they couldn't be removed. The absence of stuff made the room feel almost luxurious by prison standards. This amount of space for a single prisoner would have made them royalty in the Pits—or a target.

Talania Dedria sat on the lone bunk, knees pulled tight to her chest atop the thin mattress. Her power blazer and trousers had been replaced with a rough, flimsy tunic and slacks—all too familiar to Aaron.

The thin curtains of her hair were tangled and crinkled, bunching around her ears and threads clinging to her forehead like errant spider silk. Her brown eyes stared into the floor, almost as though she refused to acknowledge the movement outside of her cell.

There was no sign of strain, but small lines were carved in the muck on her cheeks, where tears had blazed trails to the laminate floor.

He knew silent grief all too well.

Aaron stood at the door of her cell. "When?"

Talania didn't move, her eyelids hanging heavy, fluttering.

Aaron had to shake all of his expectations of her. The Queen had used her form, bringing with it an alien distance and formality. But even Talania's trademark brusque and bullish self had been purged from its shell. Eliciting expression would require some animus to be left in there.

Except Riley had been here, with his canteen and his lies. Perhaps he had broken whatever horrible news personally, or he had let her deduce it herself so that the revelation would shatter her. However the method, she was a husk of her former strength.

The crowd hung at the door as Aaron approached, crouching low into her field of view.

Her eyes flickered, refocusing past him. She didn't want to talk. Fine. He would do it all.

"You can't let him get away with it," Aaron said, urgent and plaintive.

She huffed, a small quiver as she scoffed at the notion. "He is the Empire," she whispered back, "We are alive because he allows it."

A tape recorder, playing back final parting words from a monster.

"No," Aaron shook his head. "Your people need you. They're just waiting for somebody to follow—Tal, people are dying."

Now her eyes were tracking him, vague and frail roots to her anger taking shape again. "We were wondering when you were going to notice."

Don't back down. Meet fire with fire.

Aaron resettled himself in his squat. "You're the Voice of Vanguard. If you sit silent, he wins."

"It's suicide," she said. "He does what he wants, and the entire system defends him. I stood up for them and they...Those people out there? They sat it out. They let him do this. To *me*."

Aaron pointed at the door, at the small assembly of prisoners and soldiers. "They look like they're sitting this one out?"

"Listen up, Cap. You are nothing. I am nothing." She pointed at the faces huddled at the door. "They are nothing. If he wants to kill us, he's going to. And there's nothing anybody can do about it. The only thing you're doing right now is looking for a good reason to die."

"I was a clerk."

Talania's hard expression softened, her eyes finally fixing on his face, as though she was trying to memorize this moment.

Aaron tongued his cheek. Maybe he gives her just a little bit more, but then it all just came out. "I wasn't nothing. Didn't used to be. I...dropped out of school to help my mom pay for her medication.

"When she didn't last, the school wouldn't take me back. So I worked. I worked for the Washington Superior Court in Foggy Bottom as a Court Clerk. I took documents, dictation, recorded the proceedings, worked with the Bailiff and the Court Reporter—I was a bureaucrat. I was 'professional at being competent.' I worked schedules and covered phones. I made sure that room ran like clockwork.

"Wasn't the greatest part of town, but it was work inside a secure building. Not going to get mugged when you live and work within shouting distance of a couple dozen Peace Officers. It wasn't a good life. I paid my bills and I could afford food most of the time, if I kept the lights on low and the heater off in the winter. But it was mine and it was safe. Then..."

He paused, remembering that *gulaw* rain clinging to the back of his bloody hands. His friends and followers hung in the doorway, drinking in every word.

"Suddenly, I was standing on the wrong side of that courtroom. I knew how they worked. I'd seen plenty of cases against cop killers. They threw the book right out the window. They'd have hung me from the rafters if somebody had brought rope. The bailiff, guy named...Cliff Redding. He wouldn't look up from his file. They slapped me in iron and that was that. I was a Capital. I was locked up for defending myself."

He almost spat fire with the words. "I was *fourteen*. Capital for life."

Talania inclined her head, a reptilian part of her brain triggered, ignition in her gut.

"Everybody's been asking me what I'd do with my freedom, if I'd go back, what I'd do. Tal, I couldn't go back if I wanted to. I don't have a trade or family or nothin'. I lost all that. And it was never their's to take."

"Angry?" Talania asked, in a word.

"I was," he whispered. "For the first year. Then you..." He looked back at the people in the door. "You find a new life."

"Yeah...well, I'm still angry," Talania growled.

"Good," he said. "Then help us."

Talania gritted her teeth. "One condition," she grunted. "You and your Capital friends get their freedom as promised, if—and only if—Marcus Riley stands trial."

Aaron's eyes darkened. "He escalated a war for personal glory. He cracked down on anyone that stood against him. He imprisoned innocents & children. Instituted slavery. He tortured me, and he killed my friends."

"He killed my father," she said, all cold fury.

Aaron nodded. "He's going down. But I can't promise a court."

She smiled. "I can live with that."

CHAPTER
TWENTY-THREE
RILEY

"FIRST THEY WILL ORGANIZE, then they will organize their violence."

Riley could read a thousand treatises on it; there was no comparing to seeing it. They rose up with batons and hate, hurling firebombs at peacekeepers while hiding behind metal bulkheads they tore from the very walls around them. They had, in a matter of hours, gone from frightened to aggressive.

Perhaps that was his mistake. He had cornered the animal.

He craned his neck to look up at the city. The towering structures of Vanguard were dingy with soot and smoke, blotting out whatever light they used to cast. The obscene obelisks towered over the lesser buildings, commanding obedience they could no longer compel.

He listened to the cries of anger that echoed up amongst those towers and back down to his encampment. It was everything in him not join in that chorus, just cut loose and scream until his throat went raw.

Only a third of the populace were involved, but the rest of the colony did nothing to oppose or silence their comrades. They just watched with the muted and distant horror of a middle-class family that stopped at a memorial to early human inhumanities; 'How uncivilized they were back then' they might say to their children, while assuring their little ones they were safe from such malice.

The hypocrites.

How would this be recorded in the histories? Was it a demonstration with a streak of violence and looting? Or was it a riot with political and anti-social motivation?

Rules of engagement differed dramatically in the permitted response between the two, riot and demonstration.

To hell with the rules.

He had done this for them. He had defied orders, committed treason, and killed his career all to protect their frail little sensibilities.

His stomach froze up like he'd been punched, like there was a crimp or knot in the length of rope. Maybe he should've listened to all the flights of fancy and had the average Joe pick up a rifle, they'd have some patriotic unity with the men who volunteered for the pain.

No, they'd have broken under the stress, the demands of military life. It required a sacrifice most didn't find fathomable, let alone were willing to make. Martial law was preferable to press-ganging an entire population.

They just didn't understand. They all had complaints; no one had solutions.

Not even her.

"He has imprisoned your leaders," Talania had said in her brief chat, through bruised lip and mangy hair.

She wanted to get out her words before Allied Forces could jam the signal. Intelligence suggested she used the Hospital's emergency transmitter, and with a little technical wizardry beyond her abilities.

Aaron and his rogues gallery, of course. They blanketed the civilian airwaves for but twenty short seconds.

Talania knew how to use that time. "He has invaded your homes. He has stolen your food. He has used the crisis to consolidate power and eliminate any who might challenge him. He tells you to be frightened and beats you until you are. He believes he owns your lives."

She raised an inquisitive eyebrow like she was looking right at him. "Does he?"

And with that, the signal cut out.

The suggestion was clear enough to him. Riley had made them all Capitals, a collection of blood bags to live or die at his discretion. It was moral absolutism, dangerous and lacking in nuance.

The public so does love a simple slogan.

Riley's men had established a base camp to treat wounded and resupply squads outside the Aurora building, about a mile from the worst of the fighting. At least, it had been a mile when they set up their little popsicle stand.

What had been an indistinct din echoing off of the towers above was now clear enough to make out individual voices, even if their specific complaints were unmet.

And they only had a handful of men, a few over three dozen to contain this wildfire. With most of the defenses deployed to Wall Prefectures, the skeleton crew was quickly taxed to its limit. The battles were one-sided, as peacekeepers were under explicit instructions to hold their fire. With them so outnumbered, any attempt to dissipate the crowd with gas or batons would only endanger the officers.

Instead, Holmst had pitched a novel concept: let the rioters work out their aggression, sacrifice buildings, businesses, and a few black eyes to the whims of the crowd, and in their exhaustion, only then reinstate order.

The damage would highlight the importance of peace and civility, while minimizing any military casualties.

The only other option would turn the tables in a rather criminal direction. The Oskies and the Regulars may be outnumbered, but the citizens were not armed with ceramic plates or twenty-eight-megawatt energy weapons. Firepower was not a practical problem, but a moral one.

And besides, it would only validate their feelings and surrender the only ground he had left.

He was in the right. He had to act like it.

Riley stared out at the streets, as flickering lights and fires danced across the spires above. There had to be two thousand people out there tearing up everything they could get their hands on.

Every one of them wanted something different: their satellite television, their comfortable clothes, more rationing, or maybe to use disposable bottles again. Discord could not be rewarded, and any mob that could be bought would simply make further demands using their pitchfork and torch discount.

He didn't need their loyalty, just their cooperation.

This colony was at war, clinging to survival by their fingernails. The people had wreathed themselves in anger. They had forgotten their fear, those same heart-felt pleas they had screamed at his retreating back.

They needed to be reminded why they begged him to stay.

"Can we erect barricades on Westing and Jericho?" Holmst asked his assembly of advisors.

"We can bring up vehicles and strip the surrounding structures-"

"We're protecting the city," Holmst dismissed the idea, "Not looting it."

"A dozer might rip up the paving, make the groundwork impassable?"

"That's better. If we're going to break things, let's break public property."

Riley shook his head. "I'm not surrendering the Market District."

Holmst and the others looked up at their commander. "Sir, we're not surrendering—we've *lost* the District. We have to contain the damage, let the fire burn itself out."

"I'm not surrendering the District, Lieutenant. We're going to give quite a bit more ground than that."

Holmst narrowed his eyes. "What did you have in mind?"

"Broadcast this message, single burst in the open. I want Rebel forces to pick it up right away." Riley hung on that pause, forcing Holmst to wait in anticipation. "The Oscar Nomad and Gamma Tau

Wall Prefectures are to disband. Return to Vanguard hold points with all haste."

Holmst shifted in his boots, instantly sweating. "Clever. Make the Rebels think we're surrendering the Wall...opening them to alien attack. They might think they've overdone it, fall in line."

"Oh, no, we're surrendering the Wall. Bring 'em home." Riley pivoted to another Aide. "What's the position on Thor's Hammer?"

"Belay that order."

There was an audible gasp from some aide behind them. Riley didn't expect that response from Holmst, though he should've. Nobody else could've dared to dream of it in their most recalcitrant moments.

"Colonel..." Holmst began with the calm weight of a hostage negotiator. "Why would you need to know Thor's position?"

"Tactical withdrawal protocol," Riley said, "Surrender only ground with no value."

"Drop the textbook bullshit for just one moment, *sir!*" Holmst had to hear the ice cracking underneath him. It was daring but foolish.

Riley side eyed his second-in-command, "The Jergad will pour into the city. The citizens in their bunkers will be safe from the kinetics."

Holmst barely maintained his composure. "Say that again."

"They think they're safe because they haven't had to bleed for the ground they stand on. You have, Ilern. Your men have. Even the goddamn Capitals have." Riley growled, "I don't think the average citizen remembers why we call this place the Hellmouth. Every day we cannot maintain order, people will die. Every soldier I pull off the Wall to restore it, the more *soldiers* die on that Wall. I will not let them take this ground. Will you?"

Riley squared off with his lieutenant. He had to sell this idea or everything was lost. "No, instead—we give the ground. And then light it on fire. What do we lose? Buildings? Supplies? In exchange, we cripple the alien threat and punish them for their greed."

"Sir, do we have a BDA for that? Thor's Hammer striking inside the Green..."

Riley almost laughed. The lieutenant wanted to know what that report could possibly tell them. There was no way to accurately predict the kind of damage this would cause.

Whatever alien casualties were suffered, the Colonial Range-lands would never be 'secure' again, what with the possibility of traps laid out there. Structural damage, civilian casualties would not be immediate; it would last for years.

Riley rubbed his jaw. "Lieutenant, is it battle damage if it's a civilian target?"

Holmst pointed at the men behind him. They recoiled from his hand, desperate to avoid association with his insubordination. "We volunteered to protect people, sir."

Not you too.

Riley took a deep breath that failed at quieting the boil in his gut. "Then you can stay behind and protect the people." Riley shouldered past him, marching up to the table of Top Shirts. "Pack this up. I want all of it in the cruisers. We are going land mobile."

"Sir—"

Riley spun back, almost soft and charming. "If Aaron Havenes is correct, I won't have a target to shoot at. You will have nothing to worry about."

"Fire on the crowd," Holmst said, almost begging, "Just a few shots would put the fear of God into them."

Riley knew what burning human flesh smelled like.

"No," he said, "You can't make people fear something they already hate. They feel safe because we've made them so. Every regulation, every curfew, every action they are protesting is what has made them safe. We valued their lives so much we threw away our own. It's time to remind them why the men with guns are here at all. And when they see the horror with their own eyes, we will purge it from their sight—and they will love us for it."

Riley stooped down, plucking one of the table legs from its home, helping the nearby aide turn the surface for flat-packing. There was no time to waste. Once the Prefectures were absent, the Aliens would have access.

The little bastards burrowed at about eight kilometers an hour, so they would make the city well before the dawn. It was time to be else-where, somewhere they might secure from incursion so that they could watch the fireworks.

"You are suggesting the wholesale slaughter of the entire colony! Colonel, please!"

Holmst was too far gone. He was berating his own commander in public. He sounded like Christopher.

"I am doing no such thing," Riley said. "I'm just gambling with it."

"Just realities of command?" Holmst wasn't asking. He wasn't horrified. That was a threat.

Riley stiffened up, standing tall, "Do what you have to do, Lieu-tenant," he said, almost dismissive.

There were a few possible outcomes now. Riley knew his aide far too well. Little damn boy scout.

Holmst drew his sidearm, and charged the capacitor, "Colonel Marcus Riley, under Article Seven, Section Twenty-Two Bravo of the Uniform Code, I am relieving you of your command."

If memory served, section Twenty-Two was Temporary Insanity and Conduct Unbecoming, generally marked by an order the subor-dinate could not follow without grave insult or injury to Empire and Man. He even cited the proper regulation. He had done some home-work, checked to see if he had the grounds to do this.

He should've just pulled the trigger.

No time for pinpoint accuracy. Holmst was an Oskie with the same augmentations. In the best of circumstances, they were on equal footing. Surprise was his only ally.

Riley slipped his pistol from the holster, twisting at the waist as he did, using the turn to cover what was in his hands as he dialed the charge in: full power, wide field, short range.

To those watching, it all happened in the blink of an eye. Holmst was just wrapping his finger through the trigger guard when Riley's weapon dumped a foot wide beam into his torso.

The lieutenant didn't thrash or recoil from the blow. The beam had cut and melted; no force had been imparted. He just discovered that a majority of his internal organs were gone, a crater cut into the center of his chest, with the edges a cauterized and oozing black mess.

It almost looked like burnt sugar.

Holmst twitched as he tried to breathe, but the airways were stopped and his diaphragm was gone. It wasn't pain, but confusion, as an instinctual circuit no longer fired on command. He tried again, and the confusion grew to a realization. He wanted to speak, say some saddening passing thoughts to his mentor and commander, but there was no air to push.

His knees shook and he dropped to one knee, a tilting tower sinking into the ground. He couldn't bleed out without a heart. No, he was suffocating.

Riley holstered his weapon and turned to the Regulars and Oskies, their faces a mixture of horror. "Send the order: abandon the Wall. Rally point on the Mining Pits. We can hold there until the counteroffensive."

Holmst hadn't stopped thrashing when Riley climbed into his cruiser.

CHAPTER
TWENTY-FOUR
AARON

EVERYONE LOOKED at him like any words he might say meant the difference between a happy tomorrow and the sky collapsing down around their heads. They hung on his words, treasuring every syllable.

They were waiting for him to respond, for something inspiring to say or words of comfort. He just wanted to be quiet, maybe even have a little uncomfortable cry. Riley had been many things to Aaron; a pragmatic commander, a dismissive tactician, and a charismatic tormentor—but this?

The recording was on a loop, reiterating the disconcerting instruction in case the listeners doubted their senses the first time around. "Withdraw from your posts. Return to designated rally positions. This is not a drill."

More than a few failed to hide the terror in their eyes. With nobody manning the Wall, the Jergad had free reign. Were they friend or foe? This was a helluva way to find out.

Riley's old office had been stripped of the most important details. Aaron's fingers tapped on the edge of Riley's desk, feeling out the metal and its dents and bumps. Twin disposal units still glowed from where classified materials had been atomized. The bulkheads were barren, not even mounts betraying if there had ever been anything. It had given the room a rather unpleasant tin echo.

Everything in the room lacked aesthetic, had a simple function.

Live feed from Thor's Hammer showed the dozens of vehicles fleeing the Prefectures, most making for the Vanguard city centre with all haste. Almost heartening, a good third refused the order, holding their posts on the Wall. Riley would execute every last one of them for such insubordination.

Even still, the Wall was not going to stop any kind of incursion now. If the Jergad wanted to, they could walk right up to the door and knock like they were selling cookies.

Everyone in Vanguard heard that broadcast. Riley had not only lowered their defenses, he wanted everyone to know it. The concentrated resistance immediately dropped all pretense. Robbed of their foe and presented with an apocalypse, they turned on each other in a bacchanal worthy of the end times.

The city wouldn't need an alien threat; the Hellmouth would swallow itself.

"He's insane," Aaron said, still processing the message himself.

"Thought you said they were friendly," Solomon urged, his voice cracking ever so slightly. Even he tensed at the oncoming storm.

"Yeah," Aaron nodded, "but that's not what Riley thinks. He thinks he just put every man, woman, and child in Vanguard onto a table and rang the dinner bell."

"Sounds like him, alright," Talania sneered. Whatever poetry and political maneuvering she might have once held in such high regard was now dead weight. Not like she was terribly polite before.

Bray squared up on his former trainee. "No bullshit assessment, Havenes. We have to assume a Jergad strike force is on its way right now, burrowing under the Wall, completely unchecked. How ugly is this night gonna get?"

All Aaron could think of was Rimpau, that horde of slavering monsters that rose right from nightmares to swallow up his friends.

They laid traps, they butchered the wounded, they killed without regret.

They had so much hate in them.

"I don't know."

Bray frowned. "Not a good answer."

"I don't know!" Aaron snapped, "I'm not a *gulaw* soothsayer! They're gonna do whatever they want. Riley made sure of that."

"That's true," Keira mused, "But you're the one with the hotline to God. No idea as to their thinking?"

Jensen stood up. "This might all be for nothing. The bugs might not even know what's going on."

Aaron cocked his head, that headache swelling and falling again. The Queen was listening like she was right there in the room with them. He could swear he saw Talania's eyes flash that *fra tow* blue for just a second.

The Queen had a sense of humor, at least.

"Oh, they know everything." What they chose to do with that information was anybody's guess.

Bray was increasingly displeased with this concept, rolling his shoulders. Jensen sidled up next to the ol' Gunny, one word in his giant body: *Easy.*

"So it's only one way?" Keira asked, genuinely curious, "They know you, but not...?"

"I'll ask again," Bray said, not letting Jensen's large frame diminish his position one bit. "How bad is this going to get?"

"You and I are just going to go round and round with this, aren't we?" Aaron wondered aloud. It was a little late for Bray to hop off this bandwagon. Perhaps the old man was having second thoughts about tossing his prestigious career down the toilet bowl.

"Our first priority," Jensen interjected, "has to be getting the City calmed down."

Eden shifted in her seat. "If the Jergad are through, we have to assume the worst. Wake everybody up and get them to the transports." She leaned over to Talania. "We do have transports, right?"

Talania didn't even meet her eyes. "Riley's not going to let you get a grip on this city. You turn to run, he'll shoot you in the back."

"So let Riley pout," Nora said, shaking her head. "He can bury his head up his ass while we evacuate the-"

"He has a two-hundred-meter kinetic battery floating in geocentric orbit and he's crazy enough to do it," Talania hissed at Aaron, her words cutting the air and commanding attention. Aaron never thought he'd meet someone who could silence Nora with a word and a stare, but there it was. "You made a promise, Aaron."

Aaron bristled at that almost threat. Maybe the Queen was right to pick Talania for her form. There was so much hate. In them both.

"It's not that we don't want to," Eden countered Talania's energy. "We can't."

"When I have a boo-boo, I'll ask for your opinion." The group bristled at that, but Talania refused to back down. "No! I know this man. You back out of his face now, and he'll shove you off a cliff."

"How'd that work out for you?" Solomon clapped back from his dark corner, before returning to picking at whatever grime or blood was under his fingernails.

Talania coiled up like a spring under tension. Before, she had been a ball of energy needing direction. Now she was an active explosion at all times, eating her alive. "Suppose you just want to get down on your knees—"

"Hey!" Aaron barked, a warning, "Don't start attacking your friends, too."

"What're you going to do, shoot me?" Talania slammed right back, wise-ass till the end—a wise-ass with the high ground.

Without the consent of the civilian government, he was still a Capital. They all were. He needed her voice if he ever wanted his freedom. She decided how much worth he had.

Then again, that might've been just another empty promise from someone with no intention of keeping it. Didn't much matter to him. She might grant him freedom for his service; Riley would only grant him more bloodshed.

He'd take a *maybe* over a *no*.

"Stand easy, Tal." She bristled at the nickname and he hid his wince. Perhaps there was more than the familiarity at play when the Queen chose to emulate the young government agent. "You're right. We can't leave Riley unaccounted for. Not with four platoons of angry patriots at our heels."

"And there's also the added benefit of it being the right thing to do," Talania snarked.

"Where is he now?"

Talania rolled out—was that a sheet of actual paper? Her fingers traced out blotchy lines, and in a few seconds, Aaron recognized the geographical details. "He went to the Mining Pits?"

Bray nodded, catching on to the thinking, "Aurora's not a secure facility, never was. And the Forts are all forward toward the Wall. This has controlled access, existing reinforced buildings and terrain. And its supposedly abandoned six kilometers from the city center."

Nora ground her jaw a bit. "He let Hell inside and locked us in with it."

No, Riley wasn't going to leave this all to chance. Even Solomon could sense it, his thin fingers pawing at the map. "What's rattlin' around in your head?" Aaron asked.

"He thinks he's a hero," Solomon said, "So why is he fitting for the black hat?"

"Oh my god," Eden said, the only one looking at the monitors, "Thor's Hammer's entering launch prep."

"At what?" Bray demanded, equal parts incredulous and frightened. That was a chilling tone that Aaron never wanted to hear from a career soldier.

Eden stepped aside—the screen had a high-resolution picture of the spires of Vanguard—with the Aurora building just off-center.

Aaron settled into the chair behind Riley's desk. It was well broken in, with a mild squeak as he dropped his weight into it. It instantly felt wrong, like he was now breathing tainted air or had a knife to his back. But he had no more strength to stand.

"He's laid a trap," Aaron said, "The aliens come pouring into Vanguard to slaughter the population. And he blows the hell out of them—last ditch, big move. Then he comes back in, the conquering hero."

"The bunkers can't take that kind of punishment..." said Talania, so very cold. "He'll kill thousands."

"Gun to your head," Jensen said, eying Aaron, "What do you do?"

Aaron swallowed hard. He knew what he had done before.

Talania's eyes went dead, like she was somewhere far away. Reptilian, she turned back like a coiled snake. "You go out there and you kill the son of a bitch."

"Wha..." Aaron wasn't objecting. He was just frozen up. No cognitive function left.

"I like it," Nora chirped, sharing a sadistic look with Solomon.

"Ain't so simple," Bray chimed in. "Those Pits were designed to keep in three thousand Capital laborers. There's going to be artificial barricades that make your Detention time look like a spa day. Not to mention the natural hazards of the Mining operation itself. They can die walking across the room wrong."

Bray was lecturing a civilian on the conditions Aaron had lived in for almost a year, and the Pits had been comparatively cozy accommodations. Talania might've been horrified if she hadn't been well aware of all of this already.

"And on top of all of this," Bray said, "Riley is Orbital. And he has a complement of other Oskies with him, not to mention however many Regulars flocked to his flag. Sieging the Pits is a bad idea."

"No siege." Aaron stood up. "But yeah...I'm going after Riley."

"He'll kill you without breaking stride," Eden blurted, concern leaping out of her. There was an urgency to her tone beyond just the obvious foul prediction. She still remembered how Carmona died. She didn't want to see him die the same way.

Riley. That canteen. That firm but grinding tone that drove under his skin like a thin needle, pulling at the foundations of what he knew. He presented himself as a brother, a friend, but acted like a disappointed father. Superiority didn't give a damn about age.

"We don't come to fight," Aaron said, remembering the man he squared off within that improvised cell, "We're not going to break in, or blow our way in—none of that. He's going to let us in the front door when we show up to negotiate his return."

Jensen cocked his head sideways, eyeballing his friend. "You've taken too many blows to the head."

"Absolutely true," Aaron affirmed, waggling a finger at the big guy, "But we're going to do it anyway."

Nora shivered at the notion. "And if he decides we're all past saving?"

"Then he reduces us to molten slag at the edge of the perimeter. But he won't."

Talania planted her hands on the desk, looming over Aaron, "This is idiotic. You cannot ask for mercy from this man."

"Ain't gonna. Why did he stay, Talania?" Aaron asked, "at all. After the exodus? Why recruit Capitals? Why defy an Empire?"

"Are you actually asking, or are you on a roll?" Nora quipped at him.

Aaron pointed behind them. "Service to the People."

They all turn to look at the words—the only adornment in the room—burned into the archway over the door in block letters. The liturgical phrase looked like an ancient magical ward.

"I spent two years clerking in a courtroom. Nobody enters that room thinking they did something wrong. He thinks he's doing the right thing. He just wants to be valued for it. He *needs* it. We give him one chance to turn himself in. If he says no...we bring the fury of an entire planet down on his head."

"If the Jergad hit the city, and he drops the Hammer..." Bray cautioned, "It'll be the kind of bloodshed that gets marked up in history books."

Aaron looked up at Talania, at her eyes dark brown eyes, catching the reflection of the blue in the darkness. There they were, like they'd never left, staring back at him, almost inquisitive. Thoughtful, curious. Eager, even.

They were waiting on him.

"Bray? Trust me now. Work with Talania, get everyone you can underground. We'll handle Riley. Huah?"

Bray bristled at the order coming from a Capital, but after a second he relaxed into it. "Always thought I'd die fighting enemies of the Empire."

"Oh, Gunny," Jensen said, clasping his former drill sergeant's shoulder, "I'm sure you will someday."

"Don't touch me." Jensen recoiled. Bray nodded at Aaron, "*Zu Gloriam*, Havenes. We'll get it done."

Talania stood tall, giving Aaron a once over, like she was inspecting his face for cracks. Maybe she liked what she found, or maybe what she didn't find. She squinted for half a second, before shaking her head. "Give me a reason to believe, Capital."

And with that, she went for the door, Bray on her heels.

Aaron looked to his team: Eden, Nora, Jensen, Keira and Solomon. They stood around him, the Fifth Floor clan—what was left of them. They looked back at him with a mixture of faith and fear. The Queen's words echoed in his head.

It is in the story, in the telling, that they are lionized: the acts in which people become legends, and the legends are remembered.

They were about to do something worth remembering.

CHAPTER
TWENTY-FIVE
RILEY

THEY SAUNTERED up to the Pits with their proverbial hats in their hands. But there was no amount of groveling or empty promises at Riley's feet that would stop what was coming.

The Jergad were tunneling toward Vanguard with all haste, unabated by the litany of defenses Riley had once offered so freely. It was a little late for the citizenry to cajole him into doing his job after so explosively telling him where he could shove it.

It was less convincing coming from the famed Aaron Havenes, Capital extraordinaire and resident flower child gone feral. Riley would've had the perimeter snap his spine in half at two hundred meters were he not personally curious as to what the Capital had to say.

Was he here to present himself to justice, at which point a ranged execution would be a kindness? Or was he here to sue for some kind of status quo, a return to normalcy with soldiers on the Wall and control restored?

But there was one curious truth to it: the current state of affairs might be considered a victory for him were he truly a traitor to the Empire. Aaron was not as compromised as he had once feared.

No, this was something else. Human error and human growth?

Mistakes were made, and now we made the honest effort to make amends.

How adorable. With a wake of casualties behind him deep enough to buoy a gunboat, there was little restitution that could be made.

Crimes required justice.

Or worse still, he was here as an undercover agent all right—but not of the Jergad.

The Capitals had shown their true colors, as every advisor had warned him they would. As his own gut had warned him. When the Ministry came knocking, they would not point the finger at a young man drafted into the service in a desperate time with little training or conditioning; they would blame the Commander.

Unless Riley could give them some other meat.

The Oskies searched the prisoners at multiple checkpoints as they advanced deeper into the Pits, each subsequent search more thorough than the last. Against all expectations, they were clean—not so much as a sharpened bit of wood on their persons.

Six soldiers, no weapons.

The mystery deepens.

Riley ordered them separated and observed, isolating them into individual blocks. Together, they would direct all communication through Aaron, but alone they might let slip their true purpose. Curiously, they sat silent with a rather conceited demeanor. They did not engage the cameras or the interviews in any way, like they would rather wait for what punishments may come.

It was highly disquieting. Something was wrong, but they just weren't finding it.

Time to be drastic.

Riley's command center had been cobbled together on the top floor of the Apartments, sweeping away a half dozen small shrines and altars someone had constructed in vain pagan rituals. There were no walls or delineations like the lower floors, but a wide-open loft, allowing the Oskies the freedom to establish themselves as they wished.

The giant studio was now strewn with barely organized equipment, nearly a dozen different screens and feeds, including Thor's Hammer satellite photography and closed circuit feeds from Vanguard population centers. There were frequent recorded broadcasts urging the citizens to seek shelter in their bunkers, sealed away until reinforcements could secure the city.

Such reinforcement hadn't even been dispatched. The hundred or so Regulars who had assembled were in such disarray that they were enjoying a warm meal in the Apartment's lower levels. But that didn't wash the foul taste from their mouths. Humans were in danger and they were on orders to sit it out.

Grumblings of discontent had made their way to Riley's ears, but that didn't stop them from following their orders or carrying out their duties. These were the Empire's battalions; their families were safe light years away.

Even still, those were their charges being left out to bleed. It didn't sit well. With anyone. Even Riley's neck itched.

Two of the more obedient grunts brought Aaron for presentation, his forearms bound together behind his back and irons clasped about his ankles, like they were bringing him as the accused before a magistrate.

He looked terrible—dried blood gone crispy on his forehead, a bloody bandage soaked through, and his clothes stained with mildew. It had been months since he'd had a shower, and a patchy beard adding to his feral look. He looked like a man dead several times over, but refused to stop walking.

"Did they fish you out of a dumpster?" Riley asked, genuinely concerned at the man's condition.

Aaron looked down at his clothes. "You like 'em? They were free."

"The previous owner is...alive?"

"No idea," Aaron said, "There has been a lot of killing tonight."

Riley leaned on a table, sitting on one hip as he gnawed on a ration bar. He sniffed away the grime that had started collecting in his nose from the tainted air. "That's nothing. You know, when they hit the city, the first warning is going to be a 3.2 earthquake. Rolling thunder. As they burrow. The quake will get worse...and then they hit. Whole thing takes less than a minute from first detection to first blood."

"That's when *you* draw blood, is that it?"

There was no point in feigning friendship or building a relationship now. Those ships had sailed off the edge of the map. Today's interaction would bear a bit more natural hostility to it.

And this interrogation had to have a bit more direct bargaining involved.

Riley wiped his lips, scraping the dry flakes of dehydrated paste away. "A lot of people have read about them. Only a handful will know what to expect. If they listen to the broadcasts, they'll be in the bunkers."

"You've got to go back."

Riley glanced over at Aaron, dismissive. "They didn't want me there. Your little friend was very clear on that."

"You're Master & Commander Local Allied Forces," Aaron said. "You care about being popular?"

"I care when they throw rocks at me, yeah. I think you would too, so don't get haughty with me."

"So you sentence them to death?"

Riley turned to face Aaron, leaning on the table. "No. I just don't really give a damn anymore."

"Why?"

There was the hook. Grab that and unravel him.

"You tell me," Riley said. "You're an observant man."

Aaron considered his subject for a moment, a rookie leader painting a picture. Amateur.

"You're quite the Patriot," Aaron supplied, "but that stops at the water's edge. When things go right, you'll take all the ribbons and awards, all the promotions they throw at you. When things go wrong, it's because of the world. Never you. When it's time to do the right thing, the hard thing—no praise, no reward—you choke."

Riley seethed, his skin tightening and his eyes burning. It took every ounce of his will not to wring the life out of the little *skel* with his bare hands.

"How demonic," was all he said. "And if this were a normal place in a normal command, I wouldn't blame you for that read."

"You think this is special?"

Riley blinked. "You're going to tell me it's not? I had to draft up Capitals for God's sake. This was a rather extreme situation."

"So fix it, Colonel," Aaron said, almost begging. "You didn't stay here and do all of this just to sit back and wash your hands of it. You did the right thing every step of the way."

"Damn right I did," Riley huffed, "And this is the thanks you give me?"

"Why stop now?" Aaron asked, "Those are the people you swore to protect."

"I still am. The only way they'll let me."

"You want to know what they'll let you do? You want to know?" Aaron said, shuffling on his knees, like he might edge up in his proverbial seat. "You get the credit."

Riley blinked a few times, "For what, exactly? Complete the thought."

"For the peace," Aaron whispered. "The aliens aren't coming to Vanguard. They never were. Put the gun down."

Riley pointed at the tectonic sensor behind him without even looking at it. Their Thumpers had been charting movement for hours. "Pierson Corridor scales don't seem to agree with you. The Jergad are on the move and in force."

"You gave the order to abandon the Wall twelve hours ago. Do the math. The city should be an inch deep in blood by now," Aaron said, cocking his head. "They're moving, alright. But they're not attacking."

Like a Dog at an electric fence. They were skirting edges, waiting to get punished for their hubris. And it wasn't coming. And yet, they were staying their hand.

Even Aaron's handlers were exchanging weird looks.

"It's your name they're shouting in the streets." Riley said, "I'm the one that killed their Governor."

"They'll cheer for whoever we tell them to," Aaron urged. "Bring them good news and they will erect monuments to you. You really think they'll try you for murder when they can credit you with saving every—single—life?"

The thought was tantalizing, his skin crackling and hair standing on end. He could almost taste it in the air, forcing him to swallow his pride lest it leap out of him. "And what will the Capital get? Hm?"

Aaron hesitated for a moment, his face softening. "A quiet life. My freedom. No more killing."

"Had enough, eh?"

Aaron could barely push the word past his lips. "...Yes."

With the scion of peace by his side, he could come back to Vanguard a hero. He would have proven with his action that their long national nightmare had ended. The Jergad were not coming. It was well and truly over. They need not walk on a knife's edge for a day longer. People could finally sleep.

But those towers would be torn down, the monuments defaced, and his memory ripped apart the moment the Empire finally arrived.

"No," Riley stared at the Capital, "I'll do you one better. I think our enemy is patient, and our people...complacent. I think they need the object lesson. It's only a matter of time before the aliens decide to make their push and I'll be ready when they do. A close encounter with a Drone is a rather...singular moment for a person. Don't you think?"

Aaron's jaw slackened. "You're going to hang them out to dry... out of spite?"

"Everything I've done has been to keep them safe. Everything *you've* done, too! You feel appreciated? You go out on to that field and your resumé says 'bleed for the other guy.' And when the mountain folk asked real nicely, you decided to bleed for them too. Has anybody on any side of this even so much as thanked you?" Riley thumped his chest, a bit harder than he meant to. "I did. I knew what I was asking from Day One. And I knew what I promised."

Make the sales pitch, right there.

"Freedom, Aaron Havenes. It was a heavy cost for a heavy item. And it's still on the table but let me crank it up a notch."

Riley took a knee in front of Aaron, pinching the man's face between thumb and forefinger like he was inspecting his food. "You... are a helluva soldier. You should be one. Not just free. I could sponsor your commission in the Imperial Navy. Serve with honor for a change, fight for something with meaning beyond yourself. Gain a family. So what do you say, one last time? Freedom...for a little obedience?"

Aaron took a deep breath, and the guards squeezed on his arms, as if to say 'try nothing.' Not like the boy was in a position to do much of anything. Riley could dispatch his prisoner like he was swatting an insect. Aaron was no threat, and there was nothing hanging on decency.

Riley had to get the statement he needed. A Capital could not have instigated a rebellion all on his own, with nothing but supposition and mythology.

"Who told you to do this?" Riley asked, pointedly.

"Do what?" Aaron blinked. "I surrendered myself. To get here. So you would come back."

"Think bigger," Riley urged. "Who told you...to be *you* for the last few months?"

Aaron glanced aside, like he was scanning through the video footage of his memories. Satisfied with what he found, he looked back up at Riley. "You know who."

"No," Riley maintained. "Who told you to say that?"

"They did."

Riley shook his head. "And we spent months trying to corroborate that with no success. I'll ask again, Capital. A broken Wall, a destroyed Howler, and dozens of casualties—not to mention your existing record—all up in the air. Who...told you to do it?"

It was a small motion at first, like Aaron was having a seizure, but the rhythm was too even. A half second later Riley realized he was laughing.

Aaron lifted his head, a big dumb smile across his face. "I'm sorry. I just got it. Sorry...I've had no food for a bit, I'm a little slow."

Riley stared daggers at the laughing Capital, a man chuckling in face of devastation. He was truly a madman.

Aaron finally settled. "You think...*Talania* told me to. You think she saved my life all that while ago...and I owe her. You think *she's* behind everything—the riots, my story—"

"What I think happened is irrelevant, Capital." Riley hissed, trying to force the train back onto the tracks by intimated threats and willpower alone. "I want to set down for the record what *actually* happened."

"Bullshit," Aaron sneered, clearly having given up on politics and niceties. "If you get me to finger Talania, suddenly your failures are one grand conspiracy starting at the very top. If it's her, then you were set up to fail...and all the deaths tonight are on her head. Not yours. You're absolved."

"Did she?"

"No. You drove her right into me," Aaron shrugged, "Sad to say."

"I can fabricate all the evidence I need, Capital." Riley was done with implications and covert action. "I don't need you alive. Cooperate or die. Those are your choices."

"You think any court in this world or the next is going to be strengthened by the testimony of a convicted Capital, a man excommunicated and banned from the Pilgrim's light?" Aaron jeered, almost daring his captors to do their worst. "Riley, even you seem to think I'm more important than I am. This whole thing...is going to go the way it's going to go, with or without me."

Well, that's a damn shame.

"Iron sulfide, when exposed to air, produces Hydrogen sulfide. Smells like rotten eggs. But you knew that already, didn't you?"

Aaron's eyes darkened a bit, but Riley was on a roll.

"It takes your eyes first, then your lungs rupture. In appropriate doses. We'll be administering an inappropriate amount."

Aaron looked like he might snarl, a caged animal. "Am I taking somebody else's spot? 'Cause I wouldn't want to impose."

It was almost a threat. Amusing.

Riley drew his pistol. "I lied. You and your friends were never going to get your freedom."

"You say that like you're disappointing me."

Riley pursed his lips. "Well, then..." Riley looked up at his men. "Prep a sled. You're not going to want to drag this sack all the way to the Tailings Dam."

"Last chance, Riley," Aaron pursed his lips. "Go back to Vanguard."

Riley shook his head. "Anybody else tired of his voice? Because I'm tired of his voice."

Wide beam, soft focus, full power. The pistol moaned to life, like it was waking from a long slumber.

And Aaron just smiled, psychopathic, the dark round cheeks of a cat and its canary-eating face. "It doesn't matter either way."

Riley's eyes narrowed. "How's that?"

The ground shook under their feet and a fine powder fell from the ceiling like an industrial rain.

Aaron's eyes darkened and for a split second, Riley thought he saw a flash of blue cross the dry brown. "They're not going to the City, Riley. I'm hooked into their network. They know exactly where I am. And they're coming to me. Dead or alive, they know the only way to peace...is through you."

Riley tapped a comm code into his tablet. "Thor, authorization code Kilo Zebra Epsilon—"

"You don't have to do this!" Aaron shouted. At Riley, at the crew in orbit. At everyone.

Riley scoffed and squeezed the trigger—and the ground rolled underneath him.

The shot slid wide of Aaron's head, scorching a spatter of carbon on the floor in a long trough. The building seemed to revolt against the attack, melting into a fluid and then a following sea, lashing against his ankles in unpredictable shoves as though it were fickle and abusive.

His augments kicked in, tracking every conceivable detail. His officers held their arms wide as they tried to hold their balance, while Aaron had crumpled to the floor on his side.

Cracks ran up the wall, drawing their charcoal fingers along the slate and concrete with a loose hand. Light bulbs hanging from the ceiling hummed to some alien frequency, as they tilted in unison to one side, like a line of chorus dancers.

Far below them, amongst the sounds of crunching stone and creaking beams, he could make out the occasional chitter of busy little Drones carving up the terrain.

And that's when the floor fell away, as the building found the ground it founded upon had been removed.

When Riley opened his eyes, he could hear water flowing. But that couldn't be water...

CHAPTER
TWENTY-SIX

AARON

A ONCE STURDY STRUCTURE, weakened by the years, had just been proverbially thrown down the stairs. An entire building kicked in the knee and brought to heel. The problem with that, is buildings don't like being dropped.

Aaron awoke in a hallway, with bits of the cement draped over his back. The roof and upper floors were now propped on the support pillars, leaning the whole building to one side, like a hat settled onto a decapitated neck.

He had punched right through the crumbling slate floor, slamming through two whole floors. The dust cloud hung about him like a fog. His shoulder screamed, and his head rung, but at this point, when didn't his head hurt?

He expected the Queen and her cavalry to make a grand entrance, sure. Maybe one of her beasties would surge through a wall or reach up through the floor to snag a guard in a dramatic upheaval.

But no—we brought the building down to them.

The gurgle of a heady stream or a lazy river snapped him to his senses. Somewhere below him at the edge of hearing, there was moving liquid.

Strange, as the Apartments had their aquifer disconnected and the plumbing extracted to seal the building for prison habitation. What possible—

The smell hit him like a knife up his nose. The Tailings. There were toxic chemicals flowing en masse into the lower levels, which would push right on up like a gas line of death. He could start taking shallow breaths, or he could be tasting the inside of his lungs in short order.

A chitter at his back, the deep-throated croak of something large. He knew that sound all too well: the battlefield muttering of a two-ton hostile angry organic bulldozer.

Time to put up or shut up—were they friendly?

The arm bone of its scythe brushed against his forearm, teasing, almost like it was stroking him, perhaps savoring a kill.

Or was this subterranean demon petting him, cooing and shushing him? Though if it were trying to soothe his fears and pains, maybe doing it with a three-foot blade was the wrong way to do it.

Aaron closed his eyes, welcoming whatever came next. It wasn't like he had any say in the matter.

There was a swift jerk on his wrists and the bindings slackened, his hands dropping to his sides. He felt the stiff blade nudge his side—

Nudge. The force alone flipped him right over, bringing him face to face with the cosmic horror from his nightmares. Despite that bifurcated jawbone and the crushing teeth, the leathery mottled flesh and the blank hollow stare, he felt some comfort in its pure blue eye.

Eye, singular, because the other had a vicious scar hollowing to a pit. A knife scar.

His knife.

Scar nudged him again, that strange purr rolling from somewhere deep in its throat.

Get up.

Aaron looked down at his feet, trying to direct focus down. His ankles were still bound too.

It hooked its immense scythes on either side of the ankle locks, pinching them together and crushing the bindings like they were simply stale bread. The metal sang out with a soprano tone and was silenced as soon as it began.

Scar stuck its scythe-finger out, holding the backside to his chest like he was some unit of measurement. It was nearly half the length of his body.

And it took a short jerk from the alien before Aaron realized it was offering him a hand.

Aaron had to override every single instinct in his body to stick his fingers inside the scythe's bladed edge, hooking around the knuckle of the blade high above the natural serrations near the leathery knot at the joint.

The bone felt porous and light, like it might be hollow. He remembered that stone he plucked from the mining rig all those months ago and it occurred to him that the bone had been more...fresh than he had thought then.

The Jergad raised its arm, hefting him up from the floor like he was weightless, its impressive natural strength made for carving stone rendering his tiny frame meaningless.

Aaron looked the monster from crested head to taloned toe, finally resting on that familiar blue eye—the Queen's eyes. "Maybe next time, your Highness, give me a heads up you're about to drop a building I'm *still inside!*"

"Shoot it! Shoot it!"

The Jergad swooped around, presenting its skull fan to the voices. Gunfire rang out and Aaron hunkered low behind his protector, as shots skipped off the leathery hide and chunking the stone around them. The beastie croaked and chittered with the assault, taking fierce blows.

An inhuman cry came as one clean shot punched through the shield, impacting the wall behind Aaron, bits of blood and bone showering over him.

Furious and pained, Scar gripped the floor with its taloned feet—scratching long lines in the concrete—and drove forward. Aaron stumbled along behind it but there was no keeping pace with this runaway freight train as it barreled down the crumbling hallway. The ground dented underfoot, sinking—and in some cases, collapsing—under Scar's weight and aggression.

The two Regulars at the end of the Hall had emptied their magazines in the vain notion that many bullets is what the situation required and not careful placement.

Two tons of angry leather and blade slammed into them, tossing the first soldier to the side, as it had selected his friend for ruin. The sickening crunch and squelch implied the result had something in kind with paste.

The surviving Regular fumbled the magazine into the well and dropped the bolt. The Jergad had left its vulnerable thorax exposed.

The Capitals had been assigned the JP-36 assault rifle: antiquated and flawed. The Regular was shouldering something newer, more modern. But it looked similar enough.

And the soldier was...preoccupied with his target.

Aaron reached up from behind the Regular, lifting the rifle at the magwell. With his thumb, he depressed the release, sending the magazine flying free. It looked like he had half-heartedly tossed a rock at the Jergad's rugged hide.

One shot in the chamber and that was it—which promptly went into the roof.

Aaron dropped his boot into the Regular's knee before shoving him to the ground. The rifle spun in the air, like it was wistfully searching for its owner. Aaron snatched it like a baton.

The Jergad whirled about, looking for the commotion. It loomed over Aaron, even in its hunched position.

It was an intimidating sight, Aaron and monster both menacing over the collapsed and quivering Regular. He couldn't even muster the wherewithal to point at the Jergad, his hands shaking and horror in his eyes.

He had likely seen the critters before, but nobody had ever been this close and come away without damage. And despite his fear, he couldn't look away from Aaron—who stood with a genuine demon at his back—the prophet of peace. The man soaked in the impossibility before him.

Aaron reached down to the prostrate man, plucking two fresh magazines from the man's vest. He pocketed one, slapping the other home in the rifle.

The creature hissed somewhere behind him, its hot breath buffeting around his bare neck. Aaron looked back at the beast, with its scarred skull fan and a fresh wound. Its blank expression scanned him over, waiting for some instruction. Where to, how far, and who was in their way?

He looked back at their captive, as he shouldered the rifle. "Empty hands. And keep your head down. Whatever you do, don't look back. Go, now."

Aaron marched away, leaving the frustrated Jergad to give one last threatening hiss before falling into tow. That man would have to clean his face of spittle before he could think about moving.

Exiting that hallway might have been the single worst decision of Aaron's brief and terrifying military service. Sounds of battle echoed up and down as though it came from everywhere and nowhere at once.

The warm tone of discharging lasers and cracks of ballistic fire were the rhythm to a cacophony of screams, fear, and frenzy in equal measure, metered only by the dull echoes muted against the stone walls. The occasional ring of falling brass shells pierced the air, but most of the ordinance being delivered went without the corresponding report.

Heavy footfalls filled the empty spaces, dozens upon dozens, so as to blend into one continuous march. But those were not human boots challenging the gunfire for command of the air.

The Jergad had brought their full force.

Beyond the sound, a dull haze hung on the air, a blend of the cement dust kicked up by the collapse and the sulfide moisture leaking up from below, clinging to any particle it could find in a yellow mist, like toxic veils.

Aaron had no idea if the Jergad was going to have issues with this, but *he* had to get up and away from that lethal cloud.

Aaron took the stairs two at a time, his uniform pulled over his mouth as a makeshift air filter. The taste of it hit him in the back of his mouth, stinging his throat and coating his tongue like it was wrapped in an acrid paste. It felt like someone had jammed a rusty spoon in his mouth—blood.

He didn't think the thin fabric was doing him much good, but he wasn't about to lower what little defense he had.

He passed holes in walls and cracks thick enough to shove his arm through. The building had been riddled with damage *before* it was dropped onto bedrock. Lord knows how the building was still standing at all.

Of course, he found his high-minded escape stopped short. The stairs to the top floor had collapsed, the brittle and aged struts finally sundering under the abuse. After all, a building had slipped a full twelve feet into the ground, and no part of it was built for that kind of stress.

Aaron would have to find another way up.

"On the left!"

He knew that voice, strained, dry, almost like it was being shouted through a fan.

Keira. His friends were somewhere on this floor.

He turned, darting between chunks of fallen detritus. He probably looked a tad ridiculous with the organic tank rumbling behind him.

It was his Fifth Floor dormitories—his old home—crumbling walls and tilted furniture. If he hadn't committed its brand of mess to memory, he would not have blinked, but the blood and gore added a new texture to this horror show.

Corpses littered the hallway, almost a dozen armed and armored Imperial Regulars. It was like a spirit had come through and drawn their souls out of their chests through a series of high caliber exit wounds.

He saw the muzzle flash before he saw anyone, pale yellow strobes illuminating the hallway's distressed edges. Hidden from view somewhere in the rubble was a shooter, and an aggressive one at that. The rifle reports came in brisk chirps, groupings of hostile cracks.

As violent and random as it might have appeared, there was careful trigger discipline, letting off only short controlled bursts despite the constant fire.

He saw her red hair first, thinning at the scalp and stringy at the ends.

"Oy!" Keira barked, as she poked her filthy grimy skull out from behind the rocks. "You made a friend."

Aaron threw a glance at Scar behind him as he took stock of the carnage around him. "You seem to have things handled."

Solomon popped up from their little hole, facing the wrong way like he was presenting himself for a headshot. His hair was smeared in other people's blood like he'd been massaging his neck with the stuff. "Who is it?"

"It's Aaron!" Keira pointed, and Solomon spun about.

Aaron's jaw dropped, seeing the 'war paint' Solomon had adopted. He had actually smeared it on his neck, under his eyes and nose—and done so with care.

Scar purred somewhere behind him—its reaction was far more delighted than Aaron's was.

He tried to shake off the sight. "Where's Riley?"

"No idea," Solomon said, pointing down the corridor to the pile of bodies around him, "Maybe good ol' Ugly there can sniff him out?"

Aaron looked back at the Jergad—perforated skull fan, missing an eye, and despite its hideous countenance, was able to cock its head like a confused shepherd dog.

Did these things even have a sense of smell? Scar sure as hell wasn't going to say, but Aaron's memory of the mountains implied otherwise.

Movement beyond, past Solomon and Keira. He recognized the threat by their uniform. An Orbital officer rounded the corner, their curious laser rifle tucked against their hip.

The impressive little bunker of rock and debris that Solomon and Keira had taken refuge in was about to be as effective as plaster.

Even Aaron's personal bodyguard wouldn't do much against that.

And, of course, Scar hissed at the new threat. Without a word, Aaron looked back at Scar. With a chitter and a twitter in response, it plowed right through a wall and out of sight to the left, off to flank its new threat.

The Oskie raised his rifle, thumbing the capacitor. As dangerous as Aaron might be, they couldn't let that Jergad flow freely through the battlefield. A tight beam no broader than a pencil drove through the wall, guessing a path where the beast had to be.

Aaron didn't hear any protest from Scar, so the shot must have been wasted.

But the beam - or Scar for that matter - must've sawed through something of import, as the building lurched again, sagging in its muddy foundations. Everyone stubbled and staggered, trying to find their footing in a building rapidly losing its own stability.

Keira surged from her hole at the stumbling Oskie.

The element of surprise was damn near insignificant. Her hand found their rifle, and they seemed to pirouette the damn thing out and around her hands. They were so fast, she mostly discovered where they were before they blinked away again.

She was twice their size, but found their hand at her throat, heaving her up into the air.

They studied her like a curiosity more than a threat, carefully presenting her to the world as a shield. Aaron could swear he heard the augmentations and implants grind to life, tiny servos leveraging chemical batteries for the impressive strength.

Whatever alloy bands held those arms taut, whatever motors and processors lent their aid, made them more than mere man.

Solomon saw the Oskie and saw Keira—saw her in danger. It was like a switch flipped, or a string snapped. He didn't make a sound, as he lunged forward, coated in blood like an archon of death. He hopped in the air, reaching out with his rifle to find an angle around Keira's large frame.

He found it and fired. Adorable.

The Oskie stepped forward, simultaneously lurching out of the shot's vector and slamming Keira into Solomon, sending them crashing back into their foxhole. One—if not both of them—had probably broken some ribs.

Aaron snapped his rifle up, snug to his shoulder. He had seen Riley step out of the way of a shot trained on the back of his skull. He had seen Holmst throw a grenade before Aaron could open his mouth. Was it even worth the trigger pull?

Do it.

Aaron tapped off a shot, center-mass. The muzzle brake spat fire up and to the sides in a three-pointed star, like he was brushing aside the fresh dust with tongues of flame. The vibrations shook the walls, a knock on the doors of Hell.

The Oskie watched it come in, the copper jacket just another particularly annoying family pet. They pulled to the side only just far enough to let the bullet slide harmlessly past their shoulder, the sudden jerk launching a curtain of dust in the air like a billowing cloak in their wake.

The focus in the eyes was electric and hypnotizing, as they tracked a dozen items in just a blink, almost soothing in their hyper-perceptive state. Aaron swore he could see flashes of yellow light in the dark of those pupils.

They lowered their rifle, training on Solomon and Keira without even turning their head.

Aaron snapped off more shots. He didn't have a prayer of hitting the Oskie, not at this distance. Each shot was met with more blurs of motion, but he was noticing something—the Oskie was gasping for breath. They may be more than man, but they were hardly machines.

Aaron might not be able to break this stone, but he could wear it down.

"Keep up the pressure!"

The Oskie heard the order as much as his allies did. They squeezed the trigger and blasted the makeshift cover shielding Solomon and Keira, scorching the stone to a black powder—along with anything hiding there.

Comforted by the lack of blood-curdling screams, Aaron snarled and resumed his fire, forcing the Oskie back to his own cover. But it was a short time before Aaron's weapon clicked empty in his hands—and Scar was nowhere near close enough, still barreling through apartment walls.

The Oskie leveled their weapon at Aaron.

And found Keira charging in again, this time swinging her rifle like a bat.

The Oskie slid deftly out of the way—slamming on Solomon's quick knife, rammed to the hilt into the Oskie's gasping open mouth.

The Oskie gurgled and choked. Solomon held two fingers to his lips, shushing the croaking pains.

"Checkmate, friend," Solomon said, like a good sportsman shaking the hand of a worthy opponent.

The tip of the blade had punched clean through and actually lifted the Oskie's helmet off of the nape of their neck.

Keira had forced the Oskie to move or be hit—and Solomon was waiting at the only place left to go. It was a teamwork pinch at its finest.

Scar peeked around the corner, and Solomon cocked his head: monster meet monster. Solomon clucked his tongue, like he was calling over a horse.

The Jergad stomped over, towering over the kill. Solomon nodded toward the Oskie. "For obvious reasons, I can't let 'em loose. Would you mind?"

"They don't really speak--"

Aaron stopped as the Jergad slammed a claw into the Oskie's chest.

Solomon plucked his knife from the impaled victim, wiping it on his sleeve like he might a camping blade. Keira slumped against a wall, favoring her side. "Like I said, I think we got this handled."

Scar slid the corpse off its claw like it was dumping laundry on the floor. Solomon smirked at the display, the mess left by a pet too adorable to scold.

He glanced up at Aaron. "Go find the others."

Aaron nodded, tapping Keira on the shoulder as he jogged past Solomon's kill. That psychotic pair was going to be just fine, long as they had each other. One held up the other, always. It might even be romantic if there wasn't quite so much carnage and mayhem.

Aaron slid to a stop at the end of the hallway, half inspecting his surroundings and half scanning his memory.

Scar nudged him along, tapping his leg with one of its mandibles. Now that was a strange feeling, like being tapped with a length of leathery pipe.

"What do you want, the stairs are out," Aaron said.

Scar reached up.

"Don't—"

Too late. Scar stabbed its claws into the ceiling and pulled, tearing a chunk of roof down. Thankfully, the rebar reinforcements only bent, and the slab propped up as a steep ramp.

Scar cocked his head, with a deep cooing coming from high up in its head.

Aaron shook his head, but another voice chimed in before he could, "What the Hell, Aaron?"

Eden's abrasive voice was undercut by the wide smile on her face, "Get up here!"

Aaron scampered up the steep incline, snagging his fingertips on the ledge above. For the briefest of deja vu, he thanked Bray for enforcing all of those timed obstacle courses.

He scrambled against the ledge, working to pull himself up. Eden gripped his forearm, her soft fingers biting in with uncommon strength. More vice than hand, she braced and heaved him up through the hole.

The two crumpled together beside a table, to gather their breath and composure.

It was Riley's basecamp, now a few floors lower than before. Computers were dark, glass scattered everywhere, a power line swinging impotently, quietly the most dangerous thing in the room.

Eden gave him a once over. "You gave yourself another concussion?"

"Good to see you too," Aaron murmured.

"So much brain damage," Eden said, smiling wide, "I'm going to get you a helmet. A dorky one."

She was glad to see him, glad to see him alive, glad to see him unhurt. Just glad. Thankful.

Scar whined below them, sensing their distress. He coiled up.

"Oh, no, no - don't!" Aaron tried to warn the critter. With all the structural harm, there was no conceivable way the floor would hold the tonnage of a full grown and angry Jergad drone.

But it was not to be dissuaded. Scar leapt up through the whole, clearing the gap and clean over Aaron and Eden's post. Its landing was almost graceful, still shaking the entire floor.

"Friend of yours?" Eden asked from between the beastie's legs.

"I mean, we've met before."

Snaps and cracks of bullets skipping off the ground around them, ripping and chunking through the wood like the mere inconvenience it was. They had cover from sight, and that's about it.

The only defense they had was that they weren't the target.

The shots were deafening, the sounds echoing off the walls and bouncing back to marry with more, making for louder and louder chaos.

Scar dropped its head low, assuming a defensive stance with its skull fan up and face unnervingly close to Eden's. It somehow roared with a thunder to challenge the fusillade, forcing Eden to clasp her hands over her ears.

It crawled over the cover like it wasn't even there, advancing on the unseen threat.

The Jergad was offering protection, both literal shielding and drawing some focus.

Time to go.

Aaron took off running, Eden close behind, as the barrage peppered into Scar's leathery hide. Whatever harm the beast was absorbing, it had little concern for its own safety. Its life belonged to a greater whole, to which Aaron also belonged now.

Aaron could see the shooters now: three Regulars huddled behind their own table, barely sighting in as they sprayed entire magazines at the marching demon. They might not have had accuracy, but they were doing enough.

Scar stumbled as a round drove through its knee. The titan whimpered and chittered, dropping onto its face. It tried to prop itself up, drag itself forward, onward. Refusing to die.

The Regulars crept out from cover, ready to finish the job.

"Hey, assholes!"

Whatever half-second pause that offered was enough, as Nora popped out from behind a pillar, steel rebar in one hand and empty pistol in the other. She went to work, smashing heads and legs.

This was no fluid ballet; this was an angry woman who had grabbed anything at hand.

One Regular went down hard, dropping within Scar's reach. The beast reached out, snagging the poor sod with a claw and dragging him into range of the half dozen weapons it had available. The term wheat thresher came to mind, as it reduced him to a pulp in seconds.

Something about the violence—maybe the adrenaline or the sheer force of will—brought Scar back up onto his crippled legs, exerting years of hatred down onto one man.

Nora finally met resistance, as the Regulars remembered their training—fire and tenacity were no match for actual hand to hand skills.

With the element of surprise removed, they soon had her gunpoint.

"Capital bitch!"

She just smirked back at her executioners, bloody gums and pearly whites. For they had forgotten about the rest of the room.

Aaron and Eden fired two shots, so synchronized they sounded like one, and the Regulars fell. Nora flinched a bit, as a chunk of lead split through the wall over her shoulder.

The Regulars hadn't even hit the ground before she was complaining.

"You almost hit me!" Nora shouted, pointing at the impact.

"Somebody *did*," Eden said, pointing at the deep gash in Nora's thigh.

Nora looked down at the stained red patch of flesh and cloth, with even some black scoring from the muzzle flash etching a scatter pattern. One of the Regulars, here or in some former skirmish, had gotten off a lucky shot.

She cursed the wound, more out of her level of stupidity than out of pain. "Yup. Yup, now I feel it."

She reached to prop herself against a wall and found Scar's hide. She favored the leg, electing to lean completely against the Jergad's massive frame.

Scar chittered some apology, almost a purr. It's only then Nora recognized what it was. She stared at the big beast, wary of it, fully able to read its intent but months of conditioning urging her to beware.

"You're losing a lot of blood, lady," Eden scolded, "But it just skipped off your quadricep. Nothing primary."

"I'm bleedin', you're bleedin'. Tell me something I don't know. Like," Nora must've felt the Jergad move again, as she popped off of him. "What is *your* deal?"

Scar murmured something. Did that big guy just shrug?

ALLEN A IVERS

That was Keira, Solomon, Nora, Eden. Who was missing? Aaron stepped up. "Anybody seen Jensen?"

"Not since we checked in to the Hotel Deplorable," Nora sat on the floor, wincing as she extended her wounded leg for Eden to see. "But I know where Riley went."

Aaron's eyes darkened, and Scar growled deep, a mutual and silent oath. "Where?"

"Down," she grunted, "Gas mask and all."

Aaron chewed on that. Riley was going into the fumes, where the unequipped heroes couldn't follow.

Sulfide poisoning was a nasty way to go, and Riley knew they wouldn't throw away their own lives for an admittedly small chance of apprehending him.

"No," Eden snapped, "I know that look! It's suicide in three different ways."

"You're assuming he's not going to come quietly," Aaron said, looking back at Scar. "He's a reasonable guy, right?"

He could swear, the big guy actually smiled, pulling its mandibles back high and tight.

"You don't have to do this anymore," Eden barked.

"He's got Thor's Hammer trained on fifty thousand people," Aaron shot back, "and nothing to lose."

"They won't shoot at civilians. They won't do it."

Nora huffed. "You want to bet?"

Aaron walked up to Scar, rubbing a hand across the rigid hide. He had never actually touched a Jergad before, not in a moment when he could think about it. It felt coarse, almost like sandstone, porous and rough. Might be why the bastards were so fast if it was both strong and light.

The several wounds had already stopped bleeding, the deep red almost black, mixing with the concrete powder into a toxic mud that could not be healthy. It stained his fingers, smearing like oil.

He remembered the blood on his hands from a murder so long

ago, washing away in the rain. "Just one more," Aaron said, marching across the top floor.

Eden left Nora leaning on the wall, stalking after him. "His forces are scattered, he's just a single man now. He walks into the desert, you think the Jergard are going to let him be?!" Scar growled at that thought. "He has no power anymore. It's *over*, Aaron. We won!"

It was a tempting notion, to walk away now, take the chips down and call it a day. Riley wasn't going to surrender; maybe just let the planet hunt him. The Queen could amuse herself with dogging his heels until she finally pinned him to a corner and etched all her pains onto his flesh.

And how many people would Riley kill in the meantime? How many shots would Thor's Hammer take against the 'rebels' while Riley roamed free?

Aaron had killed a lot of people to get here. No choice in the matter. This one time, he was going to choose to. Maybe that would make all the other times feel better?

"The front door's probably buried by now," Aaron said, working out the problem, "He'll want—what, the third or fourth floor?"

"Don't do that to me, Aaron!" Eden bellowed at him, "Do not-! You've died. Twice. Left us all behind. Maybe you're casual about it now, but we're not!"

Aaron looked back at her, the tears she steadfastly shoved back in her eyes, leaning into the rage, refusing to let grief take the stage. Every fiber of her was shaking, vibrating like a plucked string, but her footing was solid.

She was a Doctor first and foremost, and she would absolutely prevent her patients from coming to harm; but she was also a Capital, trained and conditioned to die in place of another. There was a respect, a belief, and an admiration in her eyes that seemed to bake into a form of dread, a reverence surrounding the most common man poisoned by the unfortunate truth.

She cared about him more than her Hippocratic oath would allow her to admit.

Walk her back from that now. He had to let her go.

"A young man has a gun, Eden. And he feels betrayed, angry—and now he's alone." Aaron said, "What do you think happens next?"

"Don't go. Please." That's all she had left. He didn't blame her.

"This world goes spinning on without little ol' me. What we've started, isn't going to stop. But Riley...he can move whole mountains."

He bit his lip, feeling his own stomach churn at the truth he was contemplating. She was right. He wasn't coming back from this. "Me for him? I'll take that deal."

"If it was a clean swap," she blurted too fast, as she tried to walk back her own overstep, "You for him? I'd say 'sure.' But this isn't that! This is just a chance!"

"And a terrible one at that," Nora chimed in.

Aaron shook his head. "We're wasting time."

He turned and slung himself onto Scar, a dark rider astride a demon's back. It was probably fifty feet to the ground below, and he was betting on a crippled alien's fortitude to get them there. This was going to be an interesting ride.

"Aaron—"

"We didn't choose to be here," he said, catching a look of her brown eyes and matted hair one last time.

She shook her head and drew a shaky breath, "We just choose to do something about it."

He opened his mouth, as if he might say something more, a button on it all, but nothing came. In that moment, he failed her. He couldn't say goodbye or promise to see her again. He had hurt them before but never so purposefully.

He was on that mountainside, forcing them to watch as he deliberately ended his own life. This wasn't a kindness; it was torture. His choice was not limited to him, but it would leave a wake of damage in its passing.

There was no good option.

He had to choose, which pain he wanted for his friends. A lifetime of servitude to pay, or a lifetime of freedom bought.

"For what it's worth, I'm sorry."

And with that, Scar charged at the wall. Aaron crouched low, hiding behind Scar's crest. There was no time to make out the details of the wall, as he was suddenly bathed in sunlight.

It took two seconds. He counted. Just two seconds from crashing through the wall till the ground punched him in the chest.

Scar's wounded legs took an impressive amount of the abuse, but they had just jumped out of a sixth story window, for all intents and purposes. They should be goo, and instead, Aaron just had to catch his wind.

Aaron looked back at the structure. It wasn't just collapsed, it was actively sinking, a bobbing cork. He had lived for years in that building, a casual unknown to guards and friends alike. The fifth floor he had felt so warm in was now the third and soon to be the second. Yellow gas eked out of the lower levels, and the raucous battles inside could still be heard bleeding from the walls.

Scar propped itself up, standing tall on its battered and broken legs, no thought for its own suffering. Aaron might have thought it was out of some sense of loyalty or determination, but the Jergad had suffered far greater pains than this. This was an arm of a larger creature, and it could be motivated by a will far grander than any Aaron had concept of.

A bullet to the leg was not going to kneecap an entire species.

He dropped the empty magazine from his rifle, slapping his last one home. Secure the magwell, check the safety, wrap the trigger and press the shoulder.

Both eyes open. Aim small, miss small.

"Where is he?" Aaron found himself saying out loud. A flash across his vision, coupled with a blinding circle etched into his corneas, like a highlighter around anything he looked at. He felt the oncoming headache like a spike through his left eye, straight through to the back of his neck and crown of his head.

313

And in that instant, the Queen looked back at him. That highlighting ring settled onto a particular window—the new 'ground' floor, third from the left. And moving away. And just as quick, it was gone.

Aaron pulled his shirt up over his nose, securing it over his mouth to give him the barest of protection against the fumes to come. It would help, maybe buy him seconds, but it was better than taking deep breaths of the noxious haze he was about to be swimming in.

"Thank you," Aaron murmured, spurring his heels into Scar's flanks.

Scar turned his big head around, glaring at Aaron with his good eye, as if it to scold Aaron. The nerve of some people. "What am I doing? You know where to go," Aaron said, clinging to Scar's hide.

Scar huffed, his horrid breath kicking up a tiny cloud. Aaron felt the creature coil underneath him, muscles tightening underneath the mottled leather plates. And they took off, Scar's heavy talons pounding the dirt with a terrifying percussion, more runaway train than concerted charge.

Aaron was riding a living battering ram, a siege engine made flesh. Like some kind of lunatic. Maybe he ought to follow in behind, not ride the demon-steed on the highway to poor judgment?

Too late. He hunkered down.

The wall was six inches of reinforced concrete, rebar, and drywall. It might as well have been made of glass. Large chunks of building rocketing through the air. What a sight this must have been, to see two tons of angry sentient blades erupt from the wall.

Instantly, Aaron clamped his eyes shut, regretting the entrance. The sulfide in the air stung his eyes, tiny needles rolling under his lids and piercing at the whimsy of a malevolent power. His lungs felt as though they were halved, and they felt hot in his chest, rattling with each breath.

Aaron doubted anybody actually saw him past the much more interesting attraction. He didn't really see them either.

But he could feel Scar underneath him, wasting no time shred-

ding...someone. The soft crunching and awful mulching was probably best left unseen anyway.

With that task done, Scar whirled about, eager for its next amusement. He had to help. Aaron forced his eyes open, letting that fire
pour in.

There he was.

Riley stood tall, squared up against the Jergad. Steel crates scattered at his feet where they had been dropped. A spattering of blood
across his face, splashed up from the bodyguard Scar had just pulver-
ized. A gas mask clung to his face, a simple filter and respirator that
held flush against his jaw and goggles that clung to his cheeks,
pressing in for a good seal.

Through the transparent shell, Aaron could see Riley's eyes flash
with a yellow light.

Scar hissed and hacked at Riley's midsection. As if that would
work.

Riley slid underneath the strike fast enough to kick the claw as
it went by, throwing the big creature off its already unsteady footing. Scar moaned in pain, a soft but dulcet tone, pulling at the
heartstrings. The beast pushed through with the momentum, spinning in place to bring both scythes around to Riley anew, but Riley
was so fast he may as well have been part of that dreaded toxic
mist.

It was as though the strike simply passed through him. Riley
seized the opportunity and drove his quick knife into Scar's exposed
belly, sliding past the banded plates to the vulnerable flesh beneath.
Scar let loose an agonizing roar, croaking and cut short with a gurgle.

It lashed out at the man underneath it, but Riley had vanished
again, sliding under Scar's legs. The knife bit into Scar's ankles,
slashing under the leather plates at the precious muscles underneath.

No amount of willpower could keep Scar standing now. The
creature crumpled to the ground with a wheezing whimper. Riley
stood tall, cracking his neck and bringing the knife to Scar's spine—

To find Aaron staring him down, rifle tucked tight into his shoulder. Mucus, blood, and sweat streamed down Aaron's face as he cut loose with the rifle.

The bullet was traveling at eight hundred meters per second. They were mere feet from each other. In theory, the bullet would hit Riley before he'd even be aware it was fired, let alone have time to dodge it.

And yet.

Riley wove his way around every shot, side-stepping and leaning away from each burst. Riley was working so hard, his skin was starting to steam, the white moisture distinct from the hostile yellow haze that hung in the air.

Between Scar's assault and Aaron's surprise, they were wearing him down. Which is what made the click of an empty chamber that much more disheartening.

Riley sneered, lunging, and it was all Aaron could do to stick the barrel of his rifle out to greet him, like a single pike holding the barbarian at bay. Riley pressed himself flush against the hot muzzle, the knife held inches from Aaron's throat.

If Aaron could smell through the blood and pain, he might have a wretch-inducing sample to couple with Riley's obviously singing flesh. Between overwhelmed cybernetics and the branding heat of the barrel, Riley was cooking to a crisp.

Riley's voice was stifled by the mask, muted and muffled. "I'm not sure how you thought this would work out, Capital." Riley leaned to one side, teasing. He could easily roll off the barrel and drive his blow home. Aaron was at his mercy. "You're real quick to throw your life away."

Aaron coughed through the blood pooling in his mouth. "Not my life to lose."

"Do you have any idea how many people died down here?" Riley asked. "Their blood is on your hands!"

The knife slipped low, its fine tip grazing Aaron's neck. Aaron couldn't keep his eyes open a moment longer, clenching them away from both the stinging air and the inevitable. Riley sneered. "When I take my first shot, I really hope it kills that little bitch. Because if it doesn't, I'm gonna plow that whole city into dust."

And a battle-cry caught Riley's attention.

In a flash, Riley turned to meet the oncoming foe, knife at the ready. Jensen threw himself onto the knife's tip, going too fast to do anything else. Riley and Jensen tumbled to the ground, releasing Aaron from his chopping block.

Aaron gasped, every breath hurting more than the last. He could feel Scar wrestling to breathe underneath him, the big guy rattling with each rise and fall.

Riley sat atop Jensen, a knee to the throat. Somewhere in the fall, his respirator had been ripped free, exposing Riley's sweaty visage. Every inch of his skin was flushed red. Bits and pieces of his augments glowed in the fog, sparklers just under the skin, the light catching off every little particle.

He threw blow after blow at Jensen, a thousand pounds of fury. "I offered you bastards everything! What did *you* give *me?!*"

Aaron had to stop this now.

He rolled off of Scar and found himself in slime and muck. The sulfide tailings? No, that was the remains of a person, the unfortunate recipient of Scar's entrance.

In the man's holster. Pistol. Locked and ready.

Bleary eyes. Bones hurt. His chest creaked with every breath. Fingers shaking.

He pulled the pistol free.

Riley slowed his abuse, heaving labored breath. He elected instead to twist his knife in Jensen's gut, "You know, sometimes killing is hard. Just a reality of command. And other times, it's a real pleasure."

"You're fast..." Jensen croaked out, with a blood-stained smile, "But you faster than light?"

Riley's eyes slid back to Aaron. Propped against a wall, pistol in hand. Aaron cranked the capacitor, and it whirred to life.

In an instant, Riley was in his face and reaching for the pistol. Too late.

Aaron pressed the pistol into Riley's chest and fired. Aaron was intimately familiar with the damage.

The laser heated Riley's torso to a blistering eight hundred degrees in less than a second. Liquids in the skin and muscle snap boiled, bursting the chest cavity, creating the signature crater common to laser weaponry. The temperatures reduced anything in direct contact to a black carbon crust, almost fragile. But blood still burst from the popping 'bubble' that used to be Riley's stomach.

Aaron's hands were coated with its warmth.

Riley's eyes froze, staring at Aaron's face, a potent mixture of shock and confusion, a confrontation with what he long believed impossible. His expression didn't change as the lights of his eyes dimmed into nothing.

Riley slumped against Aaron, and the two fell to the ground together.

Maybe just lie here, let the fumes take them away. No. Something nuzzled his hand, pushing him up. As battered as Scar was, it still urged him on. It stared at him with its one good eye, a single commandment.

Get up.

It took everything he had, but Aaron was able to drag Jensen out of the sinking apartments to the safety of the mining grounds, Scar staggering behind them the whole way. Aaron collapsed beside his friend, drinking the fresh air in.

He could hear the whistle to Jensen's breathing, as it came lighter and lighter each time.

"What were you doing?" Aaron asked him, shaking his head, "That was so stupid, man. You tryin' to kill yourself or somethin'?"

"Look who's talkin', boss," Jensen murmured, his voice hollowing by the second, "Jus'...found somebody worth it, is all."

Aaron let out the shallow breath he didn't know he was holding, all concern and finery melting away, as he lost themselves in the soothing blue of that endless sky.

Jensen whispered, soft and distant, like the last wisps of a refreshing breeze, "Like tamin' a dragon..."

Aaron let his head roll over to look at his friend. His big smile was as potent as ever, a charisma that wasn't stopped by the blood drenching his abdomen.

Jensen's eyes panned over the sky, hunting for some unspoken dream left unfulfilled. Or perhaps, he was self-satisfied, sated with his time and was simply looking for the call of the horn that would call him to rest.

The quick knife stood tall in his gut, quivering against the failing heartbeat, each stroke of the drums causing the faintest tremor. Jensen smiled, his eyes focusing on nothing at all. "Let's go, short-stack. Let's..."

Jensen let out the breath and did not draw a new one in.

Aaron chuckled, letting that painful catharsis of broken ribs and bleeding lungs grow into an uncontrollable wave of tears. It was a long moment before Aaron realized he was laying in that dirt, weeping alone.

EDICTS FROM THE MINISTRY

EARTH DIRECTIVE

RE: VANGUARD INSURRECTION

BY ORDER OF THE MINISTRY OF CIVIL DEFENSE

HOSTILE OCCUPATION OF REPUBLIC MINING COLONY
HR-2056 IS DEEMED AN ACT OF REBELLION

ALL FORCES ARE TO DISARM AND AWAIT
ADJUDICATION

ALL CRIMINALS WHO RAISE THEIR ARMS AGAINST
THE CONSUL WILL BE HELD TO HIS SWORD

IMPERIAL FORCES ARE EN ROUTE TO PACIFY
RESISTANCE AND RESTORE ORDER

YOU WILL SURRENDER OR YOU WILL BURN

ZU GLORIAM

EPILOGUE

IT WAS the only place in the world Aaron didn't feel insane anymore. He stood on that plateau in the mountains, where Holmst had abandoned him to die, looking out on the basin below and the sparkling jewel of Vanguard.

The smoke pillars had died down, and the mild commotion of hurried transports more resembled a mirage. The vista felt like a painting just out of reach. He stood at the lip of the cliffs and drank in that pastel morning view.

And it was quiet. No more congratulations or condolences, just the kiss of the wind on his rugged cheek. He needed a shave. Every touch of the world felt like sandpaper.

Someone must've tattled.

Talania approached him from behind, waving off her body-guards. She wanted to talk to him alone, or at least with the appearance of it. She took to leadership like a hammer to a screw—never mind the intent of the design.

"Let me guess," Aaron grumbled, hating the sound of his own voice, "They said we could have a three-week head start, and they promise to be sportsmanlike."

Talania paused, the gravity of the situation weighing down her smirk. "In so many words."

"Well, Governor...are you going to surrender?"

She stepped up to his side, taking a sip of that humbling landscape. "I actively participated in the violent overthrow of my military. I don't think surrender is going to provide an improved result for me."

"And the people?" Aaron asked, pointed. If she was only concerned with her own hide...

She didn't answer for a long second, taking a full breath of the crisp mountain air, the altitude robbing the heat from the savannah and refreshing with the moisture of the fog. "Now I know why you come up here. Clears the head."

It didn't need to be said. The Empire wasn't going to selectively determine who participated and who didn't. As far as Sol was concerned, the entire Colony was locked arm in arm, and they would drop the hammer with the certainty of it.

Now, that absolutism was going to be hard to convince any holdout loyalists of. Some people were just so faithful, they would—even out of fear—lay their own necks on the block.

It turned his stomach, and he knew exactly why. Quinn, Carmona, Jensen...they laid down their lives to stand up against that system. Even Holmst had done the same in the end.

She took one last draw of that revitalizing open-air elixir, before turning back to her bodyguards and the waiting Howler. "So, we get ready?"

Aaron shrugged. "Not like they're leaving us much choice."

She nodded, her mind off imagining the horrors she had only sampled this week. That gleaming city in the distance would burn.

Talania turned and strode toward the waiting Howler, powerful clean strides. He wished he had an ounce of her conviction, even if it was all for show. She stepped up into the machine, grabbing a handlebar for support.

Only then did she look back at him, as if suddenly realizing he hadn't followed her. She beckoned for him, but he just shook his head. One more thing left to do.

She pursed her lips and shrugged. The Howler lifted off with a huff, scattering the loose gravel at Aaron's feet, before whispering off into the blue tableau of the sky. Aaron watched it go, feeling a tingle on the back of his neck. That particular sight had some rather foul associations to it.

"She will need you before the end, *ak'thun*," he heard the Queen whisper on the wind. "They all will."

Aaron eyed the Howler as it disappeared into the distance. Maybe Talania was staring at the rolling fields underneath her, scanning for the active Jergad now grazing openly in their fields again, sifting for what scant vegetation had returned. Maybe she was looking toward her city, a cracked crystal catching the mid-morning sun and scattering it into a dozen impotent shards.

Or maybe she looked back to Aaron and witnessed the smokey silhouette he knew hung behind him on that plateau. Hell—she probably couldn't see that. It was all a projection in his head.

He turned—and indeed, there she was. The Queen's human form stood in stark contrast to the stiff double who had just departed. This illusion's posture was loose with twisted shoulders and a cocked hip, like twisted silk hanging off some invisible rod, like she didn't quite know how to naturally stand—an observation only magnified by the billowing darkness, the veiled titan that hid itself in the vaulted shadow of the mountain.

There was a part of him that hoped he never met whatever that really was.

A curious flicker in his heart, as several Jergad staggered forward from their caves and their hidden places—it was always unnerving how something so large could hide in plain sight. Poking his ragged head from the pack was Scar, hobbled but healing well, croaking and whining like a large mutt.

The Queen studied his eyeline to Scar and the others. They were not separate from her, after all, and his admiration for the big guy was probably akin to someone finding her hand more valuable than herself. "We will need you, as well."

"Why?" Aaron said, eying the twisting black more than her human counterpart. He chewed on the implication like it was shoe leather, some indigestible concept that revolted every part of him. "Everyone I know seems to think I'm some kind of hero. Like they just can't go on unless I'm leading the charge. I didn't overthrow Riley yesterday, or end a war. It was a big...community effort, but somehow everyone keeps thinking *I'm* the light at the end of the tunnel!"

The Queen smiled softly and leaned forward, like she might try to nuzzle his cheek from twenty feet away. "You are more than one of the crowd. You led them from bondage. You led them through blood-shed. You led them—"

He couldn't listen to this anymore. "I led my best friend to his *death*! I led them—were you asleep for the last seventy-two hours?! I *turned* them on their own people! I have personally killed more than my share. And for what? A good six months of freedom? What was it all *for*?!"

The Queen's stare held no judgement. He wished it had. He had killed. He had killed by choice. He had decided to kill Riley. He had wanted to. He wasn't even sure if that was wrong. He needed someone to judge him, punish him.

He had gotten used to the cage, after all.

Aaron pointed at the city below. "There are loyalists down there in that city that would like me drawn & quartered; there's a couple hundred Naval Regulars who are somewhere between blood-thirsty and scared gutless; and by the way, some of us Capitals ain't the nicest people either.

"Yeah, sure, the next few days are goin' to be a party. But none of it is going to matter terribly much when a megaton of kickass shows up to wipe this planet back to the Stone Age—for the second time! We have fifty-two thousand civilians down there. God knows how many you have."

Aaron rolled his head back, staring up at the sky above that hid distant danger. "And now *they* have an axe to grind. They're not coming back as colonists, Your Highness. They're coming back ready for a war. And we're not even *in the neighborhood* of something we could call 'ready'."

The Queen welcomed his rage, absorbed it, and then: "What would you need?"

Aaron huffed, like he was being asked to run another mile after having just declared himself spent. "I'm no general. I wouldn't know where to start."

"Then think in the simplest of terms. What would you need?"

More time. Professional training. And more than anything, a real army.

And even with those things granted, the Imperial Army had just gotten through quashing a rebellion a hundred times this size. This would be a speed bump, a police action, peace delivered through fire —and the blaze that rendered Vanguard to ash wouldn't even register as bright as the candlelight at Jensen's vigil. Their end was all but absolute.

What he needed was impossible.

"Where would I find any of it?" Aaron blurted, incredulous. "Nobody's going to come protect a small mining colony. Or a group of convicts like us." He pointed down at the city, his voice cracking and his throat squeezed shut. "Those people...they believe I'm going to save them. And I—I can't tell them how. I can't tell them that their friends and family fought against a psychopath and died—for *nothing*! I'm their 'Hero' and I—I've got nothin'!"

Scar led a chorus of quiet murmurs, somewhere between purrs and crackling. They wanted to soothe his discomfort but made a noise that seemed to materialize his pressure into the real world.

The Queen inched over to him, and he could feel a warmth wrap him like a wool blanket against the cold mountain wind.

"You are not a hero, *ak'thun*," she said to him. "Heroes are stories told to the people to enshrine honorable qualities. Heroes can never measure up to the stories told about them. They were just people.

But you...you have a privilege and a responsibility. You will get to tell your story yourself. The only one who will define your worth...is you."

He closed his eyes, taking a deep breath of air, feeling the crisp, dry refreshment fill him to the brim until he was sure it would spill over into tears. He was back in that jail cell, consigned to labor out endless debts, not of his choosing. He could wait for the end, drink up his freedom until a boot fell onto his neck. It was inevitable.

Aaron didn't start this. Neither had Talania, no. Guilt was a paralytic that would cause one to bow their head unto the block. Aaron had done everything asked of him and more. He had risen to every challenge.

No more. He was done following.

"Your Highness," Aaron said, his voice still shaking, "we have a lot of work to do."

She smiled. "Well, then...we'd best get started, shouldn't we?"

AFTERWORD

This book has been a long time coming. I first wrote this story when I was seventeen years old, turning it in as a completed manuscript for an English project Senior year of High School. Then, I re-wrote it as a screenplay at least twice.

So when I dipped my toes back into fiction, I had to take another swing at the beast that started it all. It ended up launching my very first series!

Aaron's story continues in
Ranks of the Blood Service.

And the ripples of Aaron's actions touch far more than this one world
Coming June 2023
The Iron Service

If you're enjoying the Capital Adventures, please rate & leave a review on Goodreads & Amazon. It really helps small authors like myself.

And if you need more thrills right now, you can get another

adventure absolutely free by signing up for the Newsletter on my Website:

https://www.authorivers.com/

The Dollfaces, a Cyberpunk Action/Adventure set in the Capital-verse.

As part of the Newsletter, you get that exclusive story that you can't get anywhere else, along with other free stories, updates on my latest work, thoughts on books or video games I might be immersed in, along with other news.

I also have a cat. I will likely be dropping pictures of her there regularly, as she is a consistent part of my office day. She is bad at being a cat, but she is fat and good and adorable. Sign up and see!

ABOUT THE AUTHOR

Allen Ivers started writing original stories at the ripe age of eleven, largely trying to figure out why the Disney villains on the television box were the way they were. Villains, monsters, and politicians have always fascinated him with their behavior. Twenty years later, he's still fascinated by bad people and the bad things they do.

Allen first wrote this book when he was but a wee lad in sun-crazed San Diego. After spending ten years as a screenwriter and as a creative consultant, he decided to revisit the tales he wrote as a boy.

He now lives in beautiful Juneau, AK somewhere in that fluffy snow drift. You can find his thoughts about writing, politics, and the odd cute cat on his Twitter.

facebook.com/AllenIversSFF

twitter.com/AllenIvers

ALSO BY